KUROSHIO

ARSENAL
PULP PRESS

KUROSHIO

The Blood of Foxes

Terry Watada

ARSENAL PULP PRESS
200 – 341 Water Street
Vancouver, BC
Canada V6B 1B8
arsenalpulp.com

The publisher gratefully acknowledges the support of the Canada Council for
the Arts and the British Columbia Arts Council for its publishing program, and
the Government of Canada through the Book Publishing Industry Develop-
ment Program and the Government of British Columbia through the Book
Publishing Tax Credit Program for its publishing activities.

Text and cover design by Shyla Seller
Editing by Brian Lam
Cover illustration by Helen Koyama
Author photograph by Tane Akamatsu

Printed and bound in Canada

This is a work of fiction. Any resemblance of characters to persons either living
or deceased is purely coincidental.

Library and Archives Canada Cataloguing in Publication:

Watada, Terry
  Kuroshio : the blood of foxes / Terry Watada.

ISBN 978-1-55152-233-3
  I. Title.
PS8595.A79K87 2007   C813'.54   C2007-903935-9

AUTHOR'S NOTE: Japanese terms in dialogue are not italicized to indicate the
character is speaking Japanese. Conversely, italicized English words in dialogue
are "spoken" in English.

Dedicated to the memory of
Dr. Wes Fujiwara and Jesse Nishihata,
two of our great storytellers who shared so many secrets with me.

1. Monday, March 11, 1940

The woman sat in the well-worn office chair, daring not to fidget for fear of making it squeak. She kept her head bowed sullenly, obsessively rubbing one of the clear red buttons of her Sunday-best dress. Cut like a jewel, the glass ornament usually sparkled but not so in the inert fluorescence of the small, airtight room.

Yoshiko Miyamoto, normally a young-looking forty-one-year-old, appeared haggard as if she hadn't slept in many nights. Perhaps it was the light, but her face was tight and pale. The lines at the corners of the eyes were deeper, darker than usual, sharply defined. But her skin held its resiliency and her hair, pulled up in a tight bun, was as black as her teenage daughter's. Yoshiko was the picture of a once-delicate woman grown old without looking much older.

Behind the heavy oak desk across from her sat the *oyabun*, the gangland boss of the Powell Street area, leaning back in his own creaking chair staring at the ceiling fan as he contemplated each slow revolution. The diminutive Etsuji Morii wore an oversized three-piece suit. Yoshiko had heard that the head of the Black Dragon Society was cheap, unwilling to go to a tailor, and so bought off-the-rack even though no department store carried his exact size.

"Can you help me, Oyabun?" Yoshiko pleaded unexpectedly.

Morii raised his thin eyebrows and his hand to silence her. He crooked his index finger to scratch the nub of a moustache beneath his bent nose. A stalling tactic. His narrow, secretive eyes, tight mouth, and clenched jaw bore the signs of decadence and decay – the collapsed cheeks, the broken nose, the eroded complexion predicted a fall to ruin.

Not knowing what to say, Yoshiko averted her gaze, surveying instead the Nippon Club office. The wooden file cabinets were stuffed to the brim with paper, threatening to collapse with the next passing freight train. The walls were a dull green, plain without moulding or baseboards, but freshly painted and adorned with a pinned-up *Hinomaru* – the proud Japanese flag in full red sunburst – championship judo ribbons and the treasured framed certificate, awarded just last year by the Kodokan Judo headquarters in Tokyo, proclaiming Etsuji Morii a third *dan* black belt during the tenth month of the thirteenth year of the Showa Era, 1939. It was a room that revealed only what everyone already knew of its occupant. Perhaps that was more than enough since it was also the only office in the building, the true testament to the *oyabun's* stature within the Japanese sector of east Vancouver, an area simply called "Powell Street" after its main drag.

Yoshiko's eyes settled on a grainy photograph of a fog-bound bridge, its obscured identity revealed in the unmistakable spider's web of girders and suspension wires. The fabled Golden Gate.

Biting her lower lip, she stared at the picture and ached to be in San Francisco even though she had never been to that saltwater city. Her face flushed hot with the thought of him laughing in the embrace of another woman. She grew angry in her vulnerability, wanting to lash out but daring not to in her pocket of futility. Instead, she sat wringing her hands so hard they turned a bloodless white.

"Miyamoto-san," Morii finally said, "you come to me with this ... this horror story and all you want me to do is bring him back?"

"I don't know what else to do!" Yoshiko burst out loud. She instantly withdrew, knowing she had violated the unwritten rule against the display of emotion. She sought escape in a damp handkerchief taken from inside her sleeve.

"Naniyo? Stop crying!" Morii admonished, suddenly angry. "I won't have blubbering women here!" His wide, tight mouth grimaced as his small fists slammed his desktop.

Yoshiko raised her eyes to come face to face with the devil. She trembled at the fury roiling in Morii and held her breath.

"Can you help me?" she pleaded in a whisper. It was clear Yoshiko was desperate, grasping at any string of redemption. "No one must know, Oyabun, I couldn't bear the shame."

"Shame? What're you talking about, woman? If he comes back, shame'll be the least of it. There's a lot more at stake here than your bloody reputation," he jeered and then turned his back on her. "Shame!" he scoffed. "Do you have any idea what's happening in the world? You don't, do you? You can't see what damage your selfishness could cause. You just can't see how everything could be brought down." He looked at her again.

In a moment of helplessness, Yoshiko reached out and touched his suit sleeve.

"You've brought dishonour to our people," Morii admonished as he pulled away. "You've brought dishonour to me."

She lowered her head, choking back tears. "Forgive me, Oyabun. Forgive me."

He paused. "All right. All right, I'm going to help you. Just stop crying!"

Yoshiko took a deep breath to compose herself.

"Who knows about this?" he asked.

"Only me, I think. Probably others."

"Do others know or not?"

"No, no one."

"Are you sure? Friends? Relatives?"

"I had a cousin in Steveston but she's dead." She blurted out the lie easily. "Everyone I have is dead."

"Listen, you go home and I'll go see my Mountie friends."

Yoshiko visibly stiffened.

"Look, I said I'd help you," he said. "Not so much for you but for the sake of the Japanese here."

"But —"

"The police don't have to get involved with this. I'm going to keep this quiet," he said with resolve. "I do so much, you don't know. I work … I sacrifice so much but boke-nasu Japanese like you live in your own little selfish worlds. Without any respect for all I do for you until you get in trouble!" he said, nearly boiling over with anger. "I'll call on you."

His words fell like a hard rain as Yoshiko gathered herself together and rose to leave. As she walked to the door, she forced a perfunctory smile that quickly disappeared when Morii bid his farewell.

"Well, we've set up an obligation here. Haven't we?" the *oyabun* said, almost under his breath.

Yoshiko shuddered and wondered how and if she would ever be free of such an obligation – of such *giri*.

The cold humidity of that cloudy March day enveloped her when she left the darkness of the hulking, anonymous building on Alexander Street. She pulled her faded cloth coat close to her and scurried to get away from the weather eastward up the rise of the street. As the cold chased her, she imagined the accusing stares of the Nodas, whose Yoshino Restaurant occupied the first floor of the Empress Rooms, a boarding house a couple of store fronts away from the Nippon Club. *They're such gossips,* she thought to herself. Not that Kikuno and Yoneko Noda knew anything, but they viewed any visit to Morii with suspicion. Fortunately, the curtains in the restaurant's large picture window were drawn.

Yoshiko knew that going to Morii was a desperate measure, a last resort, but the situation warranted it. She ached for the return of the way things were: afternoons with him in his room, the sun slicing through the darkness, caressing their bodies.

His hands were soft, not like those of a woman but of a man of grace and civility. They ran over her skin like warm water, streaming into the crevices of her body. A shiver of pleasure.

A life so different from what she had when she first came to Canada. The cost was heavy, but she was only too willing to pay it, perhaps because the consequences, as in most cases, were only now becoming apparent. Still, it could've been worse: she wasn't wracked with guilt, keeping as she did the horrible thoughts about what she had done at bay like a dam against a swollen river. She sneered at the *oyabun's* disgust; she knew full well what was at stake for her. Little did she care about the world.

She crossed Dunlevy Avenue and soon the Japanese Hall came into full view. The squat, grey cement-block building, simple in its architecture and empty at that moment, was where most of the Japanese locals took their children for after-school language lessons. It was adjacent to the original school, a wooden structure whose classrooms were reserved for the junior grades. She had considered taking her own daughter, Mariko, there, but decided the child had had enough trouble in English school to justify risking further embarrassment. She jerked her head away, catching sight of Burrard Inlet with distant seagulls rising above it, undulating like newspapers caught in the updrafts beneath the peaks of North Vancouver's mountains. The salt air felt good.

She walked to the corner of Alexander Street and Jackson Avenue and stopped in front of the Three Sisters Café, the place where everything had started six months before and perhaps where everything would end. Yoshiko squinted through the large front window obscured by partially open Venetian blinds and made out the long linoleum-topped counter with its four metal stools. Focusing on the second stool from the left, the one with the ripped vinyl, she hoped against hope to catch sight of him sitting there once again, but it was empty. Her heart sank – the memory of him in his cashmere coat lingered before fading away.

To the right of the counter, a set of stairs led to the rooms on the second floor where the real business of the establishment took place. All of a sudden Hatsuko Yamada, the eldest of the three sisters, emerged from the backroom kitchen and looked up, seeming to stare directly at her. Yoshiko, startled at being discovered, rushed away southward toward Powell Ground, a bleak clay field nestled in the heart of the Japanese section.

The park was empty, but opposite it on the north side of Powell Street, the line of stores, garishly painted in primary colours and covered with flat tarpaper roofs and clapboard siding, bustled with shoppers. Mrs. Sawada, a shrunken and nervous woman, came out of Union Fish with that night's dinner wrapped in newspaper under her arm. Kids swarmed in and out of the Star Dairy and Confectionery, the community's *miriku-ya*. Haruo, a fat-faced ten-year-old, clutched his prize of penny candy as he carried away the bottle of milk he had been sent to buy. Burly Mrs. Fukushima stood in the doorway, laughing heartily at the children who wrestled one another for show. She held the pain in her stomach in check as she turned to reveal her full, round face.

For fear of being noticed again, Yoshiko quickly crossed Powell and pushed along Jackson Avenue, moving quickly by the United Church's stained-glass gaze, past the glum *Japanese Gym* next door, and finally arriving at her boarding house, a drab two-storey with gabled roof and exterior shiplap siding crouched directly across from Powell Ground. She opened the front door and walked into the comforting anonymity.

The hallway was dark. The telltale fumes from the basement furnace tickled her nose and triggered her memory, pulling images into sharp relief. She began to shake and then cry, the dust in the air reaching out to grab her throat. She tried shaking it off but the acrid smell of camphor conspired against her. Spinning around, she began choking and coughing until the tide of illness subsided.

Recovered, she removed her shoes and groped for the light switch in the front sitting room. With no boarders, the house was quiet, the gloom closing in on her. The deep darkness of the corridor ran the length of the house, passing a dining room and leading to a sizable kitchen. The back extension of the house consisted of two small bedrooms, reserved for the unusual but telling sleeping arrangement of Yoshiko and her sixteen-year-old daughter Mariko in one and Jinsaburo, her husband, in the other. Upstairs were four roomier apartments: three she rented to the transients of the logging and fishing trades and one she optimistically kept vacant, ready for its lodger's return. She sank into the front-room chair heavy with the burden of recent events.

Out of the corner of her eye, she saw that the family altar in the corner, an indulgence purchased during her recent brush with prosperity, was open, the pictures of long-dead relatives displayed prominently within its rich mahogany confines. In front of it, there were two stacks of *mochi* rice cakes both crowned by a fresh Mandarin orange, the offerings resembling meditating Buddhas. Mindful of the recently departed, Yoshiko decided she should light an incense stick. It was then that she noticed her hand shaking involuntarily. Must be the cold, she dismissed.

"The Buddha is always near," preached the Reverend Eon Mitsubayashi the last time she had attended a church service. *Even for me, sensei?* she had wondered. She rose to go to the kitchen, the intention fixed in her mind for later.

The small four-element gas stove seemed inadequate to cook for four boarders plus her family, Yoshiko remembered thinking when she had first moved in, but she had fed work crews of ten or more on a crude wood stove or open fire during her nomadic years in the lumber camps and mining towns of the Interior. She put the kettle on to boil.

She eased into her favourite kitchen chair, threadbare and rickety, and contemplated the silence of the house with a cup of tea. Her ears rang as she undid the knot in her hair, letting it fall loosely. She warmed at the thought of his fingers becoming enmeshed in it, like a swimmer in seaweed.

The ringing seemed to grow louder as she picked up her cup and teapot, the newly-bought green set with gold trim so much like her mother's wedding gift all those years ago, and returned to the front sitting room. Her mind cleared after a few cups of jasmine tea. The sitting room had an open ceiling, the rafters exposed. Yoshiko stared at them, mesmerized by another vision of her own making.

She shook her head and moved to the altar. Three tall incense sticks stood in the pulverized ash of the kanagoro, *a small, circular brass container. She swept her loose hair away as she struck a match to light all three sticks at once. The smoke quickly rose and accumulated in the empty space above her head. Startled at the amount, she turned away from the altar, the* butsudan.

The air grew thicker until the light of the overcast day faded from the front window. From the billowing clouds, an image emerged, slowly yet insistently: the body of a girl, her eyes white, the pupils sunk into the recesses of the sockets, hung from one of the rafters. Her hair wet and straggly. Her dress a simple chemise, faded green, torn and ragged. Her hands limp and bruised by her sides — the crude rope digging into the tender flesh of the neck.

The sound of distant howling filled her ears.

Overwhelmed, Yoshiko opened her mouth to scream but could utter nothing. She collapsed to the floor with camphor and incense clogging her lungs. The presence of the Buddha.

The image lingered, the animal cries persisted, until she blinked and both vanished along with the smoke. She suddenly felt the cup hot on her fingertips and quickly put it down onto the coffee table. She chuckled. *My mind is playing games with me*, she thought, nearly saying it out loud. The vision was not unfamiliar to her because she had seen the mysterious child many times before. In her dreams, recent and past.

ॐ

August 1917

The chanting floated atop the smoke from incense sticks burning before the grave markers of a humble yet overcrowded cemetery lying in the mountainous area on the Sea of Japan side of the country. Unseen crows called from above as the droning voices, modulating only a half-tone here and there, had a hypnotic rhythm, causing Yoshiko Hayashi to drift into a daydream. The attending *bonsan* with closed eyes was lost in the Sanskrit of the Buddha Dharma, the Teachings of the Buddha. The clear ring of the ceremonial bell vibrated out in concentric circles, like the wake of a frog-spirit after plopping into water.

Standing nearby in the wilting summer heat were the relatives whose common ancestry lay before them, marked by wooden staves with the ideograms of the Hayashi clan inscribed.

The eighteen-year-old Yoshiko Hayashi paid no attention to the commemoration. It held little significance for her, just another ritual in a ritual-rich season. Her quarter-moon eyes ran up the rising mountain-side where the trees leaned acutely toward the distant, hidden peak, the smoke drifting amongst the branches like ghosts observing from a distance and buoyed by the soft, indistinct cries of the wilderness.

She enjoyed Obon, the Buddhist commemoration of the dead, the *odori* folk dancing, socializing and the lantern boat ceremony called the *toronagashi*, but the graveside visitations bored her to tears. Anyone could see it on her face, the liquid downcast eyes and the clear skin tight with inertia. Still, she stood with hands respectfully folded in front of her demure *kasuri kimono*, a confining cotton garment with a pattern of stars cascading across it; the fall of her hair came to a sharp point about halfway down the back without a strand out of place.

When the *bonsan* began his discourse about her grandmother, who had died the year before, Yoshiko forced herself to listen, if only as a matter of courtesy – it was an important anniversary, after all.

Obachan, Yoshiko's grandmother, was a woman with eroded skin, thin hair, and world-weary eyes, and had never travelled anywhere. Born not more than a mile from the cemetery, she had grown up to marry one of a hundred rice farmers in the village of Kiyama, so named for the "mountains of trees" surrounding it. After the Emperor Meiji abandoned Japan's feudal system, the modern-thinking couple eventually bought their own farm and cultivated rice. They raised eight children, all of whom married other villagers and raised their own children in turn. Obachan, after burying her husband in his sixty-ninth year, grew old on the farm and never left the village, not even to visit Tokyo. She herself died at the beginning of August in the fourth year of Taisho, 1916.

Yoshiko's parents were more adventurous. Although both were from a rural setting, her mother's village was by the sea, thus leaving the family home for stretches at a time to harvest fish or to go to market was not altogether unfamiliar. Still, her parents were surprised when Yoshiko approached them last month with an outlandish proposal.

"I've never heard of such a thing!" Naka Hayashi declared to her husband, setting down her rice bowl and *hashi* chopsticks.

Jinshiro's knuckles turned white as he squeezed his hands tightly.

"Okasan, I've made up my mind," Yoshiko said obstinately. "I don't want to end up like Obachan!"

"Quiet!" said Jinshiro, her father, his face growing red with anger. "Such disrespect! Your grandmother's not dead a year yet."

"What do you mean by that?" demanded Naka. Ignoring her husband's admonishments, she watched her daughter with great concern washing over her face, a slight bend in her back, presaging a widow's curve, becoming more pronounced as the discussion continued.

"She never went anywhere. I want adventure. I want more than Obachan ever had."

"So being a rice farmer isn't good enough for you?" Jinshiro abruptly stood up from the table and slid open the rice paper door, nearly knocking it off its track. He glared back at the tableau of his wife and daughter kneeling glumly before the simple meal of steamed vegetables, yam noodles, and pot of rice. He snorted his dismay and stepped into his *geta* to walk outside, the clip-clop of his wooden sandals penetrating the tranquility of his garden with its lush vegetation and chortling water.

"I want to go to *A-me-ri-ka*," she declared, enunciating the foreign word carefully. Although somewhat shamed by her father's words, she felt the courage of her conviction. "It's time for me to marry, Okasan. Please find me a husband who'll take me there."

Yoshiko loved her family but knew that the years ahead offered, at best, marriage to a farmer, an eldest son, without vision or ambition to see the world. A tyrannical mother-in-law lurked in the mist as well as if seeking to imprison her. And as the wife of the eldest son, she was destined to take care of her in-laws in their dotage. She winced at the years of drudgery to come, at the callous whim of tyrants.

Naka Hayashi had said no to her daughter right away and continued to say so throughout the evening until they sat together on the *tatami* straw mats of the sitting room that looked out onto the house's small enclosed garden. She recognized the yearning to travel in her daughter, since she had felt it once herself, to no avail. She had been the good daughter, after all, who implicitly obeyed her father's commands. Mindful of changing times, however, she resorted to reasoning with her daughter. A trickling waterfall underscored the singing of the cicadas.

In a gentle tone, Naka spoke, "Yoshiko-chan, I need you here. Your two sisters are gone far away and now you want to go even farther. I'll be all alone."

"You have Otosan."

"But I have no help."

"Michiko-chan and Harumi-chan are nearby," Yoshiko said, referring to her brothers' wives.

"They have their own families to take care of."

Yoshiko scoffed at her mother's trepidation. *As if two able-bodied daughters-in-law couldn't "help" her,* she thought. *She just wants me to stay at home to torment me.*

"If you wait," Naka said, with a note of desperation, "your otosan and I can arrange for you to marry well. How about the eldest Watanabe boy? You'll live a very comfortable life."

Yoshiko's face turned sour immediately. "I will not be under the thumb of some awful mother-in-law, especially someone like old lady Watanabe! She's so mean, she'd work me to death saying no thanks whatsoever."

"I will not have you talking like that!" Naka chastised. "That is your duty, you urusai child!"

Yoshiko bowed in shame. Twice now she had forgotten herself before her parents. Has there ever been such a disagreeable child? she wondered.

In the advantageous pause, Naka posed, "*America?* There's nothing there but devil men and ghost women."

"That's just a child's tale," Yoshiko answered with a smile. "Okasan, remember how I felt on the pier in Yokohama two years ago? Remember? I told you."

Yokohama Harbour bustled with the commerce of Pacific trade. Ships bound for Kowloon, Singapore, and San Francisco groaned with their cargo. They were ready to set sail. Yoshiko stood on the pier, her sixteen-year-old eyes fancifully scanning the horizon for any glimpse of America. The whitecaps danced for her in the distance – the surface movement of the current below. She raised her arms toward the Pacific, stretching out as if to catch the watery swirl. The Kuroshio – the Black Current – lapped at the fingertips, pulling away pieces of her, dissolving her like an iceberg in tropical waters. The hands disappeared. The arms melted and the hair wavered like seaweed. Her thoughts drifted into the outflow of water, sea, and air. She rode the Kuroshio, like Urashima Taro on the back of a benevolent sea turtle, travelling along the submerged trail within the Pacific Basin to the other side of the world.

"I must go to *America*," Yoshiko insisted. In the silence that followed, she noticed her mother's face harden. The cicadas' singing rose and ended in a screaming crescendo.

That had been a month ago. She had felt badly immediately afterwards, but that soon dissipated and she was proud of standing up for herself. Okasan has got to learn, she reasoned, that times have changed. The Emperor had said so.

Despite the fact that a silent chill, pierced by occasional bouts of argument, now prevailed between Yoshiko and her parents, she smirked at her own audacity as she stood in the darkness and random light of the *toronagashi* ritual by the river.

The silhouettes of men light the candles inside the paper lanterns affixed to foot-long wooden slats. The bonsan *begins chanting while girls in kimono and short jackets called* haori *launch the flotilla into the river. After hesitating a moment, the crude boats, once caught by the unseen current, float toward the sea.*

It is the end of Obon, the festival of the dead. The lanterns flicker as the spirits of ancestors flutter around the flames like moths. Slowly the black water infuses the thin paper walls until they can hold no more, and the beacons cave in, extinguishing the flame and releasing a puff of smoke. Ghosts rising to the Pure Land. Goodbye, goodbye until next year.

Yoshiko, having changed into her broad-brimmed hat, dark green chemise, tight cummerbund, and black skirt, stood among the shoreline bamboo trees, mesmerized by the candle lights on the indistinct river. She had discarded the constrictive *kasuri kimono* for the evening ceremony because it was time to think and dress Western, like the Emperor Meiji had advised when she was a child. "Only a fool fights change," the Emperor had said. *Some fools fight change.*

"Yoshiko-chan," asked a youthful voice, "are you awake?"

She jerked to attention. "Of course I'm awake! What a silly question."

She dismissed her sixteen-year-old cousin with a flash of disdain.

"Well, you looked so lost." Akiko giggled, her round chubby face growing more animated with her teasing. "Thinking about some boy?"

"As a matter of fact I was," Yoshiko said smugly.

"Really? Who? Who?" Akiko spoke rapidly as her body shook with sudden excitement.

"Why should I tell you?"

"Because ... because ..."

"Stop hopping like a frog!"

"And you stop teasing me!" Akiko pouted as she rearranged her cherry blossom kimono.

"Oh, stop. I don't know who the boy is. I asked my parents to arrange a marriage for me!"

"Yoshiko! That's wonderful! I bet they call on the Watanabe family. They're so wealthy and have three sons."

"Well, I don't think —"

"And they're all so handsome. Maybe I can ask my otosan to arrange a marriage for me too. We'll be sisters-in-law!"

"Stop it, Akiko! I'm not going to marry one of the Watanabe boys. They all have weak eyes and big noses."

"They do not."

"Well, their thick glasses don't fit very well on their faces."

Akiko broke into an exaggerated laughter.

"It's not final yet, but I asked my parents to find me a husband to take me to *America*."

Akiko's laughter sputtered into choking surprise.

Yoshiko sat with her legs folded underneath her in the sitting room again, watching the darkness settle as the evening wore on toward midnight. In the small room with a low-lying dressing table and ornate mirror mounted on top, her only company was the strong yet fragrant aroma of summertime mothballs that hung in the air.

She closed her eyes, listening to the mice clattering across the ceiling and oblivious to her presence. The tightness of her pleated hobble skirt made sitting difficult as she waited patiently for her *okasan* to come into the room with bad news. She thought of lighting the candle on the floor beside her but then she heard the telltale soft padding of her mother's *tabi* stockings approaching.

"It's so dark in here," complained her mother. "Yoshiko, why don't you…." Her voice trailed off as she fussed about the room lighting lamps with conveniently placed matches. Despite a sigh of exasperation, Yoshiko remained still and waited for her *okasan* to finish. As the gentle glow of the lamp played over the sombre rice paper walls in waves of chiaroscuro, she noticed her mother's hunched posture, a physical feature which always made her feel inexplicably guilty. But it was her mother's permanently pained expression that made it difficult for Yoshiko to confront her.

"How was the toronagashi? Everyone there?" Naka asked.

"I saw Akiko."

"Ah," she sighed. "Still as flighty as ever?"

"Okasan, she's nothing like that!" Yoshiko insisted.

"The men get the boats off?" Naka asked, changing the subject.

"Very pretty … the lights on the water. It reminded me of …"

"Did you see Obachan's boat?" Naka interjected.

"… sad departures."

"Did you see the boat?" Naka repeated. "I paid good money for that."

"Oh, why didn't you just go down to the river bank and look for yourself!" Yoshiko asserted, startling herself and her mother. Though her mother wasn't generally cheap, Yoshiko hated when this side of her emerged.

To avoid embarrassment, Naka quietly settled herself. Her impoverished childhood produced in her a need to save money, but her spoiled, brash daughter wouldn't know anything about that. Again, she changed the subject.

"Your otosan and I have been talking."

The pause was deafening.

"We really are against you travelling so far away and to such a dangerous foreign country."

"But …"

"But we've decided it's your life," Naka continued. "After a month of your nagging, we can see no amount of arguing is going to change your mind. You're such a stubborn, urusai child!"

"So you'll find me a husband who'll take me?" Yoshiko asked anxiously.

"Your otosan will contact my family friend, Miyamoto Iwakichi, in

Mihama. He has a son overseas. We're going to need a good picture of you."

After this, Yoshiko didn't hear much more of what her mother was saying.

Landscapes loom before Yoshiko. Lush evergreen trees, reaching for the sun, spread branches in a welcoming embrace. The sweet smell of cedar fills her senses and her mind reels with the intoxication. Distant mountains seem to move to lend their strength to her. Her pores open. Her mouth opens. From deep within her spews a current of water, strong and abundant, pouring her essence onto the land in a ritual blessing of her new home. The Kuroshio has delivered her safely.

The shadows were intensely dark in the field between the neighbours' farms, even with the moonlight lapping the thatched roofs like waves on the beach. Yoshiko had promised to meet Akiko late, but she soon had second thoughts as the two stood on the dirt road looking across the swampy rice paddy to the smudge of mountains on the horizon. She was the *onesan*, or big sister, in Akiko's life. That carried a lot of responsibility, but now was the time to cut free. A faint harmony of animal calls chilled her in the strangeness of the night.

"Shimatta ne!" Akiko cursed, breaking the mood.

Yoshiko quickly scolded her. "Don't talk like that!"

"But there's mosquitoes out here!" she whined as she tried to slap them away.

The shrillness of her cousin's voice was something Yoshiko would not miss. She was so immature. "Stop being a baby," she insisted. "I've something important to tell you."

"Is it about your husband and *America*?"

"Shi! Be quiet," she commanded. "If I tell you, will you promise not to tell anyone?"

The young girl beamed, her pouting mouth professing loyalty while her body pressed forward, anxious for the news.

"All right then. My parents are arranging a marriage to Miyamoto Jinsaburo."

"Who's that?" Akiko exclaimed.

"Shi! I told you to be quiet! You want to wake everyone up?" The half moon had just about set, its meagre light now gently bathing the distant mountain peaks.

Akiko looked shamefaced.

"I don't know him either but he lives in Ban-ku-ba. Ka-na-da," she said, carefully pronouncing the strange new words. "*America*! Owns a big boarding house … rich.…" She spoke in fragments, as if trying to convince herself as much as her cousin.

"What's a boarding house?"

"I don't know exactly but my oka says it's like an inn, like Shimano-san owns," Yoshiko said. "I'm meeting his family –"

"Oh, why do you want to go so far away?" Akiko said, her eyes starting to well up. "From me … from me?"

"Quiet! Be quiet, you little girl," Yoshiko said to comfort her. She reached out to her cousin and touched her shoulder a moment before drawing her hand away. "Don't be silly … don't be silly.…" Tears came to her own eyes as she sensed she had betrayed her cousin somehow. Was there ever going to be a time when they were together again?

"I'm not going yet," Yoshiko assured. "You can help me get ready. Come over tomorrow and help me pick out a photograph."

"What for?" Akiko managed to get out.

"To send to *Canada*."

Akiko smiled and nodded.

The road to her mother's birthplace was crude and dusty. Mihama was about five miles away, along the flat lands, far from the mountains of Yoshiko's own village. From the road, she saw acre after acre of rice paddies, their intense green surface of long slender shoots fluttering in the hot breeze. Adjacent to the fields, crisscrossed bamboo structures towered over everything, like skeletal giants teetering in the wind with their coats of drying rice harvest.

So elated was she about the prospects of the day that from time to time as she walked with her father, she called out to neighbours and strangers alike working in the fields. Some looked up, flashing a grin of recognition from beneath their broad, cone-shaped *mino-gasa* hats as they waved at her. Yoshiko felt special, as if she were royalty greeting her people. The prospect of being mistress of an inn made her beam uncontrollably. But her father said nothing to the well-wishers.

Jinshiro Hayashi was a stoic man who resembled his mother, Yoshiko's *obachan*, having inherited her sad, stony demeanor. In Yoshiko's mind, her father's weary eyes and creased face were the scars of a life full of constant worry and endless work. Jinshiro, as the first-born son, had taken up the challenge of saving the nearly bankrupt family farm after his father's stroke. Even though he toiled long, back-breaking hours in the fields just to make ends meet, he never complained.

Nor did he put on airs when times grew better. Instead, with the help of his two sons, he quietly refurbished the old farmhouse with fresh *tatami* mats. He fixed the roof, enlarged the cooking area, and managed to install an enclosed garden with a small fountain and lush vegetation as an oasis in the constant struggle to keep ahead of the creditors.

Yoshiko only hoped that she was not fated to bear such scars.

Jinshiro's relationship with his children was at best distant, but at times he was capable of kindness and poetic understanding. One such incident occurred five years earlier, when Yoshiko was thirteen.

In the middle of the summer of 1912, she had come home from the village store in tears. The sun was high and the sea playful, both out of step with her feelings. The first person she saw was her *otosan*, and she ran to him.

"Yoshiko-chan, what's wrong?"

"The Emperor ... the Emperor," she said, subsiding to a whisper, "is dead."

"Who told you that?"

"Shimizu-san, the postman," she said, stifling a sniffle. "Is it true, Oto-san?"

"Yes, it is," Jinshiro confirmed as his stern face melted at the sight of his distraught daughter. He put his arms around her and held her tightly. The beloved Emperor Meiji, the ruler who had brought the modern world to Japan, had died in the night, leaving a nation in mourning.

Although unaccustomed to such a show of affection, Yoshiko appreciated the warmth of her father's embrace.

"The time of Meiji is now gone, Yoshiko-chan," he said, "but maybe you can keep its spirit in your heart." His voice softened as he spoke. "Today is the first of August, the month of Obon – when the dead come back to comfort us."

As they walked buoyantly toward Mihama, the daughter properly behind the father, Yoshiko and her *otosan* said very little. Japan was at war but there was little negative effect on the people, rice farmers especially. Everyone knew the country was becoming a world power as part of the

Allied Forces, and the people swelled with pride that their military had ousted the Germans in the Marshalls, the Marianas, and the Carolines in the Pacific, not that Yoshiko or her contemporaries knew of their significance or even where these places were situated. But many salivated over Japan's foothold on China's Shantung Peninsula, the beginning of extensive machinations in that country.

In silence, Yoshiko admired her *otosan's* formal black kimono, brown felt fedora, and travelling slippers. The family crest of a white fan enclosed in a circle was positioned in five spots on his outfit: each side of the chest, on each sleeve, and in the middle of the back just below the collar line. The material was the traditional *habutae*, a glossy, lightweight silk cool enough for a hot summer's day. He looked so different from his usual work shirt, leggings, and *hakama* workpants, the garb of a rice farmer. No, today was a special day, and everyone knew it by the way he was dressed.

Yoshiko too was clothed in an informal kimono that her *okasan* had sewn, a pattern of red maple leaves tumbling over the garment as if caught in the wind. The material a light and therefore cool blue cotton, the kimono was worn loosely – ideal for a long walk in the stifling, sticky weather.

With the smell of the sea in the air, Mihama soon came into view. The fishing village, appropriately named the "Three Beaches," was built from the delta of the Tsuruga River at the Sea of Japan, spreading out along both banks of the river's curve. The land was generally flat, running to forests so green the vegetation hurt the eyes in the naked sunlight.

Yoshiko and her family had been there a few times in her lifetime to visit her mother's relatives. The Shinodas lived close to the beach in a modest house, typically decorated with a chaotic nest of fishing nets. Large globes of green glass floats accentuated the mass of webbing. In all likelihood, the family was out to sea and her father told Yoshiko that they would not be visiting. A distraction she didn't want anyway, though she did wonder, for a moment, what her mother was like when she was her age.

Mihama's houses were similar to those in Kiyama, simple square wooden structures with thatched roofs seemingly cobbled together, all identical except for the Miyamoto estate which stood on the only promontory above the Tsuruga River. Iwakichi Miyamoto had built himself up from modest beginnings to become the region's largest landholder, rice purveyor, and lumberman. Proof of his success resided in his grand house of crimson brick foundation and cedar panels overlooking the village from the highest vantage point in Mihama.

Yoshiko felt the thrill of her expectations as she approached her new life.

"Hello! Hello!" called an old man, his legs bare and curved by rickets. He smiled broadly as he rushed forward to greet them. "You must be very tired. It's such a hot day."

Yoshiko smiled back, thinking what a funny-looking servant this was.

Iwakichi nodded his head to her father, who bowed in return. "Hayashi-san, so nice to see you again," he said. "It's been too long. How is your wife and family?"

"Very well, Miyamoto-san," Jinshiro replied. "This is my daughter Hayashi Yoshiko."

Yoshiko wiped the smile off her face, realizing this was her future father-in-law. This is not a good start, she thought. She bowed deeply as if apologizing.

"You are a pretty one," Iwakichi said.

Yoshiko blushed, but smiled secretly, thinking she had gotten away with something.

"Well, come on then, let's go inside, out of the sun," Iwakichi continued, showing them in. As Yoshiko entered the house, she couldn't help but gaze in awe at what she saw. She nodded her approval as the gleaming oak floors and faintly golden *tatami* mats took her breath away; it was the brilliant electric lights, however, that made her gasp in amazement.

"I like to have the lights on all the time," Iwakichi said. "But that generator is so damned loud!"

Yoshiko began to relax, giggling quietly at her future father-in-law's irritation at the buzz of the generator outside that could be heard everywhere.

"So you want to marry my son." Iwakichi's voice was full of gravity, but he smiled gently. His face, a study of scars and leathery skin, bore the years of hard work without regret.

"Do you have a picture?" she said abruptly, startling even herself.

"Naniyo Yoshiko? Don't be so rude," Jinshiro scolded. "You're not buying a cow!"

"It's all right. It's all right," chuckled Iwakichi, waving Jinshiro's objections off. "I expected this. The girl's got a right to know what her husband looks like." He reached within his kimono and pulled out a photograph. "I'm afraid this is the most recent one I have. He was younger then."

With a heightened sense of anticipation, Yoshiko gingerly accepted it and examined the image of a dour boy in his dark, militaristic school uniform staring back. The small face in the black and white photograph was grainy but the uncertain, tentative look of adolescence was clear. With a pockmarked complexion, squinting eyes, and thin-lipped mouth, his youth swam just beneath the surface. At first she was disappointed at such a distorted and out-of-date picture, but she imagined a handsome face emerging with the onset of adulthood.

"Here's one for your son," Jinshiro offered, magically producing his own photograph.

Yoshiko gasped. "Otosan! Not that one!"

The sepia-toned picture depicted a trio of two brothers and Yoshiko posed in rather formal, subdued kimonos, with joyless, sullen expressions on their faces.

"Yoshiko-chan!" her father admonished. "It's good enough."

"But Akiko and I picked one out," she whined as she pulled out her own, a photo of a young woman demurely dressed in a lightly coloured kimono and holding a bamboo parasol, looking expectantly into the distance.

Jinshiro shook his head in dismay.

"Please, Miyamoto-san, send my photograph to your son," Yoshiko asked earnestly.

Iwakichi laughed heartily, suggesting to his future daughter-in-law the message that she had won the day.

"I'm so sorry," Jinshiro said. "My daughter asks for the world."

"No, no. She's a good match for my son. Jinsaburo always writes home about his large boarding house in *Canada*. He's become a good business man." Iwakichi spoke like a proud father as he called for tea and sake from one of the hovering servants, a pretty young woman who offered a tiny smile to Yoshiko. "He'll need a partner who knows her own mind!"

"Why did he leave ...?" Yoshiko ventured.

"Damare! That's enough," Jinshiro scolded, even though he knew it was a fair question. Why would the sole heir to an obvious fortune leave for an uncertain future in such a faraway land?

But Iwakichi let the question hang in the air, and the two men then carried on as Yoshiko silently sipped her tea. A dowry was offered and the deal sealed. Iwakichi said he would register Yoshiko's name with the family temple and then get in touch with his son to make arrangements to sponsor his bride overseas.

That night, the late August moon hung full and high like a jewel, suspended in the window frame of her guest room somewhere deep in the Miyamoto compound. Lying on her back, Yoshiko's mind raced with all kinds of thoughts: travel overseas, the wedding celebration, Akiko. She and her younger cousin had always fantasized about their ideal husbands, but that was schoolgirl talk. Yoshiko had never told her of her dread of a traditional marriage. She knew Akiko would be content to marry some farmer and fulfill all the expectations of a Japanese bride and never, ever understand Yoshiko's motives.

No, the man I marry will be adventurous and have the strength of ten men. His eyes will be clear and black like coal. His hair too, long and dark like fertile earth. He'll stand tall, proud of his accomplishments as seen in his straight back and great flexed muscles. He'll have lived in the land of white devils and ghost women and will be their master. And I will be his wife.

She rolled over and pulled out his photograph. Holding it close to her heart, she swooned in a young girl's reverie. *Do you see the moon, my love? We are together despite the miles of ocean between us.*

She pushed away the heavy *ofuton*. The evening was too hot to be covered. Loosening her *nemaki*, she struggled to stand up. The breezes felt cool on her skin. She closed her eyes as the moon expanded, enveloping her in its brilliant glow. Her garment fell away and the air currents tickled her full breasts before drifting across the pale-white expanse of her abdomen, then finally diving into the blackness between her legs.

She angled her pliant cheek to his clean-lined jaw and pressed her breasts against his chest. The flesh flattened and then moulded into the crevices like soft dough. Her hands traced the curves of his muscled upper arms. Her legs opened to him. She moaned weakly and squeezed her eyes.

On the floor by her feet, she noticed the pool of light had shifted. As she stepped back into it, her body glowed blue and the wind ran through her hair like gentle fingers. She knelt down and offered herself with arms spread wide and palms open to the cold beauty of the moon and the subtle movement of night drafts.

2. Monday, March 11, 1940

Etsuji Morii lounged in his office chair after hearing the confession. Even after an hour, he could smell Yoshiko's cheap perfume clinging to his jacket as if she were still grasping at him. The situation was bad enough, he conceded, and then began to chuckle incredulously. "She's worried about her reputation! Damn these stupid Japanese over here. She could ruin everything!"

The *oyabun* had been looking after the Japanese in Vancouver and in most of the west coast communities since the turn of the century. Though most feared him for his tactics, he considered them to be his children made to swallow bitter medicine from time to time for their own good. The money he made from his illicit schemes was merely tribute for his "services," much of it put to good use in the Japanese community, or so he believed.

He pulled at the ends of his moustache, the pinprick pressure points on his skin stimulating thought as he considered his options. At length, he reached across his desk for the telephone. Crooking the receiver between two fingers, he dialled a familiar number with his free hand.

In slow, Japanese-accented English, he said, "Please to speak to Sergeant *Gi-ru*."

A voice accommodated him quickly, automatically.

"*Gi-ru-san*? This Morii. Yes, I want talk to you ... late ... tonight, at *dojo*." He hung up, rose to his feet, and tugged at his loose-fitting suit. As he appraised himself in the office's full-length mirror, he smoothed his moustache and then tamed the renegade strands of hair on top of his balding head. It was a useless gesture – wisps of hair stood tall with the static electricity. Giving up, he at least brushed the telltale dandruff specks from his shoulders before clenching his fists to make his arm muscles bulge. "Not bad," he judged. "This is a bad business," he then hissed, and relaxed the tension in his arms.

The cold March sky was as grey as slate, its cloud ceiling pressing down on him like some invisible weight. As he pulled his black topcoat in closer and held his bowler against any stray wind, he considered the Yoshino Restaurant down at the corner for lunch. But they make lousy donburi rice dishes, he remembered. Besides, he couldn't stand that Noda woman, calling her a "*kuchigitanai*" to his boys, a low, foul-mouthed, gossiping fishwife. Maybe I'll get something at the club, he decided.

He glanced at an upstairs window and just caught the startled face of the mousy proprietress of the Empress Rooms before it disappeared behind lace curtains. "Her too," he said out loud, and then thought to himself: *these useless Japanese and their dirty mouths.*

He stormed westward past the various rooming houses, shops, and homes until he reached Powell Street, where he ran into Rikimatsu, his tall, angular *yojimbo*, his first lieutenant.

"Where'd you come from?" Morii asked, startled.

"Ah, Oyabun," Rik-*san* greeted as he picked his teeth. "From lunch."

"Oh, where'd you go?"

"Tengu's. Best nabeyaki udon around here."

"Ah, you like it cuz it costs thirty-five cents!" Morii scoffed.

"No, it's really good."

They laughed and then walked together toward the Showa Club.

ॐ

Not much was known about Etsuji Morii – his origins, his "business" dealings, his ambitions, his fears, his loves. His *yojimbo*, Kintaro Rikimatsu, may have been his only confidant. Certainly he had known him the longest and played witness to and participated in various schemes of his, but he generally kept his own counsel when it came to the *oyabun*. If the truth of Morii's life were a pure white light, it could only be seen through a prism as disparate colours, inconsistent and disconnected. Isolated incidents, anecdotes, and testimony given during the two times he stood trial could be strung together into something of a coherent story, but the end result was always thought to be unreliable, mere conjecture.

In one version of the truth, Etsuji Morii first came to North America in early 1904 via Portland, Oregon, as a *shosei* student with a small stipend. The wind slid across the ocean's surface toward shore and streaked upwards and across the docks buffeting two young men in identical dark suits and fedoras, their eyes shut tight in the onslaught. Both were thin, nearly scrawny, but fresh with optimism. After all, Etsuji Morii and Yosuke Matsuoka, who had become good friends on board ship, were looking forward to four years of study at the newly established University of Portland. Morii, being from a family of "free thinkers," had been part of a high school insurrection in Japan and thus took advantage of a government program, which provided students with opportunities for higher learning at American universities, to escape prosecution. His father was a great help through his socialist contacts. Matsuoka, on the other hand, was highborn and projected the confidence of someone whose future was assured. These were not typical *shosei*.

In fact, they were met at the docks by a university representative and escorted to their dorm rooms, probably out of respect for Matsuoka's station in life.

"Matsuoka-san," Morii said as they rode in a grand touring sedan, "they know of your family." The sharp angles of his cheek bones and jaw relaxed in the presence of so much attention and luxury, as if he were born to it.

"I'm sure my otosan sent word," the young aristocrat replied matter-of-factly, then folded his manicured hands on his lap and fell silent.

Morii rubbed the rich leather upholstery and wondered about his future.

All seemed well until the suspected radical learned about the fate of his fellow *shosei*. Many Japanese students in fact had come to this alien land to evade possible government persecution or prosecution. Unfortunately in pursuit of an education, they quickly ran out of money, becoming idle and destitute. In desperation, they gave up their lofty goals and took jobs as servants, waiters, or cleaners, embarrassing not only themselves but the Japanese government as well. To the local Consulate officials, these once honourable *shosei* became known as *dekasegi mono*, menial labourers. Morii, in deference to his upbringing, grew steadily incensed at the government representatives' consistent willingness to criticize without offering any solutions.

At the same time, the highly principled young man with ambitions had no intention of seeing himself lowered to the status of *dekasegi mono* even though his own stipend was hardly adequate. To this end, he decided to let his university classes slide to join the Nihon Seinen Kai, a student political group aimed at harassing the Japanese government – through their embassies and consulates – into protecting their fellow Japanese in America. Eventually Morii, using his initiative and cunning, made his way to the group's headquarters in San Francisco, where he soon devised means of extortion and blackmail in order to rescue the *shosei* from the depths of desperation.

Underpinning his socialist and radical outlook was his Buddhist upbringing, common to most Japanese families of the time. This fit in well with his *shosei* concerns. He practiced what he himself called a "social Buddhism"; that is, a melding of Buddhist principles and a concern for social justice. How he reconciled his "Buddha nature" with his violent nature as he sank into the depths of gangsterism was a mystery.

Back in the day, however, Matsuoka remained diligent in his studies, and Morii, despite the different path taken, did not burn that bridge, perhaps foreseeing a time when a well-placed contact like his friend was going to be valuable.

⌘

October 1905

In the swirling heart of the San Francisco fog, at the corner of Laguna and Post, across from the Northern California District Buddhist Church with its ornate Japanese shale-tiled roof, stood an impressive Victorian building with angels caught in the architecture, a feature odd for the area. The fourth floor housed four offices with high ceilings and tall windows, its blinds perpetually closed to the curious. Its clammy atmosphere gave visitors or intruders a chill, a definite advantage to the tenants.

There was little furniture – a battered desk of cheap wood in each room, a few wire-fastened chairs that creaked to the touch. No file cabinets, no coat rack, no shelving to speak of. An oil lamp stood on each desk, but none seemed to have been used in a long time. The walls were blank: no paintings, no fixtures or adornments except for a ceiling gaslight with a few art nouveau flourishes in its design. Nothing to give away the occupants' identities.

In another era, the place served as headquarters for an association of San Francisco's Japanese brothel owners – the Gorotsuki Club or the Hard Crowd Club formed in 1892. Less than ten years later, the place and presumably the members were taken over by the Black Dragon Society. In 1905, the building still remained anonymous and, even though everyone suspected what went on inside, only a few knew exactly what did.

A large man whose overhanging belly spoke of his romance with food pulled his new charge into the smoky front office. Hideo Kameoka, clothed in a dark double-breasted suit, pushed the shy seventeen-year-old inside to stand with head lowered, shoulders hunched, before a group of men. The boy's own suit was tight-fitting, frayed at the edges, the cuffs of his pants precariously falling just above his ankles.

"Oyabun, this is Morii Etsuji," he announced. "Bow, boy!"

The skinny teenager with a ferret-like face, coughing as the tobacco smoke attacked his lungs, looked back to the hallway. Kameoka instantly slapped the top of his offending head. Morii snapped around to face forward again and bowed deeply.

The *oyabun* emerged from behind the desk to tower over the shivering boy. He too was dressed in a dark suit with matching cravat and handkerchief.

"All right, stand up straight," Kameoka commanded.

The *oyabun's* face was obscured by the smoke and shadows of the room, but Morii could make out a ragged scar down the left cheek, the surrounding skin hardened into ridges as a result.

"What's his name again?" the *oyabun* asked.

"I'm Morii –" A fist slammed him to the floor before he could finish.

"Baka! Speak when you're spoken to!" shouted Kameoka. "Morii Etsuji, Oyabun."

"You say he's going to work for us?" The *oyabun's* voice seeped through the haze of Morii's pain as he lay in a lump.

"He did a good job at the Seinen Kai. Nakamura vouches for him."

"Seinen Kai? Well, we'll cure him of that. We can't let our youth be open to such influences." The *oyabun* glared at the boy with an intimidating intensity. "Stand up," he ordered in a whisper.

Morii rose to his feet gingerly, rubbing his neck.

"Morii-san, don't mind Kameoka. He's a stuffed shirt, likes the old ways." The *oyabun* smiled as he reached out to Morii's shoulder. The boy flinched, but the hand was as gentle as the voice was soft. "Yes, the old ways, the time of loyalty, of Yamato-damashii, when a Seinen Kai wasn't even considered possible." The *oyabun* turned his back on the boy and continued his diatribe. "The Japanese today have forgotten that they're Japanese, especially in this kuso country. But that will change. The Russo-Japanese War is but a mere example of our superiority. The Emperor will continue to lead us to greatness!" His voice rose with emotion.

Morii stepped back, trembling like a frightened dog.

The *oyabun* faced the boy again. "You seem to be an ideal candidate to join us," he said, then suddenly looked up to include the others in the room. "But first we must teach you the spirit of Yamato! You must not fail the Emperor and bring dishonour to Japan. You will never forget that you are Japanese!"

Everyone cheered, "Banzai!" but Morii said nothing. His mind raced, evaluating the situation, his eyes raised at the degree of Emperor worship. His father would have been appalled.

"Listen, my little rebel," continued the *oyabun*, "you're going to need someone to show you our ways."

Morii nodded tentatively.

He waved to a black figure in the deeper shadows of the room. "This is Rikimatsu Kintaro. He'll take care of you."

Emerging into the light, the lanky man was a frightening presence. Standing two heads taller than Morii, he had a ruddy complexion, close-set, inkspot eyes, and a wide mouth full of brown pegs for teeth. His face was straight out of a nightmare.

The *oyabun* once again receded into the smoke with the others in the room as Morii and Rikimatsu shook hands. The two new companions left, ignored by the new business at hand.

Post Street was cloaked with its typical early evening fog. The young Morii strained to see the Victorian houses of Pacific Heights, the glum ladies of old money, but his field of vision was maybe twenty feet ahead as the street sloped into the heart of what was called Little Tokyo. The chill with its touch of winter forced him to pull in the narrow confines of his suit jacket.

The buildings tightly lined the street making misdirection hardly possible, but Rikimatsu led the way with a crooked gait, rocking from one hip to the other. His strange walk combined with his checkered vest and black suit gave him a clownish air. Morii knew better.

Two blocks later, the duo stood before what appeared to be a massive wooden wall. Morii soon discovered it to be the decorative false front of a local *nomi-ya*, a drinking place called Naniwa-ya. Rikimatsu insisted they go inside.

"What kind of joint is this?" Morii asked dismissively as he shook off the outside cold. The large open room flooded his senses, his cheeks flushing instantly. Loud conversations, choking smoke, and the cloying smell of stale beer floated above the crowd of mainly rough Japanese men playing to heavily made-up women sipping on drinks made of sugar, seltzer water, and ice.

"This joint, as you call it, is owned by the oyabun," growled Rikimatsu as he pointed to an empty table.

The young Morii was impressed. He knew the Black Dragon Society generated a lot of money for its members, and just how much was plain to see in this bar.

A waitress appeared like an apparition.

"You want biru or sake?" asked Rikimatsu in his gruff, gravel voice.

"Uh … biru," he replied hesitantly.

"Nesan. Biru onegaishimasu!"

The waitress nodded and drifted back into the smoke.

Now that they were seated, Morii noticed Rikimatsu's heavy-lidded left eye and the misshapen socket housing it. "Can I ask what happened to your eye?" he asked.

"Accident."

"On a boat?"

"How'd you know that?"

"Your hands. They look like those of a fisherman."

"Not a fisherman. Merchant marine." Rik-*san* shifted as if uncomfortable talking about his past. "I jumped ship here smuggling some jewellery and got caught."

"Customs?"

"Customs? Hell no! By my captain. He was the one who done this," he said, pointing with his thumb to his eye. "Stuck a spike in it and left me for dead on the pier."

Morii paused in awe before a grin cracked across his face. "Bakayaro! You take me for an idiot or something?"

"You're pretty sharp." Rikimatsu winked his good eye at the boy. "What'd you do at the Nihon Seinen Kai?" he asked while continuing to size up his young companion. "Personally I hate political clubs."

"I circulated rumours about Maikawa."

"The Consul General?" he said in astonishment. "That's something. What'd you say?"

"I said he liked little boys."

Rik-*san* burst out laughing just as the waitress brought two bottles of beer with tall glasses. "Don't tell the oyabun this!" he advised as he slapped the table. "What were you trying to get? Money?"

"No, I was just trying to convince him to help an old lady I know get her son out of jail."

"Heh?"

"The shit got drunk and beat up a police officer. That ketsuno ana, bringing the keto cops down on us like that."

The waitress didn't hide her curiosity well as she lingered by the table, pouring the beer.

"What did Maikawa do?" Rik-*san* asked. His eyes narrowed as he waved off the nosy waitress.

Morii attempted a tentative sip but then sat back proud at being so clever. "What do you think? He got the son out."

"Hey, don't you drink?" Rik-*san* had noticed the boy's hesitation.

"Of course I drink. I'm just not thirsty now."

"What's being thirsty got to do with anything? Drink!"

Morii looked up fearful of being found out and quickly lifted his glass to his mouth. He took a long draught until he choked on the acrid liquid, coughing violently and betraying his lack of experience.

Rik-*san* laughed even more and pounded his new friend on the back. "You're all right, Morii-san. You're all right!"

After his fit had subsided, Morii breathed in deeply.

Rikimatsu picked up the questioning again. "So tell the truth. You get money out of the old lady or Maikawa?"

Embarrassed by his lack of drinking prowess, Morii wanted to avoid revealing much more of himself. "What did you mean about not telling the oyabun?" he asked carefully.

"Heh?"

"About Maikawa."

"Oh, because he's an Emperor worshipper. Or didn't you notice? 'Honour and loyalty above all else!' Me, I don't care about such things. I told you I don't like anything political or the like. I'm just warning you so you don't say nothing bad about the Emperor or Japan," Rikimatsu advised.

"So ... what if I don't want to join the society?" Morii asked gingerly.

"You got no choice. The oyabun is aware of you now," Rikimatsu explained. "Who do you think brought you in? Not that fat bastard Kameoka. That kusotare could never recognize raw talent if it hit him in the face."

The boy sank into silence. *No choice?* The revelation bothered him. He didn't like being told what to do and this sounded as if he were in a trap – one he could not extricate himself from easily. The soft luxurious feel of leather seats entered his thoughts.

"So did you get money or what?"

"I told you no," he replied with irritation in his voice. "I didn't want any money."

"No?"

"No."

"Then why bother?"

"I got something better than money."

"What's that?"

"Obligation."

Etsuji Morii made quite a name for himself after his induction into the Black Dragon Society, even at the tender age of seventeen. On his own initiative, he boldly went to Chinatown in search of Japanese patrons, down narrow staircases leading into cramped and noisy basement gambling dens on Grant Avenue and thereabouts. At first, he was intimidated by the lettering of the ubiquitous signs. He could read the ideograms like any Japanese could, but what if some damn *Chankoro*, Chinaman, spoke to him? They would find him out for sure.

Swallowing his fear, the teenager made himself inconspicuous by wearing his ill-fitting suit with a bowler hat and a heavy woollen overcoat. In this way, he hid his youth as well. He looked like the anonymous Englishmen in a newsreel of London, England, he once saw. These white men seemed to be of no consequence. Perhaps no one would notice him, much less want to talk to him as a result.

Fortunately, he was correct, as the Tong strongmen paid the boy no mind. He moved amongst the crowds of the basement enclaves undisturbed until he spotted an *issei* card player, waited for his chance to sidle up to him and then talk some sense into him.

"Hey boss, what're you doing here?" Morii asked in a conspiratorial tone.

"Looking to win back my shirt," the *issei* said, startled somewhat at hearing Japanese in the Chinese den. Nonetheless, the distressed labourer, his slumping shoulders and curved back bearing the burden of bad luck, continued to sit, riffling through his remaining money and accounting for his losses.

"Why are you giving these Chankoro all your money?" Morii said.

"Heh?"

"Gambling's no good, you would agree, ne? Bad for you, your family, or your future family."

"But I could win."

"Win? You'll never win," Morii said grinning. "Look, the *fan tan* dealer? He's a cheater, a well-known cheater. At least well-known in Chinatown."

"He is?"

"If you insist on gambling, why not do it with your own kind? Keep the money in your own community."

"Say, who are you?"

"I'm one of you. Japanese. You should be at Naniwa-ya, where all the Japanese are."

More often than not, his words did the trick. He always sported a wry smile as the *issei* made their way back to Little Tokyo and his *oyabun's* club. Like a teacher and her students, he knew their character: their strengths, their weaknesses, and what was good for them.

Any qualms he had about joining the society quickly dissipated with his share of the profit the returning players produced. He didn't spend it in any obvious way, as he was too clever for that, and it would be too much of a betrayal of his nature. Instead, he secretly donated to the Seinen Kai, his old political club, or created obligations amongst the Japanese families.

If he felt any guilt about exploiting his own, he never showed it. The men were weak, forgetful of their obligations to their families. Keep the money in Little Tokyo, not to be enjoyed by the despicable and godless Chinese. He saw that the Society members were obligated to set an *issei* straight if he went too far in his wagering. And there were the envelopes of money placed in suffering mothers' hands.

Eventually, Morii came to the notice of the *oyabun* and was summoned once more to the austere office at Laguna and Post.

Discarding his overcoat, the boy, dressed in a thin jacket and cheap tie, shivered once more in the chilled air of the room. The fat Kameoka was off to the side, restraining himself. The *oyabun* stood as he always had, behind the desk, his face as ever in the shadows.

"So Morii-san, you have done well for us," he said in his quiet manner, "and in such a short time." He moved in front of the desk to talk to the boy face to face. "You're right to think we can't let these Chinese dogs take advantage of our people. And you've brought back a lot of business to us."

Morii smiled broadly as Kameoka sneered at him.

The *oyabun* continued, ignoring the exchange. "I've a new job for you. There's a place north of here called *Vancouver* with a fairly large Japanese population. We own a club there that can't keep our people loyal. Many of the Japanese go to Chinatown, and of course, get taken advantage of. You go there and work your magic. Bring them back to their own, where they belong. The oyabun there is Shiga Mitsuzo. Rikimatsu will go with you."

Morii remained silent as he bowed acceptance.

"One last question," the *oyabun* asked suddenly. "Where'd you come from?"

"From Hiro —" The *oyabun* interjected by raising his hand.

"Never talk about your past, where you come from. Only the present is important. The past is a curse."

As Morii walked out of the office, he noticed Kameoka rushing forward as if anxious to have his say. From the hallway, he heard a loud slap and a flurry of harsh words. He turned around to see Kameoka on his knees begging forgiveness and holding the side of his head.

Morii was the first to admit that he was bewildered at being sent as a troubleshooter to a Black Dragon holding even if it was, as he later found out, to some hick town in another country. Maybe the *oyabun* wanted to put his first lieutenant in his place by assigning a young buck instead of him. Or he wanted to revitalize Vancouver with fresh, energetic blood. In the end, he concluded out of arrogance that it was because of his particular talents. After all, he had risen to fairly rarefied heights in an inordinately short period of time. He savoured the image of fat Kameoka on his knees, grovelling for forgiveness.

On a cool, clear spring day in 1906, Morii and Rikimatsu arrived in town and found a couple of rooms in the New World Hotel on Powell Street, the main thoroughfare of Vancouver's Japanese community. The long flights of stairs to their fourth-floor rooms were dark and narrow, like the gambling dens in San Francisco's Chinatown, but the place was clean, if rundown. Morii especially appreciated the fact that people kept to themselves.

The next evening, Morii with his derby cocked and Rikimatsu with his rocking gait made quite a pair as they set out along Powell west to Gore Avenue. The teenager was struck by the beauty of the mountains to the north, the panorama scarred by plumes of black smoke coming from what he later discovered to be Hastings Mill. Dwarfed under the landscape were Vancouver's characteristic flat-roofed buildings with their Victorian cornices, forlorn windows and weary foundations. In a fanciful frame of mind, Morii began to identify with those buildings. He was as insignificant in the presence of greater beings yet, at the same time, he was undeniably being observed from afar. His need for success despite his isolation from the lively action of San Francisco's Little Tokyo area or even Chinatown's lights and forbidden women became clearer to him now as they continued walking down the street.

Around the corner on Gore, they found the Raku Raku Restaurant, which occupied the bottom floor of a solid-brick building of anonymous apartments. Only a small, crudely painted sign in Japanese identified the place. The broad storefront window was closed with drawn shades.

The place was a dump, a dive. Morii suddenly realized the *oyabun* meant this to be his baptism of fire. He would have to make it here in this backwater town in a largely untamed land or never be heard of again. He certainly couldn't go back to San Francisco if not successful. He bristled at the thought of Kameoka's glee over his failure.

Morii angrily knocked on the solid wood front door. No answer. He knocked again and kept on knocking until the lock disengaged from the inside.

In the grey interior, the two gagged on the odour of dried sweat, spent tobacco, and camphor emanating, evidently, from a group of four men – rough-looking, and standing around in rolled-up shirt sleeves, hard expressions on their unshaven faces. The dimly-lit, one-room restaurant with a greasy checkerboard floor and rundown kitchen in back was as inviting as a den of wolves. The worn tables and chairs in front were empty of customers. The apparent boss of the group, a stocky man with the tired look of general booziness, was slumped in a wobbly chair, riffling a deck of cards on a table in front of him. With the intrusion of outside light, Mitsuzo Shiga squinted at the two interlopers.

"You the pros from the oyabun?" he snarled sarcastically. The others chuckled.

"Have more respect," Rikimatsu warned, straining to hold his temper. "This here's Morii Etsuji, and I'm Rikimatsu Kintaro."

Another scoffed at them. "How old are you two? Still sucking at your oka's chi-chi?"

In one swift motion Rikimatsu stepped forward, cocked his leg, and kicked the insolent henchman in the face, blood exploding from his nose. The man fell back and knocked himself unconscious when his head hit the floor. Two others moved to counter. Morii stepped into them and, with a neat body throw and leg sweep, toppled both men to the floor.

The boss stood up roughly, awkwardly, nearly falling down himself. In a panic, he shouted with hands raised, "Now wait a minute. Take it easy! We're all on the same side here."

Morii and Rikimatsu stood breathing heavily, their hands poised for more. "What kind of business you running here?" asked Morii, spitting out the question like venom. "It's nearly seven o'clock and you're still not open? No gambling going on? No wonder all the customers are headed for Chinatown."

"Now hold on –"

"No, you hold on," Rikimatsu interrupted. "Things are gonna change around here."

As his henchmen dragged themselves to a corner in defeat, the boss came out from behind his table to try and calm his assailants. Scratching his two-day-old stubble, he smiled crookedly. "Say, you boys are pretty good at judo!"

"What of it!" Morii barked.

"Learned it in Korea," Rikimatsu added.

The boss raised his eyebrows. "Oh, you Korean then?"

Rikimatsu grabbed the man by the shirt with one hand, the other curled into a fist, threatening to strike. "What'd you call me?"

"Wait! I was just asking."

"Don't ask about the past," Morii warned with his finger pointing. "The past is a curse."

It was clear to the two "pros" that the Black Dragon group in Vancouver was not up to the standards set in San Francisco. The men here were weak, lazy, and unimaginative. In a couple of weeks, Morii let it be known he was the new leader with Rikimatsu as *yojimbo*, his right-hand-man. No one challenged them.

The only provision Shiga got right was the alcohol. In 1897, the Alien Labour Act prevented Japanese from obtaining licenses to buy and sell liquor to the public. According to Black Dragon methodology, he then employed farmers in nearby Abbotsford and thereabouts to set up operations to distill alcohol and brew beer. Rikimatsu had little trouble in convincing the hapless farmers to continue doing business with the new "management."

Morii then hired a carpenter, Goro Kaburagi, a fireplug of a man, to fix up the Raku Raku inside and to put up a proper sign in front so people knew they were open for business. Retaining a cook and bartender, the young *oyabun*, as he started calling himself, soon had a restaurant that attracted a fair number of customers. The fresh vinyl booths, white clapboard walls, and good food and alcohol were a welcome change. It could have been a place for families to enjoy an evening out if not for the gambling room in back with four tables, low lighting, and smoky atmosphere. The former boss and his henchmen resided there, their glum faces long and defeated as they dealt out cards to the patrons: itinerant workers such as lumberjacks and railroad men. Eventually, Shiga faded into various Powell Street enclaves, just a mere shadow in the night.

Morii had no intention of opening a place for families. The Japanese in Canada were as weak as those in California, and just as easily led astray. He decided then and there he would provide a place for the men to play out their vices while at the same time become a pillar of the community. In this way, he could fulfill the demands of his masters in

San Francisco and satisfy his own sense of altruism.

Another amenity of the place, instituted six months later, brought in a different, more advantageous clientele: the most successful businessmen in the area. Upstairs from the Raku Raku, the entire second floor became the Hinomaru, an exclusive club catering to only the rich.

Through his Black Dragon contacts in San Francisco, Morii brought in young women to act as waitresses and hostesses – but not the broken, diseased, and desperate kind who worked as prostitutes or *joro* in the bawdy houses on Alexander Street, or who met their johns in the bramble of the junkyard lot farther along Alexander, east of Princess Avenue. He paid those women no mind, though once in a while he kicked at one, laughing when she flinched.

At his establishment, for a certain amount of money, any patron could hire a "wife," fresh-faced and comely, for an evening's conversation, before retiring to one of several discreet rooms in the upper floors of the building.

This new accommodation was not always convenient. Some of the women whined about the cut they received. "Not enough!" they complained. Others refused to sit with, let alone have sex with, those they considered to be "smelly," "ugly," or "too old." The troublemakers were sent back to San Francisco, but at great cost. After about a year, Morii hit upon another scheme to cut back on his overhead.

"Soga-san," Morii breathed into his lascivious customer's ear. "You like Michiko, don't you?"

Soga nodded, his jowls jiggling in his excitement.

"Yes, she is a pretty one. How would you like your pick of Michikos? They could be the 'wives' that suit your mood."

Like a schoolboy in a candy store, Soga again nodded, not saying a word, not even taking his eyes from the waitress serving the table next to his, her sensual hips swaying in her tight kimono.

"I tell you what," Morii continued, "I can arrange passage for as many 'wives' as you like. All you have to do is pay for their boat fare from Japan and rooms at the Empress Rooming House and they'll be yours any time you like."

Astonished at the thought, Soga turned to Morii. "Am I made of money?"

"Soga-san! You own the biggest department store in the neighbourhood. Everyone goes to your store. Besides, a man of your prominence deserves the best."

Looking sheepish, Soga added, "But I've had trouble with Michiko. You know, getting her co-operation, if you know what I mean."

"Don't worry. I guarantee these 'wives' will be co-operative."

After calling in his marker from the Japanese Consulate soon after the 1907 riots in Chinatown and Powell Street, Morii was able to set up an advantageous relationship with the Consul General. Using the "Guarantor Authority" the Consul bestowed upon the Nihon Jinkai, the *oyabun* (who had tremendous influence in the Japanese Businessmen's Club) could then control all Japanese immigrant documents and easily bring in these "sponsored" women for his club. By holding their passports "in trust," he could also force them into service by threatening to have them arrested by the RCMP for entering Canada without the proper documents.

The sudden scream tore apart the prevailing evening quiet of the Hinomaru. Morii and Rikimatsu abandoned their glasses of whiskey with water on the side and scrambled upstairs to one of the anonymous rooms to find the fat and old Soga-san cowering in a corner clutching his nakedness. By the bed, Michiko shuddered in her outrage, her breasts wobbling in a game of hide and seek beneath her open yukata of maples and rain.

"You shit," she accused at the top of her lungs. "Shit ... shit ..."

Soga swivelled away to hide as the oyabun and yojimbo entered.

"Damare!" commanded Morii. "What's going on here?"

"That kusotare!" she cried out, almost incoherently.

"All right. All right. Soga-san, tell me —"

"I told you. She always gives me trouble ..." he whimpered.

Michiko lashed out at him. "His chinpoko is dirty. It stinks! I won't do what he wants! Not with my mouth!" A sudden slap across the face choked off her words.

Morii seethed in his rage. "Shut it! He's the customer." He slapped her again, hard, crumpling her to the floor.

Rik-san as if on cue covered the distraught Soga with a convenient yukata and escorted him out of the room.

"You're the little shit," Morii hissed at the quivering, somewhat recovered Michiko. "You made me look bad in front of my best customer. You're more trouble than you're worth."

"But he never washes! He farts all the time!" she complained in rapid-fire succession. "His wife doesn't want him! Why should I?"

"Because I make two hundred every time he comes in! You ... I'm giving

you to the Mounties. And then they'll deal with you in Tokyo. You'll never bring shame to me again," he promised. "Too bad, you had such a pretty face."

Her cries went deep into the night.

In this way, Etsuji Morii and the Black Dragon Society prospered in Vancouver.

ॐ

Monday, March 11, 1940

The Showa Club was located in the 300-block of Powell Street, upstairs from Shibuya's clothing stores, women's apparel to the left, men's to the right. A single door opened to a well-worn stairway that led up to the men's club. Just inside the vestibule to the street, the "watchman," a grizzled old man with pockmarked and jaundiced skin, sat on a metal chair. He was always dressed the same, in a rumpled jacket, stained pants, and suspenders over an undershirt, no matter what the weather.

At the top of the staircase, a single bare light bulb led the way to a large, well-lit hall with buzzing fluorescent lights, three billiard tables and assorted chairs along the walls. Across the ceiling and down the walls was the telltale trail of renovation work. The continuous wound of exposed studs and plaster, work started and abandoned in the 1920s, marked how the space had been divided into smaller rooms for let. Many complained that it had been twenty years, and it was time to get the work finished, but Morii dismissed his critics and told them to pay for it if they wanted the renovations so badly. In the back of the place were three doors.

Kichitaro Akiyama, a handsome man with thick hair and a winning smile, was the manager. Before World War I, he had owned the Momiji Pool Hall, one of three popular establishments where most of the Japanese men wiled away the evening hours before reporting for the morning shift at the Hastings Mill or catching a boat to a remote logging camp. Perhaps it was for adventure or to prove his loyalty to Canada, but Akiyama, or "Aki," wrote to his wife in Japan that he had volunteered for the army at the outbreak of war in Europe.

Do not grieve for me no matter what happens. I will do my best to be a good example for our children to become good citizens. Aki

So proud of his grand gesture of patriotism was Aki that he recited the contents of his letter to anyone who cared to listen. Other than being surprised and amused at his candour, some thought his signing the letter with his nickname was indicative of his flippant attitude toward marriage. Others guessed that perhaps he was telling his wife he had decided to become Canadian. Many, especially Rikimatsu, treated the whole thing as a joke.

In any case, Aki was reported missing in action on April 26, 1917. By the end of the war, everyone in Vancouver's Japanese sector presumed him dead. So there was quite a commotion in 1928 when a familiar figure walked into what was once the Momiji Club.

The patrons in fact stopped their gaming and drinking and fell silent. One dropped his pool cue.

The man standing before them stared back for a moment, then said, "What? You never seen a ghost before?"

A voice cried out. "Aki? Is that you?"

"In the flesh!" he said, thumping his barrel chest.

"But you're dead!" another voice shouted.

A diminutive stranger stepped forward and bowed. "Akiyama-san? I'm Morii Etsuji."

"Oh yeah?"

"Welcome to my club, the Showa Club," he said, sweeping his arm across the air, "and welcome back to life!"

The moment prickled with tension.

Aki breathed in deeply and glared. "Glad to be here!" he finally said and let out a belly laugh, as did Morii and everyone else in the place.

He had indeed survived the war and even taken a *hakujin* wife, Michelle Dubois, a French woman who thought all of Canada spoke her native tongue. Although disappointed, she came to Vancouver with him to settle in the Kitsilano area, away from the disapproving eyes of Powell Street.

No one talked to him directly about the wisdom of marrying a *keto*, but speculation did arise in the endless barroom gossip: "Ten years ago they would've lynched the asshole. Maybe the both of them!" ... "Ten? Try five!" ... "I can't believe the Kitsilano Japanese would let 'em live there. They're so 'proper' over there!" ... "Why'd he marry one anyway?"

… "You don't know? They got big tits and big, round bottoms! And I hear they do things no respectable Japanese woman would do."

Aki soon learned Morii and the Black Dragon Society, in his absence, had amalgamated the Momiji, Toyo, and Shintani Pool Halls into the Showa Club. He asked for a job and was offered the manager's position; he readily accepted. No public mention was ever made of his abandoned wife and children in Japan. How he felt deep down about losing his place of business was also anybody's guess.

The rumble of feet and lively conversation up the stairs heralded the arrival of the *oyabun* and his *yojimbo*. Morii first entered the room and removed his derby to reveal his balding head and grinning face, made hard by his runt of a moustache. Following him like a loyal dog was Rikimatsu, regaling his *oyabun* with a story about the old days.

"I saw the notice in the *Tairiku Nippo*! I swear."

"Rik-san, I don't believe it."

"Yeah well, we'll see." Rikimatsu looked around the room, half-filled with lumbermen in the city from the Interior waiting for their next job, before settling on the manager behind the counter.

"Aki," he shouted. "Ain't it true your wife put an ad in the paper looking for you? You know, just after the war? Your Japan –"

Morii chuckled as he elbowed Rik-*san* in the stomach. "Damare, you're embarrassing him."

"Oh sorry," said Rikimatsu in Akiyama's general direction. "Maybe he's planning on getting another one," he whispered with a smile. "You know, 'over there' with the new war."

The bartender went about his work as if nothing had been said.

The two took a seat near one of the pool tables and called Aki over.

"So how's business?" Morii asked casually of the manager.

Aki shrugged. "Not bad. Not good. It'll pick up tonight."

"So ne," Rikimatsu agreed. "Two beers and a chicken-rice donburi for the oyabun. Make sure there's plenty of shiitake in it!" He returned his attention to Morii. "Hey, remember the first time we met? We were at that bar. What was the name again?" He scratched his chin, the rough stubble making a rasping noise.

"Naniwa-ya."

"Yeah, that's it. You couldn't take it. You coughed up beer everywhere!"

Akiyama walked away, sensing trouble. Only Rikimatsu could get away with laughing at the *oyabun's* expense, but not entirely.

"Yeah, I remember," Morii said, scowling at his minion. "I couldn't take it. Long ago, when I was a kid and you had a nose."

Rikimatsu stifled himself abruptly, knowing he had gone too far. The *yojimbo* was not handsome; in fact, he had a horrible-looking face with gouges and craters in his skin, and a distorted and scarred left eye. And if not for the badly reconstructed skin to accommodate his nostrils, Rikimatsu would not have any semblance of a nose.

Such an omission not only drew attention to his face but also raised questions about Rikimatsu's ethnic origin. It had always been in dispute. His name was Japanese, but he just didn't look it. His skin was sallow, distinctly like a Chinese, some observed. Others felt he was Korean, especially when he demonstrated his knowledge of Korean-style judo techniques. No one knew for sure and he wasn't talking.

"Oi, Aki! I told you to get over here," Morii called, having put Rik-*san* in his place.

"One minute. Ya want beers or don't ya?" Aki shouted back. The manager carefully balanced the two glasses on a tray before making his way back to the table.

"You heard about anything unusual happening around here? In the neighbourhood?" Morii asked as he took his drink in hand.

"Well, I heard old lady Seto got cheated at Soga's," he laughed. "Soga, that bastard, probably shortchanged her!"

"No, no. Did you hear about any arguments, fights? Anything?"

"Oyabun," Rik-*san* interjected, "what're you driving at?"

Morii hesitated. "Anyone missing?"

"I heard about some money missing. In Steveston."

"What's going on?"

Morii took a big gulp of beer and stared into his glass. "Murder," he whispered.

3. May 1920

The Yokohama sun was at its peak with no clouds floating overhead to mar the perfection of the day. The May winds were strong, insistent but pleasantly warm. Yoshiko Miyamoto breathed in the salt air and she felt its sting deep inside her twenty-one-year-old lungs. She rubbed her cheeks rosy as she revelled in the anticipation.

It was the height of the Yoboyose Jidai, the "Summoning of Relatives Period" or "Restricted Immigration Period" (1908–1924), and everyone was caught up in its spirit of adventure. Very few brides were fortunate enough to meet their suitors beforehand. Some of them married successful men who had returned to Japan to select wives for themselves; most, however, married through the picture-bride system. Yoshiko fell somewhere in between. Her husband was rich enough to come home but chose not to, so here she was standing on the docks with all the other picture brides tightly clutching their photographs of distant strangers. Each woman appeared anxious to get underway, most hoping the man they had married was honourable enough not to have misrepresented himself. But Yoshiko was confident in the certainty of her fate, and kept her new husband's picture in a pocket close to her heart.

The *Canada Maru*, a modern ocean-faring ship with steam engines and three smoke stacks, gently bobbed in place as it sat waiting for its passengers, held by its moorings. The Yokohama docks buzzed with the goings and comings of emigration. Yoshiko's trunk was already down below in the cargo hold. She herself stood with her parents, father-in-law, and cousin Akiko, awaiting the signal for her to board. Beside her were two packages of clothes gathered together by *furoshiki*, knotted aquamarine spreads of square cloth decorated, in this case, with stylized evergreens. She was dressed in her best kimono with a brilliant pattern of pink cherry-blossom *sakura* and red maple leaves streaming across the material. Her mother had objected to making it since she would only be able to wear it as a newlywed, as a *yomesan*. It wasn't sensible, especially since she was off to a foreign land. Shortly, Yoshiko would be considered an *okusan*, a homemaker, and the kimono too garish to be seen in polite society.

"Yoshiko-chan," Naka called out to draw her daughter's attention. She held out a cedar box with the ideogram for tea on the cover.

Yoshiko smiled as she accepted the present. Opening it gingerly, she discovered six bright-green teacups and matching teapot, all rimmed with gold. She bowed in gratitude. They had been a wedding gift given by her *obachan* to her mother, Naka. She remained for a time with her head lowered, turning over in her mind how bad a daughter she had been in the weeks leading to this moment.

ॐ

Yoshiko Hayashi entered the Miyamoto family at the end of August, Taisho 7, 1919, almost two years to the day the proposal of marriage had been made during a similarly hot August day in 1917. The "wedding ceremony" itself consisted of the unceremonious registering of her name in the *koseki* family register at the temple in Mihama.

In early adolescence, Yoshiko had dreamed of preparing for a traditional wedding. She and her cousin Akiko had giggled for hours on end about it, promising that the other would play a significant role. Akiko would act as her dresser. She winced every time she imagined her sincere yet clumsy cousin using camellia oil and cosmetic paste to pull, comb, and shape her long hair into the formal bridal hairstyle called a *takashimada*.

"Ow! Be careful," Yoshiko complains. "You're hurting me!"

"Sorry! I'm so sorry." Akiko juggles the black mass of hair and gambols about as she tries to keep the gooey oil from dripping onto the floor.

"You clean your hands before you touch my favourite comb! It's real tortoiseshell, you know."

"This stuff is so slippery."

"What a mess! I just hope my hair is all right."

Akiko next smears Yoshiko's face with thick white powder paste, then etches her eyebrows with a pencil and paints red miniature lips on her mouth to give her a demure appearance.

"Hold still!" Akiko insists.

"I can feel something in my ear."

"I'll clean that out after I do your lips. Oh no."

"What've you done?" Yoshiko asks suspiciously.

"Don't worry, I can fix it."

Looking in a hand mirror, Yoshiko declares angrily, "Even if your life depended on it, you could never draw!"

If that isn't enough, her cousin then has to deal with all the ceremonial clothing: a wraparound underskirt, cotton undershirt, a long white silk crepe under-kimono, and an outer kimono, a formal montsuki, which was embellished with hand-painted designs.

"Too tight! Too tight! I can't breathe," Yoshiko complains as Akiko ties a long silk obi sash around her body to keep everything together.

The final accoutrement is the tsunoka kushi, a pure white hood, placed on the bride's head to hide the horns of jealousy women are fabled to possess. Akiko naturally pricks the scalp in the effort.

"Were you born to hurt me?"

"I'm sorry, Yoshiko. You know how I am … I'm … I'm …"

"Oh, stop, you little girl, before you start crying. I'll recover before the wedding! I'll get my revenge when it's your day!"

Not that she was much older now, but Yoshiko had to chuckle. That was when she was a schoolgirl. It was okay for Akiko, she was still a silly girl who could afford to fantasize. Yoshiko did worry about her immature cousin, but her duty was clearly to cross the ocean to join her husband. Akiko would have to grow up on her own. A week after registering the marriage, she was on the road again to her new family's estate. This time, she travelled in style.

Her father and mother accompanied her on the bus that carried all of her worldly possessions. They sat saying nothing to each other, quietly enduring the heat and dust. Jinshiro, of course, wore his *montsuki kimono*, while Naka had on an understated one, perhaps as an example to Yoshiko of how a wife, newlywed or not, should dress in public. Both outfits took on the random patterns of blowing white dust as the journey continued.

After arriving in front of the Mihama post office and grocery store, the trio made the rest of the way on foot. Yoshiko breathed in the invigorating sea air, almost tasting the seaweed combed by the steady currents. The simple, low-lying houses of the village were weather-beaten with fish netting draped on drying racks in front, seemingly poised to ensnare anyone who walked by. She thought that perhaps her mother was thinking of her own wedding day when she and her parents walked these roads towards Kiyama. In the distance, she heard the roar of waves, catching a glimpse, every so often, of the whitecaps beyond the sea wall. Yoshiko stopped a moment, chilled by her imagination.

Fingers of the current wrapped around her and pulled her down. So far down, the light faded and all became dark. But the river within, the current Kuroshio, was a deep and profound black, blacker than the absence of light. It entered her heart and she held her chest in pain. She cried out as the cold, anonymous water inundated her. Everything disappeared.

Around the bend of the incline to the Miyamoto estate, a crowd of strangers greeted Yoshiko and her parents.

"Hayashi-san! Welcome! Welcome!" they shouted in unison.

The throng took Jinshiro and Naka aback but Yoshiko revelled in their enthusiasm.

Men grabbed their luggage and led the way to the house. Women gushed over the bride's sumptuous silk kimono. Iwakichi Miyamoto stood as bowlegged as the first time, teetering on his front steps with a wide grin stretching across his face.

"Ah, my new daughter-in-law! My wife would've been so proud," he said sincerely, sadly.

Inside, the house was filled with the aroma of *ogochiso*, a feast of seafood, rice, and multicoloured sweets. After Iwakichi escorted them to the dining area, Yoshiko and her parents knelt in their places of honour before the longest lacquer table Yoshiko had ever seen, her delight mirrored in the depths of its luxurious surface.

She began filling up with the realization that she was about to lead a life of wealth and privilege. Pride settled in her breast as she took a deep breath and grew into her new role.

Soon a crowd of guests joined them and servants appeared from behind sliding doors to serve the miso soup, *tai* fish, ginger crab, scented rice, silken tofu, flavoured seaweed, and multiple bottles of sake. Yoshiko's eyes grew wider. The dishes seemed never-ending.

In due course, Yoshiko spotted a familiar face, the impertinent serving girl, and gave her a hint of a smile as a secret gesture of familiarity.

"Eat! Eat!" encouraged Miyamoto.

Jinshiro laughed and helped himself to a succulent piece of *tai*, the good-luck sea bream.

"Hayashi-san. When do you think I'll have a grandson?" Iwakichi asked.

Yoshiko hid her face as she blushed.

"Come on, is she fit enough?" he added.

"Of course she is!" Jinshiro said. "Look at the fat around her stomach. She's bound to be fertile!" Jinshiro's face was beet red, his eyes puffy; he was already feeling the effects of the rice wine. He caught Naka frowning at him and flashed a silly grin at her.

"Just like my wife!" he shouted. The room broke into applause and belly laughs.

The conversation and merriment mixed with a blur of faces as the hours climbed to their midnight summit before sliding down the sluggish slope toward daybreak.

"Oi! Oi, wake up!"

The woman's voice was crude, harsh enough to break the bonds of Yoshiko's sleep, but the effects of the previous night's celebrations weighed heavily upon her.

"Get up!" the voice intruded again.

Yoshiko cracked open an eye and spied a large, if blurry, woman with a soiled apron, thick arms, and short hair cut in an unattractive, boyish manner, her wide mouth mashing words like a barking mongrel dog forecasted an ugly day. With too much to deal with at the moment, Yoshiko tried to tell her to go away, as sausage-thick fingers began to poke at her. She let out a low groan until finally she managed to speak. "Go back to the kitchen. I didn't call for a maid."

"Maid? Maid?" said the voice, now sounding indignant. "I am Miyamoto Hisa, eldest daughter and mistress of the household!"

Consciousness shook Yoshiko awake as she rolled to her feet, only to discover she was still wearing her wedding kimono. Mortified, she tried smoothing it down and straightening her tangled hair.

Hisa Miyamoto had inherited her father's round face but not the kindness of the eyes, the compassion of his voice. A heavy woman, she seemed about to splinter and crumble to the floor under the extra weight if not for her two sturdy legs. Even her oversized garment, an informal kimono, strained in the effort to contain her girth. "What a spoiled brat!" she declared. "How are you going to survive in *America* if you're so lazy and disrespectful to boot?"

Yoshiko said nothing. *How could I be so stupid?* she thought. *Didn't I meet her last night? Who can remember?* Even her muddled condition could not excuse such an insult.

Hisa shook her head in disbelief. "All right, come with me."

Yoshiko followed her down two long hallways with rice paper walls until they reached the familiar dining area littered with the previous evening's spent food and soiled dishes.

"Clean it up," Hisa ordered.

Yoshiko couldn't believe the mess. It looked as if there had been a riot. "Where are the servants I saw here last night?"

"I told them to leave it for you," Hisa chuckled as she started to walk away. "If I were you, I'd change clothes."

Yoshiko Miyamoto's introduction to the family was thus less than auspicious. It had been a rude awakening in more ways than one. Not only had she brought on the ire of Hisa Miyamoto, but also having slept all morning long, she had missed her parents, who had risen early in order to pay their respects to Naka's family before leaving for Kiyama.

In the days that followed, Yoshiko came under the intense scrutiny of her older sister-in-law, who made her do chores around the estate, the more menial the better. In quiet moments, the irony of the situation struck her painfully: she had married a *gaijin* to get away from a despotic mother-in-law and here she was for an indefinite amount of time under the thumb of an unrelenting tormentor. Had she made a mistake?

On the second night, Yoshiko began hearing voices, echoing off the walls and ceiling beams in the darkness. She ventured forth in her night-clothes down the halls to a room in a remote part of the estate. Careful not to reveal herself, she stood near the entrance where the candle-light emanated with a dull reluctance. It was her father-in-law Iwakichi Miyamoto standing over the impudent serving girl, the one who had smiled at her on her first visit. She was kowtowing before her employer, who was obviously berating her. All the poor girl could do was mutter a contrite "hai … hai." What was he angry about? Yoshiko couldn't be sure because she quickly slipped away, wishing to remain discreet. After many more nights of the voices, she realized these lectures were going to occur on a nightly basis at about the same time. *What had the girl done that was so bad?* A creeping ache of loneliness began taking her over for some inexplicable reason.

Though curious, Yoshiko had her own problems with her sister-in-law. Her heart broke a little more with each onerous task.

Gutting and cleaning the fish was perhaps the worst – something she had never done back home on a rice farm. Of course, no effort on her part was of any value. No amount of work was ever good enough.

One night, while getting ready for bed, she pulled back the sleeves of her *yukata* to find a number of hideous cuts on her hands and arms. Blood still oozed from some of the wounds. Yoshiko's stomach turned queasy. Acid rose to the root of her mouth, and her eyes seeped tears.

The waves are cruel at night. The sea conspires against her. Sharp-edged, black kelp reaches up, cutting her as she passes. Seabirds swoop to snatch morsels of flesh. The hands of the current pull her along as she comes apart in pieces. But in the distance is the land with sunlight breaking over the horizon. Just beyond the horizon.

A hand touched her shoulder. "What's wrong?" asked a soft, kind voice. Yoshiko's eyes widened as she focused on the compassionate, fresh moon face of a young girl. Yoshiko stopped sobbing.

"Aren't you the servant –" she asked tentatively.

"I'm Miyamoto Hiroko."

"Miya …?" Yoshiko said, suddenly realizing. She bowed deeply, mostly out of shame than gratitude. "I didn't know. I treated you so badly."

"Don't be silly," Hiroko said smilingly. "Forget about that. What's important is that you're all right. Are you?"

The bedchamber was dark but the light from the hall lapped at the doorway. Yoshiko looked toward the entrance in a questioning manner.

"Oh, I was passing by when I heard you crying," Hiroko explained.

Yoshiko hid her hands and looked away, guessing where her newly discovered sister-in-law was going.

"You must miss your family," Hiroko said and coaxed Yoshiko's hands into view. Her face, pale and glowing in the stray light, quickly turned to concern at what she saw. "Oh those cuts look nasty." The skin was raw and red with anger. "Look, I've got a salve. It'll help get rid of the pain."

"You … you brought …?"

"I know how hard my nesan's been on you. You're plenty tough to last this long."

The greasy ointment cooled over the heat of the wounds. Yoshiko sighed.

"Why is Onesan so hard on me? What have I done to her?"

"Ever since Okasan died, Hisa has taken her place. She thinks you're her daughter-in-law."

Yoshiko fell silent, wincing at the irony once again. From that moment on and throughout the months that followed, however, she and Hiroko were the best of friends. Whenever Hisa gave a particularly unctuous task to Yoshiko, Hiroko would volunteer to help. Her life became a lot easier.

Perhaps Oshogatsu, the three-day New Year's celebration, was the grandest time of all. The crisp air, the constant winter rain, and the dull roar of the sea in Mihama conspired to depress Yoshiko, allowing her to give in to dark thoughts, but with the approach of 1920, she felt the promise of change in the wind. Along with Hiroko's kindness to bolster her, she was able to hold back her sense of isolation, even though she knew it was always there.

She hadn't received one letter from her husband since as far back as her engagement, but that was to be expected. Her father-in-law told her that Jinsaburo had been busy dealing with the various bureaucratic tentacles of Canadian immigration. All she could do now, since she had become a married woman, was to be patient and everything would be taken care of within a year. Still, she often passed the time with her feet under a comforter before the brazier, craving for a letter during the quiet of each new day.

Fortunately for her, life became distracted by the preparations for the New Year's holiday. The first task was the *mochitsuki*, the process of making *mochi* or rice cakes. Yoshiko was assigned the job of pounding the steaming rice in the mouth of the stone mortar (called an *usu*) with a *kine*, a large wooden mallet, while Hiroko and Hisa kneaded the rice until it became a smooth whole. Timing was essential. A disruption in the rhythm of beating and manipulating the dough could result in a bruised or bleeding hand.

"Yoshi! Yoshi!" Hiroko called out as she literally punched and folded the *mochi* between Yoshiko's strikes. Hisa grunted with her effort.

Yoshiko, for her part, had to rest frequently. Back in Kiyama, her father and brothers took turns swinging the heavy *kine*. In Mihama, it became her job, another torment conceived by her nemesis, her fat, ugly sister-in-law. The weight of the mallet and the exertion of keeping up the pace was hard on her. Hisa exhaled in disgust every time Yoshiko stopped. After a while, Yoshiko had to resist the urge to delay her timing slightly in order to wreak vengeance.

Once the glutinous rice was ready, the three then transferred the dough to a table covered in flour in order to make the smooth, round dumplings. As she rolled the *mochi* in the palms of her hands, Yoshiko thought of the snowball fights in the mountains back home with her cousin Akiko.

After they filled several trays with *mochi*, the women then used them in various ways: as offerings to the Buddha and dead ancestors, as the key ingredient for *ozoni*, the good luck soup, and as a treat, fried and drizzled with a mixture of soy sauce and sugar. Before eating it, Yoshiko loved to stretch the molten *mochi* in the air after breaking through its caramelized surface with chopsticks. She found great solace in the familiar flavours.

Next came the planning for the New Year's feast. Magohachi Ryoji, the best cook in the city of Tsuruga, was hired to supervise the cooking.

"Make sure the rice has the proper amount of vinegar," he barked. His own ample girth and imperious look warned everyone not to cross him. Even Hisa seemed intimidated. Yoshiko privately took pleasure in her *onesan's* indignation when ordered to slaughter a pig for roasting, even though in the end it was she who was delegated for the onerous task.

"Handling pork is work for eta!" Hisa growled at Yoshiko. "Just right for lowborn like you!"

During the Oshogatsu feast, food glistened on the lacquer table: the pink shrimp swam amid the cucumber salad, the *inari-zushi* wet with the sweet juice of rice vinegar and sugar, the *sashimi* bursting with plump succulence. On the first day, the village men came by early and in large number to partake of the banquet. They particularly enjoyed their exchanges with Iwakichi Miyamoto, the *oyabun* of their town.

"The war was good for Japan," opined the local barber. "The Allies respect us now!"

"We've really become a military power in the world, ne?" Iwakichi replied to the gathered guests. "Look how we captured that German fortress at Tsingtao! Classic manoeuvre."

Their faces went blank.

"On the Shantung Peninsula, in China! Don't you people know anything?" Iwakichi had followed the military campaign with great interest, since he held absolute belief in the Emperor's divine right to rule all of the Orient. Japan was the roof over the house of Asia, after all.

"We should take over China next!" the barber slurred.

"All in good time my friend," assured Iwakichi. "Yoshiko-chan, more sake, onegaishimasu!"

She responded quickly and poured more of the cedar-flavoured rice wine into their cups. As she did so, she conjured in her mind a letter half-written.

The New Year shines brightly with the moon overhead. Husband, are you biting into the thick, silken mochi, the kind with the sweet bean filling? Are you living a good life in America? Send me a letter. Send for me to start our life together.

The light and warmth of the approaching spring brought a welcome change into Yoshiko's life. One day during the turn of the season, as she and Hiroko were cleaning out the horse barn, Yoshiko took a moment to rest and leaned against her shovel.

"Hiroko-san? What's my husband like?"

Hiroko continued to work, not even to look up. "We'd better finish before nesan comes by."

"No, really," Yoshiko continued. "I've got a photograph but I can't tell much from such an old picture. I want to know. I haven't heard from him ... not even one letter!" She gazed at Hiroko expectantly. She and her sister-in-law had become more like sisters in the past few months, especially when talking about Yoshiko's future after Mihama.

Hiroko emptied one last shovel-full before she stopped and relaxed, resting one boot on the head of the shovel.

"Oh, he's all right, I suppose. I was only a little girl when he went away to *Canada*. Tall ... strong ..."

"Handsome?"

"Now that's something you're going to have to find out for yourself. He's my onisan, after all!"

They both laughed.

"There is one thing that I've been wondering about," Yoshiko ventured.

Hiroko looked up.

"Why did he go? I mean, he was to inherit all this, but he went overseas instead."

"Well, as I said, I was a little girl when all that happened, but I think it had something to do with the Emperor and the times —"

"Oi!" The all-too-familiar voice bellowed from the barn's entrance.

The two scrambled for their shovels and began to work again.

"I want this place clean by the end of the day, you know!" Hisa stood with her hands on her hips in her customary dirty apron, glaring with anger. "Today's not a holiday!" As she turned to go, she remembered something. She reached into her pocket and took out a crumpled envelope.

"Oi, you!" she called to her underling with a snort. "This arrived for you."

Yoshiko rushed over when she realized what it was. Finally, word from Jinsaburo.

Greetings to my new bride! Life is very good here in Vancouver. The boarding house prospers. I may buy a second one soon. I need your help. I have finally arranged matters with the authorities here for you to come. Don't delay. My otosan will make the arrangements there. Get your papers in order and let me know when to expect you.

Miyamoto Jinsaburo
Taisho 8

Yoshiko was ecstatic. She began shovelling again with a new-found strength. Her vigour impressed Hiroko, who pitched in but couldn't keep up and ended in a heap in the hay, gasping for air and laughing at the same time. Hisa watched for a bit before turning away to leave with a slight smile on her face.

The next day, Iwakichi Miyamoto and Yoshiko boarded the bus headed for a distant municipal building to apply for emigration. Upon their return, Yoshiko dutifully filled out all the forms, and Iwakichi mailed them to the authorities with the money for the fees and taxes. She would now just have to wait for the official exit visas to arrive.

The days went by as they had before – full of farm chores, Hisa's bad temper, and Hiroko's goodwill, although the work seemed not as distasteful as before; either Yoshiko had become used to them, or Hisa wasn't as hard on her. No matter, for Yoshiko, still buoyed by the letter she kept carefully folded with the photograph in her pocket, the time went by quickly.

On a bright, sweet-smelling day in late April, an excited Hiroko came to Yoshiko in her bedroom.

"Your papers have arrived!" she screamed out loud, her eyes animated with joy.

"Really?" exclaimed Yoshiko, rising from the *ofuton*.

"Go down to the post office now!"

She immediately dressed, put her hair up, and rushed from the house in straw *zori* down the hill toward the centre of town.

Ten days later, the preparations for the journey were almost finalized. Naka Hayashi arrived shortly before the departure date.

"Yoshiko-chan, you're so fat! They must spoil you here!" Yoshiko sighed happily at the sight of her mother, even if her first comment was a criticism.

The subsequent evenings spent with her mother were deep with conversation. Her mother seemed older to Yoshiko, with obvious streaks of white hair, the faintly visible skein of lines on that sorrowful face, and the ever-curving back. Yoshiko began to feel pangs of guilt within but dismissed them so as not to ruin her own mood.

"Okasan, the time has finally come!" she exclaimed gleefully on the day before her departure.

Seated on a thin cushion on the floor, Naka gazed sadly at her daughter. "Your otosan and Akiko-chan will be at the pier. They're in Yokohama making final arrangements and waiting ..."

But Yoshiko didn't hear a word her mother had said. Instead, she continued to pack, crouched on her knees before an open steamer trunk. With eyes beaming, she held up a simple western dress with a matching jacket and hat.

"How do you like my new clothes? Miyamoto-san bought these and others for me. They come all the way from Tokyo! I look just like an *America*-jin!"

"Yes, Yoshiko-chan," whispered Naka. "I haven't talked to you about …" She hesitated long enough for Yoshiko to notice. There was concern in her face.

"About what, Okasan?"

Naka cast her eyes to the floor and had her hands folded on her lap, saying nothing.

"About what?" Yoshiko repeated, a note of irritation in her voice.

Naka's cheeks burned with embarrassment as she lowered her gaze. "About … about the wedding night."

Yoshiko was caught off guard. Her mouth dropped open, and she could feel her face growing hot. "No … no … you haven't," she replied.

"Do as your husband says," her mother advised with a note of urgency, "but don't let him take away your dignity." She paused to let the point take.

"Yes, Okasan," Yoshiko replied with compliance and folded her own hands across her lap.

Naka physically relaxed with her daughter's acknowledgment, thinking perhaps that her daughter had understood.

A calculated silence rose between them.

The anticipation of the next day kept daughter and mother up to well past midnight, but soon thereafter fatigue set in and their eyes began drooping.

"Here, get under the covers," Yoshiko's mother said. "Go to sleep."

Yoshiko adjusted herself under the *ofuton* and settled in. She gazed at her mother as Naka stroked her brow.

"Okasan, tomorrow's going to be a great day."

"Yes, Yoshiko-chan," she whispered again. "Now close your eyes."

"Tell me a story," Yoshiko asked, like a child wanting to stave off sleep.

"What? How old are you?"

"Oka, please. Like when I was your little girl."

"You haven't called me 'Oka' since you were ten," she said smiling, the creases in her eyes clearly defined.

"So will you?" Yoshiko prodded. "Tell me a story?"

"This is silly. What kind of story?"

"Tell me one about a fox."

"You always liked fox-spirit stories."

"They're so magical. They can do anything, go anywhere, be anything they want."

"But they're so mean. Nothing good comes from foxes."

"That's not true. They live under rainbows. That would be so wonderful. So beautiful."

"They never forgive if you cross them," Naka warned, "and they're always plotting."

"Come on, tell me a story!"

"Oh all right, you urusai girl," Naka relented. "Now which one should I tell?"

"The one about the Fox and the Jewel Maiden! That's one of my favourites," Yoshiko said.

Naka smiled and began.

Mukashi, mukashi, the bonsan Genno, after a long weary pilgrimage, came to rest under a great stone by the side of the Hokkaido road. The moment he sat down, a spirit suddenly appeared and warned in a ghostly deep voice, "Do not rest in the shadow of this stone. This is the Death Stone and men, birds, and animals have died just by touching it!"

"Really?" Genno said, astonished. "Great Spirit, pray tell me the story of the stone."

And so the spirit began. "Long ago, in the time of the Emperor Toba, there was a beautiful maiden at court. So fair was she that she was called the Jewel Maiden.

"During the summer, the Emperor held a great feast, gathering all the wisdom, beauty, and wit of the land. It was a wonderful dinner with sweet, delicious food and drink, but during the evening the skies became choked with cloud and a mysterious wind arose howling like mad dogs.

"At midnight, it whipped through the palace and blew out all the lanterns. The darkness caused the guests to panic and rush about. Someone finally said that they could see a light, a faint light coming from somewhere, when suddenly the lanterns reignited and all was well again. Except that the Emperor had fallen ill — so ill, in fact, that the alarmed attendants called for the Sorcerer Kamo, a grizzled old man with a scar across his eye from a long forgotten battle. No one knew where he came from or his age or the depth of his powers.

"Upon seeing the Emperor, he stood and pointed a finger at the Jewel Maiden. 'She is the one! She is evil and has caused the sickness to enter His Majesty's body!'

"With the accusation, the Jewel Maiden began to shine with an eerie light. Spinning and reciting a sutra, she magically changed into a fox. She muttered a last incantation before escaping to the Death Stone and entering it."

Her mother's words drifted as Yoshiko fell asleep.

She awoke when daylight came pouring into the room and sat up to find her mother sitting beside her.

"You up already?" she asked. "How long have you been up?"

"I didn't go to sleep."

"You didn't? Why not?"

"I … I just wanted to watch my daughter sleeping as I did when you were a baby."

Yoshiko shook her head questioningly.

"This'll probably be the last chance I'll have," her mother said, and her eyes filled with emotion.

Yoshiko turned away. Waves rippled through her. It suddenly occurred to her she would, in all likelihood, never see her mother, her cousin, her family again. She of course had considered that prospect in her brooding at night but, for the first time, it really struck her. Her ambition for adventure had turned to vanity. Perhaps it wasn't too late to stay in Japan, marry a farmer, and raise more farmers. *No, no, no*, she insisted to herself. Her husband will bring her back to Japan. And what a day that'll be, she fancied. She'll walk the roads of Kiyama in the finest clothes like the prominent wife of a rich and successful man she is destined to be. Her family, and everyone in the village, will come out to see her and be guests at the largest, most sumptuous feast they have ever seen. She must go and be with her husband. *Only the foolish fight change.*

The day was bright with only a hint of early summer heat in the air. Townsfolk loyal to the Miyamoto clan arrived at the homestead about mid-morning to help carry the luggage, a steamer trunk, a valise, and a couple of *furoshiki* packages, to the bus stop by the post office, which was no more than a vegetable store blessed by the government. As the volunteers went ahead, Yoshiko emerged and walked to the edge of the promontory overlooking the Tsuruga River. With a sombre look, she mentally traced the route from the fragmented delta, through the town, past the Miyamoto compound, and on to the distant mountains where Kiyama lay in its quiet obscurity.

She had played in the cool waters of that river as a child. Even then she imagined the river flowing to the sea where the Kuroshio, the Black Current, resided. Now, the splashing of water had given way to the rolling of waves. She was about to ride a great current to her husband and a new life.

Iwakichi led the procession, followed by Naka Hayashi, Yoshiko, Hiroko, and Hisa, an odd collection of bodily shapes and sizes. Yoshiko wore her western outfit with pride even though the shoes, despite their low heels, were hard on her feet. The hip-hugging dress, lace-trimmed bodice, and wide-brimmed hat with a small feather attached, on the other hand, made her feel grand. As she walked, she became self-conscious for a time as she noticed villagers gawking and then trading comments with one another, but then Yoshiko smiled to herself, enjoying the attention.

By the time they reached the grocery store depot, the bus was waiting. Hiroko's eyes were wet and swollen as she embraced Yoshiko in the western manner.

"Hiroko!" Hisa scolded. "There are people watching!"

"It's all right," Iwakichi interceded. "Your sister's losing a friend."

"You take care of yourself," Hiroko said not knowing what else to say.

Yoshiko could only manage to nod an acknowledgment as she fought back her own feelings.

The bus driver honked his horn announcing the luggage was loaded and calling for the Miyamoto party to board. With a flurry of activity and rushed goodbyes, Yoshiko, her mother, and father-in-law boarded and found their seats. As the bus roared to life and started on its way, Yoshiko waved from the window to Hiroko and Hisa, both dressed in light-coloured kimonos. Hiroko waved back furiously and mouthed her farewell; Hisa remained as stoic as ever. The sisters' contrasting personalities were consistent to the end.

Hisa probably wasn't as bad as she made her out to be, but Yoshiko realized she could now afford to be charitable toward her tormentor. She would miss Hiroko, the only reason she survived her stay in Mihama. She continued to wonder why her sister-in-law was subjected to the nightly torment, but during her entire stay, Yoshiko had never mentioned it. There was no need to embarrass and possibly alienate her close ally and friend. Perhaps they will meet again during a visit home whenever that may be and all will be well. "When my husband and I are rich," she whispered.

The journey to Tsuruga was not long but the dirt road made for a bumpy ride. Yoshiko knew the city from past trips and her history books. Tsuruga, specifically its fabled castle with its stone walls and tiered and tiled roofs, was the scene in 1868 of one of the final acts of resistance staged by those loyal to the Tokugawa Shogunate following the Meiji Restoration. *The foolish cannot win against change.* Her eyes grew damp again with her childhood memory of the Emperor.

What she wasn't prepared for was how modern a city it had become in the five years since she was last there with its myriad paved roads, bustling vehicles, thatched houses, and concrete buildings. Yoshiko stared in amazement at the number of automobiles and factories.

Since Iwakichi Miyamoto only had business connections and no relatives or friends in town, the party stayed at the Matsumiya Hotel, a small inn near the train station. The rooms were cramped with a writing desk, one ornately upholstered chair, and an oversized western bed.

"The sheets are changed every day," boasted the proprietress, the rotund and accommodating Tomoko, widow of the long-dead Matsumiya.

Yoshiko shared a room with her mother while Iwakichi had his own. Naka seemed more at ease with her daughter's leaving by the time they settled into bed.

"This is so uncomfortable," Naka complained. "Too soft."

"No. It's wonderful! I feel so ... so rich!"

"Ah, you're going to be spoiled by these gaijin ways."

"So let me be spoiled!" Yoshiko threw her arms up over her head and looked smugly at her mother. Her spirits soared in the anticipation of seeing family again, even if she knew it was to be for a short time only.

Naka turned away and buried herself in the pillow as she tried to hide her own delight from Yoshiko.

The next day, the three boarded the steam-powered train and began their cross-country journey to the major port city of Yokohama. Of course it was impossible, but Yoshiko swore that as she gazed through the coal-sooted window beside her seat she could see in the great distance the Tsuruga River. It shone like a mirror in the early morning sun, perhaps an omen of good things to come. She warmed to the thought that the river was guiding her still. As she smoothed her clothes, she noticed that the colour of her green blouse had somehow paled in the morning light.

Yokohama, the great seaport, was a day away and the trip was boring to Yoshiko with the relentless clickity-clack, but as the train turned the last bend, the city's looming presence took her breath away. If Tsuruga was a city, then Yokohama was a metropolis. Masses of houses and buildings spread in every direction. White smoke rose from myriad chimneys as a testament to life. Vehicles of all kinds raced along paved roads parallel to the tracks until they veered off into some mysterious and enticing enclave of the city.

Yoshiko felt her mother's hand under her chin. Although she had visited at the age of sixteen, she was not prepared for the enormity of the panorama before her and her jaw had dropped. She pushed the hand away with a jerk and flashed her mother a look of adolescent disdain. Eventually, the train lurched to a slower pace as it moved cautiously under the latticed canopy of the terminal station.

From her seat, Yoshiko saw Akiko on the platform, rushing forward, searching the windows of each car. She anxiously jumped up and left the Pullman to meet her cousin before her mother could stop her.

"Akiko! Akiko!" she called from the steps.

Her cousin waved, her pudgy face beaming as she ran. She was dressed like a schoolgirl in a navy blue skirt, long matching blue tie, and gleaming white blouse, and her hair was in pigtails.

They met on the platform, bowing slightly while grinning from ear to ear at each other.

"Look at you!" Yoshiko gushed, breaking with formality and grabbing at her cousin's pigtails at the same time.

Akiko squealed with delight, words failing her.

Approaching from behind the two, Naka and Jinshiro appeared from different directions. "Now stop that, you two!" Jinshiro reproached. "Yoshiko, where's your luggage?"

"Right here!" Iwakichi called from the train, loaded down with suitcases and *furoshiki*-wrapped packages. Jinshiro called for a porter, who just happened to be wading through the oncoming crowd.

The reunion was grand. They all went to a local *ryokan* to have a celebratory *sukiyaki* dinner that ended with a glazed blueberry tart, which both cousins oohed over. But the sweet delicacy could not distract Akiko and Yoshiko from their main preoccupation during the meal: gossip, punctuated by their girlish laughter.

"Matsumiya-san was this big, jiggling woman! But she was so nice to us," said Yoshiko. "And the beds. Akiko, you should have seen the bed in our room! A gaijin bed."

"Yoshiko, they have gaijin beds here too. I'm sleeping in … what do they call it? A double?"

"I bet it's not as comfortable."

"Well, I don't know, but I sink into it until I'm nice and cozy!"

"I bet my husband's beds are just as wonderful." Her eyes sparkled. "In the boarding house."

"Oh, I might be getting married myself!" Akiko said.

"What? To who?"

"Watanabe Etsuo."

"One of the Watanabe boys?"

"The middle one. His matchmaker approached my otosan before I left."

"That's wonderful, but …"

"But what?"

"Get a good eye doctor!" Yoshiko said, remembering the family's characteristic weak eyes and large noses.

They laughed out loud, bringing disapproving glares from patrons around the dining room.

The Palace Hotel in downtown Yokohama was ten storeys high and western in motif, with a grand foyer of small black and white tiles, floor-to-ceiling mirrors, and a wide staircase to receive its guests. Their rooms were on the second floor. Yoshiko and her mother stayed together again, although Yoshiko spent most of her time with Akiko. The beds were just as comfortable if not more so than those at the hotel in Tsuruga.

"She was so mean and fat … I hated her. I used to call her a devil woman behind her back. A fat onibaba."

"Then I hate her too!" Akiko concluded. "Let's see your husband's picture."

Yoshiko reached into her night garment's breast pocket and pulled out the grainy, creased photograph. "Here he is."

Akiko squinted in order to gain a clear image of Jinsaburo. "He's too young."

"Bakayaro. This is when he was a school boy," she chided as she hogged the picture for herself.

"I was just saying.... How old is he?"

Yoshiko paused a second. "Actually, I don't know. Twenty, I guess. It did take him a while to get successful."

"I bet he's handsome."

"His sister thinks so. Strong too."

"The onibaba said that?"

"No, Hiroko-chan, the youngest. The nice one." Yoshiko stopped and sighed heavily.

"Anyway, you're lucky to have such a wonderful husband. What do you like about him the most?"

Yoshiko beamed and once again shared the photograph with her cousin, wondering what Jinsaburo did with her photo.

"He went to Canada instead of staying in Japan. He could've stayed and been a rich man, but he lives for adventure, not money, not for tradition and not for the old Japan."

"You are lucky ..." Akiko admitted as her voice trailed away.

"We're going to have lots and lots of children and live a rich life," Yoshiko said as they nattered long into the night.

Two days later, the party of five found themselves on the pier of Yokohama Harbour, waiting for the *Canada Maru* to set sail.

At ten minutes past ten o'clock, the ship blasted the "all aboard" signal. Yoshiko turned to the teary-eyed Akiko and bowed deeply, dabbing her own eyes at the same time. The warmth between the two lasted only a moment but felt like a lifetime.

"Hayaku. Hayaku," encouraged her father. "They want you on board," he said as he patted Yoshiko's shoulder.

Naka indiscreetly blew her nose into a handkerchief, knowing the time to separate had arrived. She appeared grateful for the piece of cloth that hid her sorrowful look as she bowed slightly to her daughter. As a last gesture, she reached out and gave her daughter one last gift: an *omamori*, a rectangular amulet encased in silk. Inside was a small book filled with the Buddha Dharma. "It'll protect you."

Yoshiko grasped it tightly and bowed deeply, at the same time whispering, "Arigato." She, along with her mother, fought back the tears.

Iwakichi and Jinshiro smiled at each other and moved to speed them along. "Women! They're always little girls at heart," Iwakichi said.

Yoshiko pulled away from her mother, her face awash with the melancholy of departure.

From the deck, Yoshiko stood alone in the crowd of passengers as she surveyed the gathered throng on the pier. She thought she spotted her family but … no, it wasn't them. She vowed to return one day, though in her heart of hearts, she concluded that it wasn't likely. The events of the recent past came to her in a whirl of sentiment that made her feel dizzy. She would write to her parents, and Akiko and Hiroko, her true sisters. Pebbles of tears rolled down her cheeks as she tried to focus on her husband, Jinsaburo. The past is a curse. "It's the future that counts," she said to herself with conviction.

Streamers fell from the ship to the people on the dock below. A final connection made, Yoshiko grasped a paper streamer as she felt the boat start to move away. Three blasts from above told her she was on her way. The current had taken hold.

Like sliding on glass, she was swept out to sea on the back of the Kuroshio, the Black Current. Its whitecaps carried her until she began to sink beneath the Kuroshio's depths. Colour corroded as the dark reaches of the ocean bubbled to the surface.

With a slight tug, the streamer snapped and fell to the water. Yoshiko looked once more into the mass of faceless humanity and tried to conjure up the image of her proud *otosan*, her poor, suffering *okasan*, and her childish cousin Akiko. Above the crowd, the city rose and, above and beyond it, the bright emerald landscape ran into the distance towards Kiyama. Japan steadily slipped away from her, her family faded from view.

4. Monday, March 11, 1940

"Murder." The word hung over the Showa Club like a bad smell. No one said a word. No one moved. Even the lone occupied pool table fell coldly silent, like a slab in a morgue.

The metallic clink of a lighter broke the tension. The rasp of the flame igniting and the inhalation of cigarette smoke sounded like the exaggerated clearing of a throat.

Rik-*san* spoke tentatively. "You involved?"

"Bakayaro!" Morii exploded.

Rik-*san* shifted away quickly, knowing he had made another faux pas. The 1921 Yamamoto case came to mind, but the mention of the incident on Alexander Street would have been imprudent, given his boss's reaction.

"I just want to know if anybody's heard anything." Morii, a sense of impatience building in him, lit his own Chesterfield cigarette, the exhaled smoke masking his face. "I can't go into details, but I'm thinking there's been a murder. About three days ago."

"What do you mean, you think?" Rikimatsu complained. "Was there or wasn't there?"

"Damare! No matter what, the damn keto are gonna think so and come down on us!" Morii asserted. "Anybody know a Okihara Koji?"

"Never heard of him," Rik-*san* answered immediately. "He the stiff or did he do it?"

"*Nem mind!* You notice any strangers in town recently?"

Rikimatsu's eyes sparked with a memory. "Now wait a minute, is this Okihara guy a fancy pants? Soft hands like a woman's? Probably never worked a day in his life?"

"Yeah, might be him."

"You know this guy?"

"From a long time ago, maybe. So you know this guy or what?"

"Yeah, yeah. I think I ran into him at the Sisters." Rikimatsu scratched his head and then related his encounter.

With winter winds foreshadowing the ruining weather ahead, Rikimatsu adjusted his tie as he descended the rickety stairs of the Three Sisters Café. He stopped to chat with Kifumi Yamada, the youngest of the sisters and his favourite. At the foot of the staircase, he noticed a fastidious dandy perched on a stool at the counter with two blueberry tarts in front of him.

"Hatsuko-san, who's the pantywaist?" Rik-*san* called to the eldest sister, waiting on the stranger. The *yojimbo* only respected strength in men, anything less offended him.

"Damare, Rikimatsu!"

The man pushed off his chair, coming to his feet, and shot the *yojimbo* a look of disdain. "Okihara Koji, desu," he said curtly.

His voice grated on Rik-*san*, its tone somewhat effeminate. "You got a sweet tooth or something?" he asked, pointing to the two sugary treats on the counter.

"I'm waiting for a lady friend, if you must know."

"A lady friend? I get it, you're the kind that gets women to buy you things, right? You smell like one."

Koji frowned and scoffed, "At least I don't pay for a lady's company."

Rikimatsu rushed forward and grabbed the miscreant by the silk lapels of his cream-coloured suit. "Kusotare, who the hell do you think you're talkin' to?"

Hatsuko quickly wedged herself between them, forcing Rik-*san* to let go. "Stop making trouble, you two! I don't need no trouble!"

Koji smoothed the material of his outfit as he apologized to the proprietor. "Please tell Miyamoto-san I'll be back when the air clears. Save the tarts for me." He bowed curtly before leaving in a huff.

"Ketsuno-ana," cursed the *yojimbo*. "Goddamned asshole."

"Good, good," Morii said. "You go find him and bring him to me. I need to know a few things from him before I can act."

"Act on what?" Rik-*san* leaned closer. "You're not gonna protect these Japanese again, are ya? They don't appreciate it. Never have, never will." The *oyabun's* compassion for those they victimized really bothered Rikimatsu. Take their money, demand their respect, even do them a few favours, but don't coddle them. He never understood the concept of obligation, though during the "evacuation" and later in Toronto he himself would soon be known for protecting "these Japanese," perhaps to create an obligation, but in all likelihood not.

"You want the police down here? Looking into every corner, meddling in our business? This is just the excuse they need!"

Rik-*san* shrugged his shoulders. Aki walked away.

"And if I don't protect 'these Japanese,' who will? They'll just die in some keto jail. That'll make me look real good!" Morii inhaled with a look of disgust, thinking of his betters in San Francisco and His majesty the Emperor in Japan. "Our people are better than that," he uttered in an exhalation of smoke. "We've got to take care of our own." His voice subsided to a whisper, "Take care of our family."

の

Summer 1907

Three years before Etsuji Morii married in 1910, U.S. union leaders came to Vancouver in September to organize members in demonstrations against Oriental labour. Word soon got out that the Asiatic Exclusion League, whose sole purpose was to engage in "active hostility against the Orientals on the West Coast," was involved.

On a Thursday evening during that same fateful month, four or five hundred white men, with just enough drink in them to make them act on their anger, raided the local mills and bunkhouses just across the U.S. border to attack the Sikh and Hindu workers sleeping in their beds. They beat their victims senseless and dragged them to the city limits. Six were hospitalized.

As a consequence, the police jailed four hundred Sikhs for "their own protection." Pursued by the chant "Drive out the Hindus!" some seven hundred and fifty others made their way to Canadian territory, hungry, exhausted, half-clothed, and seeking shelter with their status as British subjects.

Early in the morning of Friday, September 6, 1907, the destitute Hindu and Sikh refugees poured across the border from Bellingham, Washington. At about the same time, the steamer *Charmer* chugged into Burrard Inlet carrying five hundred Japanese immigrants. The public reacted swiftly to voice their "concerns."

Although preparations had been in progress for months, the *Vancouver Daily Province* decided to give a huge anti-Oriental demonstration extraordinary coverage that evening: "Thousands will line up in parade. Arrangements are complete for the big demonstration and parade to be held tomorrow under the auspices of the Asiatic Exclusion League. Many citizens in sympathy with the movement will also aid in the demonstration."

In the still heat of the Raku Raku, Etsuji Morii, the young boss, sat stiffly in his new oversized suit lasciviously running his thumb over the smooth, butter-browned skin of a *manju* cake resting in the palm of his hand. He had bought a batch at Nagami Kashiya earlier in the day. It was his favourite dessert; the feel of it had the same firm pliancy as a young woman's abdomen.

His bow tie was especially uncomfortable as sweat collected under his collar, but he ignored it to concentrate on the greater issues at hand. He had been ensconced in his position for less than a year, and he knew he was facing his first major challenge as *oyabun*. He could see that fat Kameoka laughing at him if these *keto* drag him down to defeat.

Both the *Canada Shimpo* and *Tairiku Nippo*, the Japanese-language newspapers, reported the facts of the Bellingham riot and the imminent Vancouver "parade" and demonstration, unfortunately without any words of warning, trepidation, or even irony. Many readers as a result planned to go see the spectacle.

"Bakatare. They're all bakatare," Morii grumbled as he popped the *manju* in his mouth. His face grew a dark red as he chewed the confection vigorously.

Rik-*san*, puffing on his cigarette and desperate for a little calm, paced the floor of the small office in back of the restaurant bar. Smoke clouded his head like some distant mountain. His beady eyes pierced through the obfuscation like two red-hot coals.

"Damn keto! If they come here, I say we get rifles and shoot them dead in their tracks."

"No!" Morii commanded. "The Reverend Sasaki and church elders came to me and asked for no bloodshed."

"You're not gonna listen to 'em, are ya?" Rik-*san* insisted, his grimace contorted into a devil's scowl.

"I don't want the police down here, but we're going to fight back. You do as I say."

A motley brass band cobbled together from the Vancouver Presbyterian and First Baptist churches led the parade along Hastings Street toward City Hall. The day was sultry, the sun burning in everyone's eyes. Some marchers wore white shirts and thin ties with their sleeves rolled up to just above the elbows. Others wore plaid work shirts and dungarees. Stress and exertion blackened the underarms of the union workers as their tempers sparked and sizzled with every step. In the crowd that had gathered along the street were several Japanese men with cautious, expectant looks on their faces, some having made a special trip from nearby lumber camps and sawmills. A few wore their uniforms from the Russo-Japanese War, their decorations shining proudly in the sun.

The parade proceeded inexorably until it split into two factions – one group to City Hall, the other larger one funnelling into the Sand Lot, a narrow field at the foot of Carrall Street, for an open-air meeting. Adjacent to the gathering was the entrance to Chinatown.

By nine o'clock in the evening, the sun had dipped into the Pacific Ocean and the crowd began to feel the liberation of cool night breezes. Speaker after speaker spoke of the inevitability of a "Mongolian province," the diluting of Anglo-Saxon blood that made up Canada, and the emasculation of the Canadian worker by cheap Oriental labour. Finally, the most prominent speaker rose to the dais: the Reverend G.W. Wilson, an impressive man in an immaculate black suit trimmed with the ministerial collar of Christian respectability. He paused before speaking, fanaticism the cosmetic masking his face.

I am of the opinion that this province must be a white man's country. I do not wish to look forward to a day when my descendants will be dominated by Japanese, or Chinese, or any other colour but their own. The result of the Hindu trouble in Bellingham today is that there are no Hindus in Bellingham.

As if on cue, someone threw a rock crashing through a nearby store window; its swirling configuration of Chinese lettering disappeared in a shower of glass.

Then suddenly, in a scene of mass hysteria, the mob swept along Pender Street like breakaway water from the dam of pent-up feelings into the centre of Chinatown. Rioters smashed windows, ransacked buildings, and looked for victims. Chinatown in a matter of moments lay in waste, the inhabitants and the one or two policemen assigned to the area escaping to hide during the melee.

Like raging flood water, the mob then turned and streamed up the streets and tributary alleyways toward the Powell Street area. They moved within seconds to the outskirts at the intersection of Westminster Avenue and Hastings Street. Uchibori's Dress Shoppe stood demurely on the corner with its plate-glass window displaying the latest fashions. The glass shattered with one well-placed shot, and again with the signal given, the mob rioted.

Earlier, from his vantage point on a rooftop above the corner of Westminster and Powell, Morii peered into the dark streets below, seeing no movement, sensing no presence. Throughout the evening, he had been receiving reports of the demonstration's progress from Rik-*san* and his cohorts who were standing with the Russo-Japanese war vets at a strategic distance from the crowd. He had even assigned translators. So he knew what was going on.

In his shirtsleeve garters, waistcoat, and bowler hat, Morii waited for the mob to pour into the heart of the Powell Street area. With his face shining in the stray light, he looked like some ancient *shogun* ready to command his samurai into battle. This was his war and he was ready.

He also knew they were waiting, the huddled mothers with their newborn babies in the backrooms of Powell Street – their arms held tight around their children in the blackout that he had ordered a few hours ago. He knew the children born in this *kuso* country sensed the danger and held their breaths, as did their mothers in the wake of strangely absent fathers.

No one here had the comfort of an extended family, having given that up when they left Japan. They had no one to depend on except themselves. A tight-knit community was the only logical result, and the *oyabun* was determined to be the head of that community, the head of the family.

The murmur of distant voices grew to a steady roar. Morii's eyes narrowed, straining to catch sight of the coming hordes. The sound of footsteps of the steadily approaching mob, heavy and slow through the darkness, was punctuated by glass shattering. He eventually saw a black mass moving north on Westminster Avenue. In a few seconds, he would give the signal and, in a heartbeat, his war would begin.

The rioters poured into the intersection at Powell Street. Inexplicable to them, barriers blocked their way on three sides. They were caught in Morii's bottleneck trap. Suddenly shadow men popped up on the surrounding rooftops and began hurling fistfuls of solid night down on the *keto* below. Here and there, the rioters let out screams of shock and agony before collapsing. They were sitting targets as the unrelenting flow of their cohorts behind pinned them against the barriers facing them. Panic set in and frustration grew in the realization they were trapped. Many covered their blood-splattered faces with their hands, only to be hit by a rock, bottle or brick in the back of the head, cracking the skull. Some fell to their knees. Others cried out trying to escape. Their spirits broken, they were animals led to the slaughter.

In relief from the halo of the city's light behind him, Morii raised his arm as he gazed down upon the scene with an "enigmatic smile" (as the *keto* newspapers would later call it) on his face. He then put his arm down and, as if out of nowhere, platoons of men, armed with wooden clubs, iron bars, broken bottles, and other makeshift weapons, converged on the intersection from three directions. The crush of nine hundred rioters left the unionists and bandwagon jumpers at the mercy of the vastly outnumbered Japanese.

A chorus of voices roared an eerie "banzai" above the mob scene. At the head of the retaliatory force was the enraged Rikimatsu, his raised samurai sword waving and then slicing into the melee. The weapon, so blunt it couldn't cut butter, was the compromise for the prohibition against firearms. Morii shook his fists above his head as encouragement.

The two irresistible forces met in a stupendous clash of scuffling, desperation, bludgeoning, and screaming. Row after row of rioters fell. Bodies crumpled beneath the weight of unconsciousness into indiscriminate piles. Blood splattered with the merciless contact of wood to skull, glass to skin, blade to body. Limbs twisted into unearthly positions.

In a matter of moments the battle royal ended, the dazed and wounded retreating into the enclaves from whence they came. A slow but steady cheer of victory ascended like a storm of enraged angels to the roof where Morii stood, legs apart, waving his arms at the men below.

In the days that followed, patrols were set up to deal with any attempt at counterattack, but soon the rains came and washed away any remaining taste for rioting in the echoing union halls downtown.

ॐ

Monday, March 11, 1940

"You remember the 1907 riots, Rik-san?" Morii shouted, his alcohol-slurred voice reverberating throughout the nearly empty Showa Club. "We took care of our own. We didn't need the police then and we don't need them now."

Back then, the *oyabun* had seen the building of racist unrest in the white community as an opportunity to establish his power and influence as a Japanese community leader and acted accordingly. With the Reverend Senju Sasaki and a deputation of Buddhist Church leaders, he contacted the Vancouver city police the Friday before the riots to ask them to stay out of the area. Morii promised they would organize patrols, establish barricades of wagons, benches, automobiles, and barrels, and take care of their own. The police readily agreed.

Afterward Morii made sure the Japanese-language newspapers gave credit for defeating the *keto* to Saburo Yoshie, an official from the Japanese Consulate in Vancouver. The stern, impressive-looking Yoshie had approached Morii to volunteer to organize a defensive force. The *oyabun*, after all, possessed a commanding presence within the community.

Yoshie directed the collection of armaments, like bricks, rocks, bottles, and baseball bats, and organized the men into fighting units, but it was Morii's consent in the first place that gave the Consulate official the credibility to be followed.

The *oyabun* himself saw the value in celebrating Yoshie: it kept his name out of the newspapers and it set up an obligation in the Consulate which he soon exploited to his advantage. Through Yoshie, Morii acquired the "Guarantor Authority" for all legal immigrant documents on behalf of the Nihon Jinkai, and he became chairman of the adjudication committee within that businessman's association. In this manner, he approved or rejected passport applications for all brides coming to Canada, which included his Hinomaru Club "wives."

Morii spent the rest of the afternoon at the Showa Club holding court over the patrons and his minions: Aki, Rikimatsu, and the burly Tanaka and Moriyama, Rik-*san's* two best henchmen, who had come in from the cold about halfway through the oft-told riot story. With his particular fondness for the Japanese mushroom, the *oyabun* had wolfed down his generous bowl of chicken-rice *donburi* between sentences. *Shiitake*, with its smooth, slippery texture and musky, earthy aroma and flavour, reminded him of the allure of women and the corruption of men who would win them. He had also switched sometime during the proceedings from beer to Canadian Club whiskey with a glass of water on the side and was becoming more boisterous as a result.

Rik-*san* shied away from the table, holding his tongue even if his intense eyes smouldered while he listened. He had been there in 1907. He knew the police were not interested in protecting the "Orientals" of the city. He doubted they had any intention of showing up in the first place; after all, they had initially offered only one officer for the Japanese sector. He knew most of the buildings damaged in the riot were owned by *keto* and only rented by Chinese and Japanese businessmen. He also knew that shortly afterward, a group of optimistic Japanese immigrants had come down the gangplank of the steamer *Charmer* only to be met by a brigade of white men, who beat them and threw them off the Canadian Pacific Railway Wharf into Burrard Inlet.

In the aftermath of the riot, twenty-four persons had been arrested, nine were fined, and one was jailed for six months. Rik-*san*, much to his embarrassment, was the only Japanese arrested. He was fined ten dollars for "carrying a concealed weapon." He complained over many whiskeys that his sword was hardly "concealed." *Damn keto*, he cursed to himself.

Furthermore, he knew the Asiatic Exclusion League worked to force the governments of Canada and Japan to come to the "Gentlemen's Agreement" of 1908 to limit if not halt altogether male Japanese immigration. His question then was how did "we take care of our own" when *keto* insurance paid for the damages to *keto* property, several "New Canadian" Japanese ended up in the hospital and entry into Canada was restricted as a result of events of 1907? Of course, he knew better than to raise these points with the *oyabun*. The man had won his war, after all.

By seven o'clock, Etsuji Morii's face was quite red and more than a little bloated. The harshness of the Canadian Club had grown progressively softer with each new glass; however, Morii, at some instinctive moment, tipped his eyes upward at the far wall clock and a clear light broke through the fog. He remembered an appointment. Pulling himself to his feet, he groaned, "Yokkorisho. I've got to go. Practice."

"Oi oyabun!" Rik-*san* spoke up. "What do you want us to do about this … murder you mentioned?"

"Find Okihara. And keep your eyes and ears open."

The early evening air was crisp, the grey, muted light nearly gone. His head cleared. Again, Powell Street was empty as he pulled his heavy topcoat tight and walked toward the park until he came to the New World Hotel at the corner of Dunlevy. The second-floor corner room housed the offices of *The New Canadian*, the upstart *nisei*, English-language newspaper. Morii disliked Thomas Yamanaka, the editor, for his youth and democratic, "British sense of fair play" attitudes, especially when it came to the situation in China.

What irked him even more was the fact that the *nisei* were insinuating themselves into his Nihon Jinkai. By 1934, the businessmen's association was the co-ordinating agency for over twenty Japanese organizations in all of British Columbia, a measure seen as a necessity in light of the Great Depression's "Japanese problem." The so-called "young idiots," who first came in to conduct surveys and work as clerks and who were now being elected to the board of directors, recently changed the Nihon Jinkai's name to the more acceptable Canadian Japanese Association or CJA.

Vice-president Bunjiro Hisaoka welcomed the "new blood" into the organization. "They are the future," he often said. But Morii was not of the same mind, publicly expressing his regret for having approved their hiring. Although the organization was still under the *oyabun's* control, the truth of the matter was that the second generation just didn't recognize him or his ideas with the appropriate amount of deference. In fact, they were at times downright disrespectful.

Etsuji Morii was well known for his support of Imperial Japan's campaign in China. His speeches on his homeland's imperialism and his wife's efforts to organize the women to put together comfort bags for the soldiers were popular amongst the *issei* but anathema to the editorial staff of *The New Canadian* and the *nisei* board members of the CJA. In time, the *oyabun* decided to take steps to stop the university graduates like Yamanaka. Japan, after all, was a "divine country" in a "holy war" against China. He must uphold the honour of the Emperor. It was his duty.

There were times in the evening at home, usually alone since his wife was often out at some social gathering, when he struck up a conversation with a bottle of whiskey. He chuckled over his misspent youth, a time for railing against the government as his socialist father had done. Now in his middle years, he accepted that the divine Emperor looked after the best interests of His subjects. It was the government that exploited, manipulated, and ruined the people.

Morii especially saw the rich and the greedy as the worst in shirking responsibility for the welfare of their fellow Japanese in Canada. *The Buddha Dharma tells us desire causes suffering.* He saw it as his duty to exploit their weaknesses, whether it be money, women or whatever, for the good of the people. In return, he expected loyalty from those he benefited, achieved one way or another.

Across the street, the naked park grounds of hardened clay looked as desolate as a wasteland could be. Shallow furrows of eroded earth sloped down its width. He imagined warmer times when the Asahi baseball team played, showing off their athletic prowess to the admiring throngs. Now that was something the young *nisei* could embrace to build pride in the community, he grumbled to himself. When the team played the *keto* and beat them, his heart swelled.

The *oyabun* grunted and huddled in his overcoat as he turned north to head up Dunlevy away from the park. The cold north wind had sobered him up almost on contact. Half a block away was the Vancouver Honbu, also known as the Vancouver Judo Club. The organization occupied the first floor of a hotel with two large front windows closed shut with curtains. When open in hospitable weather, they allowed passersby to watch them practice.

Bodies confronted each other in loose white *judo-gi* uniforms. A pull of material here, a sweep of leg there. Overseeing the sparring at the head of the *dojo* was Tadasu Kojima, a barrel-chested instructor wearing his ego on his sleeve, his wide, glowering face constantly evaluating students.

Morii had to chuckle at the serious demeanour of his long-standing friend, a friendship that had grown over the years to mutual benefit.

Shortly after coming to Vancouver at the age of nineteen in 1922, Tadasu Kojima went to see a vaudeville show at the Capitol Theatre on Granville Street. On stage were two Japanese "entertainers" in a mock fight using fake judo skills. Kojima sat shocked, his youthful bearing swelling with outrage. The men in purple and pink *judo-gi* and slicked-down hair appeared more like clowns than serious students of the martial art. Not only that but their movements were clumsy, lacking any kind of skill or style. However, what really dismayed him was the fact that the audience loved it.

"Those bakatare," Kojima complained to his friend and boss Toshiaki Nagami, owner of Nagami Kashiya, a Japanese sweets store on Powell Street.

"Don't upset yourself. They're just doing it for money," Nagami advised, a lighthearted man in general.

"But they're bringing shame to all of us who're dedicated to judo."

"I suppose so, but what can you do about it?"

Kojima, an extraordinarily young black-belt champion and teacher of judo in Japan, did do something about it. After two years of preparation, he began the Vancouver Judo Club in 1924 in the house of a Nagami acquaintance, Kanzo Usui, another dedicated follower. With the living room cleared of its furniture, its delicate Japanese doll, dressed in red kimono and silk *obi*, carefully moved to an upstairs bedroom, Sensei Kojima taught the basics to two students at the beginning. Fortunately, the thick Persian rug cushioned their falls and the ten-foot ceiling easily accommodated a flip or hip toss.

The membership steadily grew with dues affordably set at five cents a lesson. Finally, when the organization was large enough to cover rent, Kojima moved the club into the bottom floor of the Richmond Hotel on Dunlevy. In time, he put in thick, interlocking *tatami* mats with green woven surfaces to cushion falls and expanded the club to include a dormitory with a few cots in a back room of the hall for poor students and out-of-towners needing a place to stay. An English school was also started on the premises for newly arrived Japanese students. No fees were charged for either of these services.

Both were supported by a generous grant from an anonymous donor, anonymous to the public anyway. According to some, Kojima was often seen in the *dojo*, kowtowing before Etsuji Morii in an odd expression of respectful obligation. Odd, since Morii was Sensei Kojima's student.

Besides being an excellent pupil since his childhood in Japan and now well on his way to the rarefied heights of the black-belt hierarchy, Morii also had a practical interest in the club. In February 1933, the Kido Kan ("Return to the Spirit") Judo Club, appropriately renamed after a prominent member of the Olympics Committee had visited the club the year before, decided to hold a tournament at the Japanese Hall and Language School on Alexander Street. Among the notable guests was William Morrow, Chief Superintendent of the Royal Canadian Mounted Police from Ottawa. So impressed was he with judo and the club that he asked Kojima for a demonstration.

During the exhibition a month later, Morii fidgeted in his seat, a squeaky wooden chair. Feeling more than a little out of place, the *oyabun* sat fingering his trademark suit and his bowler on his lap amongst a capacity audience of RCMP administrators and officers in a cavernous gymnasium at the downtown YMCA and wondering about the unusual match taking place in the boxing ring before him.

A left jab followed by a quick right – Tadasu Kojima easily avoided the potentially contest-ending blows. The boxer, a heavyset Irish officer with closely cropped curly hair, advanced steadily against his relatively short opponent. Kojima's stocky legs were surprisingly agile as he dodged another left-right combination.

"C'mon, you little jackrabbit. Stand still!" the boxer yelled, his face turning red to match his hair. The audience laughed.

A roundhouse right – Kojima saw his opening. Stepping into him, he avoided the extended arm and threw an elbow to the solar plexus. His opponent stunned and at a loss for breath, he then grabbed the Irishman's arm, moved his hip inside, and flipped him to the floor.

The crowd exploded with applause. The match was over.

Two weeks later, Kojima talked with the RCMP about giving lessons to the local constables at the club. Morii immediately started English lessons at the *dojo* school to brush up on the skills he had acquired as a student in Japan. He could see the value of negotiating with the Mounties himself.

☙

By 1940, judo was well established in British Columbia with Kojima's club at the centre of the activity. The *oyabun*, being a third *dan* black belt, held strenuous classes, imbuing his Japanese students with a sense of the Japanese spirit known as *bushido*, while offering his RCMP charges other incentives for their loyalty.

In Kojima's office after practice and after the hour had chased most home, Morii sat in his *judo-gi* mulling over the Miyamoto situation with Sgt. Benjamin Gill, an impressive man of sybaritic tastes with auburn hair and full moustache.

"So Mr. Morry, you called. What can I do for you?"

"*Gi-ru-san*, I just want to know something," Morii began in tentative English.

"And what's that?"

"Have you heard anything from police?"

"Heard anything? About what?"

"Anything wrong."

"Strange, you mean? You're not being very clear."

"Any murder?"

"Murder, well, now that's a different kettle of fish." Sgt. Gill scratched his head. "No, haven't heard a thing. When was this to have taken place?"

"Three day ago."

"Hmm. Tell you what, I'll go make some inquiries and get back to you."

"I would like to keep quiet. You know, we care for own."

"Sure, sure. But first, Mr. Morry, I have a bone to pick with you. My box of chocolates this month? It was a little light."

Morii's eyes widened. "Heh? I sorry, *Gi-ru-san*. You know, I take care of you."

The sergeant rose to his feet and made for the door. "I've got a feeling you're gonna have to take real good care of me on this one."

5. May 1920

The cabin of the *Canada Maru* was small but comfortable. There was a simple, uncomfortable-looking *gaijin* bed, a plain dresser made of some lacklustre wood, and a porthole to view the passing panorama of white-caps and endless sea. In the room's full-length mirror, Yoshiko Miyamoto admired her western outfit of a simple hat, white blouse, and long-waist-ed navy-blue skirt. She worried over the appropriateness of her bare legs. Her exposed calves were of considerable concern to her mother. It must be okay, she concluded. Why else would Miyamoto-*san* have bought such an outfit for his new daughter-in-law?

Her mood had brightened considerably since leaving port. Holding her *omamori* in her clasped hands, she gave thanks to the Buddha and to her father-in-law for his generosity in providing for her passage in such relative luxury. Bowing next before her husband's photo on the night table, she finished by offering words of gratitude to Jinsaburo for making all of this possible in the first place.

She knew of the immigrants below her in steerage: all second and third sons destined for poverty in Japan but now holding on to hope for prosperity in America. Housed above them with the other so-called picture brides, taking pride in her new clothes and anticipating the wild adventure of a foreign land with a new husband, she was keenly aware of her unique status.

Yoshiko often talked to fellow passenger Nofu Furukawa, a stern-looking woman with a gruff disposition, a trace of a chin, and a practical outlook. Those times on deck during the first part of the voyage, before the ship stopped at three other Japanese ports to pick up additional passengers, were the best, when the sea was calm and the sun was high.

"So your man owns a boarding house in … where again?"

"Ban-ku-ba," Yoshiko replied, careful not to stumble over the syllables. "He may even own two by now."

"Two! Well, you are set, aren't you?"

"Maybe you can visit us … or stay with us?"

"Not me," Nofu said distinctly. "I'm off to some godforsaken place called Pu-rin-su Jo … no, Pu-rin-su … oh, I can't even remember!"

"Where is it?"

"How do I know?" she shot back.

Yoshiko was taken aback, her face flushed with embarrassment. She had met such hard, rude women before, Hisa Miyamoto for one, but none were so sharp, so rude, during a normal conversation. It would take time to get used to this one. "Maybe … maybe it's close. You can come for a visit. Stay for free!"

"That's kind of you but I doubt I'll be travelling anywhere decent once I join my husband."

"Why?"

"He's a lumberman. I'll be cooking and cleaning for the men in camp."

"Really?" said Yoshiko, revealing her sympathy.

"Oh, I don't mind hard work. At least I answer to no one. It's better than living in Japan with the eldest son for a husband and a mother-in-law!"

Hisa Miyamoto's face appeared before Yoshiko, ugly and unforgiving. The constant barking hurt her ears, causing her to shiver back to the present. "That's exactly what I said … to my family, I mean," she said cautiously.

"Oh, you were wise to leave," advised Nofu. "I just said to myself, if there's going to be a mother-in-law making life miserable for some wretched girl, it had better be me with my son's wife!"

Yoshiko covered her mouth as she laughed.

By the end of the following week, the *Canada Maru* headed out to the open sea, her hold full of cargo, human and otherwise. Yoshiko overheard the crew say that the voyage should take about another two to three weeks. The thought troubled her a bit; after all, she was anxious for her new life to begin.

She surrendered completely to the pull of the Kuroshio. There was no drag of land behind her. The water ran through her veins, rippled over her skin, streamed through her hair. She was one with the Black Current, always would be. Yet she looked skyward and saw the moon, its round, pregnant aura descending toward her, its light expanding to envelop her. Her watery arms reached out to embrace it, to embody it. A premonition of life stirred inside her.

For most of the passengers, the trip had become boring by the time the ship set sail for Canada, but for Yoshiko, the anticipation only grew stronger and her conversations with Nofu more fanciful.

"Furukawa-san, what's your husband like?" she asked, her eyes beaming.

"Like? Like? How do I know what he's like? I've never met him." Nofu was ever the practical one, her stern face cemented in its severity.

"No, no. I mean what does he look like?"

"Oh, I don't know. By the picture, he appears like any other man. Tall, I suppose."

"Is he handsome? Muscular? With a small-diamond shaped birthmark on his shoulder, like mine?"

"You've been with him?" she asked, startled at the revelation.

"No, no, no."

"Then how do you know about the birthmark?"

"In my dreams."

"Oh … well, that's silly."

"I could tell by his picture, he's a kind man, tall like yours and very generous when it comes to friends."

"All that by his picture? I just saw a man uncomfortable in his Western suit and with big feet."

Yoshiko giggled. "How many babies do you want?"

"Ten, mostly boys. I come from a family of fourteen, good breeding stock," she replied matter-of-factly.

"Oh, I don't want that many. Four, maybe five," she asserted. "I need time to take care of the boarders and greet visitors."

"You do have plans, don't you?" Nofu threw her an ironic look.

Yoshiko looked out to sea. The horizon appeared deep blue, holding up the azure lightness of the sky. The colour of the water deepened until it turned into a rich and boiling green beside the ship, as if emanating from the black current below.

The tenth day outbound brought late spring storms, not entirely violent but strong enough to whip up the winds to rock the boat and disturb stomachs. Most passengers retired to their cabins, hoping for relief. Seasickness, a malady most had never experienced, had wreaked havoc aboard ship.

Yoshiko periodically forced herself up from the web of sleep and mucus of illness to look through the porthole window. A sad rain fell from grey clouds flattened against the sky, the rolling of the waves and the ship unrelenting. The storm lasted another five days, numbing her into a lingering apathy.

My god, do I have to endure this every time I go back for a visit? she thought to herself several times before invariably returning to bed. *Oka ... oka....* Maybe she should've stayed home. Whatever had possessed her to think this was a good idea? Maybe her thoughts were a byproduct of her homesickness but she did want the voyage to be over and magically be transported back to Japan. Sleep was a blessing; at least, she could dream.

... and the moonlight reached down through the water and pulled her to the surface. Her face, wet with the anonymity of the depths, opened to the cold light. She began tearing up, blinded by the brightness, and placed her hands on a solid surface of wood. She suddenly realized she was in a room, an empty room.

... and looking down upon her was a little girl in a pale green chemise hanging from somewhere above; she saw it as the face of death. Her pupils lost up behind her eyelids, her hair torn into shreds, her bruised arms down by her sides. Her face, long-nosed and feral, in torment, in agony.

Yoshiko awoke screaming ...

... only to find herself encased in a silent nausea.

On the seventeenth day out of Japan, a steward came around to announce a port of call: Vancouver, Canada. Anticipation revived Yoshiko as she picked herself up from the bed and moved to the porthole. As usual, the ever-expanding breadth of the sea met her blurred vision.

Outside her cabin door, she heard voices and the rapid shuffling of feet. After throwing on a handy *yukata* and coat and hastily pinning up her hair, she opened the entryway to find passengers rushing to the deck upstairs. Everyone was anxious to smell fresh air, dispel the fetid cabin air – and see land. On deck, Yoshiko managed to find Nofu Furukawa, holding herself steady on the railing.

"Miyamoto-san, look," Nofu called as she pointed off the forward bow.

Yoshiko cast her eyes toward a smudged stretch of brown horizon.

"Is that *Vancouver?*" she asked.

"It's gotta be *Canada!*" someone yelled.

It was too soon to see, but Yoshiko imagined a verdant landscape of forests and mountains. In a few hours, she would arrive.

Everyone later learned what she had seen, what they had seen, was Vancouver Island. It took a little more manoeuvering to enter the Strait of Georgia, First Narrows, Burrard Inlet, and finally, Vancouver Harbour. To the east of the Pacific port, great plumes of black smoke rose to the heavens above. A crewman who noticed the pretty passenger's fascination with the massive clouds explained to her that the waste burner of the Hastings Mill chimney was the navigational beacon most ships used in Vancouver Harbour. Yoshiko could see its usefulness.

Beyond the smoke were the mystic forests of North Vancouver, which reminded her of her home village nestled among the mountainside trees. She was now so far from home, she would never easily return to see that familiar landscape again. Her loneliness had not been completely left behind on that Yokohama pier so long ago, it seemed; her fears and doubts always circled on the edges of her senses like a restless pack of wolves smelling prey. Anxiety needled her, and she sought comfort in thoughts of her only saving grace: her husband.

When the *Canada Maru* finally docked at CP Pier B-C, the young bride nervously took in the enormity of the coastal mountains above the tree line and the city nestled far below. She made an effort to survey the waterfront, the bulwark of the grey city mass behind. Docked nearby and gently swaying in the sea's wash was the giant yet elegant *CPR Empress* ocean liner. Yoshiko couldn't pronounce the ship's cursed English name, but she imagined the finery and luxury contained within and promised herself a berth back to Japan someday on that floating palace.

Rain fell as the rebellious clouds abruptly cut off the sunlight, but Yoshiko didn't mind as she returned to her room to pack. There was so much to do. She had finally arrived.

Breathing in the ocean air on the pier, she decided it smelled differently from Japan, unusually sweet even though it was tinged with smoke. Before she disappeared into the crowd, Nofu told her it was the pulp from the local mills, from the massive log jams in the water. Vancouver pulsated with the buzz of industry.

Yoshiko was truly excited. The nagging thought of home still bothered her but she knew there was no turning back now. The challenge was before her; fortunately, she was not about to face it alone.

What she didn't like was the sight of so many white men. Rough-hewn, unsightly noses, booming voices, and a rainbow of different hair colours, they seemed more like beasts of burden toiling in the field than human beings. *Rise above it*, she told herself. *Ignore these animals.*

"Join that line," ordered a gruff Japanese voice. A man a foot shorter than Yoshiko stood in front of her, his starched high collar squeezing his head like a distended balloon. His tipped straw hat did nothing to ameliorate his officious yet preposterous appearance.

"Pardon me, I'm waiting for my husband, Miyamoto Jinsaburo."

"Well, he won't be here. You have to clear immigration first," the man explained.

She hadn't expected this, unaccustomed as she was to bureaucratic demands. The Canadian government should be honoured to have the Japanese immigrate to its country. We were favoured allies in the war, someone had told her. Why couldn't her husband accompany her through the red tape or used his influence to cut through at least some of it?

"Get in that line."

"But my luggage?" she asked. In a panic, she clutched her *furoshiki*.

"It'll be taken care of." With that he pushed her toward the line of picture-bride women and steerage men waiting to board buses.

The ride was short but revealing. Yoshiko sat with her head leaning against her slightly open window to get away from the unseemly man next to her. He had obviously been staying well below deck and not had a chance to shave or bathe probably during the entire voyage.

There was nothing to do but accept the situation. Just one more step to go through before she would join her husband, she assured herself. Just a few more hours.

The paint-chipped fleet of buses travelled along a dingy and deserted Vancouver street composed of dirt, gravel, and patches of worn, broken pavement. There was a horse-drawn buggy and a few automobiles, driving on the left-hand side just as she had seen in Tsuruga and Yokohama, which clogged the narrow waterfront road. Mostly dilapidated garages or warehouses, their walls sagging and rotten, lined the back street. Row after row of them made the city seem melancholy if not foreboding.

At some point, Kawasaki Mamoru, as the official on the dock had identified himself, ordered everyone on board to have their papers ready for inspection. The blur of the passing cityscape, the anticipation of the day, and the noxious presence in the seat beside her made Yoshiko feel dizzy, but she nonetheless rummaged about her person for her documentation.

The buses came to a stop as they reached the crescent of the hill they had climbed. From Yoshiko's vantage point inside, she saw that it sloped down into a vast tract of land spider-webbed with railroad tracks. On the other side of the expanse, like a silent castle deep inside a forest of thorns and bramble, lay a squat, brooding building, its windows all barred. Kawasaki announced the stop in front of the Immigration Building.

After carefully negotiating the maze of railway tracks, the long line of immigrants trudged through the double doors in single file. The building consisted of two wings with four floors each and a middle section, which featured a fifth with peaked roof. The first floor windows upon closer inspection were not only barred but also boarded up – an ominous portent of things to come.

His bug eyes accentuated by his round, wire-rimmed glasses, Kawasaki watched them closely as they streamed past. With such a large mob pooling inside the small alcove of dark, musty walls and a low ceiling, it quickly became claustrophobic. Yoshiko and all were relieved somewhat when they were directed upstairs by anonymous white men.

On the fourth floor, they emerged into a large room lit by barred but open windows, with southern exposure. Bathed in light, she breathed deeply to catch her breath. An officious, lumbering *gaijin*, straining in his white shirt and narrow tie, addressed them in a language that sounded like loud chewing. As Kawasaki interpreted, the men and women were to be separated – the men scheduled for washing and something called *delousing*, and the women taken to an office in a distant wing of the building.

Yoshiko wondered how long this process was going to be, as unease continued to churn in her stomach. Surely, her husband could and would rescue her.

After removing their clothes, a violent spray of some vile chemical and an embarrassing and intimate inspection by large, silent female nurses, the immigrant women, after dressing, were brought to another large room somewhere in a dingy recess of the building filled with tall, latticed windows and rows of metal-framed cots, a vulgar, earthy smell emanating from the damp canvas. Yoshiko expressed dismay when she heard she was to sleep there with all the other brides.

"This can't be. I thought this would be over today!" she complained. "I was to meet my husband on the docks!"

"Your husband isn't going anywhere," Kawasaki snorted. "And neither are you."

Her face melted but she refused to cry. She wouldn't give them the satisfaction.

Yet another *gaijin*, a tall muscular one this time, demonstrated the use of the toilet, a water closet with the tank above. The device puzzled Yoshiko. In Japan, she had used the *benjo*, an outhouse, but this was a mystery.

After they were left alone, Yoshiko and her adjacent bunkmate, Chitose Kiyomoto, a plain-faced woman with a faint moustache and short, unattractive hair, examined the water closet. Yoshiko pulled the chain and water came rushing down the pipes into the bowl. They laughed, but soon realized the water was not stopping.

"It's broken!" exclaimed Chitose in a panic. "It'll flood the place!"

They ran into the dormitory area. Chitose tripped over herself, then scurried back into the washroom the next moment. Yoshiko followed. The water was still gushing, unwilling to stop. In a panic, Chitose hopped around like a wounded frog.

"What'll we do? What'll we do?"

By this time, the others had noticed the slapstick chaos and ventured to investigate the roaring toilet as well. No one had any idea what to do.

"Call that gaijin! The one with red hair!"

"Somebody get him!"

"Where?"

"No, get Kawasaki-san!"

"Where?"

At long last, the contraption stopped on its own and returned to normal. Everyone breathed a sigh of relief.

A bell rang an hour later. Kawasaki appeared and ordered everyone to dinner downstairs in the basement.

The dank staircase opened at the bottom to a large hall filled with noise. Light came from overhead, institutional fixtures only, for no windows existed. It was then that Yoshiko realized how many were imprisoned here in the Immigration Building. The dining hall took up the entire basement, packed with long wooden tables and chairs and occupied by all manner of immigrant from various countries. As she ventured farther into the hall, she was hit by the unfamiliar smells, foreign smells. The *hoi sin* of China, the curry of India, and the *kimchee* of Korea combined with fetid body odours caused her to gag. She automatically gripped her throat to quell an embarrassment.

She slumped onto the bench, feeling the weight of unanswered questions. Was this her fate? How long was she to be a prisoner? Wasn't she better than most of these immigrants? She was a Miyamoto! Where was her husband? Her husband of consequence? Is he really so powerless to help?

She looked around. Evenly spaced on the conjoined tables were pots of steaming white rice. For each person there was a plate of nondescript fish served by taciturn white women in full-length aprons. Unarmed but uniformed guards were placed strategically around the room.

The meal was tasteless, and the fish had copious tiny bones, but Yoshiko was impressed the officials did provide soy sauce.

Back in her bunk, she unwrapped her *furoshiki* to find her toiletries. Amongst her mementoes of civilization she found the photograph, *omamori*, and a piece of paper, a letter home she had started aboard ship.

May, Taisho 8
To the Hayashi Household,
The sea is beautiful and the going is very easy. Please, do not worry about

me. I am making many friends here, even gaining weight from all the eating.

I am so grateful to my father-in-law. Without his help, I would not be enjoying all the wonderful food and the wonderful view of the ocean.

I am looking forward to landing in Canada and meeting my husband. I am sure we will have a good life together. Perhaps one day we shall all be together for a reunion.

The weather is getting hotter.

Yoshiko raised her head and watched the shadows of the window bars growing long across the bunk beds. The bedding was shaped into lumps from the many anonymous bodies beneath. Even though it was only early evening, most had taken to their beds out of exhaustion. She closed her eyes and considered how far she had fallen. That morning on board ship, she was in relative luxury anticipating her new life with great excitement. Her perhaps rash decisions made in youth were now coming back to haunt her. She reread the unfinished letter. The optimism mocking her, she decided not to finish it, vowing not to send any letters home. At least not until her circumstances were better. She couldn't lie, and if she told the truth, her family would have to endure such shame. Dampness rose in the corners of her tightly closed eyes as she thought of her mother. Homesickness settled in her stomach like a cold, damp rag. She wiped her face dry on the scratchy pillowcase when she lowered her head. Maybe she would dream of returning home in triumph.

Fatigue fell upon her and, without changing her clothes, Yoshiko squirmed underneath the covers, not even caring about the wetness of the canvas that insinuated through the thin blanket, to her garments, and to her skin, or the sour smell that threatened to become part of her. She drifted to sleep as the sound of shifting tides swelled and crept in through the windows.

Kuroshio-san.

She failed to dream, even as woeful mongrels called out to her in the mysterious foreign night.

6. May 1921

For Vancouver, the spring of 1920 was a time of great optimism. The spirit of free enterprise rose in the air like a fresh breeze coming out of the north. The city's very vitality enticed to industry a population burgeoning towards a half-million. "Opportunity" was the catchword of the day. The Panama Canal was now open, making Vancouver *the* port of Western Canada. From all over the Pacific, immigrants came to a land of prosperity where the "easy life" was the golden promise.

In the Powell Street area as well, Japanese-owned businesses flourished, and families became immersed in the Canadian way of life. Churches were well established. Organized picnics and festivals (religious and otherwise) took place. The community's own Asahi baseball team of the fledgling International League had won last year's championship for the first time and, with returning players like Junji George Ito (a great sacrifice hitter), the dedicated Harry Sanzoku Miyasaki, and Eddie Eizaburo Kitagawa (top of the batting order four years running), they were expected to repeat as champs.

Everybody lived with great expectations.

Unfortunately for the Asahi, the new season was not going as well as had been hoped. The ball team was second overall but trailed by five games. Perhaps not a great margin, but their surprisingly sloppy play and their too-frequent bench arguments did not bode well for a second championship. In particular, their style of baseball, identified as "brain ball," was not working as well as last season. Bunts went awry, steals produced no advantage. Still, "Bariki" Kasahara, the fast-talking coach so nicknamed for his stamina and stubbornness, guaranteed a repeat and staked his job on it.

Etsuji Morii sat with his constant companion Rikimatsu in the paid section of the wooden stands along the first base line of Powell Ground. Morii, in his characteristic bowler hat, tipped a greeting to as many of the married women who happened to pass by as possible, expecting an acknowledgment, a show of respect, from each in return. After all, every *yomesan* and *okusan*, bride and housewife, owed her presence in Canada to him through his guarantor committee within the Nihon Jinkai.

Rik-*san*, a straw hat awkwardly perched upon his skull, felt no such responsibility and paid little or no attention to the women or the game. Being stuck in a "hick town" meant nothing to him – he reputedly had been in all kinds of ports of call, after all – as long as he could make money, and he hated anything that distracted him from acquiring it. He was squinting as if in pain in the wash of the radiant sun. Exposed as he was, he preferred the night with its shadows that offered anonymity, and always hoped each day for cloudy or foggy weather. At an opportune moment, he brought up a subject to divert attention from the ball game.

"So you think we can open this new gambling club?" the *yojimbo* ventured.

"Sure, it'll be the biggest around these parts. Oh, Nikaido-san, and how is your husband? Recovered from the flu, has he?" Morii smiled, then whispered an aside in the next breath. "It'll take a while to set up but it's a way to keep the money out of Chinatown permanently."

"Where would this place be? And how do we keep it away from the police?"

"*Nem mind,*" he said in heavily accented English before returning to Japanese. "Enjoy the game."

On the mound, Mickey Kitagawa, Eddie's brother, waited solemnly for the Humbly Sawmill Spitfires' ace batter to step up to the plate. "Ty" Johnson, a Negro ballplayer, could hit the ball all the way to Jackson Avenue on the other side of the park. The pitcher with a slightly sloped abdomen and his big feet firmly curved to the mound stared down the batter with narrowed eyes. The posturing was to no avail.

After a few pumps of the bat, the gigantic first baseman was ready with a mean look of his own that had chilled many a pitcher's resolve, rookie and veteran alike. Mickey went down into his crouch and began his windup. His arm came over his shoulder and, with its trademark snap, the ball blistered into Yo Kitagawa's catcher's mitt. Strike one.

"Oyabun, I gotta go ... back to the Hinomaru."

Morii waved off his *yojimbo* as he kept his eyes on the game.

The second pitch – high and away. One and one. The defense over-shifted, anticipating a ground ball. A looping curve ball off the plate to the outside and Johnson's bat made contact. Not the overpowering homer of legend to left field, but an opposite field hit toward Cordova Street just south of the park.

"Chikusho! That Kurombo hurts us every time," Morii shouted as he and everyone else in the stands rose to their feet. "Look at those outfield-ers running around like Chankoro."

As Johnson rounded the bases, the sun gleamed on the man's teeth, his burnished skin emphasizing the white elements of his face.

The Asahi managed to eke out a win with a remarkably long homer by George Ito that crossed Jackson Avenue to Dr. Uchida's front porch (so remarkable the good doctor went straight to the team manager to complain even though no glass was broken) and a rare double steal by Miyasaki and Ed Kitagawa. Miyasaki was caught at second but, with only one out, Kitagawa made it home in time. One errant throw and a costly error by the Spitfires but a great manufactured run by the home team. "Brain ball" had made a triumphant return, albeit briefly.

Even though they improved their play throughout the season and ac-tually made it to the championship rounds at Powell Ground, the team did not repeat as champions. When all was said and done, the *oyabun* talked extensively and for many nights over sake and *donburi* with Dr. Seitaro Nomura, the team's manager and the First Vice-President of the Vancouver City Baseball League. Morii, witnesses say, suggested a need for change.

The next year, the coach, "Bariki" Kasahara, was gone and the Asahi found glory on tour in Japan. The season following that, Harry Miyasaki became the new coach, thus starting his remarkable run of multiple championships with the team in the harder-hitting, faster-paced Termi-nal League.

All was well for the Asahi, but a year almost to the day that Dr. Uchida complained about possible broken windows by exceptional homers, the *oyabun* couldn't be found cheering from his usual seat. He was sitting in the Cordova Street police station being questioned for the murder of seventeen-year-old Haruo "Harry" Yamamoto.

⌘

Etsuji Morii examined his fingernails carefully for any grime collected during the four-hour interrogation he had just endured. They were clean; in fact, his entire demeanour was hardly ruffled despite the ordeal. His full head of hair was neatly in place. His shirt was still crisply white, the crease in his pants sharp, the bay-rum scent about him fresh. He sat alone in the straight-backed creaking chair as calm as he was when first brought in by the police. Closing the door behind them, two officers re-entered the interrogation room in the basement of 236 Cordova Street. The room itself consisted of four unblemished, institutional-green walls (with the exception of the calendar featuring the popular Gibson Girl, the look on her face at once cool and condescending), a lone table, a few chairs, and a single light bulb casting a severe light. Both men were identical in appearance: clean-shaven with greased-down hair and coal-black eyes. Their dark grey suits were off-the-rack from Woodward's department store. The only difference between them was that one had an unseemly full head of red hair. They both appeared haggard, betraying their frustration in dealing with this case.

"All right, Morry. Let's start all over again," said the redhead with a deep breath.

Morii glanced at him before returning to his stony expression.

"We know you did it," asserted the other detective. "We just want to know why."

He remained mute.

"You killed that poor seventeen-year-old kid right out in the open. We got an eyewitness who'll testify to it."

Morii looked up in defiance, but with perhaps a hint of surprise and fear. He clenched his jaw.

"That's right, Morry, we got you."

"Someone's come forward since we nabbed you."

"*Eigo wakarimasen,*" Morii answered.

A swift backhand caught the suspect by surprise. "You goddamn Jap, quit talking to us in that lingo."

"We know you speak English!"

He touched his cheek as he glared at his persecutors. His face was hot but the skin was unbroken; his eyes quickly turned stone cold.

In a burst of anger, the one detective grabbed him by the shirt front and nearly lifted him off the chair like a rag doll. "Tell us why you did it!"

Morii went limp, closed his eyes, and slumped back in the chair. Never would he talk to these damn *keto*. These were the people from whom he had sworn to protect the Japanese: the big, dumb, vulgar *keto*.

There was a knock at the door. In came a tall man, impressively taller than the two detectives. Every strand of his wavy brown hair was in place; his suit seemed tailor-made judging by the ease with which he moved. He even smelled clean.

"Gentlemen, I have business with your prisoner." His voice was smooth and pleasant.

"Who's this swell?" asked the one detective, thumbing the other.

"Constable Benjamin Gill, RCMP," he replied.

"What can we do for you, sir?" asked the other respectfully.

"This Mr. Morry you have in custody, I need to have a talk with him about immigration fraud."

"Yeah, well, we got him for murder!"

"Gentlemen, I only have an hour before I have to return to head-quarters. Shall I call in your captain?" he threatened as he retrieved and clicked open his Birks gold pocket watch.

"No. No need for that," said the one as he looked to the other. "Let's go. We need a break anyway."

The other nodded.

"Unless you need us to stick around?" said the one, his fist offered as an inducement.

"No, gentlemen," Gill said, pocketing his watch. "I'll let you know when I'm finished."

The two detectives collected themselves and walked out of the room, both sneering at Morii as they passed.

Alone with the prisoner, Gill sat across the table from him.

"Murder is such a nasty business, isn't it, Mr. Morry?" he began.

"*Eigo wakarimasen.*"

"Oh now, now. Don't play that game with me," Gill replied as he took out a pack of cigarettes. He patted the bottom of the package before selecting one and putting it to his lips. "I know you speak English." He produced a silver lighter with the RCMP insignia embossed upon its gleaming surface and flicked it to ignite. He drew on the cigarette and blew out a stream of smoke. "In fact, I know a lot about you."

Morii felt sweat under his collar.

"You immigrated here about fifteen years ago in 1906. Funny thing, though, you didn't come from Japan like most of your compatriots. You came from San Francisco. Why were you in San Francisco, Mr. Morry?"

Morii squirmed. *The past is a curse.*

"No matter. The authorities down there are doing a little checking of their own. I'll be hearing from them soon, I'm sure. "Now then, you soon took over the Raku restaurant and became the local big shot with the Japanese businessmen. A lot of women seem to pass through that place. Why is that, Mr. Morry?" Gill bent down, moving closer to Morii. "Hmm, no answer, eh? Well, then, it seems you really made it big after the 1907 riots."

Morii looked agitated but remained silent.

"Then a happy event." Gill sat up straight. "You went and got married back in Japan in 1910. To a Misao, now let me get this right, Ma-sue-o-ka," he mispronounced slowly. "She's a high society type from what I gather. Now what does a high-toned lady like her see in a reprobate like you?" He paused for a reaction, but none came. "Now there's this murder. What's that all about, eh?"

Morii smirked enigmatically.

Gill smiled back at the prisoner. "I really don't care about some seventeen-year-old you happened to have business with. That's the Vancouver police department's worry. I want to know about the box of chocolates."

Morii loosened his tie. His brow furrowed at the mention of the box, and broke out in a thin sweat. "May I have cigarette?" he said in accented but clear English.

Gill's mouth pulled back into a grin as he provided Morii with one.

After a long puff, Morii relaxed in the camouflage of cigarette smoke. "What chocolate box, Gi … Gi …?"

"Gill. Constable Gill. I understand there was a problem with a Mr. Moriyama last year with immigration. You know Moriyama, a big strapping fellah? Works at Nagami's sweets shop on Powell and seen in your company. No?" He smiled in the pause. "Seems he entered Canada under false papers, for which somebody paid four hundred dollars. Rumour has it the local judo club put up the money. Now why would such a cash-strapped organization like that put up that kind of cash? You wouldn't know anything about that, would you?"

The *oyabun* shook his head, staring back hard at the constable.

"Well, I have a report that says Moriyama was found out and was about to be deported when Mrs. Moriyama, so distressed by the prospect of losing a husband, approached you with a box of chocolates." He paused again. "No chocolates, I gather, but enough money in that box for you to act."

"Me? To do what?"

"That's what I want to know," Gill said, leaning forward. "Moriyama was released within a week after his wife's visit to you. Aside from his bakery job, he seems to be working for you now; at least, he's seen in your company a lot of the time."

"I never talk about past."

"Well, you're going to talk to me," he said in a raised voice, banging his fist on the table. "Who did you bribe in immigration? If there's any corruption, I know you're the man to give me the details."

"*Gi-ru-san,*" the *oyabun* answered calmly. "You smart man, *ne*? Smart enough to know make-up story when you hear one."

"Mrs. Moriyama's testimony seems pretty convincing to me."

"You say so and I tell you real story if you want, but I am here for murder."

"Maybe I can help you there."

"*So ka*? Then maybe I help you better."

"How's that?"

"Maybe you like own box of chocolate?" he ventured as a gamble.

Gill sat straight up. It was obvious he wasn't expecting such a possibility.

"Maybe once a month, every month," Morii added, jumping on the hesitation.

Raising an eye, Constable Gill spoke. "What are you saying to me, Mr. Morry?"

"I want you as ... friend. I take care of friend."

"And what would I have to do for this friendship?"

"Help me with murder."

"And for that I would get a box of chocolates?"

"Then every month," Morii stated.

"You know that's bribery."

"No bribe. Gift ... for help with question." The *oyabun's* eyes sharpened and grew dark looking for acceptance. He felt the advantage now his.

The officer caressed the fine wool of his suit lapel. His own eyes darkened. Benjamin Gill had been born into poverty and didn't enjoy living on a constable's wage. "Tell me more, Mr. Morry."

"In my business, I have question, many question. Maybe you help answer question."

"And what business are you in?"

"That is something I not tell my friend." Morii inspected his interrogator quickly yet thoroughly. "That is nice suit you wear."

"Thank you," he responded.

"Tailor make?" asked the *oyabun* as he smoothed the coarse material of his own suit pants.

"Local man. I'm working my way up to Savile Row."

"How much money you make, *Gi-ru-san?*"

"Now that is definitely something you don't tell friends."

"But you need money?"

"We all need money."

Morii forced a smile despite taking another draw on his cigarette.

"But chocolates, Mr. Morry, we all *like* chocolates," Gill added as if he had made a decision.

"So you are friend?"

"What about Moriyama? I have my own questions that need to be answered."

"You help me," Morii said, grinning, "I help you."

Constable Gill's face grimaced and he abruptly came to his feet. "I think I've got all I need here, Mr. Morry." He stepped toward the door.

"*Gi-ru-san?*" Morii asked.

"I'll be in touch."

"*Gi-ru-san?* You forget one thing."

"Yes, Mr. Morry."

"What I do about murder?"

"Hirano ... he's your man of interest."

"Hirano? The hardware man?"

"You know him, then?"

"I know everyone."

"Of course you do," he said with a smile. "He's the eyewitness for the police." Constable Gill nodded knowingly as he stepped out of the interrogation room.

Left alone, Morii pondered the advantages of having the RCMP on his side. He didn't know how to gain more of that influence at the moment, but he also knew the way would eventually make its presence known to him.

Morii was cleared of the first-degree murder charge, receiving instead a suspended sentence for manslaughter, the result of a lack of corroborating evidence. The chief witness for the prosecution had for some reason disappeared.

．ゝ

Tuesday, March 12, 1940

Dream and memory. Until 1921, Morii seemingly hadn't let guilt bother him whenever he used violence; it was a means to an end. He claimed it was only employed as a "last resort to gain co-operation." Do what you must to find your way to enlightenment, devout followers of the Buddha like the Abbot Rennyo had said. Even violence? the *oyabun* wondered.

Witnesses, however, observed that when dealing with the "unco-operative," Morii seemed to enjoy meting out his "justice." Brutality was used as punishment and he reveled in its power.

But in the Yamamoto case, the *oyabun* was the cause of someone's death. He slept uneasily, woke up in tears of rage more than he cared to admit. Guilt became his constant companion and tormentor, and because of that teenager's untimely passing, he was driven to seek redemption, not a Buddhist imperative but a Japanese one. They must be made to understand, he reasoned. Oh, there was the talk that Etsuji Morii had fatally wounded a police officer in a San Francisco barroom brawl. His *oyabun* sent him to Vancouver under the watchful eye of Mitsuzo Shiga as a result. There was even a rumour that he had killed an officer during a student protest in Japan, which was the reason he found himself with Yosuke Matsuoka on a ship headed for Portland, Oregon, in the first place. But that was all talk, none of it ever substantiated. For his part, Morii did nothing to set people straight. He had learned early that that kind of reputation was good for business.

Now with this Miyamoto business, he found sleep hard to come by once again. Just thinking about another possible murder in Powell Street, he feared history repeating itself. The intensity of the feelings swirling inside, in fact, surprised him to no end. He wasn't responsible in the least bit, but he knew he would be blamed somehow. All he wanted was respect from his own community. He wanted to see it in their eyes. He wanted to feel it in their treatment of him. But murder is a dirty business, with little hope for redemption.

The hour was late. It was the night of the day after that Miyamoto woman came to see him, and his face sagged with weariness as he sat drifting toward sleep but never quite making it behind his desk in his Nippon Club office. As the events stemming from that early evening nearly twenty years ago were resurrected in his mind's eye, the *oyabun* started to well up with emotion.

The sound of a gavel being pounded pierced the air. The young Yamamoto, frozen in his youth, stood before him in his office, with no fear in his eyes, burning with resentment. His judo men, Tanaka and Moriyama, sat nearby, one of Tanaka's fat legs up on the oyabun*'s desk. Rik-san was conspicuous by his absence. "Yamamoto-san, you're a good boy to do your father's bidding. Come here and shake hands. A gesture of good faith." "Saibashi" was all the boy said to Morii. Inflamed eyes, heavy breathing. The chase out of the office and down the street was short. Slaps about the head. The boy swung his right fist. Instinctively, the oyabun grabbed the boy's arm and tossed him over his head. The teenager fell with an ugly crack; his neck broke. The gavel rapped again.*

Morii rubbed his palms together until the sweat turned to curds of dirt. It was easy to murder. No, it was easy to kill. Murder is planned, murder is foreseen. Killing happens without thinking. There's no decision to make. The *oyabun* was so surprised at how fragile the boy was. Here one minute, gone the next. He saw life in him, the anger at the hard-nut centre of his accusing eyes, and he felt the strength in his arms even as he fell to the ground. Extinguished like a light bulb. *Life is suffering.*

In his drowsiness, the *oyabun* could almost reach out and touch the dead boy's scuffed shoes, torn dungarees, and soiled shirt. The bruised neck, bending the head into an unnatural position, and the eyes, the round, clear, glassy eyes of a dead fish lying cold on the sidewalk, horrified him.

Morii suddenly recalled the several heated arguments with Ryuichi

Sato, the fishermen's association president from Steveston, which had escalated at one point to deadly levels. The *oyabun* had actually pushed the president down a flight of stairs. What was he thinking? Was he really capable of murder?

Sato had survived. Why hadn't the Yamamoto kid? He bristled at the memory of that police interrogation room. He never should have been arrested, and never would he be arrested again, he vowed. He held to the conviction that the kid had been stupid, brought on his own death.

For all that he had sacrificed and planned for his people, like any father, how dare that kid question his authority. If that imbecile had paid his *otosan's* debt to him in the proper way, bowing and with respect, he'd be alive today, Morii reasoned.

Despite his rationalizations, he had moments of self-doubt. Had he been too arrogant with the boy? Yamamoto was justified in his anger. His father was weak and had lost a great deal of the family savings. Why hadn't he been more compassionate, more understanding? The Buddha said that the ego creates desire and desire causes suffering. Why had he given in so easily to his own weaknesses? The *oyabun* would never know.

At least Hirano, the eyewitness, came in handy. When Constable Gill staged a raid, looking for his "box of chocolates" immigration-fraud suspect, what he found was "proof" that Hideo Moriyama had boarded the *Yokohama Maru*. Records in Yokohama showed that the felon had landed and entered Japan three weeks later. He then promptly disappeared.

Constable Gill reported to his superiors that his suspect had absconded overseas, back to his homeland. The case was closed and he made sergeant for his efforts.

What was odd to the residents of Powell Street about the Mountie raid was the fact that it wasn't Moriyama's house. Morii's goon lived in the Empress Rooms, a cheap boarding house. Everyone outside heard a woman's voice pleading for the *gaijin* officers to find her kidnapped husband: Hirano, the hardware man.

What had happened to the star witness was anyone's guess, and no one looked into it to any great extent. Not even his wife, she knew better.

The telephone suddenly rang, shocking the *oyabun* out of his ruminations.

"Mr. Morry," said the worried voice on the other end, its smooth tone instantly recognizable as Sgt. Gill's. "I must see you right away."

"Yes *Gi-ru-san. Dojo de* … one hour," he replied and hung up, then quickly donned his hat and coat. Obviously, the RCMP officer had something to tell him. He held out hope for something of value.

Similar to Morii's office, Kojima's was adorned with black and white photographs of judo gods, awards, citations, and not much else. In one corner, two filing cabinets acted more like dust catchers than storage for paper records. One worn desk and two loose-jointed chairs comprised the furniture for the sparse room.

The *oyabun* paced the floor constantly. It was nearing midnight, the overhead light the only evidence of life in the club.

About ten minutes past the hour, Gill walked in cautiously and removed his heavy overcoat and felt hat before sitting down in the creaking chair. His face was grim.

"The city police have found a body," he said succinctly.

"Where?" Morii asked with trepidation. Had the police found out?

"CP rail yards. Decapitated."

"*Nani?*" he asked, his face plastered with questions.

"His head was cut off, probably by a train," Gill informed. "Looks like murder. He was stabbed several times."

Morii remained silent, pondering any connection to the Miyamoto woman. Okihara may be mixed up in this. Find him and answers will follow, he concluded.

"It happened two maybe three days ago. They've been gathering evidence … against you."

"Me? Why?" he exclaimed, surprised at the turn of events.

"Because they want you," Gill said without equivocation.

"No, I not do such a thing."

"Well, you're the man of choice for the moment. The identity of the man is still unknown. For the time being anyway. They found some damning proof on the body."

"What?"

"I don't know. They won't tell me." He paused before continuing. "Maybe something connected with that club of yours. They're planning on a raid," Gill said solemnly, "for selling liquor without a license."

"But I pay … pay plenty to –"

"I know," Gill confirmed, "but your man on the licensing board won't be there. The liquor violations are a smoke screen. They really want to look for more evidence in the murder case. My guess is they'll arrest you at the same time. They'll get you for murder and break your operations all in one go."

"Can you stop?"

"No."

The *oyabun* considered his options. Worry lines dug deep across his forehead.

"May I make a suggestion?" Gill said.

He nodded.

"Find a fall guy."

"*Nani?*" he asked in Japanese, forgetting whom he was talking to for the moment.

"A fall guy. Someone to take the blame," he suggested. "How about your henchman, Rick-*san*? He looks made for the part."

Rikimatsu? Turn in Rikimatsu? Betray my lifelong friend? Can't be done.

"My records say very little about the man," Sgt. Gill revealed. "His point of origin and age are unknown. Is he Japanese, Chinese, Korean? No one seems to know. All I know is that he was found on a San Francisco dock one day in 1902 half-dead from a beating. No one knows what he was doing there. It looks like the Black Dragon Society helped him avoid investigation and probable deportation. He came here with you, obviously."

Morii said nothing.

"What happened to his nose?"

☞

Autumn 1906

Six months after the devastating San Francisco earthquake, the city was beginning to re-establish itself. It was also the chance for the Black Dragon Society to consolidate its holdings. Farther south, the four leaders of the west coast operations met in the back room of the Mikado Restaurant at the corner of First and San Pedro Streets in Los Angeles's Little Tokyo. The basic greasy chopstick with its trademark clapboard booths, long counter, and cherry-top stools was crowded with Japanese railway workers in from Sacramento or Fresno eager to partake of the Blue Plate special – sliced *teriyaki* chicken, greens, and mashed potatoes for fifteen cents, with a dessert of stewed fruit thrown in for free.

In the private eggshell-coloured room decorated with a few Hoku-sai prints, Shinichi Sera of Los Angeles, Sadaki Matsuda of Seattle, the *oyabun* of San Francisco, and the young Etsuji Morii of Vancouver were served home-cooked Japanese meals by discreet women in kimonos.

The *oyabun* spoke first after dinner. "I would like to thank Sera Shin-ichi for the wonderful hospitality. The food was excellent. The sake even better."

Sera, the gaunt and ancient gambling boss of LA's Little Tokyo, nodded his gratitude for the acknowledgment. Morii once again noted the long scar of the *oyabun's* face.

"The earthquake in San Francisco has devastated the city," the *oyabun* continued. "Not so bad in the Japanese quarter but Chinatown has been laid to waste. It's now our opportunity." He paused. "I believe it's time to fulfill our duty to bring back the Japanese from the Chinese gambling halls."

"Yes! Yes!" the excitable Matsuda exclaimed. "Our people are losing all their hard-earned money to the godless Chankoro with no chance of bettering themselves."

"My men tell me that some $150,000 goes out of our communities up and down the coast every year!" Sera added as he picked his teeth openly. "Families are being ruined by the fathers taking their savings or borrowing money at impossible interest rates from the Chankoro just to gamble it away."

The *oyabun* continued. "We all know of cases where Japanese went into those Chankoro dens and never came out. Never seen again."

"But what can we do?" Sera asked. "Forgive me, but our people are such simpletons."

In the flurry of ensuing laughter, the *oyabun* took his cue. "Let me introduce you to Morii Etsuji, our man in *Vancouver*. He's young, but wise beyond his years."

The adolescent stood up awkwardly, not knowing how else to react. He was happy to have made the trip "home" as a celebrated son, but Los Angeles was a new experience. He liked it despite its differences from his favoured San Francisco. Though he was just recently out of the world of student activism, Morii had begun to see the advantages of *bushido*. Loyalty to the Emperor and the ideals of Japan opened up a whole new world of power and influence. At the same time, the Black Dragon Society afforded him an efficient means to protect the Japanese from the devious and dangerous *Amerika-jin*.

The room of men shifted uncomfortably. Morii's shoes were pinching him. He nervously twitched as he was determined not to move his hands to scratch an itch in an indiscreet area of his thigh.

The *oyabun* sat back and gave a casual wave of the hand. "Morii, tell us what you've been doing."

"Well … I …" he began tentatively.

"He's going right into those Chinatown dens and talking our people into coming back!" the *oyabun* interrupted before laughing at the audacity of his young charge. "He started doing it for me in San Francisco!"

Morii relaxed as the others around the table expressed incredulity and then delight. The *modus operandi* was set. Each gang would infiltrate the Chinatown gambling dens to look for Japanese patrons and either encourage or threaten them to come back to Little Tokyo. There was no telling how the Chinese bosses would react.

﹀

Rikimatsu's job had changed in early 1921. He was still Morii's *yojimbo*, but he had taken on the extra task of scouting Vancouver's Chinatown, which he didn't mind since he felt he was undermining the business of a rival. With his ink dot eyes, sallow skin, high cheekbones, and long, wiry body, he could easily pass for Chinese. Morii himself was busy with an idea for a new gambling establishment.

Rik-*san's* problem was his mouth; it always got him in trouble. It was in the basement of the Ho Yuen Restaurant on East Pender Street where the *yojimbo*, as he was to tell later, was chatting up a young, wayward *nisei* gambler named Tadashi Yoshida when a burly Chinese bouncer, who had heard the cursed Japanese coming from the disfigured stranger in the corner, shouted at him in the guttural Toisan language before grabbing him by the back of his collar and throwing him to the ground. Before Rik-*san* could react, three others jumped on him. Kicks to the kidneys and then stomach and groin as he squirmed to get away. His face contorted with agony. Jagged words in an incomprehensible language rained down on him. He floated on the verge of unconsciousness when he caught a glimpse of metal.

Fear grabbed his instincts and wrestled him awake. Invisible hands raised his head by the hair into the lap of one of his tormentors. His eyes bulged in horror at the sight of the knife. He couldn't move, pinned by alien hands, of his bruises and broken bones. An angry Chinese boss stood above him yelling tortured sentences.

The hot, sustained pain of being cut flooded his mind. Spurts of blood blinded him. He covered his face with his hands and felt an emptiness. Rolling to the floor, he screamed into unconsciousness.

The owner of the Empress Rooms, Shigeko Kaminishi, found Rikimatsu in the alley behind her rooming house. She hurriedly reported to the *oyabun* who was enjoying a late supper of chicken and *shiitake* hot pot at the Chidori-tei Restaurant.

Once Morii himself found his *yojimbo* lying face up with his nose sliced off, his life bleeding out of him, he called for Tanaka and Moriyama to take the injured man to Dr. Miyazaki. Rikimatsu ended up in St. Mary's Hospital.

ॐ

Wednesday, March 13, 1940

"He's the perfect fall guy," Sgt. Gill repeated in the hushed tones appropriate for the pitch-black hours of the morning.

"No, I not give Rikimatsu," Morii said in a fatigued but succinct manner.

"Then you'll take the fall."

Past the old, sleepy guard, and at the top of the long flight of groaning stairs, a sign hung over the entrance to the Showa Club giving good advice and perhaps fair warning.

> *Bakuchi-wa suruna. Surunara Showa kurabu.*
> *(Do not gamble, but if you must, gamble here at the Showa Club.)*

The crowd was good for midweek. The loggers and miners were in Vancouver waiting for the next job and looking for diversion during the evening. They all seemed to start at the Showa Club before heading for the *joro* houses up on Alexander east of Jackson, well beyond the annoying moral presence of the United Church. Some did partake of a bath and a woman at the *furoba* bathhouses on Powell or have a meal and other delights at the Three Sisters Café, but most liked the possibility of winning money at the Showa Club.

Few did, of course. The games of chance, like *gaji*, a gin rummy-like card game, and various *gaijin* games of *poka*, poker, provided ample opportunity but little return. In addition to losses, each player paid a certain amount to the manager Aki for time taken at the tables, for alcohol and for food. But it was the possibility of winning that kept them at it, all night for some.

At about ten o'clock on that Wednesday night in March 1940, Aki was busy behind the bar heating the sake and installing a new keg of draft beer. Morii sat by himself in the corner, appearing to be waiting for something. His face dark and ominous, no one dared approach him. Rikimatsu was encouraging some older customer on in his game. A victory yell came from another corner of the club. Kazuto Sugimoto had just won his fifth consecutive game of *gaji*.

In the next instant, the ceiling lights flickered off and on three times. Suddenly, a cool and efficient movement ensued. Morii himself rose to his feet, donned his hat and coat, and pushed a convenient button near him. Hidden compartments in the walls opened, and Showa Club employees pushed tables with gambling money and paraphernalia into them. Others lifted the gambling tabletops to uncover the three pool tables, their green fields of worn felt shining in the light. Still others flipped large sections of the immovable tables to hide the gambling markings. Aki, in a practiced manner, concealed the keg within a handy wooden box, stashed sake and beer bottles under floorboards, and drained drinks in a nearby sink. In a matter of moments, the place was transformed into a harmless clubhouse with billiard tables, shoe-shining facilities, and a restaurant counter.

A loud rumble came up the staircase. Into the room burst the watchman, his face animated with panic. Following him a mob of Vancouver policemen, their truncheons drawn, flooded into the hall. Their faces were angry with purpose and red from the exertion. The lead group of men headed straight for Morii.

While others quickly searched the room and ushered out the members and patrons, two grabbed the *oyabun* by the arms. He offered no resistance.

"All right. All right," he said in English. "I go."

"You're under arrest, Morry, for the murder of Gin Miyamoto."

7. June 1920

The ocean lay mute as Yoshiko Miyamoto stood outside the Immigration Building. Despite the ugly briar patch of railroad track in front of her, the thick pine tar caked on orphaned railroad ties, and the rusted spikes discarded haphazardly, she could taste the heavy saltiness of the sea in the air and feel the Kuroshio draining into the land, being absorbed by all the souls who had emerged from its depths seemingly so long ago. But she could no longer hear the ocean's voice, the steady roar and boom of hope and memory of home.

She in fact hadn't heard the Pacific for the two weeks she had been imprisoned in the building for bureaucratic clearance. The experience had left her feeling quite empty despite the anticipation of meeting her husband, the man she still envisioned, albeit with diminished conviction, with strong arms and sharply defined features standing tall in the sun. He was all she had left, her only hope since she started to accept the fact that she was truly without family. Perhaps there was still the tingle of excitement somewhere within her, but she dismissed the sensation as a dull irritation.

On the morning of her release, the sun was hardly visible. Low-lying clouds pressed the atmosphere to the ground, flattened it against buildings straining at the seams to endure the weight. It was the weather that had deprived the sea of its voice.

And the absence of sunlight had robbed her of any chance of enthusiasm. At least the sting of a bright day might have awakened her somewhat from her complacency. Instead, the dull atmosphere spoke to her of her life of the last two weeks: the daily grind of waking up in an uncomfortable metal cot beside a stranger more than likely moaning from the ache caused by the inconvenient bar across her back; a quick splash of water on the face from a cold, prosaic basin; the toilet rituals out in the open without semblance of privacy; and then shuffling down to the dining room with all the other anonymous immigrants. She surprised herself when she noticed how quickly she had got used to the rancid smell of perspiration, fermented urine, and alien cultures. The food of watery rice, thin miso soup, and a bit of bland fish offered little escape from the boredom and loneliness. The bars on the windows, the grey-green institution walls, the sombre *keto* guards, the scowling kitchen staff depressed her, isolated her.

Without the sun and the voice of the sea, she lacked what she had come to realize was her nourishment. She had been deprived of Japan, the brightness that is Japan. The rich blackness of the ocean's depths had disappeared, only to be replaced by the enervating atmosphere of a leaden sky in a foreign land filled with white devils yammering in an incomprehensible tongue.

Even as the prospect of meeting her husband became imminent, she went through the motions of preparation, donning her best western out-fit consisting of wide-brimmed hat, white lace blouse, and black tailored skirt over medium-heeled shoes. The simple half-jacket was short in the waist but covered her arms. Her only misgiving was the wrinkled state of her clothes. The immigration officials had not provided an iron. There was nothing she could do after she had asked for one. *Shikataganai.*

At least, she no longer needed his photograph as reference, having committed his image to memory long ago. She would keep it safe in her jacket's breast pocket.

Kawasaki-*san* had informed her that her husband was waiting with her luggage at a prearranged meeting spot. A bus took her and several oth-ers down what the unctuous interpreter announced was Burrard Street toward various drop-off locations in the Japanese area of town. Her stop, the Patricia Hotel, stood at the corner of East Hastings and Dunlevy.

Yoshiko was confused. She couldn't understand why she couldn't go directly to the boarding house. The thought nagged at her at first, but in the end she reasoned it must be convenient for all the other brides and hollow-eyed men. *How stupid of me!* she chided herself as she grew warm at the thought of sleeping that evening in her own "double bed" with her husband by her side. *Tsuruga. Matsumiya Hotel.*

Vancouver's avenues seemed broad, much wider than she had expected. It soon began to rain, lacquering the asphalt black and shiny like the Miyamotos' dinner table she marveled at what seemed like decades ago. The automobiles jammed the downtown streets trying to make their way past the streetcars and avoiding the swarming pedestrians struggling against the afternoon drizzle.

The bus veered onto a bustling street decidedly different from downtown. On East Hastings, Yoshiko gazed with wide-eyed fascination at the garish buildings festooned with light bulbs flashing an invitation to customers to enter their intriguing interiors.

The dullness of the day subsided, as did her apathy.

"*Patricia Hotel!*" Kawasaki shouted, his small arm crooked around a metal pole to balance himself.

Yoshiko settled her gaze straight ahead and gasped at the number of Japanese people milling in front of the six-storey concrete and brick hotel. "*Pa-tsu-ri-sha Hoteru*," she mouthed as she strained to catch sight of her husband.

The passengers rose en masse and began their shuffle out of the bus. The scruffy man next to her reached above him and pulled down her *furoshiki* to hand to her. She smiled at his kindness, but she moved on quickly in an effort to distance herself.

When her foot landed on concrete, she imagined she heard a rumble in the air, like the rolling of waves. She raised her head and caught a whiff of the ocean before slipping into the crowd of reunions and introductions. Not knowing what else to do, she stood still somewhere in the middle.

"Miyamoto-san?" called out a voice.

Yoshiko spun around but couldn't determine the source because of the congestion of noise and bodies.

"Miyamoto-san," came the voice again. "Miyamoto Yoshiko-san!"

She manoeuvred slyly to the right to the open sidewalk, a short distance away from the throng. There a man, vaguely familiar, walked toward her with photograph in hand, his eyes darting back and forth between her and it. He was about her height, perhaps a shade shorter, his fedora making him appear taller. His topcoat went down to his knees. Beneath it, he sported a broad-stripped tie like those men in the business offices.

His face was weathered, his complexion ruddy, but not unattractive.

Her mind flashed to the student picture in her pocket. His eyes had grown melancholy with a telling droop. His nose was long, disfigured, perhaps broken a few times in the past and only recently healed. Once high, well-defined cheeks had sunk under the strain of heavy work and his face was streaked with lines. His mouth was wide, tight-lipped, and the dull light of day played hide-and-seek with the teeth, which seemed to range from caramel to grey. Age had set upon him with its characteristic cruelty.

"Miyamoto Yoshiko-san," he said as an introduction, "Miyamoto Jinsaburo, desu."

In the awkwardness of the moment, Yoshiko hesitated before bowing. Her spirit had sunk: the apprehension had not lived up to the anticipation.

"Ah, I was not what you were expecting," Jinsaburo observed as he stuffed the photo inside his coat pocket.

"No ... no," she tripped, "that's not true."

"Your face is red."

Her hand immediately rose to hide her embarrassment.

"I suppose I'm a little old ... for someone like you," he said, a sad but edgy look on his face.

"No. No. That's not true," she insisted again to assure him, though she knew it to be true. This was a man whose youth had been worn down, almost to nothing.

He smiled broadly. "Come. Let's go to our room."

She looked at him not understanding.

"In the *Patricia*," he said, anxiously pointing up. With a wink he added, "We're staying in style for the wedding night."

She followed him, close-mouthed in her shock over the lie of his age and confusion about the accommodations. Why not go directly to the boarding house?

The hotel room appeared claustrophobic with busy, red-flecked wallpaper, overstuffed furniture, and crudely framed photographs of posed Victorian ladies. A dark ornate carpet nearly covered the entire floor, its faux Persian design faded and frayed from overuse. Resting upon it, a massive wardrobe dominated the room with its mahogany panelling. Beside the only window stood a chair and the bed, its sheets and blankets pulled tightly across the surface. *We change the sheets everyday.*

She stepped gingerly around the fifth-floor room, the smell of camphor irritating her nose. The place seemed entirely too closed-in to be comfortable, and too profoundly silent, as if it harboured many secrets. She placed her *furoshiki* on the bed.

"Miyamoto-san," she began, "where's my luggage? Kawasaki-san said they would be here."

"Eh?"

"My trunk and bags?"

"Oh, they're at the boarding house," he said, exposing his brown, uneven front teeth. "Sit down."

Relieved at the mention of the boarding house, Yoshiko carefully pulled the long hairpin out and removed her hat before sitting on the cool mattress, soft like a true *gaijin* bed. The subdued daylight caught her face and defined the lines sharply as she turned in profile to place the hat and pin on the floor.

"You're very pretty, you know that?" he opened. "Your picture doesn't do you justice." He awkwardly pulled out the crumpled photograph and held it up to her.

It took a few seconds, but she recognized the girl with the bamboo parasol and the sunny expression of better days on her face. His grubby hands had crushed and stained it badly, but the optimism and hope shone through still.

"I've been holding onto it all this time, imagining what it would be like to meet you in person." He couldn't help but stare. "Now that you're here, I can't believe my good luck!" he beamed and then sighed. "I'm not what you expected, am I?"

She looked away. Maybe she had been foolish, indulging in girlhood fantasies, but she was disappointed. The reality of the situation pressing upon her, she began to accept her fate. The price she had to pay for reaching so high.

"I admit I'm not as well-off as I could be. But I'm ambitious. I've got plans for you and me." He began to pace across the carpet. "I could've stayed in Japan and gotten all my otosan's wealth. I'm the only son, you know. Yeah, but my otosan. My otosan, that son of a bitch, he made me feel like I should strike out on my own. Make something of myself. Like him! Ha! Like I could on my own in this country. Yeah, well, now I'll show him. I'll show him." His voice rose with his rambling thoughts.

"I just need you to have a little faith in me. You can do that, can't you? Can't you?"

Yoshiko, a bit alarmed at her husband's odd behaviour and mounting anger, nodded as if assuring him. "But you have shown him. Your boarding house and the second one you want to buy —"

"Heh? What's that? Oh, the boarding houses, yeah. I forgot." Jinsaburo quickly removed his topcoat and suit jacket before moving to sit beside her. "You know, you do make a wonderful picture bride. You're just the ticket to help me make it. I like that. I like you."

The bed creaked as she heard him gasp. Warmth flushed throughout her body. She shivered slightly away as she suddenly became aware of his body odour. Being so close to him, she noticed the unshaven skin, the uneven jaw line, the hunched shoulders. She felt a surge of revulsion as he pushed aside her jacket to squeeze her breast. She squirmed away.

"Nanja?" he growled, then roughly pulled her jacket away and tore at her blouse.

She let out a scream that echoed into an indifferent hall. His weight pinned her to the double bed, smothering her, silencing her. Whiskers scratched as the wetness of his tongue spread across an exposed breast. Unseen hands roved elsewhere.

Clothes tore open, fasteners unsnapped, garments slid off. A cool breeze whistled from under the door and rushed along the floor to the bodies undulating with the shortness of breath.

Her body craved to sink into the bed away from the gravel surface of his body. Her skin recoiled with the touch. The aura of sex rose but curdled within the smell of his unwashed body. She screamed again, but not even a call of curiosity came. Just the gymnastics of his grunting and positioning ... and then the pain.

The ocean breathed in her ears as a montage of sound swelled into one great wave. Cruel, mocking laughter skittered across the floor as plaintive animal cries filled the room. The black rush of sound came over her like raging water just as night entered the room.

The dawn cracked with bright sunlight. Yoshiko awoke in bed, crying and exhausted. She had slept fitfully: dazed and crying before falling asleep, and then waking in tears of anger and shame only to fall unconscious again, exhausted. She sat up and a tide of aches and malaise came over her until, in time, a tolerable numbness allowed her to comprehend her surroundings.

A profound sense of isolation, even deeper than what she felt when she was released from the Immigration Building, washed over her. Her only companion was the lonely cackle of an animal she heard amid the morning traffic sounds outside her window.

The sheets, bunched up like frozen waves, were demurely gathered around her shoulders. The creature she had to acknowledge as her husband from that day onward slept next to her, snoring and breathing in a regular manner. Her eyes burned holes through his coverings, through his back, through to the hard, cold centre of his heart. If she had the strength, she would've reached out and choked the very life out of him.

She pictured his slumped face in the moment they had met and knew then that not only had he lied to her but also his father, Hisa, and maybe even Hiroko had been in on it. No, that she couldn't believe. She and Hiroko were like sisters – Hiroko was not like her tormentor or the fat, cruel *onesan*. Her spirit slumped, her heart broke, yet she refused to cry anymore. Conspiracy and betrayal made her look the fool.

But why had he so humiliated her last night? The degree of brutality shocked her then, horrified her now. *The photograph ... the look, a schoolboy's look.* The contorted face of lust, abandon, violence. The thinning of the face, the hardness of bone in the shallow depths of his skin, the grating stubble. *Against apple wet skin.* The attack had been swift and vicious, yet brief. But the damage had been done. When he rolled off her, leaving her in shock and dripping in shame, he immediately fell asleep, spent and exhausted, like a predator having had his fill of the carcass. Yoshiko shivered in revulsion and sought to cover herself, feeling her body had been scraped by claws and bathed in saliva. Darkness wasn't her friend either; she tossed and turned in the incredulity of violence.

It was not as she had imagined it when she and her cousin Akiko giggled about boys, the act of love never mentioned but understood, or when, in her most private moments, she conjured up the romantic lover intent on seducing with gentility and love. The gulf was as wide as the ocean that separated her from her childhood.

Surely her parents knew how old this monster was. Then again maybe not, since they didn't know the Hayashi family all that well. She was such the *urusai* daughter, she probably wouldn't have listened anyway. *Oka, forgive me.* Her parents were not as stupid as she thought they had been.

With so much weight pressing down on her, she decided not to send any letters home. They would have to consider her lost.

As she moved, the pain came back. Fighting it, she slid out of the bed, careful not to wake him. Her clothes were strewn across the floor, some torn, most rumpled and soiled so as to be unwearable. She collected them despite the fatigue and efficiently untied her *furoshiki*. Inside, she found clean undergarments and another blouse to wear and her mother's amulet, which immediately reminded her of his photograph. In a soundless motion, she recovered it from her jacket and tore it to shreds in a fit of anger.

After further manoeuvering, she was dressed, her damaged *Amerikajin* clothes folded inside her *furoshiki*. She then searched his discarded topcoat for her photograph. It was as she had first seen it in his hand: stained, worn, and slightly ripped. She moved to destroy it as she had his, but no. Holding it to the light, she saw the bright-eyed girl with the parasol as a symbol of a time of unblemished skin and an absolute belief in a prosperous future. It will be a good reminder of how absurd her optimism had been.

Yoshiko placed the photograph with the *omamori* in her *furoshiki* for safekeeping. She then sat in the chair by the window, breathing heavily as the bitterness began to fester. "Do not let him take away your dignity." Her mother's words crystallized in her mind. In the mirror, she contemplated her own tired but youthful face. A faint teardrop trickled from the curve of her eye and rolled down her plump cheek. She mouthed a voiceless "okasan" and then broke down thinking about her future. *Babies?* How could she start a family with this monster? She felt herself drowning amongst languid waves. "Why do you want to go to the land of devil men and ghost women?"

After an hour, Jinsaburo awoke. He groaned and ran his fingers through his greasy hair before snatching his underwear as if suddenly aware of his nakedness. He sat upright at the edge of bed, his head hung down in an effort to fight off his fatigue. Once his head cleared, he looked around and seemed surprised to see Yoshiko seated in the chair fully clothed, looking like she was waiting for a bus.

"What the hell are you doing?" he shouted indignantly.

She pursed her lips and paused a moment before she asked pointedly, "How old are you?"

"Nani?"

"Your age. What is it?"

He rubbed his face to wipe away the dust of sleep and to gain a moment. "I'm thirty-two," he said finally.

Her stomach ached with a small agony.

"So what?" he asked gruffly.

"I was led to believe —"

"That I was a lot younger? Isn't that right?" He burst into hoarse laughter. "Would you have come if you knew?"

She wilted with his mocking.

"My father knew you wouldn't so he showed you my old school picture!"

Yoshiko sat paralyzed. Her suspicions had come true.

"Oh yes, he told me all about it!" he confessed. "Funny how my sisters never told you. I could see Hisa really enjoying the joke. Don't you see? Would've been too late by that point. You were already committed to me. Too late."

She thought she should cry but no tears came forth. Instead, her face hardened.

Iwakichi Miyamoto sat in front of her with legs folded underneath his body. He was wrapped in a billowing garment though there was no wind. His kind eyes spoke to her of his sincerity. His palms held open and outstretched offered a gentleness she had never known. Lights glowed behind him, softening his face. She turned her attention to the long table beside him. It shone in the light, its luxurious black lacquer deep with mystery.

As he spoke, the words distorted and his eyes turned white. His face melting into its skeletal skull, he opened his garment to expose a rib cage with bits of meat hanging in fetid decay. Contemptuous laughter, Hisa's laughter, and Jinsaburo's yowling.

The sidewalk seemed hard and forbidding in the clear light of day. The sun had returned. *Too late. Too late*, she thought. Jinsaburo walked quickly in front of her, impatient of her slow and awkward walk. His fedora was crushed against his head, his topcoat loose. She limped behind as a dutiful wife, quickstepping in a painful effort to keep up.

They walked through the shadow of the Patricia Hotel toward the mountains, partially concealed by the characteristic black beast of smoke from what she knew to be Hastings Mill, until they encountered a large open area full of dust and stray people roaming across its expanse. "Powell Ground," Jinsaburo pointed out.

Near the southeast corner of the field, an animated Japanese man stood proudly with both feet planted firmly on the sidewalk just outside the perimeter of the park dressed in full military uniform. He spit out his patter with an earnest look about him. Yoshiko, listening at a distance, was intrigued by what sounded like gibberish spewing forth from the man.

"*Vimy Ridge*," he said with religious vigour. "I caught the mustard gas. I suffered so you would all be free. Listen to my tales of the horror of the trenches. The Shintani brothers died right before my eyes. I saw many young men, your young men, wither before the onslaught!" he preached in Japanese like an impassioned man of religion. "And yet I would gladly do it again, not for my country, but for the Japanese in *Canada!* We can hold our heads up high because of the medals I wear. See here, how many I have."

As she stared, Jinsaburo pulled at her arm to move her along. "That's Crazy Iizuka. He thinks he won the war by himself!" He scoffed in a voice loud enough to be heard by the preposterous lecturer.

"Not by myself, my good man. This medal of bravery represents the many deaths of my comrades-in-arms!"

Yoshiko kept looking back as she was dragged away. She had never seen insanity before.

Back in her village, the rumours about Shigeishi-*san*, a Russo-Japanese war veteran, buzzed about her youth like mosquitoes. He had been wounded during a barrage of Russian shells, which greatly affected his mental stability. He came back a haunted man with emaciated body and black circles around the eyes and remained holed up in his house, subject to rumour and imagination. No one ever saw him. Children, including Yoshiko and Akiko, were afraid of even passing the shut-in's house for fear of being dragged inside, never to be seen again.

Mental illness was whispered about, never confronted or even mentioned in polite conversation.

Jinsaburo led his bride across the street at the corner directly north of Iizuka's corner and continued walking away from the park until they came to a particular building. The sign in Japanese and English above the picture window identified the place as the Three Sisters Café. Yoshiko could see through the glass that it was a restaurant with various tables, chairs, and booths, as well as a long lunch counter with fixed stools in front of it.

Inside, she noted a sociable woman, the probable proprietress, behind the counter, chatting with the customers. She reminded Yoshiko of Mrs. Matsumiya, the jovial innkeeper in Tsuruga. Behind and above the counter was a large rectangular open window to the kitchen where someone was banging pots and pans while preparing meals.

Jinsaburo led her to a particular booth in the corner of the room. She stood before three men, an older man with a balding head and the air of a businessman about him, another who was slight and young-looking with an intense gaze and bearing of potential danger, and the third, an even younger man with beautiful eyes. Impeccably dressed, he sat quietly.

The trio hardly looked up when Jinsaburo cleared his throat and bowed to them.

"Forgive the intrusion, Taniguchi-san," he began, "but I am Miyamoto Jinsaburo."

"Yes, I know," Taniguchi, the older man, said matter-of-factly.

"I am here to let you know my wife has arrived."

"Wife, well! Is this her?"

"Yes. Yes," he confirmed as he nudged Yoshiko forward.

"She is a pretty one," said the intense-looking one, sitting up to notice.

"Oh, Miyamoto-san, you know Morii-san," introduced Taniguchi.

"Oh yes. Oh yes," Jinsaburo said in an ingratiating tone.

"And this is Okihara Koji. He's in from out of town as a messenger –"

Okihara stood quickly to cut off any further revelations. As he bowed graciously to the newlyweds, he kept his eyes on Yoshiko, shooting her a faint smile at the same time. The bride felt a tingling somewhere deep inside her.

"Oyabun, may I introduce Miyamoto Yoshiko," Jinsaburo said, ignoring the unimportant "messenger."

Yoshiko bowed as Morii beamed, obviously impressed.

"I hope you keep your looks," Morii said in a cold whisper that frosted Yoshiko's spine.

Jinsaburo moved to his wife's side and interrupted, "We'll be staying at Taniguchi-san's place."

"I'm sure you and your yomesan will enjoy the accommodations. Very private," Taniguchi said knowingly. "It is your honeymoon, is it not?"

A silly grin spread across Jinsaburo's face as he backed away. "Yes. Yes, it is."

Yoshiko, confused and simmering with anger, had many questions, but decided to wait.

On the street one block north of and parallel to Powell Ground, they entered Taniguchi's Boarding House, rundown with peeling paint and dilapidated porch. Breathing a sigh of relief, Yoshiko found her missing luggage in their room on the second floor. Everything was intact.

The accommodations seemed like the hotel except roomier, containing a dominating double bed and a settee, miniature table, and lamps representing the style of the times yet cheap in construction. The floral wallpaper was dingy and curled at the edges. There was no window, which made the room rather gloomy. Again, the accommodations felt close-mouthed, dumb to any confession.

Once settled in, Yoshiko could no longer contain her curiosity. "Miyamoto-san," she said, confronting her husband, "I don't understand. Why don't we stay at your boarding house?"

Jinsaburo stood as if surprised by the question. "Boarding house? You think I own a boarding house?" In a gleeful frenzy, he fell to the bed. "I thought you were only kidding last night! Weren't you listening to what I said?"

Yoshiko became indignant, the soft features of her face growing hard. "Why are you laughing?" she asked on the verge of tears.

"Because … because …" he started, choking on his words. "Because you believed me!" The outburst continued. "You actually believed the letter I sent." He pulled her onto the bed. "Didn't you wonder why it took me three years to bring you over? From the time our fathers set the dowry to the marriage registration took two years. It took me another year to tell my otosan to put you on that damn boat! Didn't you ever wonder what I was doing?"

She shook her head. The betrayal was now complete. She was humiliated and made to feel like an absolute fool.

"I'm a poor man. Can't you see that? I was working to get the money in the bank to get permission to bring you here," he said as he began to fondle her. "Now come on, be a good wife."

As his tongue traced a wet trail about her cheek, she shivered once again in revulsion and lashed out, striking his repulsive face. She then bolted from the bed as he covered his throbbing cheek. "You lied! You lied about everything!" she screeched. "About the boarding house, your age, everything!"

Jinsaburo lunged forward and knocked her against the wall. He raised his hand and slapped her face several times. "Baka!" he shouted. "You want my father to be ashamed of me?" He slapped her again.

"Every night he stood over me to tell me what a shit I was, how I was going to be a failure if I didn't strike out on my own. Be like him. Don't depend on him for money. Be my own man! Every night ... every night...."

The young man trembled as he kowtowed before his imposing father. "Don't wait for my money. Be a man. Getting an inheritance from me means nothing. Earn it yourself." The boy buried his head in the candlelit darkness and muttered agreement.

They fell to the floor. While Yoshiko sobbed uncontrollably, Jinsaburo pawed at her dress until her legs were exposed. "Now be a good wife."

8. Thursday, March 14, 1940

Morii's chair toppled underneath him with the impact of the punch to his chin. He fell heavily to the concrete floor. His mind spun and a black oil slick crept across his consciousness. His groans were automatic as several hands came upon him pulling him to his feet.

"Goddamn Jap!" cursed a voice.

"Let me have a whack at him," said another. "Hold him up."

The interrogation room in the basement of the Cordova Street Police Station had not changed in the nearly twenty intervening years since the *oyabun* was last there. The single light bulb sharply defined the space. The furniture was spare and mean: a couple of skeletal wooden chairs and a solitary table. The barred windows were opaque, blind to the street, black with the night. At least, the calendar had moved on in time, the cool Gibson Girl illustration replaced by a curly-haired country girl with a sunny disposition about to take a sip from a bottle of Coca-Cola.

Morii's tormentors seemed familiar to him. *Were they the same as last time?* Each had his particular shade of dirty blond hair. *No nigiyakana red head. That's a change.* Each had the dead-cold eyes of a sadist – and the zeal for meting out justice with brutal severity.

One detective clenched his fist while the other held Morii up by the armpits. Defenseless, the *oyabun* smirked slightly just before his tormentor began pounding his stomach. Blow after blow came with merciless regularity. He soon tasted blood.

Eventually, the man stopped and the other lowered Morii onto the uprighted chair.

"Now, let's start again," the chief interrogator said. "Morry! Morry, look at me! Don't pass out on me, you bloody Jap."

Morii opened one swollen eye.

"Why'd you do it ... why'd you kill Gin Miyamoto?"

"Did not kill," he said groggily. "Train kill...."

"Sure, you'd like us to think that, wouldn't you? The train cut his head off, sure, but before that he was stabbed three times. It's got your filthy Jap ways all over it."

Morii waited for more.

"He owed you money ... from gambling at that club of yours."

"Not my club." He struggled to take off his tie and open his shirt's top button to breathe better.

"Now don't lie to us, Morry. Your boy, Aki, he told us your take is two hundred a month and Gin owed you something like four hundred which he wasn't gonna pay. So you got your payment another way. Ain't that right?"

"*Eigo wakarimasen.*" A bad taste burned at the base of his mouth.

"Hiding behind that lingo again?" he remarked as he waved his partner back into action. "Detective Adams, he's being unco-operative again."

With a wide swing, the hulking police detective struck Morii to the floor. The concrete grew warm with the molten film of his sweat, saliva, and blood.

"Okay, boys, that's enough," an authoritative voice called out. Sgt. Gill had finally arrived, just past three in the morning. "Did you get anything?"

"Tough little runt, this one," was all that Detective Adams said as he flexed and massaged his own swelling hand.

Maintaining his composure, Sgt. Gill waved the police officers out of the room. They complied, although the other couldn't resist telling Morii on his way out, "We'll be right back."

Once alone with Morii, Gill stepped outside to retrieve a cup of water. He then pulled up a chair and sat down beside the diminutive *oyabun*. He pulled out a linen handkerchief from his grey suit pocket, wet it, and applied it to Morii's wounds. The *oyabun* flinched, and then relaxed as the cool water offered some relief.

"Well, this feels familiar," the sergeant remarked. Back in 1921, the then Mountie constable decided to play along with Morii after the suggestion of bribery to get incriminating evidence out of the gangland boss. What he hadn't counted on was the effect of the box of chocolates: one hundred dollars a month. It meant he could afford Savile Row suits, meals at the Hotel Vancouver, and maybe even a place in Shaughnessy.

Breaking the Moriyama case with misinformation from Morii wasn't bad either. Not only did Gill get a promotion but he also became known as an expert on the Japanese community in British Columbia, a valuable and unique asset according to the white-bread feds in Ottawa.

"They really worked you over, Mr. Morry."

The *oyabun* grunted.

"Sorry I couldn't get here sooner. I had to do a lot of explaining to a lot of people why the RCMP would be interested in this case."

After a time and a few draughts of cold water, Morii had regained some of his composure, even trying to straighten his attire. It was useless to wipe away the grime and blood on his suit but he did tuck in his shirt and smooth down his hair. He searched the room for his derby but then remembered it hanging outside in the hall.

"*Giru-san arigato* for coming," he said, nodding his head slightly.

"Don't worry about it," Gill replied. "Now why are you taking all this? Tell them what you know."

"I no can."

"You can't? So you know something. Why can't you tell?"

"You remember *Titanic*?"

Gill fell back in his chair incredulous. "What does a cursed ocean liner have to do with anything?" he said, with a touch of exasperation.

"On boat was Hosono Masabumi. He work for government. A coward. Like a little girl, he jumps in lifeboat. Save self, did not die."

"Forgive me, Mr. Morry, but so what? That was, what? Twenty-five years ago!"

"You don't understand. He full of shame in Japan. He should die. Just like me. If —"

"Now wait a minute! You want to commit *hari kari*?" he questioned.

"No ... no ... if I talk," Morii said, completing his sentence in a raised voice. "I not bring shame to Japanese ... here or in Japan. I will tell police nothing."

Sgt. Gill stood up and walked around Morii. He ran a hand over the sheen of his oiled-down hair. "How are you not going to prevent the

Japanese from losing face if you go to jail?"

Not waiting for an answer, the good sergeant sat down again when another thought crossed his mind. "You know, soon Japan's going to be doing a lot more to lose face than you'll ever do!" he said with a grin.

Morii ignored Gill, as he had other things on his mind. *That damn Miyamoto woman.* He recognized the last name of the dead man found in the CPR yards to be the same as his charge as soon as the police had said it. But she had made no mention of her husband's death. Was it related or a coincidence? She was becoming as bothersome as an unco-operative prostitute. What were Okihara's and her role in all this?

And what of Akiyama? He was a traitor. The one thing the *oyabun* couldn't abide. He hated it in 1921 with Hirano, but this was especially heinous. Betrayal was an indictment of his reputation: that his respectability wasn't deserved. But why Aki – one of his own? The only explanation he could think of was that he had a *gaijin* wife and didn't live in the Powell Street area. That was the only way Morii could explain the treachery. To the *oyabun*, it felt like Aki had struck his father or spit in the Emperor's path.

The questions grew to plague his mind.

"Give them somebody. They know they don't have much of a case against you. That's why they're beating a confession out of you. They want someone as high profile as you for sure, but they'll settle for anyone as long as they can get their captain off their backs."

Morii remained still.

"How about Rick-*san*, like I suggested before?"

"No, not Rikimatsu."

"Then one of your other boys. Just tell me who."

"Moriyama," the *oyabun* rasped, without much consideration.

Gill's eyes widened. "Hold on there. You want them investigating me? Moriyama's supposed to be in Japan, remember?"

Morii lowered his head, the bony skin surface rippled with anxiety. "Akiyama then. Give them Akiyama."

"Aki? The bartender? But they had him and let him go."

"He manager. He keep Miyamoto-*no* marker for the money."

"It won't work. They want you and he gave you up."

"You try!" Morii commanded.

As Sgt. Gill shook his head and moved to the door, Morii called out, "*Giru-san,* after … you help me help Akiyama-*san ne?*"

"You sure are something, Mr. Morry," Gill said, astonished. "Sure, sure, anyway I can. But first, let me get you out of here."

⌥

1925–1926

The ten-year period following World War I afforded Morii much opportunity to expand his empire and to set in motion his plan to keep the Japanese out of Chinatown permanently. He first set his eyes on the three clubs in the Powell Street area where men went to play pool and gamble in the back rooms.

The Spanish flu epidemic of 1918 in Vancouver took the life of Isamu Sakiyama, owner of the Toyo Club. At the funeral, Morii approached the widow to offer condolences and an envelope of money to buy the club. Kazuyoshi Shintani lost two sons at Vimy Ridge, something that Crazy Iizuka, the doughboy, loved harping on in his daily Powell Ground diatribes. In his protracted grief, Shintani inevitably sold his Shintani Pool Hall to the *oyabun* in 1921. Now, finally, with Kichitaro Akiyama missing in action, the Momiji Club could be easily taken over.

During a cool spring night in 1925, the stairs up to the Momiji rumbled with the feet of several men. Through the club entrance burst Morii, Rikimatsu, and two strong-armed men filled with "judo spirit," as Kojima *sensei* described practitioners of his art.

The one open room contained three pool tables with heavy legs, worn green felt, and leather pockets. Several men holding cues stood around them, looking startled. A skinny man in wire-rimmed glasses casually gazed at the intruders while continuing to wipe down the counter of the long oak bar.

"You," Morii called out to him. "Are you the manager?"

"I guess I am," he replied nonchalantly. "I'm holding down the place until my friend comes back from the war."

"Bakayaro!" roared Rikimatsu. "He ain't never coming back! Never, you hear me?"

Morii narrowed his eyes. His henchmen, towering over him, gathered around their boss. "I'm taking over this place. From now on, this is Black Dragon property."

Rikimatsu grunted an order and one of his men promptly dragged the manager out by the collar. The *yojimbo* then swaggered behind the counter as if taking ownership.

Morii addressed the largely indifferent patrons of the club. "If the owner ever comes back, he'll have a job here. I promise you that!"

His chest swelled as he realized he now had control over the three places where most of the Japanese men in Vancouver spent their time. Violence used as a means to an end. *Enlightenment perhaps? Or karma.*

After the *oyabun* closed the smaller establishments to consolidate his holdings into the spacious Momiji Club, he decided to improve the new club's facilities; hence, Morii appealed to San Francisco.

A month later, Koji Okihara, the elegant, young messenger with ebony cane and silk top hat in hand, showed up at his office in the Nippon Club with a thick package. In it was $10,000 in small bills. A note attached provided an ominous message.

Consider this as koden.
Kameoka Hideo

"That fat bastard!" Morii shouted. Okihara smiled discreetly and made his exit. It was obvious Kameoka was warning him that he had better succeed or the money could be used as *koden* or funeral money, his funeral. It worried Morii to think this might also be a warning from his own *oyabun.*

With the bankroll, the *oyabun* called upon an old acquaintance. Goro Kaburagi was a craggy little man. Even as a young man in 1906 when Morii first hired him to spruce up the decrepit Raku Raku, he seemed older than his years. His skin was ruddy, looking like well-worn leather, from his apprenticeship as a carpenter's helper. Naturally he had workman's hands, big, scarred and callused, but his eyes were close-set, narrow slits protected by ridges of skin, like an ancient lizard basking in the sunlight.

By the 1920s, he looked so worn down he had become a mere nub of a man. Skin and bones, bowlegged and nearsighted, he was reclusive, often sneering at the world when he engaged it. Yet, he was a skilled carpenter, the one most relied upon for special jobs. Such was the case when Morii met with him at the Raku Raku on a sweet-smelling day in July 1925.

"Kaburagi-san! Welcome, welcome," Morii said as he greeted his guest with an exaggerated grin. "As you can see, we've improved on your handiwork."

"Looks the same to me," he replied gruffly.

As they moved to a quiet corner, a waitress brought a bottle of sake to the table and poured two small cups. The two men drank quickly and then had another before Morii dismissed the waitress, telling her to leave the bottle.

"Kaburagi-san, you're a good man," he said as he poured a third cup for the carpenter. "I need you to do a job for me."

"Aw," he scoffed. "I don't need the business."

Morii laughed, imagining Rik-*san* being there. Kaburagi would have been made to heel. The *oyabun* might have done it himself, but he genuinely liked the man for his impudence.

"No. Hear me out. I've just acquired the Momiji Club on Powell Street."

"So what? I'm happy for you."

"I want you to renovate it into a special social club."

"Special ...?"

"With some special features."

Kaburagi was intrigued and cleared his whiskey throat as he leaned in to listen closer.

Eventually the carpenter agreed to do the job, first installing a bar, restaurant equipment, and unique gaming rooms. The fine details included precautionary devices. After all, Morii's ultimate goal was to expand the gambling activities in Little Tokyo.

The Showa Club opened in the fall of 1926, the name commemorating the new Emperor Hiro Hito, not quite finished but the *oyabun* needed the revenue. Plastering walls and finishing trim were mere cosmetic details.

As a frequent and honoured guest of the club, Goro Kaburagi sat with a never-empty glass of Canadian Club whiskey in hand, speaking to anyone who would listen. It was clear he was proud of his work.

"So ne!" he would confirm to his audience of other drunken men. "This place is safe from the police. I wired a signal system from down below up to here. If you look closely at that wall...." His sunken eyes sparkled with pride even if his face was drooping with the liquor.

"Oyabun," Rik-*san* breathed in Morii's ear at the bar, "that idiot Kaburagi's talking about his handiwork again."

"I know," he snarled.

"If the police ever pick him up, he'll give everything away."

Morii snorted at the obvious.

"And we'll be in jail!"

The *oyabun* continued to stare at the miscreant.

"Shall I take care of him?"

Morii nodded again but held his *yojimbo* back for a moment. "Let him join Hirano."

Rik-*san* squinted, flashed a sardonic grin, and then nodded back, knowing what was expected. He had dealt with the eyewitness in the Yamamoto murder case quickly and efficiently. His expression darkened as he strolled over to the table where he tapped Kaburagi on the shoulder. The carpenter looked up with blurry eyes and grunted, saliva bubbling between his lips. Rik-*san* jerked his head towards the door.

Kaburagi waved a hand, dismissing the *yojimbo*. "Ahotare! Don't worry, I'll finish the job when I'm good and ready!" he said drunkenly. Rikimatsu grabbed the offensive appendage and pulled with sudden violence, rolling the carpenter to the floor. While regaining his bearings, the carpenter looked up, disoriented and shaken.

Rik-*san* threatened to kick Kaburagi, prompting the old man to curl his body into a ball in a weak attempt to defend himself. It worked. Rikimatsu calmed down enough to allow the carpenter to rise to his feet and slowly drag himself to the door. An uncomfortable laugh rose amongst the crowd.

Rik-*san* followed his victim out of the club. The Showa Club was never completed, and Kaburagi was never seen again.

꒰

Thursday, March 14, 1940

The piercing morning sun needled Morii's vision as he stepped out of the police station after a few more hours of sustained but not as merciless interrogation following Sgt. Gill's visit. He looked to North Vancouver and saw it was dark with rain. A rainbow, sparkling over Burrard Inlet, separated it from the Powell Street section of town, as if to say prosperity was just beyond reach.

The *oyabun's* suit was covered with dust from the concrete floor, the cheap gabardine material strained or torn. His shirt was bloody and soiled, his tie gone. Only his hat remained unscathed.

His eyes hollow, his tongue dry and stippled with alien debris, he needed shaving and washing, but some things played on his mind. It was time to pay that promised visit to Miyamoto-san, he decided, but fatigue was weighing heavily upon him. He would visit her but not before tending to another task that cried out for immediate attention.

One more step and he felt the pain of the blows he had endured shoot throughout his body. His kidneys ached, his legs were sluggish, and his head was spinning. As he hobbled down the street towards the Nippon Club, the *oyabun* smirked at the thought of his high-*kara* wife frowning at his haggard condition when he eventually staggered through the front door of their house. "Morii-san," he imagined she would begin, "must you? Everyone will see." And that would be that. While she left for some social function, the cleaning up was left to him and their housemaid, Kimiko Ishida.

From the outset, Misao Morii had made it clear she didn't want to know what he did to keep her in fine furniture, the latest styles, and desirable company. Like her father, a career diplomat, her husband dealt with a world unknown to women but believed to be one populated with unsavoury characters and fraught with danger.

Though they were seen together at community gatherings, she spent most of her time attending receptions at the Consul General's estate and organizing and then supervising the volunteer work of the *fujinkai*, the women's association at the Buddhist church, two activities Morii despised. He was a Buddhist, but he could never tolerate the social aspects of the church.

Coarse observers of the community speculated that she and her husband led a passionless life together, mostly apart, not only due to the energetic pace she set largely without her husband but also because of her icy personality. As well, the *oyabun* never touched any of the women under his control. It was true to a point.

When they were first married through an arrangement made in Japan, Morii at twenty-two and she at twenty, they acted like typical newlyweds in private moments: shy, unsure, and then fervent in their newfound freedom. Eventually, such ardour faded as she settled into her role of being the paragon of civilized behaviour she had been raised to be.

He too had decided to lead an "exemplary" life; that is, he would not indulge in earthly pleasures with his employee "wives." Such was the behaviour of the greedy rich, the stupid, and the morally weak. He was determined to be the model of virtue, something to aspire to and emulate. Never to be the hypocrite. He realized of course that if everyone followed his example he would be ruined financially, but he didn't mind such an outcome if he was venerated in the end, a goal that was becoming more and more of an obsession. This was perhaps his way of working off his *karma*.

"These *Vancouver* provincials need me," she was often heard saying to her bemused husband.

Morii's thoughts meandered back to the business at hand as the morning shadows subsided like an ebb tide exposing him to the empty streets around Powell. He could feel himself coming under the harsh scrutiny of the prying eyes ahead of the gossip that would surely follow. A rumble of voices sounded like waves echoing in his ears. *Kuchigitanai.*

Kichitaro "Aki" Akiyama was picked up in the sweep of suspects at the Showa Club. After questioning, he was released and back home well before Sgt. Gill initiated Morii's rescue from the brutality of his interrogation.

Early in the morning, Akiyama turned in his half-sleep when he heard a knock at the front door of his home in the Vancouver area of Kitsilano. Stumbling to his feet and careful not to disturb his wife, he made his way to the door. It was Rik-*san*, nervously shifting his gaze in every direction.

Rikimatsu did seem out-of-place in this part of town. Most Japanese in Kitsilano lived from Granville Street in the east to Balsam or Larch Streets in the west, from False Creek to the north and to 15th Avenue to the south. The main drag was West Second Avenue, the 1600 and 1700 blocks. It didn't have the allure or panache of Powell Street with its restaurants, Japanese shops and businesses, and houses of ill repute, consisting instead of rooming houses commonly known as *kyabin*, simple clapboard domiciles, and two-storey buildings that housed families in the upper floors while businesses flourished in the storefronts below: four Japanese grocery stores, Obayashi's barbershop, Murakami Laundry, and O.K. Taxi, among others. In the 1920s when Kitsilano was being established, the ownership of various buildings often exchanged hands in a quick game of chance. Today, only the slot machine brought in by one of the store owners could remotely interest a man like Rik-*san*. With the Buddhist Church and Japanese Language School standing side by side a block away on First Avenue and the Church of Ascension on Third, the *yojimbo* was on edge, surrounded by, in the opinion of most on Powell Street, the "respectable" Japanese.

Aki told him to relax. "Quit acting so suspicious," he advised as Rikimatsu continued looking over his shoulder.

"I never come to this part of town," Rik-*san* said as he pulled his overcoat tight standing in the doorway. "Hey, what the hell is that?" he asked, pointing to a skeletal tower of steel beams dominating the entire neighbourhood.

"What? Oh, that's the *Imperial* three-star sign. You can see it from *English Bay*."

"So that's what that thing says," he whispered. The billboard for the oil company came alive at night – lit up and undulating like a fireworks display, it could be seen from a great distance. "The oyabun wants to see you."

"I thought they got him for sure. When did he get out?"

"I heard from him an hour ago. He wants a meeting. C'mon, let's go."

"All right, all right, keep your shirt on."

Aki sniffed the cold March air before disappearing inside to change into street clothes. As he left the house, he pressed his fingers to his lips. "The wife's still sleeping."

"Which? Your keto wife or the one in Japan?" Rikimatsu asked smirking.

"Damare!" Aki snapped in a flash of anger.

Inside the *oyabun's* office upstairs at the Nippon Club, Rikimatsu sat Aki down in front of the simple three-drawer desk. Aki gazed at the photographs of past judo champions on the walls, then looked around when he detected the scent of antiseptic and liniment in the air.

Morii limped into the room and, refusing his *yojimbo's* help, struggled to his chair behind his desk. With pained effort he raised his head, straining to open wider his half-closed, bruised eyes to get a good look at his manager.

"Ah re!" Aki exclaimed out of sheer surprise. "Oyabun, them sons-of-bitches really worked you over!"

Morii grunted.

"They did practically nothing to me."

"I can see that," the *oyabun* said slowly, ominously. After a few more manoeuvres to settle in place, Morii drew a heavy sigh before next speaking. "I'm glad you could make it, Aki. Your wife object to you coming here so early?"

"No, I left her sleeping."

"Good. Good. You want some coffee or something?"

"No."

"Are you sure?" asked Morii smiling. "You say the police did 'practically nothing' to you?"

"That's right," the bartender confirmed, sensing something was wrong.

"And they let you walk right outta the station just like that?"

"What're you getting at?"

"What did you tell them, Aki?" Morii asked bluntly.

"What? I ... I didn't say nothing!"

Rikimatsu stepped forward as skepticism drizzled down the *oyabun's* face.

"Nothing! I swear!" Aki squirmed in a panic as if to emphasize his sincerity. "Honest, I did not say a thing."

"Well, all I know is they're coming after you this morning."

"What for?"

"For the Miyamoto murder."

"But I didn't ..." Aki started. "They let me go last night!"

"Something must've changed their minds. Could be the markers you hold."

"But they're yours!"

"Do they know that? You didn't tell them, did you?"

"No, no, no...."

Morii backed off for the moment. "Maybe it was something you said. They sure think you did it."

Rik-*san* moved to place his hands on Aki's shoulders to keep him in his place.

Morii achingly rose to his feet. "Listen, Aki, I can protect you ... save you from the hangman. Just tell me what you told the police."

"Nothing! I said nothing! How many times I gotta tell you?" He became more agitated as the weight of the situation pressed upon him.

"Bakayaro! They wouldn't be after you unless you said something! Tell me exactly what you said! I can't help you if you don't talk."

"Nothing!" he insisted.

"C'mon."

Rik-*san* made a suspicious move under his coat.

Phlegm constricted Akiyama's throat as he gasped for words. "I ... I told them about you. They had this interpreter there. Kawasaki-san. He said they'd let me go scot-free if I ... if I co-operated."

Morii sat down, disgust passing over his face. "So you betrayed me."

"No. I mean, I didn't say much."

"You lied to save your own skin. Did you tell 'em about Okihara Koji?"

He shook his head. "Who? Never heard of him."

"But you told them how much I take from the club."

Aki looked up surprised. "You ... you know?"

"Of course I know. What am I, an idiot? Did you think I wouldn't ever find out?"

He shook his head more in disbelief than denial. Emotions and uncertainty roiled within until they overflowed. "What did you expect?" Aki shouted in a burst of defiance. "You stole my club right from under me! You laugh at my wife! You don't know what I did over there! The things I seen. I've been waiting for ... this chance." Aki's words gurgled as his rant submerged into mucus and congestion.

The *oyabun* sneered in contempt. The *kusotare* mistook his philanthropy for greed. Choosing to ignore the whining, Morii stilled himself as he calmly walked behind his captive. "Akiyama," he whispered without acrimony as he bent down over him, "you remember Kaburagi? Or Hirano?"

Aki looked confused.

Rikimatsu then spoke softly into the *oyabun's* ear.

"Oh that's right!" Morii said. "You were 'over there' back then. But you do remember Nakashima, don't you? Don't you?"

Aki looked up in horror as he nodded slowly. His eyes liquefied with fright.

"You're going to join him and the others. Suffer their fate."

The manager began to shake as terror inched across his skin.

Summer 1930

July of 1930 was particularly hot in Vancouver, a time when the stench of corruption lingered irritatingly long in the cramped offices of Powell Street. The effects of the Depression were only beginning to be felt in the province. The mining and lumber industries were rapidly drying up, affecting the Japanese in particular. Markers or IOUs were always standard practice for the Black Dragon Society, but these days, the *oyabun* seemed to be accepting more and more of them. To stave off financial ruin, Morii had to entangle himself increasingly with the powers-that-be.

The *oyabun* sat in his private office at the back of the Hinomaru. The room was full of wilted shadows, a solitary flexible office lamp drooping over the papers on the desk and pooling its light in a limited area. The humidity was so thick it seemed to suspend the dust in mid-air. Yet Morii seemed undisturbed. The only sign of discomfort was his discarded jacket, which he had removed to read. He pored over his papers in his shirt sleeves, silver-buckled garters holding them in place.

He looked up at about ten o'clock in the evening when Rikimatsu announced the arrival of a contingent from the Steveston Nihonjin Rodo Kumiai, the Japanese fishermen's association in Steveston, the salmon-fishing town south of Vancouver. Ryuichi Sato, the stern president of the organization, led the party of four. Morii twirled into his jacket as he relished the idea of this meeting. He knew Sato must have been attending against his will.

"Gentlemen," greeted Morii. "I'm sorry there aren't enough seats –"

"All right," interrupted Sato, "we won't be here long."

"Please forgive Sato-san, Oyabun," chimed in the diminutive sycophant standing beside the president. "He's upset over what's happened."

"Oh, I don't mind him. We've had more than a few encounters like this."

"Then you won't mind me saying I told these fools not to come to you," Sato said sharply. "Not to entrust you with this problem we have."

"Damare!" commanded Rik-*san*.

"Morii, call off your dog!"

Rik-*san* moved to deliver a blow for the insult.

Morii quickly interceded. "Don't mind Rikimatsu. He likes the old ways," he said, throwing his *yojimbo* a smile. "Now tell me, how can I help you?"

The ingratiating young man with handkerchief in hand stepped forward again and spoke softly.

"Forgive us, Oyabun, for disturbing your evening. We would not have come if not for your well-known compassion for Japanese in trouble."

Sato sniffed his disapproval.

"If I may, I am Watanabe Etsuo, and as secretary, I would like to speak on behalf of the Nihonjin Rodo Kumiai, Steveston District One." He paused for approval. None came. After wiping away the sweat from his face, he continued all the same. "I am too embarrassed to say ... but something has happened that we cannot deal with. As you know, we formed some years ago in reaction to the canneries' stubborn practice of buying our sockeye salmon only during the peak summer season. We have no market for our catch in spring and early fall. As a result, we set up our own co-operative to process our catch during those off times. We sell directly to Japan, you see. That way we can make a living for about eight months out of the year instead of the two the canneries would have us."

"Yes, yes," urged Morii, half-yawning.

Sato's eyes flared, the insult not lost on him.

Watanabe continued unfazed. "As you can understand, Oyabun, our organization runs on a tight budget. The entire operation is so susceptible to ... economic fluctuations. In fact, we've only recently built enough of a reserve to be confident about the future. That is, we *were* confident."

"What's that? What's happened?"

"It seems the treasurer of our organization ..." he said hesitantly. "The treasurer, Nakashima Yoshihiro ..."

"Yes. Out with it, man!"

"Nakashima-san has taken our bankroll and fled somewhere."

"How much?" Morii asked casually.

"Three thousand dollars."

Morii was impressed. It was a lot of money for such an organization to be holding. "Did you call the police?"

"Yes, but they haven't done anything. Can you help us, Oyabun?"

"What's it gonna cost us?" Sato insisted rudely.

Morii sat back and glared at his adversary. "I know you don't like me, Sato-san," he said, pointing his finger. "There's no secret about that, but now you're stuck, aren't you? You don't know where this Nakashima character is. Even if you did, you wouldn't know how to get him back. Would you? The police are no help. Damn keto anyway. So you come to me. The man you hate for whatever reason. Is it really that hard for you to believe that I am a man of the people? I only want to help and protect the Japanese. How many times must I prove it? You suspect my motives, yet you come to me, even if in a disrespectful way, because in your heart of hearts you know I can help you. Isn't that right?"

Sato and his party hung their heads, unwilling to admit anything in the path of such a volley of words.

"Tell me I'm right and I'll help you," Morii continued. "Tell me."

Watanabe, the fawning secretary with a distinctive nose, raised his hand to Sato's shoulder to urge him to comply. The association leader raised his head and then nodded at the *oyabun*. A moment later, he grunted, bowing his head at the same time.

Morii knew he had them.

With Sgt. Gill's help, the *oyabun* learned that the Vancouver police were not willing to track down Nakashima who had definitely left the city, probably the province as well. Too much effort to find him and then too much red tape to bring him back. And for what? Some embezzlement case involving an obscure community group amongst the Japanese? Not worth it, they had decided. "The Japs probably brought it on themselves," one officer had put it succinctly, however illogically, to Gill. The Japanese fishermen were, after all, hurting the true Canadian fishing industry.

Morii then decided to talk to the Reverend Kakusai Tada, the new young minister at the recently established Cordova Street Kaikan, a modest two-storey Buddhist assembly hall at Cordova and Heatley. Watanabe, before he left with his Steveston cohorts, had conveyed to Morii a kernel of information: Nakashima was a devout member.

"Ah, Morii-san," greeted the minister with a deep voice, "so good to see you. Your wife does so many good works here."

"Yes, yes," Morii nodded as he shook the burly man's hand and surreptitiously compared receding hairlines. "Sensei, I need your help. I was wondering if you could tell me about Nakashima Yoshihiro," he asked. "He's a member here, is he not?"

"Why yes, he is."

"Have you seen him lately?"

"No, but then I haven't been looking for him."

"The men of the Fisherman's Association over in Steveston have a ... disagreement with him. I've agreed to help them find him."

"Isn't he at home?"

"No. He's left town, maybe even the province."

The minister took on a pensive look. "Hmm, perhaps he's gone to Raymond."

"Raymond?"

"Alberta. If I were him, I'd go there. It has the only Buddhist Church outside of British Columbia, and there's a fair sized concentration of Japanese there."

"So ka?" Morii said, nodding in surprise.

"If you'd like I could get in touch with the Reverend Nagatomi there."

"Yes, I'd appreciate that."

"Raymond's pretty much a dirt farmer's town, though."

The *oyabun* smiled enigmatically for the minister and held faith in the Buddha that he was doing the right thing.

The train ride was interminable. It took the better part of two days for the landscape of heavy rock, forest, and sculpting rivers to give way to flat, coulee-dotted land. Morii's eyes widened at the immense blue bowl of sky above him. Like the early morning streets of Vancouver, the emptiness exposed him, much to his discomfort. Completely alone, he felt conspicuous. His mind turned to Sato and the ill treatment he had received. The *oyabun* was unjustly put upon and he was getting sick of it, since it went well beyond the meeting with the Steveston fishermen. He couldn't understand why only fear and intimidation worked for him since he as well as his wife had done so much obvious good work. Why was he bothering to help these ungrateful Japanese? Perhaps Rikimatsu was right, they weren't worth it.

The train slowed to a halt before a squat, brick railroad station house, typical except it stood in the middle of nowhere oppressed by the hot, desolate wind. When the conductor announced, "Lethbridge," Morii grabbed his satchel and headed for the exit at the end of the Pullman car. Outside, in the sun-baked distance, he saw signs of life, a thin line of buildings staining the horizon. He walked a few steps in that direction when a gaunt, deeply tanned, runt of a man approached him.

"Morii-san?" asked the stranger as he bowed. "I am Higa Kyojun. I'm here to take you to Raymond."

Snorting at the sound of the Okinawan name, he nodded in response. The *oyabun* got in the vehicle without saying a word, but noted the exceptionally dark hue of his skin.

Higa appeared unmoved by the slight.

The old Ford pickup fought the road the entire twenty miles to Raymond. Morii's black morning coat grew grey with the dust. Though his wife had objected to his wearing such an inappropriate garment to travel, he had prevailed. Morii-*san's* duty was to set the example, after all.

The truck eventually pulled into the sparsely populated town, which was more like a small collection of ramshackle storefronts and jerry-built houses. *Now what would a bunch of Okinawan-Japanese be doing here?* Morii asked himself. *Eta, untouchable pig farmers all of them.*

Higa never said a word the entire trip, until he stopped the truck at the edge of town in front of an exhausted structure that served as the Buddhist Church, and said simply, "We're here."

The paint on the church was fresh and the construction simple, a plain wooden frame tilting away from the prevailing wind with a few windows and a peaked roof. A sign above the double door identified it as having been a Mormon house of worship at one time.

Inside, the *oyabun* found an empty space except for a few bags of rice. Then suddenly the Reverend Shinjo Nagatomi ran in, out of breath, in a white shirt with the sleeves rolled up. His hair was ruffled and his shirt stained with sweat. Obviously the minister had been working, expending a great deal of energy.

"Sensei, what is this place?" Morii inquired.

"Oh, this is the storage area," he said, still catching his breath. "The sanctuary is upstairs. There's talk of making this some kind of co-operative store, and that'll be good because we need our rice and soy sauce!"

The minister's cheerfulness prompted Morii to wonder further about life in this backwater. "Many Okinawans here?"

"Nihonjin," he corrected hesitantly. "Mostly farmers. Maybe five hundred. The congregation is over one hundred. Pretty good, ne? I've been here a couple of months but I can tell you the Dharma spirit is strong here. Come let's go to my office upstairs."

The minister's cubbyhole was a dusty room cramped with Buddhist tomes located just off the assembly hall, which comprised most of the second floor. The reverend was animated as he spoke. "So how's Vancouver? I haven't been there in a while. Must be wonderful weather there. Not like here. Have you been to Japan recently? Now that's what I miss the most. Could you send us some Japanese foodstuffs? We can't get a lot here as you −"

"Sensei," Morii interrupted, "I'm sorry, but I don't have a lot of time."

"Oh yes, I do prattle on, don't I? It's just that we don't get too many visitors −"

"Speaking of visitors, I understand there is someone who moved here recently and joined your congregation?"

"Oh yes, Reverend Tada wrote me you wanted to know the whereabouts of Nakashima Yoshihiro."

"Yes, I know," Morii said, now a little annoyed.

"A good man. He wants to start a men's group here."

"Where does he live?"

"Works on the Higa farm."

"You mean the man who drove me in?"

"Yes, he's the owner."

Back on the road, the truck kicked up dust again, flecking the stinging light of the sun. Morii pulled his hat down close to his eyes as he squinted at Higa.

"Why didn't you tell me about Nakashima?" he snapped. "You must've known I wanted to see him."

"You want to take him away," Higa answered.

"Yeah, so?"

"So why should I help you take away a good worker?"

Hick bastard, Morii thought. *Maybe my wife's right about these Nihonjin − even if they are Okinawans.*

The truck roared on, its owner silent until a small structure appeared in the distance. The building, with a slouching and frayed roof, stood alone against the wrath of nature.

"He's in the field," Higa pointed. "Digging for sugar beets, if there are any."

"What, no pigs?" Morii cracked as he headed into the field, dust swirling as the wind began to pick up. About half a mile in, he came across a rumpled man digging uselessly in the ground. As he approached, the man looked up, revealing a sunburnt face and tapered eyes coloured with suspicion.

"You Nakashima?" Morii asked.

"Maybe," the man grunted.

"You got the face of a man who's not used to farming ..."

"Who are you?"

"... like you just come to it recently."

"Just who are you?"

"I'm –"

"You're ... Morii-san, aren't you?" the man said, with some dismay.

"You Nakashima?"

"Hai," he answered, and bowed his head with exaggerated respect.

"You take the three thousand dollars?"

"Hai," he confessed without hesitation, at the same time lowering his head even further.

"Any of it left?"

"No."

Morii patted him on the shoulder and directed him back to the farmhouse. "Sa, iko. You've got to answer for a lot back in Vancouver."

Nakashima dropped his shovel and sheepishly went with the *oyabun* without complaint.

Once back in Vancouver, Morii put Nakashima up in the Patricia Hotel, a block south of Powell Ground. He left instructions with Rikimatsu to bring the felon to the Nippon Club after he had cleaned up. Morii himself dropped off his bag at home and bathed before heading for the rendezvous at his office. His wife was typically not home, which suited him fine.

Climbing up the stairs, he heard the murmur of conversation. Several men from the Steveston Japanese Fishermen's Association milled about his office as he entered.

"Ah, Oyabun, you're here," said Watanabe, rushing forward. "We came as soon as we got your message."

"Well, where is he?" Sato demanded impatiently.

"All in good time, Sato-san. First of all, I must tell you the bad news."

The five men stirred with anticipation.

"I'm afraid all the money is gone."

"Chikusho!" Sato's face fell. "Gone? Every cent?"

"I'm afraid so."

"We're bankrupt," sighed Sato.

"What did he spend it on?" asked Watanabe. "Horse races, I bet."

"Oyabun!" a voice called out at the door. Rikimatsu pushed forward a cowering Nakashima, dressed in clean white shirt, vest, and suit pants.

"Kusotare!" Sato cursed, lunging for the miscreant.

Morii jumped in front of the angry president. "Hold on. There's no need for more trouble."

Nakashima bowed deeply, muttering an apology to the contingent.

"Listen!" Morii shouted. "How much money can you raise to replenish the treasury?"

"What did you do with the money, you bastard?" Sato interrupted.

Nakashima was now on his knees and trembling as he recited the *Nembutsu.*

"Gave it to the horse bosses, I bet," speculated another as he backhanded the man's head.

"Stop it!" Morii commanded. "How much money can you raise?"

"We've already collected fifteen-hundred dollars," Watanabe offered. "That's about all the membership can do, especially in these times."

"Don't tell him that!" Sato thundered.

"Fifteen hundred, eh?"

"You're not getting any of it, Morii," the president, flushing red, interjected.

"You're such a crude man," Morii said, then turned to the others. "I have a proposal. Let Nakashima go." Everyone gasped at the suggestion. "No, wait. Hear me out. We don't want the police interfering down here. Drop the charges against him and I'll pay his passage back to Japan. You'll never see him back here again."

The members ruminated. "Oh, I see! No arrest. No shame to us and no loose mouths!" Watanabe said with rising glee. "Don't you see, Sato-san? Don't you all see?"

"And I'll give you fifteen hundred dollars to make up for the loss," Morii added.

Everyone stood in stunned silence. Sato moved to speak first, but was stopped by Morii's raised hand.

"All I want in return is appreciation, a little respect, and a package of Japanese groceries."

"I'm sorry, Oyabun," Watanabe echoed. "Did you say groceries?"

"Japanese, yes. And make that two. I want it sent to the Raymond Buddhist Church, to Reverend Nagatomi."

"And you want nothing else?"

"He wants us obligated to him." Sato invoked a little reality.

"Don't think of it as an obligation here. I do things for my people. Give money. Solve problems," explained Morii. "We're like a family, like-minded, loyal to each other and to the Emperor. We're all we have here in this godless land. All I ask for in return is appreciation, respect."

The party of five moved to the outside hallway to confer. Morii and Rikimatsu heard them muttering over the pros and cons. But really, what choice did they have?

Fifteen minutes later, the men reconvened in the office, only to shuffle out of the room and down the stairs in silence a few moments later. Left behind were the *oyabun* and the *yojimbo* standing over an inconsolable man who was alone in his crime, simmering in his shame and uncertain of his fate. Rik-*san* let his knife catch the light.

⤺

Thursday, March 14, 1940

"What do you know about Okihara Koji?" grilled the *oyabun*, standing over his victim. "Where is he?"

Akiyama sat with his elbows on his knees, his hands clasping the back of his head, and his body rocking in the stress of the moment. "I told you I never heard of him. I would've told you if I had."

"Rik-san says you waited on him the day before he disappeared."

"I serve a lot of guys."

Morii relaxed and looked at Rik-*san*, giving him a sign.

Aki lifted his eyes in time to see the signal, turning his face white with fear. "What're you gonna do? Ki ... ki ...?" He couldn't get the word out.

"Kill? Kill who? Okihara?" Morii asked before lapsing into a loud belly laugh. "You ... you think I'm going to kill you?"

Aki looked down and wiped his nose clean with his shirt sleeve and then began to rub his thighs nervously in his chair. "Why?" he burst forth. "Why are you doing this to me?"

"Why? Why?" Morii shouted. "Because you betrayed me, that's why!

I didn't steal your club 'right from under you.' You were dead. Remember? You came back as a ghost."

The implication was clear.

"It would've been better if you had died in the war," Morii speculated. "Can you believe this bakatare, Rik-san?"

The *yojimbo* stood with a deepening scowl on his face.

Morii suddenly grasped Aki by the shirt front. "Now listen to me, you little shit. I've never murdered anyone. Never have. Never will. You hear me?" His voice was angry, ragged, and emphatic, as if merely saying it without any hint of irony made it true.

His eyes spiked with horror, Aki nodded in agreement.

"People think I have and that's good for business. Keeps kusotare like you in line, or at least, I thought it did. But no, I'm not going to kill you. You'd be more of an annoyance dead.

"Look at the trouble this Miyamoto has caused. Shimatte-ne! If I had really done it like everybody says, I would've had Rik-san here take the body up to North Vancouver to the limestone pits there. Let nature take care of it! Not leave him lying around for the police to find."

Aki's eyes were wet with tears.

Morii narrowed his gaze at Aki. "No, I'm not going to kill you."

"But what about Hirano?" Aki blubbered.

"Oh so you do know about Hirano?"

"Everybody knows," the bartender snarled.

Morii stood up straight. "Whether he's dead or not, I don't know," he said coldly. "I hope he is, but I had nothing to do with it." The *oyabun* swung his good arm in a sweeping motion. "You're gonna disappear to Japan like Nakashima, like Hirano, like so much dust in my house."

The *yojimbo* chuckled.

"But what about my wife?" the barkeeper asked nervously.

"The keto?" Rik-*san* said in a dismissive tone.

Morii glared at him. "You've got another in Japan," he said.

Rik-*san* pulled out a short knife and pressed it to Aki's neck. "Let's go."

The manager held his breath as he rose to his feet, careful not to make a false move. Tears started, rolling down his cheeks and stinging the small cut that dripped blood down his neck.

That evening, people reported seeing a *hakujin* woman frantically searching for someone or something in the pulsating glow of the Three-Star Imperial sign.

9. June 1920

Yoshiko sat on her bed in Taniguchi's Boarding House, glad to be alone. Her husband had left her to her own devices as he went out without a word earlier that morning. *Don't let him take away your dignity.* Her mother's words now seemed like a bad joke in light of what had happened a few hours before. She smiled with contempt before breaking into tears: the heaviness of self-pity pressed harder.

Her initial impulse was to leave, but then what would she do? No one would help a woman who had deserted her husband. There was no money for a return trip. Even if she managed to get to Japan somehow, the Miyamoto family in Mihama offered no sanctuary, despite Hiroko's compassion and friendship, which Yoshiko was starting to suspect, against her better judgment. Her own family would never accept her. Coming to Canada meant she had to give up all ties to them and start anew here. But the thought of having children with this monster, this *oni*, repulsed her. Her only choice was unthinkable: *jisatsu*, suicide. She shuddered at what people would say. It was a shameful act producing nothing but embarrassment for her family, even if they had given her up for lost. Nothing, she decided. She could do nothing.

What was most unfathomable to her was the viciousness of his attack. Was it her fault? What had she done to make him so angry? Did she insult him so badly? Was this going to be a daily occurrence? The questions mounted in their insanity. Akiko came to mind and she knew her young cousin would've just crawled into a corner and died. Her mother would grin and bear it, she supposed. She didn't know what Hiroko would do. On the other hand, Nofu Furukawa would stand up to him and stare him down. Probably kill him in the end. But what was she able to do? The questions went round and round until she wept from the confusion and the unanswerable. The frustration of trapped prey.

As she cried into the sheets stained by last night's violence, she unexpectedly summoned forth the beautiful eyes of the young man sitting with Taniguchi and Morii at the Three Sisters. The large nut-brown pupils housed in soft curving eye sockets. *A kind man. A good man. I'd be safe with him.* She wondered if he had a diamond-shaped mole on his back.

Later when she had recovered somewhat, she assessed the condition of her belongings and then explored the residence. It consisted of five simple rooms like the one she was in, with functional furniture and only the barest of outside light trickling into the house, as if the sun had no business in the private lives of the occupants. A rough, concrete kitchen downstairs on the first floor, and a dining room and a laundry area in back, were obviously for boarders. Yoshiko took advantage of the time alone and hand-washed her clothes, some torn, some soiled, some bloodied.

The night breezes were gentle. The air soft. Her nakedness supple. She was his, she knew this, but he came at her like the vicious edge of a broken sword. An open wound, she bled, dripping into the black stream of water before her feet — water that gushed into the hallway, down the stairs, through the open front door, onto the streets and into the surrounding forests, cliffs, and rubble. No one saw, no one heard, and for all she knew, no one cared. The moonlight pooled near her, just out of reach.

Back in her room, she could see her laundry on the backyard clotheslines snapping in the wind, twisting like the bed sheets during her torment. She hid her eyes.

By six o'clock that evening, Yoshiko realized that she hadn't eaten all day. She was about to go downstairs to seek out the house cook when Jinsaburo burst in, his overcoat more stained than before and his suit rumpled far beyond civility.

"Hey," he greeted.

She instantly lowered her head, averting her gaze.

"They're serving dinner downstairs."

"Oh, give me a minute and we can go."

"You go yourself. I had dinner already."

"What? You had dinner without me?"

"So?" he said sharply.

"I'm your wife!"

"You're not my jailer!"

"First you lie about your boarding houses," Yoshiko snapped. "Then you and your father lie to me about your age to get me over here. Now you won't even be seen with me!"

With teeth clenched, Jinsaburo lashed out and struck her across the face.

Yoshiko buckled and then screamed. "Stop ... stop!" Her voice was desperate, raspy as if torn by a razor blade, the expression on her face pleading for mercy.

He struck again, knocking her to the floor, then stood over her breathing heavily, as if he were enjoying his power over a trembling animal.

"You don't like that, eh?" he spat demonically. "Well, I'll hit you and keep on hitting you until you start doing what I say! Until you co-operate. Chikusho! I need you to have faith in me. I'm the only son of Miyamoto Iwakichi! I need to prove myself. That's why I came here, you kuso wife. Do you think I like lying to my father? I know he knows the truth. He knows ... about my success." He paused. "Marriage was the only way to make those lies true but I'm too old and not good enough for the likes of you. So my father lied about my age. So what?"

Utterly astounded by the outburst, Yoshiko felt the heat of his blows to her face darken to an intense coldness. "You want me to do what you say?" she rasped. "You want me to co-operate?" She struggled to her feet and began unbuttoning her dress, then let it slide to the floor. She next untied her hair and let it fall free. As she slowly removed her undergarments, she said, "All right, you'll have it only if ... listen to me ... only if you never hit me ever again. You will respect me in public and in private."

Jinsaburo stared with mounting amazement. He took a step toward her.

"You agree?" she said.

He grunted.

"You agree or I'll write to your father telling him I know everything and then to my family. Everyone will know. I'll bring shame to your whole family in Japan!"

He stopped and tripped over his words, "I ... I won't let you."

"No matter how much you try and stop me, I'll write that letter and mail it. If you don't kill me, somehow, some way I will." She dropped her last piece of clothing to the floor. Unseen breezes ran up and down her body, enclosing her in shimmering air. She lay down upon the bed.

Jinsaburo approached, breathing heavily.

"You agree?" she repeated as her hair spread over the pillow. Her sea-cold eyes glazed over as if dead.

"Yes," he said, as he shook his own clothes free.

Breakfast was a simple meal of miso soup, rice, and fish, similar to that served at the Immigration Building except this food had flavour. Yaeko Ebisuzaki, a slight woman with shocking white hair and gaunt face, prepared all the meals at the Taniguchi. She had been widowed years earlier and found the proprietor's charity and wages suitable for her needs.

Around the table sat the boarders: Jinsaburo, Yoshiko, Tosuke Kato, and Hideo Yamashiro. The latter two were lumbermen from the Interior waiting for work. They spoke in a crude tongue and had manners to match.

"Oi oba! More gohan!" Kato shouted in a commanding voice.

"You'll get more rice when you finish with what you've got," retorted Yaeko.

"What am I, your baby?"

"Well, you eat like one!" she said, pointing to small clumps of rice stuck to his chin. It was obvious she gave as good as she got, a characteristic of her age.

Yoshiko looked up at them from the oblong table, her demure face remaining stern in anticipation of more food. Again she thought of Nofu Furukawa, her long-ago ship companion, and decided to adopt her no-nonsense approach to life.

Yamashiro turned the conversation elsewhere. "So, married are you?" he asked Jinsaburo. "What you doing for money? Still giving what you get to the Chankoro?"

"Damare," Jinsaburo growled, sounding annoyed.

"Okusan," he said to Yoshiko, "you better keep both eyes on your husband. He'll piss all your money away in Chinatown if you let him!"

"Fair warning," Kato added. "How many times I found him broke and in the gutter."

Jinsaburo decided to rise to the occasion. "Well gentlemen, I now have a good woman who'll take care of me," he declared. "Miyamoto-san, you'll manage all the money. I will faithfully hand over every penny I earn."

"Of course you will," she replied, mimicking Nofu-*san* on the boat as best as she could. "It's my right and duty as your wife."

Jinsaburo's face widened with surprise as Kato and Yamashiro tried to suppress their amusement.

A peace descended on the dining room with the end of breakfast. The two lumbermen had departed noisily on their way to inquire about work at Hastings Sawmill. There was always short-term work for strong men not expecting more than the twenty-five cents an hour. Yaeko Ebi-suzaki was off tending to the bedding, not willing to wait for the last two who were content to languish in their post-prandial glow.

The morning sunlight streaming through the kitchen and dining room windows beat down on Yoshiko, but indifferent to its warmth, she sat vacantly staring at her empty rice bowl. Jinsaburo lingered over his third bowl of miso soup, playfully nudging the tofu around the clouds of soybean.

"Oi wife," he said in a mocking manner, "I got you a job."

Yoshiko was jolted out of her torpor. "A what?"

"A job. We need the money."

"Where? Doing what?" she asked.

"Cleaning house ... doing laundry. I'll take you there."

The idea didn't bother her. She was used to menial labour back on the farm in Kiyama and nothing could compare to the fish cleaning on the Miyamoto estate in Mihama, but she began to buckle under the accumulating weight of surprises and indignities. "Where am I going?"

"Across the bridge. Don't worry, I'll take you there."

The sun approached its zenith as the couple made their way down Main Street. Coming upon the Georgia-Harris Viaduct, which the couple took toward the downtown core, Yoshiko enjoyed a panoramic view of False Creek industry to the south and the majestic Hotel Vancouver to the north. She paused a moment and wondered about the hidden luxuries and privileged lives contained therein.

Well past the bridge, Jinsaburo with Yoshiko following took a sharp turn to the left into a different-looking neighbourhood via Pacific Avenue. Peaceful, without the hint of desperation about it, it was an area of stand-alone houses with verandahs, some with prominent turrets, all with ample yard space in front. Every window had laced curtains, every door a shiny brass knocker. Jinsaburo finally led her up the path of one of those houses with a garden in front and potted plants on the porch. She shuddered as she realized the place belonged to a *hakujin*. *A gaijin house*.

A tall woman in short tight curls of grey hair greeted them in English. Her complexion was severely pale, with cosmetics to make her cheeks artificially rosy. Yoshiko had dealt with "Canadians" at the Immigration Building, but this was the first she would have to deal with one face to face. She was actually glad of Jinsaburo's presence.

"*Eigo wakarimasen*," Yoshiko answered and looked to her husband who was smoothing down his wrinkled suit and bowing all at once.

Jinsaburo translated, announcing the woman's name as "Follows," a name Yoshiko found impossible to pronounce. He stifled her stammering attempts and walked into the house at the mistress's invitation without removing his shoes. Yoshiko followed her husband's lead, resisting the urge to enter in stocking feet. People here are strange, she reasoned. Trying not to give him much, she was impressed with her husband's command of English, but nearly tripped him following as closely as she did.

"Baka," he spit as an angry aside.

The house was spacious compared to the boarding house and was well appointed with delicate cherry wood furniture. Paintings depicting ornately uniformed men on horseback graced the walls. It was certainly different from the Mihama estate, yet the same in its refinement.

Jinsaburo said nothing until they ended up in a clammy laundry room, with bare cement walls and floor, deep inside the house. He then listened to Mrs. Follows before giving his wife instructions on how to wash the clothes and then clean around the house. Mrs. Follows would tell her what to do. With that, he promptly left, leaving her on her own.

Yoshiko stood before her new mistress dumbfounded, certainly not knowing how to ask for instructions. Her venom for her husband immediately returned, but she soon realized that didn't help her situation. She wiped the nervous moisture from her hands on her apron dress before feeling the cold dampness of her brow. Mrs. Follows didn't seem to notice as she began to pantomime her instructions. Yoshiko was amused as the lady grew increasingly animated, but she dared not laugh or even smile. The message simply wasn't getting through.

When Yoshiko caught on, she began copying the *hakujin* woman's movements in an effort to convey her understanding. Mrs. Follows smiled and left Yoshiko on her own. In a few hours, she had finished hand washing the laundry and was about to tackle the dusting and wiping.

At the end of the day, Yoshiko again faced the lady of the house. The woman was just as mystifying as she was at the beginning of the day, but at least she seemed pleased. Yoshiko, not knowing what to expect next, stood absolutely still as Mrs. Follows reached into her purse, pulled out two shiny coins, and placed them in Yoshiko's hand. Before Yoshiko could react, Mrs. Follows also gave her two oranges from a nearby bowl of fruit.

The young housekeeper shook her head in confusion, but bowed to the lady of the house as Mrs. Follows sauntered away, humming. Yoshiko stood alone, considering what to do next, then hurried through the door to go home. She fingered in her pocket what Jinsaburo told her later was fifty cents.

As she strolled along the avenue toward where she thought the Japanese sector area was, she considered these "Canadians." Mrs. Follows was not very clean by allowing shoes to be worn in the house – are they all barbarians, letting in the outside dirt? In Japan, the *tatami* mats were fragile and shoes would weaken the fibres quickly, but surely here their carpets were just as susceptible to wear and tear. Strange customs these Canadians have, but the "lady" was kind enough to give her the oranges and the money. Whether or not it was a fair amount, Yoshiko didn't know, but at least she was paid. Perhaps these *gaijin* weren't so bad after all.

She then turned her mind to getting home. She was confident she knew the way. The viaduct was the obvious path, she and Jinsaburo had taken it in the morning. It was just a matter of finding it.

The voice of the sea came to her as she saw the bridge in the distance. A low booming and high whistle called from the tug and fishing boats in the water below. On the crest of the viaduct, she stopped again and pondered her fate. She couldn't return to Japan – maybe never, given her indigent circumstances. She couldn't leave Jinsaburo. And do what, anyway? Become at best a *dekasegi mono*, a menial labourer, shunned by decent people, cursed by young and old, leaving her with suicide as her only way out. The prospect of wealth and status faded quickly into a life of pain, drudgery, and anonymity.

What she missed the most, she suddenly realized, was the giggling, the sheer fun she had had with her cousin. Will they ever be together again? she asked herself. Where had the dreams of young girls gone? The dreams so possible in Mihama.

Within the sudden roar and decline of the sea, blown spume danced into the air, sparkling like a multitude of coins in the sunlight before descending into the dark waters raging below. A revelation.

At the corner of Main and Hastings, Uchiboro's Dress Shoppe came into view. The mannequins in the front window sporting the latest 1920s styles, Yoshiko indulged in a momentary daydream. She would have her own boarding house, she decided. *Like I was promised.*

By September 1920, Yoshiko was fully ensconced as Mrs. Follows' twice-a-week cleaning woman. She even learned a few words of English: "wa-shi" and "ran-do-ri." *Sentaku* was more to her liking but, for the patient and kind Mrs. Follows, she wrapped her mouth around the tortured pronunciations.

In the meantime, she and Jinsaburo moved to a rooming house. Taniguchi's Boarding House was just too expensive. Thirty-five dollars a month for a room and three meals a day was a luxury they couldn't afford. Their leaving was amicable and old man Taniguchi himself offered Yoshiko a job helping Ebisuzaki-*san* with the cooking, cleaning, and laundry. She accepted.

Amitani's Rooming House on Cordova near Alexander was a small house with wood-siding, two floors, undersized windows, and a tarpaper roof; the Miyamotos lived upstairs. It was close quarters but clean, or so it seemed. One night, for no apparent reason, Yoshiko woke up in darkness and stumbled into the kitchen. After turning on the light, she spied movement on the small distressed table they used for eating. She shuffled closer to see that the butter left out for the morning was covered in cockroaches. Swiftly picking up the dish, she shook the insects off and then inspected the butter to make sure it was clean enough before placing it in the icebox. *Mottainai. Can't waste it.*

Most evenings while the *oni* snored his life away and the roaches watched for another chance, she sat at the table contemplating her impoverished surroundings. How different from the luxury of the Mihama estate, so high on the hill overlooking Japan and the ocean beyond. And how far she had fallen even from the relative comfort of her ship's cabin, despite her seasickness. The sounds and smells of her home would come back to her, and her eyes strained to see her house again. But the stone samurai, the gurgling stream, and the singing cicadas of her father's garden were now but mere shapes and sounds imagined in the dark. All she could hope for now was to survive, but for what, she did not know.

It was a continuing mystery to Yoshiko what her husband did for work. He left the house at exactly the same time as she. He walked toward Powell as she made her way to the Taniguchi on Alexander or the Viaduct, and returned home in time for dinner at six o'clock, only to leave most nights after the meal, not returning until well past midnight. But every week, he gave her his earnings, ten dollars more or less. Coupled with the six dollars she made, Yoshiko watched the bottle on the bedroom bureau steadily fill up with money. In the end, she just couldn't be bothered to question her husband about what he did for his wages.

She was just happy most times he came home too late and too drunk to want her. There were the odd nights he demanded sex, and as her mother had advised, she did as she was told, but with no enjoyment, no emotion. With her eyes glazed over, she lay still as a corpse being used for his pleasure. When he finished, he would curse her, roll off, and fall straight to sleep. She would then make her way to the kitchen table to question time and again what she had done.

On a Saturday in late October, Yoshiko went to the Chinatown open-air market at Pender and Main. The bins overflowed with fresh vegetables and fruit like squash and oranges, while bleached and grinning pig heads sat atop the heavy wooden meat counter. *Eta.* But somehow appropriate for Chinese places, she thought. *Maybe Okinawans live around here!* She appreciated the low prices and she could read the ideograms. After buying the groceries, she headed home. As she opened her door, she heard a rustling coming from the bedroom.

"Hello?" she called.

A grunt.

She walked into the bedroom to find her husband sitting on the bed counting bills, the money bottle open, coins scattered all over the bed-spread.

"What are you doing?" she asked.

"I need this."

She rushed toward him, grabbing at her money. He pulled away while continuing to count it.

"You leave it alone," she cried as she reached for the bundle once again. "That's for my future!"

Jinsaburo unleashed an arm and pushed his wife to the bed.

"Bakayaro! I need fifty dollars," he grumbled.

In tears, she held her cheek and glared at him from her supine position. "What for?"

He remained silent as he stood up, pocketing the money at the same time.

"What for?" she repeated, nearly screaming.

"To pay a debt." He moved toward the door.

"You've been gambling!" she accused in desperation as she followed him. "Gambling! At some Chankoro place." She grabbed his arm and tried to pull him down to the floor, hoping her weight would stop him. Jinsaburo pried his arm free and disappeared down the hallway and steps.

She remained a lump on the floor, shaking in her sorrow and anger.

By the spring of 1921, Yoshiko found some solace at the new Jackson Avenue Buddhist Church near Powell Street; the Buddhist congregation had splintered into two groups over a controversy involving the minister. As a member of the *fujinkai*, the women's group, Yoshiko met many of the wives of prominent church members. One in particular impressed her: Misao Morii, a regal woman, tall with a back so straight her head was perpetually held high, making her gaze intimidating. Her face was pampered, smooth like the complexion of a young girl, and her manner-isms bore the upbringing of aristocracy. Gentle, delicate hands, a Tokyo accent, and an impeccable wardrobe separated her from the rest of the *fujinkai* women.

"Morii-san," Yoshiko addressed her humbly, in spite of herself. She had heard the gossip about her husband facing trial for murder and won-dered why she was so high and mighty.

Misao Morii peered down at the newcomer, who demonstrated the proper respect but still needed to be shown her place. After being relegated to such a backwater – through a marriage arranged by her father, Takashi Matsuoka, a highly placed government official – she was determined to demonstrate how a cultured and well-bred Japanese woman acted in public. She was glad of only one thing in Canada: her husband was wealthy.

"And you are …?" she asked imperiously.

"Miyamoto Yoshiko."

"Ah yes, and you are from?"

"Fukui-ken, Kiyama-cho."

"Hmm, good crabs there," Misao remarked. "When did you arrive?"

"About six months ago."

"Well, my dear, you are welcome here." She turned on her heels. "Fukunaga-san?" she called.

"Hai?" responded a plump young woman about Yoshiko's age and height.

"Would you take charge of … um…."

"Miyamoto," Yoshiko said quickly.

"Yes. Take care of Miyamoto-san. Show her what to do."

"Hai." Toshii Fukunaga led Yoshiko to the kitchen where several women worked in a flurry cleaning and slicing vegetables. "We're preparing for the new minister. He's due to arrive today."

"What happened to the old minister?" Yoshiko asked innocently.

&

The Reverend Junichi Shigeno came to Canada in 1914. The presiding minister, the Reverend Gungai Kobayashi, was a pedant of the highest order with the look of a snake about him. He found the decision to replace him an insult and so refused to leave, deciding instead to mount a campaign to discredit his replacement. He waited patiently for his opportunity.

Four years after arriving, the Reverend Shigeno received a caller in his office at the Heaps Buddhist Church. He was not a conventionally handsome man but his face filled with youthful optimism made him quite popular with the members. His charm was evident even as he gazed into the red, puffy eyes of Kimiko Nakahara sitting in his office.

"Okusan," he said gently, "you don't look well. Are you all right?"

"Oh Sensei, my husband died a few months ago ... he was ... I can't say it."

"That's all right. That's all right," he repeated assuredly.

Kimiko placed her hands over her face. "In a mental institution in *Coquitlam*. I have two children ... babies, really." She had been perspiring profusely, her blouse was dark with it.

His eyes flared at the admission, but he continued in a calm voice. "You have the sickness, don't you?"

She nodded.

"Do you have someone to stay with? Relatives? Friends, maybe?"

She shook her head. "There's no one," she confessed quickly. "Could I ... perhaps ... could I stay here?"

The minister paused a moment, his mind racing with the possible ramifications. "Well...."

Her lower lip quivered, and her arm weakened by the disease started to shake. "I have no money. No one to turn —"

"Okay, okay. You and your children will stay here. Upstairs in one of the front bedrooms. The fujinkai ladies will take care of your children while nursing you to health."

She smiled faintly as her body slumped with either fatigue or relief, he couldn't tell.

Misao Morii barely raised an eyebrow when told about the ill woman and her two children. She instead mobilized her members to help her. It was the time of the Spanish flu epidemic of 1918. The women had been preparing meals and "comfort packages" for patients in hospitals, hostels, and homes anyway; what was one more? The *fujinkai* were no longer needed to roll bandages for the Red Cross because the Great War had just about been settled. They needed a new cause.

The Reverend Kobayashi, a hungry-looking man with close-set eyes and wiry frame, prowled around the church basement alive with the activity of the *fujinkai*, whispering thoughts into straining ears. The voices echoed off the walls and filled the very rafters of the building.

Doesn't she have her own place? Not proper. What's he doing with her? She's a widow, you know. Husband was crazy! Are the children? What are they doing together in the church? Is she really sick? Sick in the head, maybe. Just how long has he really known her?

So young. Handsome too. This Nakahara woman isn't the first. He has women everywhere. Gets them drunk and has his way with them.

In about a month, Kimiko died, despite the best efforts of Misao Morii and the *fujinkai*. On her death bed, the wretched mother asked the Reverend Shigeno if he and the church would take care of her babies. Maybe they could work for him when they grew up to repay the church's generosity. The minister hesitated but ill-advisedly said yes.

Why did he agree so quickly? Are they his children? I saw them at Sunk's Grocery. Those kids sure do take after him. Honto desho! That's why he took them in.

The gossip mounted and mounted until the congregation choked on every new tidbit uttered. Eventually, Genroku Nakamura, the highly respected president of the board, decided to hold a *shinto taikai*, a conference to discuss the status of the minister. In the overcrowded sanctuary of the distant Heaps church, Naotoshi Yasuno, a man with the weathered face and hands of a fisherman, stood to speak to the quickly gathered assembly.

"Mr. Chairman, I am here on behalf of the Steveston Bukkyokai to express our sincere and total support of Sensei Shigeno. We have nothing but high regard for him. We move for a vote of confidence to get this matter over with."

A loud objection roared from the crowd. Matsunoshin Abe, the chairman, came to his feet and demanded order. Hanyemon Hayashi and Otokichi Sugiura of the Vancouver Church jumped up in opposition. "We don't need a vote! It's plain as the nose on your face. This sensei is nothing but a libertine. He's a bad example for the children. He must go!"

The conference ended with the Buddhist Church split into two, and as a result, the church on Jackson Avenue in the Powell Street area was established a month later. The Reverend Shigeno and his followers settled into the Heaps church in Fairview to the east. And the Reverend Kobayashi left for Japan, secure in the knowledge that he had reaped his revenge with his own reputation intact.

☙

Yoshiko's eyes widened as Fumiko told the tale of the Buddhist minister and the widowed mother of two. She had never heard of such behaviour by a clergyman or a congregation. The thought stayed with her as she walked home.

How could any woman do such a thing? Her reputation! A widow with his two children, and with a bonsan. How could he do such a thing? But she soon considered that maybe they were happy for a time.

The sudden image of the two lovers in one another's arms did not leave her. *Red nails left a white scar across the back.* Her thoughts turned to her husband and his cruel and crude ways. Though she could never do such a thing, she wondered about taking a lover. *The eyes were drawn to the diamond mole. The muscular shoulders gracefully sloping along powerful arms to gentle, elegant hands caressing her. A hot blade dripping with blood nestled in pure snow.* The beautiful man in the immaculate suit came to mind.

In the following weeks, she busied herself with church activities, but even while preparing the condiments for the rice for the after-service lunch, she thought about the bottled money in the bedroom. Jinsaburo would not let her hide it. When she made the attempt, he beat her severely, even with her threat to expose him and his family.

As the jar filled, she would rush from the front door to the bedroom each day when she returned home, to be reassured it was still intact. Of course, her worse fears came true more times than she cared to think.

After weeks of work and saving only to find the proceeds disappear, a physical change came over Yoshiko. She aged without maturing as her eyes grew bloodshot with despair. Thin streaks of white hair began to appear. Her face as pale as a ghost's, her body gaunt and unsteady, she drew comments from those around her.

"Miyamoto-san! You look terrible!" Toshii said when she saw her friend at church.

Yoshiko did not respond; she just looked straight ahead with trembling eyes.

Toshii quickly looked around for help. "Morii-san! Morii-san! Please come here."

The haughty woman came over and noticed Yoshiko's condition immediately. "Oh, what has happened to Miyamoto-san?"

"I don't know. It might be her husband. He's a nonbe, you know," Toshii said, referring to gossip. "She needs help."

"Come, bring her along."

"She should leave that man," Toshii offered.

"And do what? Become a joro?"

"What … what's that?" Yoshiko muttered at last.

"A woman who sells her body for money," Toshii answered with a lowered voice.

"A shameful woman," Morii-*san* added. "The kind of woman who doesn't belong in our community. You will stay with your husband."

Yoshiko winced at the suggestion that she would even consider becoming a prostitute. It had never occurred to her that such a fate was possible. Not that she knew exactly what it meant to live that kind of life, but she had heard they could be found in big cities like Tsuruga. She felt weaker still at the possibility and stumbled as the two moved to keep her from falling to the floor.

The trio made their way out of the church dressed in overcoats against the early spring wind and rain and on toward an unknown destination, led by Morii-*san*. Toshii struggled to keep Yoshiko upright as they rushed to keep up. Despite the twists and turns, Toshii gradually realized where they were going. "The Raku Raku," she said in a cloud of humid breath. A tingle of trepidation coursed through Yoshiko's muddled brain.

With a gloved hand, Misao Morii knocked on the unmarked front door of her husband's restaurant club. The door cracked open.

"Nanja?" a voice from within inquired gruffly.

Morii-*san* pushed her way into the establishment and called for her husband. "Ah ra. Morii-san! Morii-san, I need you!"

"Naniyo?" called another voice.

In a backroom, Etsuji Morii sat on a desk before Yoshiko as she sipped on a whiskey neat, which made her choke and sputter.

"That's good. Bring colour back to your cheeks." He reached down beside him. "Would you like a manju? Fresh from Nagami's. Very sweet and the skin so smooth and buttery."

She coughed to clear the bitterness, feeling more than a little uncomfortable in the *oyabun's* presence. He seemed to be staring at her exposed arms.

"My wife tells me you're in trouble."

She pulled down her sleeves at the same time trying to hide her inflamed face.

"I remember you," he declared as he stood up. "You came here as a picture bride for Miyamoto Jinsaburo. We met at the Three Sisters. I was with Taniguchi Saburo." He spoke with clarity and certainty. "You were a pretty one."

"Oyabun," she started slowly. "My … my husband. We can't get ahead with our savings."

"Oh, and why is that? I pay him a generous wage," he said, with a touch of resentment.

"You?" She looked up startled and questioned the *oyabun's* revelation. She searched his face for evidence of deception, but there was only sincerity.

"Yes. You don't know he works for me here? Cleaning jobs mostly. Some errands, odd jobs. Forgive me, but I don't give him anything important."

She sat quietly simmering in her thoughts and emotions.

"For what he does, I give him too much, but I've got a generous heart. I know he has a pretty wife to support!" he chuckled, and shot a grin at Yoshiko. "Ten dollars a week, plus I hear he works for Shintani at his pool hall. He must make an extra five to ten dollars there. Overpaid, I'd say, but that old man lost two sons in the war. I guess he sees your husband as some kind of replacement, though I can't see it. In any case, twenty a week should be more than enough for you and him to build a nest egg."

Twenty …? she said to herself.

"Miyamoto-san? Are you still with me?"

"My husband … he gambles."

"Ah, he does, does he?" he said with a certain amount of disappointment at the confession. "In Chinatown?"

"Hai."

"Well, not much I can do about those damn Chankoro at the moment," Morii mused. "But I can promise that things are in the works to keep the money here with the Japanese. Many have come to me with the same complaint." He clenched his teeth and fists. "But your husband is a special case."

She let out an audible whimper, perhaps out of fear, perhaps self-pity. The despair in her voice caught the *oyabun's* ear and he quickly turned his attention to her matter again. A change seemed to come over him; his eyes softened, his posture not so severe. "Miyamoto-san, I'll do something about your husband, but you must be prepared to live a hard life."

Questions spread across her face like encroaching shadows, but she did not respond.

"Too bad, you are still a pretty one," Morii said.

A week later, Yoshiko came home from grocery shopping to find Jinsaburo waiting for her at the kitchen table. Red-eyed, his back stooped, he had been drinking from the sake bottle kept underneath the sink.

"We're leaving," he muttered.

"What?" she asked as she put down the groceries.

"I lost my job."

She almost blurted out what she knew but thought better of it. No use opening that can of worms, as she knew what the truth would mean for her. The thought of it had burned within her for days, but as a warning, her face grew hot in anticipation of a beating.

"Fired. That ketsuno ana!"

"What're we going to do?"

"Fired," he muttered. "I'll show him one day."

"Jinsaburo!"

"Kato-san said they need men and a cook and laundry woman up near Britannia Beach. For a forty-man crew. It's the only job open to me."

"I don't understand."

"We're leaving Vancouver. I didn't want to get back into logging, but what choice do I have? Someone spoiled my name here."

She turned numb with the realization.

"At least, you'll be able to save your goddamn money," he sneered sardonically.

10.

With the opening of the Showa Club in 1926, Etsuji Morii had consolidated his power in a centrally located, recognized establishment. It seemed that every man who bounded up the long flight of steps to the club on Powell Street more or less left his gambling marker in Morii's hands.

Morii also controlled the "love trade" through the Raku Raku and the upstairs Hinomaru "gentlemen's clubs." Of course, there were the common *joro-ya* whorehouses on Alexander and the two slightly upscale bawdy houses run by the incorrigible Kiyoko Tanaka-Goto (even so, it was rumoured that the owners paid Morii part of the profits to stay in business), but by and large the *oyabun's* establishments dealt with a more affluent and discriminating clientele. Many of the prominent businessmen of the area were seen frequenting his places.

Although the upstanding and proper citizens of the Powell Street area disapproved of the goings-on, they could do very little about it. Yasushi Yamazaki, publisher of the daily newspaper *Tairiku Nippo*, tried by first tackling the problem of prostitution elsewhere, in the Interior of the province. Since attacking Morii directly would be tantamount to committing suicide, he sent a reporter to the small towns of Cranbrook and Nelson to discover the extent of the activity, and then splashed the stories across his front pages, including photos and short biographies of the *joro*, the women who actually sold their bodies for money. The reaction was swift. Prominent members of the community conveyed their outrage at such lurid stories and pictures being disseminated to the general public. In the end, Yamazaki had only succeeded in humiliating himself, his own staff, and the Japanese community.

Morii had chuckled over Yamazaki's disgrace. The *oyabun* knew that very few had an insight into his true motives; certainly, sanctimonious newspaper editors didn't, having problems with extortion, intimidation, and violence, but they never saw the greater good he achieved. *The path to enlightenment.* Some thought of him as a bully at best and a degenerate at worst. Others saw him as a benevolent dictator. Many did wonder how far he was willing to go, but feared the answer.

And far indeed he was willing to go. After the reformation of the Japanese Businessmen's Association in the early 1920s and its subsequent restoration, Morii was bound and determined to gain control of it for the Japanese community's sake. Only twice he failed to deliver and only twice did he lose control in his rage.

During the fall of 1926, yet another opportunity to "help" presented itself to Morii when the Georgia Gang, a motley crew of street toughs from Vancouver's Gastown area, staged occasional raids on the Japanese sector, smashing windows while screaming like madmen. The gang especially liked Halloween when they could roam the streets dressed as hobos while perpetrating acts of vandalism under cover of night.

"Oyabun," addressed Manjiro Okamura, president of the association, the Nihon Jinkai, his balding head bowed with the proper respect. "Can you not do something about these damn keto-jin? They're terrorizing our women and children and causing hundreds of dollars of damage."

"So ne," agreed Morii, knowing the end of October was fast approaching. He rubbed his finger under his chin to consider the situation.

The Nippon Club office was perfectly still and sombre for this clandestine late-night meeting, its dull yellow light setting the mood for what was about to take place.

"I tell you what," Morii said after some time, "I'll form some patrols to deal with the problem."

Okamura smiled broadly, making him look like a simpleton – perhaps appropriate for the moment, since he later swore he wasn't aware of what he had just unleashed.

A week before Halloween, Morii formed the *jikeidan* patrols as promised, made up of fellow judo students and, on the night of witches and goblins itself, they dealt with the Georgia Gang quite effectively. As three boys in torn jackets, soiled dungarees, and hightop running shoes began soaping the windows of Shiomi's boarding house on Main Street, a dozen of Morii's men surrounded them.

"Are you going to clean those?" Rik-*san* growled sarcastically.

The tallest boy with curly red hair swung around to curse him. At that moment, a few of Morii's men moved out of the shadows and pinned the boys by the arms while others began delivering blows about the head. Their victims soon slumped to the ground where the judo students kicked them continuously, mostly in the stomach, buttocks, and groin.

The remaining men in back turned to face other Georgia Gang members who had just shown up to see their comrades writhing on the ground. They took two steps toward the teenagers, who then scattered in a flash. No one gave chase.

Rik-*san* bent over one of the moaning gang members on the ground, the redheaded boy maybe sixteen years old. While squinting his good eye, he hissed, "Next time, I'll cut your nose off."

The boy recoiled in horror and shook his head as if to say he didn't understand. Rik-*san* grabbed the boy's nose, twisted it, and then viciously slapped his face. He laughed heartily as he walked away with the rest of his men.

The patrols continued in the weeks that followed, even though the threat soon seemed to be over. Morii joined them once in a while to talk to those businessmen under his protection.

"Soga-san, good evening to you," greeted Morii, tipping his bowler.

The chubby, grey-haired department store owner acknowledged the *oyabun* cordially but hurriedly. It was just before closing, after all.

"Any trouble? This is Saturday, you know. Lots of bad keto-jin out on the streets tonight."

Soga shook his head.

"Good. Oh, by the way, I'm going to need some money for my services," Morii said, squinting. "I can't do this for free forever. I have expenses."

Soga stood silently, refraining from saying he didn't need the service, waiting for what he surely knew was coming.

"Call it tribute money. A tribute to me for protecting you so well against damage by the keto."

"Yes, Oyabun," Soga said, resigned to his fate.

Money was a problem. It was not only proof of the *oyabun*'s status but also the means to attain his "greater good." Morii found these activities inefficient, however, involving entirely too many men, and the expense was enormous. He needed an "elegant" way in which to make a profit while striving to "protect" his constituents.

Six months after the Halloween incident with the Georgia Gang, he set up another meeting with Manjiro Okamura, once again late at night and in his Nippon Club office. He liked its discreet location on Alexander Street and its quiet – like the anonymous building in San Francisco where his *oyabun* had plied his trade.

"We have an obligation here, Okamura-san."

The president of the Nihon Jinkai kept from grinning broadly this time. In Morii's presence, most men said nothing anyway, at least when they were smart enough to guess at what was about to be said.

"I want you to step aside and let me take your place in the Nihon Jinkai," Morii said.

Okamura nodded. "Hai, Oyabun," he agreed without hesitation.

"Good. Good," Morii smiled.

ॐ

The Nihon Jinkai, the Japanese Businessmen's Association, had come together in 1897, but became a fully realized entity over a specific cause in 1900. The local businessmen rallied around Tomekichi Homma, owner of the Hifumi-ro restaurant.

In October of that fateful year, Homma with his "British-sense-of-fair-play" belief and strong constitution had decided to visit the Collector of Votes. "I want name on list," he said in a halting accent while pointing to the thick manuscript of names in front of Thomas Cunningham, an officious looking man with black-rimmed glasses.

"You want what?" Cunningham asked.

"My name Homma Tomekichi. Put my name on list," he repeated, now glaring at the official. "I want vote!"

Cunningham took a deep breath and recited mechanically, "According to Section 8 of the Provincial Elections Act, no Chinaman, Japanese or Indian shall have his name placed on the Register of Voters for any

Electoral District or be entitled to vote at any election."

Homma grimaced and then grew angry as he shouted in Japanese, "*I'll take this to court!*"

The official stared at him blankly. "I don't know or give a damn about what you're saying, but if it's registering you want you're not gonna get it. I'd rather go to jail than allow some Jap name or any other Asiatic on this here list," he declared as he slammed his hands down on the manuscript.

Shortly after the confrontation, the Nihon Jinkai rallied to conduct a campaign to raise the estimated $1,500 needed to carry out such a lawsuit. Throughout the Powell Street area, its members paraded with placards that read "Don't Let Homma Do It Alone!" The more zealous ones knocked on doors, calling on relatives, friends, and "fellow Japanese" to give. And it worked. Enough donors gave fifty cents each until the money was raised.

Although he could speak English, Homma stated his case to the Supreme Court of British Columbia through a translator and, surprisingly, Chief Justice McColl, a greying man known for his compassion for "ethnics," ordered that Homma's name be put on the provincial voter's list.

On December 1, 1900, the *Vancouver Daily Province* featured as its lead headline, JAPS CANNOT VOTE, to assure British Columbians that, even with Japanese names on the rolls, they had no right to vote in the upcoming federal election. Bolstered by such public opinion, the provincial powers-that-be appealed to the Supreme Court of Canada which actually upheld McColl's judgment. All seemed to be going Homma's way until, two years later, the government took up the matter with the Privy Council in London, England. They considered the question and reversed the decision. Homma's name, in the end, was removed from the list. The issue laid to rest, the *Victoria Colonist* trumpeted in its pages:

We are relieved from the possibility of having polling booths swamped by a horde of Orientals who are totally unfitted either by custom or education to exercise the ballot, and whose voting would completely demoralise politics.

The Nihon Jinkai continued to exist but with little effect until shortly after the 1907 riots, when Etsuji Morii, as was his wont, decided to help by giving the organization some teeth. He called on his man in the Japanese Consulate, Saburo Yoshie – the much-lauded and publicized hero of the riots – to convince the Consul General to grant the Nihon Jinkai "Guarantor Authority." Yoshie readily agreed, knowing his place. Thereafter, all legal documents pertaining to the Japanese population of Canada could be given "authorized permission" by the association. In this way too, the Consul General took on an active role in "looking after" the Japanese.

The Nihon Jinkai was now obligated to Morii, who in turn was obligated to the Consul General and his office; a relationship of mutual benefit. The *oyabun* became chairman of the Immigrant Committee, which allowed him to "import" women easily for his clientele of the Hinomaru Club as well as deport any Japanese who didn't fully appreciate his "generosity." As for the Consul General, he could use all of Morii's resources to keep the Japanese in Canada loyal to Japan.

All went well until Kaizo Kawamoto, a slender man with a keen sense of right and wrong, moved to rid the Japanese community of the Nihon Jinkai's influence. Kawamoto, in his role as columnist for the *Tairiku Nippo*, sought justice and, as a unionist, he fought against the Anti-Asiatic League's influence in the labour unions of British Columbia.

In 1921, he managed to talk the Skeena Fishermen's Association into backing his bid to form a new union of fishermen. With the Skeena membership's support, he eventually convinced the men of Vancouver Island and Steveston to form the Fishermen's Liaison Council. It took some doing, but the organization's priority was to sever all connections with the Nihon Jinkai. So outraged was the business association's board of directors that they immediately resigned en masse (although since the majority of the membership consisted of fishermen, they really had no choice). The Nihon Jinkai then came under the control of Kawamoto and members of the Liaison Council.

Of course, Morii's Immigrant Committee was immediately disbanded as a result, which caused the *oyabun* to fly into a rage not seen so publicly played out before. "Chikuso!" he screamed at passersby as he stormed along Alexander Street making his way to the Hinomaru. His eyes were those of a madman, his body shaking with unbridled anger.

"You ungrateful bastards!" he shouted to no one in particular. "You've betrayed me! Every one of you wouldn't be here if not for me!" His voice echoed off the surrounding buildings. "The risks I've taken! The sacrifices I've made! The money I've spent!" Only blank faces stared back. "Pay me the respect I deserve, you bastards!"

In his office at the back of the Hinomaru, Morii for the moment questioned his power and influence. In frustration, he chewed out a hapless serving girl as he ordered a chicken and *shiitake donburi*. Something's got to be done, he reasoned.

Tatsuo Gomyo, the Consul General, became very concerned at this turn of events. A stern man with a severely nationalistic disposition, he saw Kawamoto by virtue of his union activities and his outlandish newspaper columns as a Communist with anti-Japanese leanings.

"The Nihon Jinkai is run by nothing but a bunch of Reds," he ranted to Morii, who had been summoned to meet privately in the sedate offices of the Japanese Consulate on West Hastings. The *oyabun* nodded in agreement.

"You must take it over, Morii-san. The Japanese here have forgotten what it is to be Japanese."

"Hai, so ne," Morii grunted. *Something will be done.*

"I will be grateful if you do." The Consul narrowed his eyes as he looked for acceptance in the *oyabun*.

"Let me talk to Okamura," Morii said. "He's the weak link on the board of directors. I'll need the right opportunity."

"In the meantime, I will send a declaration to that red board reminding them that the association is under the control of the Japanese Consulate."

"You can do that," Morii said, "but you can also deny permission to the union members to bring their families over."

"Yes. Yes, that's a good idea."

"I'll plant some of my men in there to oppose every proposal they make."

Gomyo leaned back in his chair and smiled. Morii smiled in return, believing he was the right man for the job.

The plans to disrupt the organization were successful. Kawamoto immediately reacted to the pressure from the Consul by stating that the organization was registered in Canada and was therefore not subservient to the Consulate. Gomyo in turn reminded Kawamoto and the board that as long as the Japanese association had the "Guarantor Authority," it was to serve at the pleasure of the government of Japan.

Very little protest could be mounted anyway since Morii's men kept shouting down any plan to do so. The *oyabun's* personal attention soon waned. By that point, he was on trial for murder.

ॐ

Once Okamura stepped down and Morii became president in 1927, the *oyabun* effectively cut ties to the Liaison Council by slowly replacing the old board of directors with his own trusted men. Kaizo Kawamoto continued to fight but eventually gave up and reluctantly returned to Japan in 1933. In the end, Morii not only restored for himself the power to approve all visas, "picture bride" proposals, passports, and even the Japanese Language School system's curriculum ("More Yamato Damashii," he demanded), but he also made moves to acquire control over all Japanese fishing, lumbering, and farming activity in British Columbia – in effect, Morii was well on his way to becoming the most powerful man in the Japanese community, if not the province.

By January 1929, the Executive Committee of the Nihon Jinkai consisted of members that the *oyabun* could count on to extend his influence out from the city to all of British Columbia. Kijiro Tanabe owned several of the fish stores in Vancouver's Japanese sector and had certain deals with the canneries, thus giving Morii control over the affairs of the fishermen in Skeena and Vancouver Island. Tsunematsu Goto held contracts to supply men for several if not all the Japanese lumber camps in British Columbia. The fertilizer merchant, Tokuji Omasa, was a valuable middleman when it came to dealing with the farmers in the Okanagan and Fraser Valleys. All of these mostly anonymous men in the public's eye frequented Etsuji Morii's establishments, the Hinomaru and Showa Clubs.

The Executive Committee usually met late at night, a favourite time of Morii's, down the hall from Morii's Nippon Club office in a fair-sized conference room containing four large rectangular folding tables pushed together to form an even larger rectangular table. Around it the association officers sat in hard wooden chairs and made decisions affecting the Japanese community. Because the lighting was diffused, they looked sullen, washed out, indistinguishable in their three-piece suits, dull, black, and oversized like the *oyabun's*. They were like the fabled fox spirits, secretive and seldom seen but always conspiring in their den. Just the way they liked it.

"There's been a request for us to hire nisei to conduct a survey or two," the asthmatic and skeletal Goto put forward.

"Good idea," the comfortable-looking vice-president, Bunjiro Hisaoka, chimed in. "We need new blood."

"We'll get to that later," commanded Morii. "I've received an important request that the Steveston Fishermen's Association join our association."

"From who? Can't be from Sato, that ketsuno ana," Tanabe observed as he squirmed at the mention of the fishermen's recalcitrant president.

"No, of course not. The request came from our benefactor."

"Well then, how do we do it?" Goto interjected. "Aren't they still on that damn Liaison Council? Besides, there's that kusotare Sato – so headstrong. He won't allow it!"

Morii bent forward. "We'll have to wait for our chance. In the meantime, will the canneries and stores stop taking their fish?"

"Of course," Tanabe nodded. "We'll limit their fishing season to start."

The only organization the Nihon Jinkai did not have control over was the Steveston Japanese Fishermen's Association, which was an irritating thorn in the side of their powerful "benefactor," the Japanese Consul Gomyo. For the privilege of "Guarantor Authority," Morii was obligated to fulfil any wish that the Japanese government and by extension the Emperor requested, especially in light of Morii's suspected use of it during the Yamamoto murder trial in 1921.

The *oyabun's* course of action in dealing with the upstart Steveston association was textbook. Create an obligation and all would fall into place. The opportunity presented itself in short order when the treasurer absconded with the organization's bankroll. He also saw his chance in killing two birds with one stone: force the fishermen to join and replenish his coffers to stave off economic ruin. The only thing Morii hadn't expected was the unyielding and principled president of that organization, Ryuichi Sato.

෴

"You'll do as I say!" Morii shouted in a voice full of blood and rage as he rose to his feet behind his desk in the early autumn of 1930.

"The hell I will!" Ryuichi Sato retorted, his eyes on fire. "My members won't do it!"

"Convince them!" the *oyabun* demanded.

Sato snorted as he grabbed his hat and coat and stormed out of the Nippon Club office. The *oyabun* scrambled up from behind his desk and called for the insolent man to stop, then ran awkwardly after the association president. But Sato had disappeared as soon as he entered the hallway, causing Morii to look in every direction until he heard the man's footsteps nearing the staircase landing around the corner.

"Sato!" he called, holding out a hand to stop him. As he grabbed the oak railing leading to the top of the staircase, he saw his quarry waiting, cloaked in his overcoat and fedora. "You'll do as I say!" he repeated.

"I told you, my members won't do it," Sato said, enunciating every word clearly as he stared down the *oyabun*.

"After what I did for you and your damn association! You don't remember that damned treasurer of yours? I gave you fifteen-hundred dollars of my own money!"

"Bakayaro! You did it so we'd be obligated to you! You didn't do it out of the goodness of your heart!"

"Baka!" Morii thundered back. "You have an obligation!" Thoughts ran through his mind like a swollen river.

"Listen, my men don't want or need to join the Nihon Jinkai and they won't pay you any tribute money, no matter what you did for us. The keto are breathing down our necks with this 'Japanese problem' and you want us to pay you?"

"Forget the damn keto! You'll do as I say."

Sato let out a derisive laugh. "Look at this little man, thinking he's some kind of shogun who can order anybody to do his bidding," he said. "And yet he chases after me like a spoiled brat for his lost ball!"

Blood vessels exploded in Morii's eyes and he blindly pushed with all his might against his adversary. He held his breath as he felt Sato give way and then watched in horror as the man tumbled down the staircase, head over heels, before landing at the foot of the stairs in a heap.

Sato had survived. Why hadn't Yamamoto? Even after the recovery of the money and their president's "accident," the Steveston Japanese Fishermen's Association wasn't going to co-operate and join the Nihon Jinkai. Fifteen hundred dollars! A king's ransom, all for nothing. The lost money had nearly crippled Morii and his organization, there was no doubt about that. The *keto* workers and politicians were blaming the Japanese for their economic downturn. In 1930, "Canadians" began to use the Japanese community, the "Japanese problem," as a scapegoat, even though the Depression was a real threat to everyone in Canada. What irked and astonished Morii more, however, was the lack of respect … the *oyabun* had put out all the expenses to go to Alberta and drag Nakashima back. Then there were the costs of getting rid of him, all on top of the "donation." He somehow met his monthly obligations of tribute to his own *oyabun* in San Francisco while maintaining his business, why couldn't the fishermen's association?

Why had he done it – such a generous outlay? Why did he continue to care? These were the concerns that perplexed and plagued him ever afterwards.

꩜

During the winter of 1935, Morii boarded a streetcar for a part of town where he found no comfort. Vancouver had become a shabby place, still suffering from the ill effects of the Great Depression, but here the closely cropped lawns with the strategic evergreens growing tall and imposing in front of multi-winged stucco and brick houses stretching out in every direction showed no signs of economic devastation. These huge estates were the lines of demarcation that separated his life down in the mire of the Japanese sector from the perfumed and genteel lives of his betters. The residence of the Japanese Consul General was no different from the other homes in the prim and rich neighbourhood of Shaughnessy Heights. The estate featured Doric columns in front with decorative cornices above, and was painted a brilliant white with green window panes to accent the homogeneity. The *oyabun* hated it all, thinking it too British old money for his blood.

Once inside the front double doors, Morii breathed easier as he removed his heavy coat and admired the ornate but familiar pieces of Japanese decor within the echoing rotunda. He could see why his wife always had an ambition to visit, she and her high-*kara* ways. An attendant took care of his apparel before showing the *oyabun* upstairs to the private offices of Consul Gomyo.

The portly man standing behind the huge mahogany desk in the middle of the office had a high forehead with a patch of hair atop, seemingly overdressed in a grey morning coat and puffed-up cravat. He smiled as Morii entered and held out his hand, bowing his head at the same time. The grip was loose and moist, but Morii didn't mind as he sat in an armchair in front of the desk. He surveyed the various artifacts about the room and settled on the Hokusai woodblock prints. They seemed oddly appropriate for the meeting, depicting as they did the tension of humanity dwarfed by the power of nature.

The blue tidal wave stands poised above a boat crew cowering deep within its vessel. The spume blows in all directions; the whitecaps are jagged and enraged. The tiny men are at the mercy of the current beneath which is foaming in its ambition to capsize the boat and to drown all in its watery grip. Hokusai's Tsunami — at the moment between life and death.

Morii took in the symbolism and fancied it as being meant for him, the tidal wave of his misdeeds threatening to drown him — his *karma*. Doubt returned and crept into his thoughts.

"It's good to see you," began the Consul, "It's been too long since we've talked."

"So ne," Morii replied as he turned away from the painting.

"Not since that Sato matter, wasn't it? Would you like some sake?" he asked, not waiting for an answer to his first question. "The best. Comes in cedar casks. You taste the forest in every sip," he rhapsodized as he poured out two cups.

The *oyabun* took in the evergreen aroma eagerly, then took a sip, letting the cool liquid play a moment on his tongue before slipping down his throat. Morii's eyes watered as he squeezed them shut in his euphoria.

"Ah," he exhaled.

"I told you it was good!"

Morii relaxed in the moment.

"I tell you why I invited you here, Morii-san," the Consul continued. "There are things happening that you should know about."

"Oh?"

"In China."

Morii stiffened. "China," he mouthed in a self-satisfied fashion. "Has His Majesty consented to all-out invasion?"

"Well, let's just say there has been movement."

The *oyabun* knew the language of politicians but didn't tolerate it well. "What do you mean by that? Is or is not Japan going to invade?" He tightened his grip around his cup.

"Patience, my friend." The Consul raised his voice a notch. "Do you wish to serve the Emperor?"

"What kind of question is that?" Morii asked, now beyond irritation.

"I'm sorry, of course you do," the Consul said, nodding. "Listen, Morii-san, much will be made out of what Japan does in the next little while. There will be much agitation by the anti-Japanese forces here in *Canada*. Of course, our own people will be useless against them. I've said this before but many of these Japanese here have forgotten what it means to be Japanese. You can best serve by reminding them."

"Like those damn union leaders."

"Yes, but I'm thinking primarily of the young. Youth makes people stupid … well, ignorant of the ways of the world."

Morii nodded in agreement, thinking about the *nisei* on the board of the Canada-Japan Association, as they had renamed the Nihon Jinkai. How he regretted Hisaoka talking him into allowing those *ketsuno ana nisei*, those asshole *nisei*, into the organization. They don't appreciate the old ways when men of his station were to be respected, when the Emperor was to be revered and worshipped above all else. Back in the day, the editor Yamazaki would never have dared to attack him directly; these Canada-loving, British-sense-of-fair-play *nisei* had no idea whom they were dealing with. He had dealt with them well enough, but the *oyabun* was nonplussed at their active criticism of him through editorials in *The New Canadian. Bunch of know-nothing kids.*

"And who can really blame them?" the Consul continued in a conciliatory mood. "Their parents came here abandoning their family, never to see them again and only realizing too late they had given up their security. So they began anew, building a home and a new family, but their children are rootless in this foreign land, disconnected from the homeland. They don't know about their duty to their Emperor. They've no concern for honour. They have no values. It is therefore incumbent upon us, the government of Japan and you, Morii-san, to be as any head of a family and teach them, take care of them!"

The *oyabun* salivated over how he had emasculated the CJA *nisei* just last year. But then the Consul's words soaked in and Morii wrung his hands, relishing the slaughter and domination of China in a holy war divined by the will of the Emperor. The sun rose and burst upon the horizon before him, the aftermath glowing in the hum of the explosion.

Etsuji Morii soon thereafter took to the podium to make speeches.

11. October 1923

Yoshiko opened her eyes to the sparkling stars above. They reminded her of the neon lights of Hastings Street in east Vancouver: fascinating in their mystery and alienating in their distance. But no, she decided in the end, the sky through undulating treetops looked dotted with bright, glycerin tears.

The forest around her offered a vague and diffuse illumination. It was late autumn and, even without snow, the nights had taken on the pristine cloak of winter darkness. There was the kerosene lamp she had brought to the clearing, but it too gave off a dull light, allowing her to see only the dirt underneath her fingernails she had dug up while clawing at the ground.

The air was chilly but the pain at her pregnant core pumped out heat like a generator. A film of sweat covered her skin, especially on her inner thighs and hips. She felt no shame as she hiked up her ankle-length dress to her swollen stomach while taking off her undergarments before squatting down on her haunches. Far above her, the sporadic wails of unseen and faraway beasts brushed the treetops and echoed off mountains miles away.

After several hours of alternatively lying on the ground to rest and then resuming the position, she could smell the crisp evergreen mixing with the pungent prenatal excretions rising from between her legs.

The invisible winds streamed through the darkness like an ocean current. As always, she gave in to it and let go of the chaos, the various distractions and irritations that made up her life. She could now channel her thoughts to the relevant and the immediate.

"Chikusho!" She cursed at her absent husband who had brought her to this fate and had not lifted a finger to help, a fate that settled about her like the mud on the ocean bottom. She considered again her few options: suicide or prostitution. *Jisatsu … joro.*

Clouds puffed out of her mouth as her breathing became short and rapid. "Chikusho!" she screamed as the next surge of pain came over her.

℘

March 1921

The argument in their room at Amitani's Rooming House in Vancouver had continued well into the evening.

"Well it's your own fault," blamed Yoshiko as Jinsaburo slowly wrung the neck of his tormentor and only friend, a bottle of sake. He grumbled something under his breath while lifting his arm to take another drink. The eyes had grown weary, blackened with circles of torture, and his cheeks were swollen. "Someone spoiled my name here," he said.

Confession tickled her lips but she thought better of saying anything. "Maybe if you hadn't gambled away all our money," she suggested instead.

"Gambled? Gambled?" he repeated as he stood up on wobbly legs. "Who said I gambled? I haven't gambled since you got here."

"What?" Yoshiko blurted out. "What did you do with all the money, then?"

"I was paying off a debt."

"What debt?"

"Getting you here, for all the good it did me."

"Why'd you pay so much for my passage? I could've done with a cheaper room."

"Passage? My otosan paid for your passage."

She fell silent with the revelation.

"You bakatare!" he said. "You think I had that kind of money? I didn't even have the two hundred dollars in the bank to prove I could support a wife."

Jinsaburo abruptly pushed her back against the wall, pinning her with his arms. "Well, I didn't have it!" he roared. "I tried for three years to save the money for the bank and to pay for your passage. I had to prove myself! To my otosan! My damn otosan! He guessed the truth about me so he paid for your passage. I couldn't ask for the two hundred too. Too much ... too much. So I tried to get it on my own. But no, the luck wasn't with me. I'd get ahead and then lose it all and then some −"

"You're hurting me!" she cried out as she attempted to pry his hands loose.

He released her and slumped to the table. "So I borrowed the money and I've been paying it off ever since."

She rubbed her shoulders to bring back the circulation. "I don't understand. Didn't you give back the two hundred dollars when I got here?"

"Gone," he said bitterly.

"Gone?" Her eyes widened.

"Every nickel. I thought I could earn a nest egg for us while you were on the boat but no. Never the luck. Never any luck."

"Where did the money come from?"

He poured another drink and sipped it slowly without saying a word.

"Who lent −"

"That's none of your business!" he snapped. "I don't owe anymore, anyway. The loan's forgiven. I guess my leaving town is payment enough."

"It is my business."

"No, it's not!" he shouted and spit in her face as he stood up again. "It's a debt between men."

She cowered and began to sob quietly. "But I'm the one who paid ..." she cried in desperation, only realizing the consequences after she had said it.

Rage flushed across her husband's face for an instant but then he began laughing manically, his voice rising in volume until it seeped inside her, boiling and bubbling her blood in an effort to spew out and flood the mouth of her oppressor. Wolves howled, jackals gleefully yelped.

When the fog rolled in, curling along the city streets early one November morning, Jinsaburo and Yoshiko boarded a small gas boat moored at CP Dock D and left Vancouver. The chugging of the engine shattered the stillness of the air as the boat moved gingerly along the shoreline on its way northward.

Having nothing to say to her moping husband, Yoshiko gazed at the water moving past and felt something slipping away from her.

She drifted at the ever-present urging of the Black Current. Small bits of her broke off like ice floes from a glacier, leaving a trail behind her. A past melting away. Within her, something asserted itself, straining to make its presence known. A child perhaps? Fists of water formed and threw themselves against her causing her to cry out in pain with the impact. The cries escalated into animal shrieks as the pummelling refused to stop. The eyes squeezed shut until they suddenly widened at the shocking possibility of the birth of an oni *child.*

From Britannia Beach, a settlement of small buildings roughly made of scrap wood at the head of Howe Sound, the couple made their way by rowboat farther up the coast to a camp of pitched tents near the shore in an adjacent open field. The largest tent in the middle contained a rough table about twenty feet long and benches to match for dining. The Miyamotos settled into a smaller tent nearby with untreated boards on logs as a floor. There were several beds of straw, wool blankets, and sheets. These were reserved for them and about ten other men.

"I'm not sleeping here!" Yoshiko complained, her breath steaming in the frosted air. "It's indecent!"

Jinsaburo raised his head from his bedding. "There's nothing I can do about it. You don't like it, sleep outside!" he snapped.

Filled with self-pity, she had no more tears. Was a prostitute's life a possibility? Morii's words came back to her: *You must be prepared to live a hard life.* They sounded like a curse. She clenched her teeth, her tightening jaw muscles hurting her face. *Too bad, you're still a pretty one.*

Jinsaburo worked for the crew on the donkey, a huge, lumbering mechanical winch used to haul logs. It wasn't a bad job, but it could be dangerous if the wire cable snapped, whipping in a renegade, snake-like fashion, cutting men in two.

Yoshiko's duties were straightforward. At 4:30 in the morning, she arose to prepare breakfast. She did enjoy the pristine, unspoiled beauty of the landscape, and the clear, frosted air invigorated her for the tasks at hand.

First washing the rice in fresh water, she knew the loud swishing would nudge the men awake. She then cooked a substantial amount of it in a tin can full of water over an open wood fire and served it with miso soup and boiled beans.

After the meal and cleaning the dishes, she went about laundering the previous day's clothing for the entire camp. Early in that season there had been a forest fire, leaving charred wood everywhere, so each day the men came back from work coated in black from head to foot, making the laundry an Herculean task. Into an empty oil barrel, Yoshiko poured water, cut-up soap, and finally kerosene. Into this concoction, she kneaded in the whites, mostly drawers called *dorosu* and undershirts, and brought it all to a boil. She was taught this method after she had once unknowingly washed everything together, shrinking the woollens and staining the white articles of clothing. She covered her mouth in embarrassment but, fortunately, most of the men were in good humour and snickered about it.

She also prepared the other meals. Lunch, and supper too, was more rice and some canned fish (ironic since they were encamped near the ocean). When meat was available, she learned to fry the beef "*gaijin* style," as the men called it. The accompanying vegetables included potatoes, carrots, onions, and cabbage. Because of the crew's taste for salty Japanese flavours, most food was cooked with the sharp-tasting small dried sardines called *iriko*.

Once every two weeks, Yoshiko boarded the rowboat and headed for Britannia Beach to purchase supplies. The town's dress shop, located near the middle of the wooden-plank sidewalk of Main Street, always caught her eye. She usually stopped to marvel at the tailored outfits in the window. The styles weren't exactly the latest fashion (not that she knew), but the dresses were meant for church and social functions. The display reminded Yoshiko of the day, at the age of sixteen, she purchased her first "western" outfit back in Tsuruga. She sighed deeply.

In a moment of whimsy, she walked into the store and twirled into a flowing, green frock. A present for herself. She had worked so hard for so long. She bought it with money set aside for such indulgences. CPR Empress. Hotel Vancouver. "Do I dare? I shouldn't. Mottainai. Why not? I deserve it." She kept it hidden for years.

A few feet down the muddy street was a simple wood-frame building with an abundant display of fruits and vegetables in bins out front. Here at Umemoto's Grocery Store, she could buy the necessary Japanese food-stuffs. On one such grocery run, she ran into someone from her past.

"Miyamoto-san?" asked an astonished voice. "Is that you?"

Yoshiko twisted around and met a stern but friendly face, familiar yet hard to recognize at first. "I'm sorry?"

"I'm –"

"Furukawa-san!" she suddenly realized. She beamed as she bowed in greeting.

"Umemoto now."

"My, my. The last time I saw you was in the crowd on the docks."

"That's right. I was headed for *Prince George* to get married," Nofu explained.

"And I remember he's a lumberman."

"Actually, no. I had that wrong. He owned a store in *Prince George*."

Yoshiko was impressed as she warmed in the comfort of the familiar. There were a few lines here and there, the skin weathered, a few white hairs, but it was the same Nofu Furukawa as back on the *Canada Maru* with her grimace of a smile, gruff tone of voice, and straightforward manner of conversation. Yoshiko appreciated most of all her no-non-sense approach to life.

"That's what I'm doing here. This is our store. The other one went bust. We couldn't get the Japanese supplies up there."

Yoshiko nodded as if that were obvious.

"And you?" Nofu asked. "You own a boarding house here?"

"No...." Her voice trailed off. She lowered her gaze to the table.

"Ah," inferred Nofu. "Well, fortune makes fools of us all."

In the months that followed, Yoshiko looked forward to her trips to Umemoto's. She could at least spend some time with a friend who eventually informed her of her rapidly growing reputation. Word of her cooking skills reached more than a few camps in the area – especially her way with *gaijin* food. Large chunks of beef brisket were a specialty. Soon, other logging companies contracted her as a cook, offering incentives like a private cabin usually made of split cedar logs for her and Jinsaburo. One camp even had a fully equipped mess hall and a bath house. She became so much in demand that the longest the couple stayed in one place was three months. This didn't matter much to Jinsaburo, whose work seemed the same no matter where he went, but for Yoshiko the money was better with each successive camp.

Even though prosperity smiled upon her, she considered every job demeaning no matter the number and quality of the amenities. She surprised herself when she thought of how comparatively easy the work was on the Miyamoto estate in Japan. She also couldn't stand the plague of insects; mosquitoes, black flies, and horse flies came in waves during the summer, tormenting all in their path. The tiny bugs constantly buzzed about her head, periodically causing her to wince with their biting and stinging. Never again would she complain about the mosquitoes by the rice paddies back home. *I can see Akiko crying all the time here!*

"Ganbatte nasai!" was all the sympathy she received from the lumbermen. Yoshiko really didn't care for the rough, insensitive men who swore all the time and slobbered over their food. Compared to them, her husband seemed like the young gentleman she had briefly met at the Three Sisters Café all those years ago. It didn't mean she had forgiven him for his own brutish ways, every slight, insult, and caustic rape festering within her, but here in the wilderness, he could be ignored, even controlled.

Once, a runt of a man approached her carrying his spent drawers in his grubby hands. "Oi, okusan, don't forget my dorosu!" he said. When she realized he was only wearing an undershirt and nothing else, she averted her eyes, but the memory of his flaccid penis lingered for months.

On a rare bright and warm spring day in 1923, Nofu took her friend Yoshiko out for some tea and pie at a local café. The red checkerboard tablecloth was too fancy for Nofu, but Yoshiko delighted in the touch of civility.

"The life is hard, but the money is steady," Yoshiko said, just as her blueberry tart arrived.

"I hear you're doing better than when I first bumped into you," Nofu confided as she poked at her apple pie. "Maybe you could cook here," she joked, as she gestured toward her surroundings. "I'm sure you can bake just as good!"

"If only I could just cook, but these camps!" She frowned as she thought about being on her knees as she cleaned each cabin, with a bucket of soap and water in one hand and a can of kerosene in the other.

Nofu scoffed. "I'm sure you're saving lots of money for that boarding house in *Vancouver*."

"Well, I don't let Jinsaburo drink or gamble, that's for sure!"

"Good! Wasteful habits," she said forcefully. "Damn baka men."

Yoshiko's spirit seemed to fade when she thought of the chores waiting for her back at the camp. "The work is so much, I feel sick in the morning."

"You do?"

"Been so for weeks, it seems," she confessed. "Bringing up most mornings. Oh, I'm sorry. This is not appropriate conversation," she added, her cheeks flushing slightly.

"Miyamoto-san, you may be working hard, but that morning sickness isn't because of it."

"No?"

"You should see Dr. Maruno here in town."

"Why?"

"I think you're pregnant."

The suggestion shocked Yoshiko into silence. Nofu's bluntness never bothered her before but this speculation was too much. Anger flared within her, but she refused to give in to it. Blowing up at her friend would serve nothing. Yoshiko tried to avoid the subject by proceeding to eat her blueberry tart, the sweetness reminding her of better days.

"Oh, I've upset you," Nofu observed.

"No. No, you haven't," she stammered. "You have children, I understand?"

"Yes, two boys."

"Boys! Good for you. Someday I'll have boys."

"Maybe less than nine months from now."

"Oh, don't say that!" she blurted out, visibly upset. "I can't give birth in camp! It's so dirty!"

"Now, now," Nofu comforted. "Don't worry. Once you're ready you can come to town and the doctor will take care of you. There'll be plenty of time."

Yoshiko lowered her head to hide the tears.

"I'll be here to help, I promise," Nofu added. "I'll tell you all I know about giving birth. You'll see. Everything'll be all right. Everything will be all right."

In the weeks that followed, Dr. Maruno confirmed Nofu's guess. Yoshiko, who broke into curious crying jags during the quiet moments of her day, was pregnant. The idea of caring for a baby while working in the wilderness terrified her. How would she manage her chores, plus the added responsibility of a whining child? The fact that it was Jinsaburo's also gave her pause. Her only recourse was to have a perfect delivery, without pain, resulting in a perfect baby. She would expect it, she would demand it. Canada owes her that much.

"A son!" beamed Jinsaburo. "I'm going to have a son."

"I don't know that."

"A son," he said firmly.

She let it go. "I think we'd better move back to *Vancouver*," she suggested.

"Back to *Vancouver*?" Jinsaburo asked coarsely. "We have a contract here."

The Ikebata Logging Company was small but well paying, and the cabins were roomy and fairly clean. As well, Old Man Ikebata provided good food for his fourteen-man crew. On Sundays, he went off alone early in the morning, never telling anyone what he was doing. There was endless speculation about him: *He's gone to town by himself again. He's gambling somewhere. That old man's got a woman.* Finally, he confessed to Yoshiko what he was up to.

"I paddle out in the morning fog to a secret spot," he said. "It's beautiful out there. So quiet, I can hear myself think. I row out to my secret spot where I throw sticks of dynamite into the deep waters. There's an explosion, and then dead fish float to the surface. I scoop them up in my net and then get outta there lickety-split so I don't get caught by the Mounties, and come back to give 'em to you."

Yoshiko imagined the small rowboat emerging through the lingering mist above the water, like a ghost ship coming to take her home.

"But I have no doctor here," she complained. "Not even a midwife. You'll have to take me to Dr. Maruno when it's time. I'll try to hold on."

"I'll do no such thing. The boat's for important things. It's nothing to give birth!" Jinsaburo said bluntly.

Yoshiko stared at her husband in disbelief before a wave of hot blood welled up in her, her eyes burning with a damning intensity.

October 1923

Her final scream harmonized with the baby's first cry. Yoshiko collapsed, exhausted but mindful of the child lying somewhere beneath her. She struggled to see her newborn in the lantern's dim yellow light. The crying drew her hands toward it until finally she grasped it and brought it to her breast. It appeared shrivelled and ghastly in appearance like the mythical *kappa*, troll-like creatures that dwelled beneath bridges.

Having a baby had been her dream, something she hadn't indulged in a long time given her situation. Perhaps a baby was the answer. Perhaps everything would be all right. Perhaps in Vancouver, having a family will lead to happiness ... damn her husband, he could stay in the wilderness forever for all she cared. Her time was about to begin, and that meant Vancouver with a dutiful child on which to pin all of her hopes and dreams.

Yoshiko could see the steam rising from the child's muddy body, as if its soul were escaping from it. With a free hand, she drew a knife out of a pocket and held it close to her baby. Her mind suddenly flashed to Jinsaburo's callousness; he was off somewhere up the trail to the log-clearing area. He had only thought about himself, as usual. With no other woman in camp and the men totally useless in such matters anyway, she dragged herself, out of embarrassment, into the woods when her water broke. Twelve hours later, she gave birth.

A girl. I will teach her. She'll stay with me ... happy with pretty dresses, city life, education maybe. She'll do well in a gaijin world.

She remembered Nofu's instructions as her fingers, stiff in the cold, slowly tightened around the handle of the knife. Carefully she cut the umbilical cord and let everything but the baby fall. As soon as she did, Yoshiko felt a heavy exhaustion come over her. Even with the baby crying almost frantically, she could not remain awake. In her fading thoughts, she concentrated on the distant stars. She thought she heard voices calling out her name while she felt the presence of circling foxes.

12. Thursday, March 14, 1940

Etsuji Morii unexpectedly recalled the ruby red button the woman had been fingering nervously while sitting before him in his office last Monday. The colour conjured up for him her full lips before the rest of her·face fell into place: the high, rounded forehead that disappeared into the sheen of her tightly drawn, grey-streaked hair, the dark eyes moist with sadness, the luminous skin inviting a touch. Her body fit comfortably inside her plain, worn-out dress that strained slightly here and there with hints of her voluptuousness.

Her one unattractive trait was the slight bend of her back. She had aged, he remembered thinking at the time. He tried to gather all his recollections of her as he stood at the southeastern corner of Powell Ground near Jackson and Cordova. The "Miyamoto woman" had become more than an irritant to the *oyabun*; she was now almost an obsession. The implications of her suspected lies made her a danger to him. Everything told him to back out of this case. But would his world really come crashing down around him if she were given over to the police wolves? He thought about deportation, but her disappearance would create so many questions that even the intrepid Sgt. Gill couldn't answer. Against his better judgment, he once again gave in to his nature: he was compelled to help her.

It was raining slightly but his long trenchcoat was sufficient protection. That and his trademark bowler. Across the street, several policemen were swarming in and out of the Miyamoto house like ants in service of the queen, their cars strategically placed in front to discourage gawkers. Members of the adolescent basketball team, the Purple Seven Gang, who usually after their weekly game sat on the front steps of the neighbouring church gymnasium (known communally as the "Japanese gym") were hustled away, told to go home. The rain normally would've inspired them to leave, but this was too good to miss. Instead of heeding the police, they milled in the park across the street observing the outward signs of trouble.

Morii had arrived too late to have that visit he had promised Miyamoto-*san*. *Those kuso keto!* He knew giving the police the bartender wouldn't work for long, Aki's *gaijin* wife with the impossible name being his alibi, but who had put them on to the Miyamoto woman?

They couldn't have known about her lover, Okihara. Rikimatsu had told him the *kusotare* was nowhere to be found. He had definitely skipped out of Vancouver, probably heading for California. Morii sent a word of inquiry to San Francisco as a result. So what was going on in the Miyamoto house? By the look of it, it wasn't a routine visit to question her about her dead husband.

Yoshiko had aged, he thought once more as he continued his rumination, but that was to be expected given the hard life her husband had condemned her to. Still, she remained a beauty. That useless husband, he concluded. He had spent two hundred dollars to reform the bastard. It was all for nothing now. The *oyabun* cast his mind to the time Jinsaburo had made application to get married.

§

Jinsaburo Miyamoto had come to the Immigrant Committee of the Nihon Jinkai to petition for permission to bring over a bride in early 1920. He was a small-time gambler on the periphery of Morii's watchful gaze, just another ne'er-do-well destined for penury by way of the *fan tan* tables in Chinatown basements and hideaways.

"Oya ... Oyabun, I am here ... formally ... as a man ready for marriage," Jinsaburo said, standing with hat in hand and nervously aware of his surroundings and of whom he was addressing.

"You are how old, Miyamoto-san?" asked the shadow of the labour contractor for the lumber companies seated at the corner of the table.

"What's age —"

"Don't raise your voice here!"

Suddenly he felt a hand on his shoulder. He turned around to look straight into a devil's skull with brown and broken teeth, warning him to watch his step.

"I ... I merely asked ... I'm thirty-two."

There was a chuckle and a few skittering words, like conspiratorial whispers, amongst the unsettled spirit shadows around the table.

"So you want a bride? How much do you have in the bank?"

"Ah ... well –"

"Do you have enough to bring over a bride and then support her?"

"My otosan is willing to pay –"

"Otosan? I thought you were a man, not a boy!"

"My otosan will pay for her passage and papers," he concluded.

"How much in the bank?" another voice insisted.

"Nothing. Am I right, Miyamoto-san?" concluded yet another shadow. "Why do you gamble so much? You gamble away your chance to be a married man."

"Where do you gamble?" asked the *oyabun* softly from the centre of the table.

"Why, at your club," he stated with the confidence of knowing the right answer.

The hand came down again, this time crushing his shoulder with its forceful impact. He buckled where he stood.

"Not enough to lose all your money!" the *oyabun* thundered. "You go to those Chankoro places, don't you? You kusotare!"

Jinsaburo, on one knee, cowered before his betters.

Another stepped in. "You must have two hundred dollars in the bank. You must prove you can support a bride. That's our requirement. Too many of our young women are preyed upon by boke-nasu like you!"

"It's useless. How's he going to care for a wife?" asked yet another. "He's old and he betrays his own all the time."

"Yoshi. I'm going to put my faith in this ass. Perhaps I can reform him," declared the *oyabun*. Many scoffed in a chorus of disbelief. "Miyamoto-san, I'll put two hundred dollars in the bank in your name," Morii continued. "This will make it possible for this committee to approve your petition, but you are then obligated to me. Understand? Don't ever betray me!"

Jinsaburo could do nothing but nod in agreement.

"You'll pay me back with interest, of course," Morii added. "And you'll never again go down to Chinatown to gamble. Do you hear me?"

Again, Jinsaburo nodded.

"This man is weak," Morii said dismissively. "Rik-san, take him and get him set up with a job at the Raku Raku. Nothing important. Cleaning the toilets, maybe. At least, I can make sure he lives up to his obligation."

꙳

Morii turned away from the activity in the Miyamoto house to recall Jinsaburo's case without distraction. Of course, the miscreant couldn't stay away from Chinatown, and he paid for his transgression. Early one evening, two weeks before his bride was to land in Vancouver, he was intercepted in front of one of the Chinese gambling dens by Rik-*san*.

His skeletal face hard with rage, the *yojimbo* dragged Jinsaburo by the left ear back to Powell Ground. There, the powerful and unrelenting Rikimatsu proceeded to beat his victim to a pulp. He made sure he broke the man's nose first, the outward, visible sign of his punishment – a warning to all who considered disobeying. Once Jinsaburo fell to the ground, Rikimatsu then began kicking at him.

The entire time, neither said a word, did not even make a sound. Both knew the reasons behind the beating. Onlookers turned away; only the young and foolish stayed to watch.

Morii also said nothing of the incident or the betrayal. Instead, he had waited for an opportunity to settle the account in full.

A sudden bang brought the *oyabun* back to the present. The police chased a few of the Purple Seven Gang who had been leaning against a police car. Morii smiled as the overweight policemen slipped on the slick ground while the boys, who knew all the shortcuts and escape routes throughout the Powell Street area, shimmied quickly over back-lane fences.

The *oyabun* became pensive over the memory of the frightened young bride brought before him by his own wife maybe fifteen years ago. *What was I supposed to do?* he thought at the time. *So her husband was stealing the money out of the savings. Typical. Maybe he had a right to. What was that to me?*

But when he heard the husband's name, he realized it was time to even things out. The *bakatare* wasn't going to learn anything from the intermittent beatings he ordered. He'll always gamble with the *Chankoro*. There was only one answer: exile to a hard life in the Interior.

The *oyabun* had no second thoughts about what he had done. Jinsaburo Miyamoto was made to pay for his weakness, and maybe he had learned his lesson. *Karma, the result of deeds done in life. Too bad, she was a pretty one.*

In the end, it was all for nothing. Jinsaburo was dead, and what of the once young bride? Was she in custody? For murder? Was she trying to get in touch with her lover? Did the police now know what only a few had known?

⌘

Monday, March 11, 1940

Seated in his office, Morii waited as Yoshiko drew in her breath and casually let her eyes drift to the ceiling fan rotating above. She then squeezed her eyes shut and began telling her story.

"I met him at the Three Sisters Café. Last October." She paused. "Okihara Koji, my ... my friend." She paused again. "Oh, I know what kind of place the Three Sisters is," she confessed with a kind of resignation. "But I go during the day, the afternoon. They have blueberry tarts there ... It reminds me of a small ryokan in Yokohama. Seems like a hundred years ago now."

Morii appraised her faded red dress. Surely she didn't want to wear such a rag in public. It was old, out of fashion, but the glass beads as buttons helped, he thought. *Her smooth skin — manju brown and smooth.*

"Okihara-san was there one day, second stool from the left. I remember exactly. He was so handsome, like a movie star! I know you don't understand such things in a woman. But I tell you, he made my heart flutter when I saw him. He's from *America*. A salesman trying to make a new start in *Canada*. I smiled at him. I know I shouldn't have, but I couldn't help myself.

"Yamada-san must've known something was up because she introduced him to me! Teased me about him too! Brazen woman! Well, he bought me my dessert and he suggested we meet sometime ... to talk! Just to talk.

191

"So I did. To talk. I had never met anyone like him. I could say anything to him and he listened. He listened. So different from my husband.

"We became ... became ... I'm so ashamed to say. I can't say it."

Morii was surprisingly patient, perhaps guessing her secret indiscretion.

"We became lovers," she finally confessed, which seemed to relax her. "I don't know how it started. It just did. But I felt alive! If only...."

She paused again, even longer now, even though she seemed happy to unburden her secrets to the *oyabun*. He leaned in closer to capture the moment.

"Much later, we were in his room when I heard what I didn't want to hear. Mariko ... my daughter ... at the doorway. I don't know what she was doing there. She's supposed to be in school. She knows not to go into a boarder's room when occupied. My daughter just stood there, giggling at us like an idiot. I ran for her ... to explain – but she ran away and tripped over the carpeting. Those oversized shoes of hers! She fell down the stairs and broke her neck. Dead."

The *oyabun* leaned back in his chair. He didn't let on, but he was taken aback by her description of the event. She spoke as if the death, accident or not, was nothing.

"I thought of going to the police, but they'd hang me for murder. Damn keto-jin...." Yoshiko's voice trailed away.

"Who said anything about murder?" Morii asked.

"I ... I ... only meant –"

"And Okihara-san, where is he?" Morii asked, letting the question go.

"Gone. He took the body and disappeared. I don't know where."

"Do you want me to find him?" he asked, as if testing the waters.

"No ... no," she said, then shook her head. "I mean yes, yes, please ... bring him back!" she cried out.

But Morii ignored her plea. "It sounds like it could be called an accident."

"Oyabun, I can't live without him!"

"You can't live with him!" he repeated. "Not here. Not now with all the gossip that would go on."

"I don't care what people say. I can live with the shame."

"Bakayaro! There's a lot more at stake here than your bloody reputation!" he jeered, then turned his back on her. "Shame!" he scoffed. "You have no idea what's happening in the world, do you? You and your kind live your shitty little insignificant lives doing whatever the hell you want." He turned to face her again. "You leave your mess for me to clean up. And do you appreciate me? No. No." Morii took a breath. "You laugh at me behind my back. Well, understand, whatever I do I don't do for you. You mean nothing to me. You could bring...."

The *oyabun* stopped suddenly. It was her eyes, staring with the look of death at their centre. There was a total lack of grief over her only child. *Killing is so easy. Only sixteen. So easy.*

"Please help me," she pleaded, wringing her hands before him.

Three days later, Morii recounted their meeting. He knew that she had lied, but how much? What was the truth? Questions, questions unanswered, irritating questions buzzed about his head. He only knew they would not be answered standing in the park watching fat police officers tripping over themselves looking for evidence. What really stayed with him was her lack of emotion over a dead daughter. *Did she murder her own daughter? How much was Okihara involved? What was her useless husband's role in all this?*

At this point, he didn't know how much he could help her, the situation was that much more serious. Ever since the Steveston Fishermen's Association's defiance and the reformation of the Businessmen's Association in the mid-1920s, the *oyabun* had started to doubt his own influence and abilities. He knew these Japanese didn't understand his methods and could turn on him in an instant.

That evening, Morii decided to talk with Sgt. Gill again.

The usual quiet of his Nippon Club office seemed to be taking a long time to settle. Morii could hear the police still at the Miyamoto house filtering through the walls into the hallway. At least, he imagined he could. Or was it the martial arts tournament at the Japanese Hall across the way? He had been scheduled to perform his masterful sword demonstration but had begged off.

His back erect in his black kimono. His family crest discreetly displayed on his robes, proclaiming his noble lineage. His face a study in total concentration. He tenses his arms as he draws out the long, shimmering blade, the fading sunlight from windows catching it for the rapt audience. He rotates it to a position atop one arm. The opponent materializes, barking a challenge. He pays no attention to the arrogant words, targeting instead the shoulder, the neck. The eyes squeeze to concentrated slits. The sword rises and attacks, biting flesh. Blood splatters, his teeth clench, his muscles tense upon impact. The body falls to the floor but it is he who feels the pain. Cold steel, sharp grey steel, cuts him from unknown directions. He reels, but the thrusting and stabbing continues unabated. He falls to the ground and covers himself. The black, silken cloth rips, exposing his flesh that turns into a bloody pulp the next moment. He is slowly torn apart. His life slips away from his body and drains into a pool.

"They wouldn't buy it, Mr. Morry. I'm sorry." Sgt. Gill sat stiffly in the chair. Even though his head was held in place by the crisp white collar of his shirt, he managed to convey a sincere disbelief as if to say that he was just as surprised as the *oyabun* at the police department's reluctance to accept his word. "They didn't want Aki anyway. They wanted you. I told you such that night."

Morii raised an eyebrow slyly. "Why they let go?"

"Not enough evidence, again as I told you at the time."

"Why not Aki? Was it his wife?"

Sgt. Gill paused. "There's been a second murder."

"*H-h-hei*," said Morii, an elongated utterance of astonishment. He decided it imprudent to reveal what he knew for the moment.

"The Miyamoto daughter, Mary. She hadn't reported to school for a few days. A Mrs. Langley, a teacher at Strathcona, inquired at the house, but was sent away. When she reported the truant child to the authorities, word eventually got to the police. Some young eager-beaver detective at the Cordova station connected the father and daughter."

"That is why they at house," Morii said, careful not to show his hand.

"That's why they're at the house," Gill echoed, for no particular reason. "And one more thing. The daughter's body? Found in the furnace."

"*Iyarashii!*" Morii grimaced in horror. The more he learned, the more impossible it all seemed. His mind worked quickly. "So police think *oto-san* ... er, father ... kill daughter?"

"A possibility," Gill sniffed. "But then who killed the father?"

"Where is mother? Miyamoto-*san*?"

"At the station. The police tried to question her but she was in shock and her English is not good. They're holding her until they can find an interpreter. Probably question her tomorrow."

"They think it is she who kill husband … or daughter?"

"I don't know," Gill said. "Do you think it's her?"

"No, no, no," Morii protested. "I must protect Miyamoto-*san*."

"Why? You like her?"

"*Nani?*" Morii asked.

"You know, kiss, kiss." Gill puckered his lips, making himself look ridiculous.

"No, no, no," Morii repeated. "She is *Nihonjin*."

"That's what I really don't understand about you, Mr. Morry. Why you stick up for these people. What's in it for you?"

"I am loyal to *Nihon*," he declared proudly. "I protect our people. No bring shame. It is my duty."

Sgt. Gill let out an audible sigh. "Mr. Morry, you don't know the poor, do you?"

The *oyabun* looked at him quizzically.

"The poor don't care about honour or country. There's no respect, no gratitude, only contempt for people with money or power. Believe me, I'm from Cabbagetown. Back east, in Toronto – a very poor part of town. My family lived in an itinerant workers' row house. All six of us," the Mountie emphasized. "Father was a drunk. Mother's heart gave out working three jobs to keep us in the cabbages the area's famous for. I hated the rich, but they taught me one thing: I learned to scratch and claw for everything I ever wanted. Honour's not going to put clothes on your back, food in your stomach. There's no loyalty among the desperate.

"These poor Japanese you're so concerned about won't appreciate your help. Oh, they'll take it and bow and fuss before you just like you want, but they're just waiting to turn on you – to pay you back for your … help. Take my advice and forget them. Look out for yourself first."

"*Giru-san*, we help Miyamoto Yoshiko, *ne?*" Morii asked, ignoring his friend's admonitions.

Sgt. Gill snorted. "I'm sorry, Mr. Morry, I can't help you there."

"*Nani?*"

"In fact, I can't help you anymore. I've been promoted and trans- · ferred," Gill revealed. "I'm going away to a better job."

"*So ka*," Morii said when he understood.

"My superiors in Ottawa seem to think I know a lot about the

Japanese!" Gill grinned ironically. "By the reports I send them."

Morii nodded.

"The Phony War in Europe is bound to become a shooting one here, and who knows how far it'll spread. With this trouble in China −"

"Trouble? Those *Chankoro* are to blame! *Nihon* is their master in all ways! Look at Nanking! They so weak. They must learn −"

"Take it easy, Mr. Morry! That's my superiors talking. I'm not a political man ... just an expedient one," Gill offered. "And I think deep down you're one too. That's why I can't understand −"

"*Giru-san*, you help little bit with Miyamoto, *ne*?" Morii interrupted, ignoring what he didn't understand.

"Okay, okay," he laughed. "I have a week or two before heading east. I'll do what I can."

"Make sure no blame here."

"What?"

"No blame here with *Nihonjin*."

"But that's impossible. Somebody has to −"

"No blame!" Morii was adamant.

"All right, but I'll need lots of boxes."

"Boxes?"

"Of chocolate."

Morii laughed at the shared joke and shook his friend's hand.

13.

"The child is useless," Yoshiko said out loud to no one in particular. *Urusai.* Maybe it was because it was born without a doctor, in the middle of the night, in the deep woods. Maybe something went wrong and Yoshiko hadn't noticed, since she had lost consciousness just after cutting the umbilical cord. Good thing the men in the camp came to her aid shortly afterward. The baby had been saved, but there was something wrong, something that Yoshiko couldn't reconcile or forgive.

Useless. Jinsaburo was useless as well. He had begun to drink again, because illegal stills were going up all over the backwoods. Apart from considering his complete callousness toward her plight while giving birth, Yoshiko hated him for his moronic face sagging in inebriated indifference to the child, even after it was cleaned up and nursed to health. The child was not a son, after all.

But even as time went on, Yoshiko could not warm to Mariko, her daughter, either. The child did not look like the "perfect baby" she had come to expect during her pregnancy. It had been the only way for her to tolerate the fact of giving birth to Jinsaburo's child. Disappointment hardened her, deepened her bitterness. Her so-called "family" made a mockery of her dream. She often neglected the child's cries while wringing her hands white.

For Mariko's part, she was a child of no remarkable talent and had an uneventful childhood except for the two times she nearly drowned. The first incident occurred when all toddlers begin to explore their landscape.

In 1926, the family was living on a lumber raft up the coast near Alert Bay. The weather was calm and cool for an early summer day. Jinsaburo was with the crew cutting down timber deep within the wilds of Vancouver Island while Yoshiko was frying fish for dinner on the expansive raft of gigantic logs moored near the shore. Searching for adventure, three-year-old Mariko wandered outside the cabin, intrigued by the vast wonderland of forest and inviting water. While teetering on the edge of the raft, she fell in head first.

When she heard the splash, Yoshiko's maternal instincts kicked in, cutting through the sizzle and smoke of the cooking fish. She dashed out of the cabin just in time to see Mariko flailing about the surface and leapt in to save the child.

"Da-me! Da-me!" Yoshiko screamed at Mariko when safely back on board, despite the nauseating taste of sea salt in the mouth and down the throat.

The child's cry escalated to a wail trying to deal with her own shock.

"No good!" Yoshiko insisted, and began to strike her naughty daughter with an open palm to the face.

The violence of crying and hitting continued unabated.

The second incident happened four years later, in 1930, in early spring on another day filled with warmth and the promise of better times. The Miyamotos had moved into a seaside cabin in Britannia Beach temporarily while Jinsaburo negotiated their summer work contract. The small two-room cabin was functional and clean, a feature Yoshiko appreciated, having returned from a three-month stay at a camp of canvas tents at the northern end of Vancouver Island with only the winter-hardened ground as a floor. She had really resented what felt like a step backwards in her life in Canada and had let her husband know it – constantly.

Mariko, then seven years old, often played on the back porch that overlooked the bay. She loved to climb and had done so many times on the crooked, driftwood railing, balancing herself with arms stretched out, in bare feet, her eyes mesmerized by the horizon.

Kame, kame, kame-san. Kame-san yo. Oka! Oka! Look what I can do! I'm not so dumb. Look what I can do! I can climb a mountain!

That day was no different. Her parents had spent the morning bickering as usual. Lunch came and went, as did her father. Her mother washed up, loudly banging the thick, olive-trimmed chinaware plates. Mariko gazed across the water to the distant Vancouver Island, its trees so green in the brilliant afternoon sun that looking at them hurt her eyes. She imagined great waterfalls deep within its mysterious forest depths.

Almost instinctively, she then had the notion to climb the wooden railing again. Standing erect on the narrow beam, she felt confident and exhilarated while adjusting her body with every shift of the loosely fastened fence. She especially liked the feel of the knots against her heel. Then suddenly she heard from behind her an guttural, unearthly sound. She jerked her head around to discover that a seal had climbed onto the porch and was barking at her. Startled, she lost her balance.

Again her mother came to her rescue, but this time the fall was more serious. Mariko had wounded her head on the rocks in the shallow water, her blood mixing with the algae and seaweed. As she became submerged, Mariko's cotton dress with periwinkle violets absorbed the black water, rapidly darkening it. Fortunately, Britannia Beach had a hospital, where she was revived and treated.

When Mariko awoke in her hospital bed, she saw the look on her mother's face, a look of disappointment and disgust. The money, both spent and lost, the bother, and the humiliation of having to depend on others, creating an obligation. Despite her injuries, she just wanted to hide away under the sheets of her bed. The incident, however, proved to be an advantageous opportunity.

"We are moving back to Vancouver," Yoshiko declared shortly after Mariko was back on her feet. She glared defiantly at her husband as she announced her decision – she would not be dismissed or denied this time.

Jinsaburo was at the table, hunched over his homemade sake at the eating table. The news, though not totally unexpected, bothered him. "But I just signed us on with Kagetsu for the summer. Do you know how lucky we are to have a contract?" he said. "Times are getting tough for us Japanese. We need the money."

"So you can drink us into ruin!" Her eyes flashed as she steadied herself against the expected blow.

"Damare!" he yelled. "I give you all the money and you know it!"

"And it's a good thing too or else I wouldn't have any future!" she shouted, though she knew he had lied. "This is no place to raise a child. We've got to get back to civilization," she insisted.

Jinsaburo snorted, damning their child under his breath.

"Years ago, you promised me a boarding house," Yoshiko continued. "Now I have the money and I will own one. You can work for Kagetsu if you like, honour the contract. But I'm going back to Vancouver ... for Mariko's sake," she added, knowing that too was a lie.

Anger coloured his face red before he finally relented and nodded wordlessly.

By November of that year, Yoshiko and Mariko had moved to Vancouver, away from the rugged conditions of the logging camps, away from the rough-talking men, away from the seductive water constantly conspiring to pull the child into its depths. Yoshiko was ready to begin what was surely going to be a fairly decent life, even if the streets were filled with the unemployed. She had heard the rumours of violent clashes between these men and the police, but that was between the *keto*, nothing to do with the Japanese, nothing to do with her.

Yoshiko checked into Taniguchi's Boarding House, where she had first lived all those years ago. Perhaps it was the dull weather outside with its cold winds and rain-pregnant skies, but she thought the place hadn't changed in the last ten years. The same drab, caved-in furniture, the same solemn, anonymous hallways. She put a hand to her breast as she recalled the events of what he called their "wedding night." The violence at the Patricia Hotel. The hurt position her body took on the floor of the boarding house – after the beating, after the rape.

Don't let him take away your dignity. Her mother's words. Her throat constricted and tears streamed forth as she lowered her head, the hand dropping to the lap. Her body drained of vitality. Something made her look up to see her daughter staring at her with a sad, long face from the chair across the room. The idiot, she thought.

"What're you looking at?" she snapped at Mariko. *You ugly cow.*

She turned away in frustration as Mariko's lips quivered and her eyes grew wet. While constantly clenching and unclenching her hands at the thought of Jinsaburo, Yoshiko hoped he would just stay in the camps and never return to Vancouver, to his "family" with a child who was "not normal" and a wife who wished him dead.

Oka, Mama, what did I do? Why do you hate me? I know I'm ... stupid.
Not pretty like you. I'm sorry. I wish I was never born.

Within the month, she and Mariko moved to Amitani's Rooming House for the cheaper rent and then began her search for her own place. Years of working in the lumber camps had given her the money to live on at Taniguchi's, but Yoshiko wanted to live frugally since she was determined to take her time in finding the right property.

She quickly found a job as the cook at Taniguchi's, actually replacing the ailing Ebisuzaki-*san*. Her reputation as a cook in the wilderness had preceded her to Vancouver.

Fortunately and uncharacteristically, Jinsaburo also sent money from time to time. Not a lot, but enough to pay her rent and a few bills. Perhaps he was a changed man and wasn't wasting every dime on drink, she thought. He stated in a letter that jobs were few and far between, but he preferred the nomadic life and so not to expect him anytime soon.

Despite feeling relieved and maybe even a little hopeful, Yoshiko opened a bank account, just in case.

It took about five months, until the spring of 1931, but she was finally able to find a good-sized house for sale on Jackson beside the "Japanese gym." She quit her job as a cook and went to her *nisei* banker, who cautioned against the purchase during such a time of growing unemployment and racial unrest, but she was in the money, because of her savings, and the prices were down.

Although the upstairs rooms seemed cramped, she decided they could accommodate four boarders. The kitchen was spacious, but the stove looked inadequate to cook meals for her tenants if they paid for the service: thirty-five dollars a month with meals, twenty-five without. She would make do, she decided. She always had.

The exposed rafters in the front living room were an attractive feature, and she noted the convenience of the addition in back: two storage rooms off the kitchen. She and Mariko could have a bedroom each and the porch area just outside could be used immediately to take in laundry to make money while she advertised for boarders.

With some secondhand furniture, the place soon took shape. A nice touch was the white-linen cloth on the dining room table and, nestled in the middle, a teapot with four matching cups, a pale-green set with gold trim. The wedding present had lost some of its lustre, the colour faded to a near shade of white, but its mere presence lent an air of civility to the boarding house.

After finishing with the arranging of furniture and decorating the dining and front rooms for the day at least, Yoshiko relaxed with some tea, the soothing hot liquid tasting different in her Bachan's teacup. Like the sweet, fresh taste of Japan – of home, of family.

She relaxed, feeling satisfied as she mulled over her only concern: the unspoken feeling that she had moved into the house of a hanging girl.

That night. The first night. Smoke seeped through the floorboards and filled the house. With it came an eerie howling. Yoshiko arose from her bed and blindly groped her way from the kitchen through the hallway to the front room. The white smoke was thick, impenetrable. She tripped while looking for the door and fell to the wood floor with a hard thud. Above her, the smoke parted to reveal a girl's body hanging from the rafters.

Blood dripped from her blank eyes, running down her face to her shoulders, down her arms and off her fingertips. The red drops covered Yoshiko's brow, cheeks, and ran off her chin. Slowly the girl's face elongated into the bizarre shape of a fox of all things. A snarling, teeth-baring fox.

Yoshiko screamed with a wide-open mouth but emitted no sound. Her tongue stained red, she screamed again and again.

In 1935, not yet twelve, Mariko had taken on the initial adolescent signs of beauty. The hair had grown in thick and shiny, and her complexion gave off a glow, warm and inviting. Her breasts began to sprout and her legs grew long, muscular. Yet there was something in the shape of her face that conveyed something odd. The slight asymmetric position of the slitted, empty eyes, the crooked turn of the nose, and the droop of the mouth burdened with thick lips made her look like … an idiot, according to some people.

Mama, why can't I be as beautiful as you? I want to be perfect. I want you … to love me. Oka? Why?

So it came to be that Yoshiko would not let Mariko out in public except for school, only allowing her to go because it was the law. The suggestion of mental illness upset Yoshiko to no end; it was the ultimate stigma, so humiliating that no one could ever talk about it openly. It receded into whispers and gossip, like that which surrounded Crazy Iizuka in the park.

Everyone's suspicions must have been confirmed when her daughter fell behind two years at school (she started a year back and then failed a grade in her effort to catch up). *Kawaiso ne? Poor child, she's not right in the head.*

Yoshiko also put her daughter to work in the rooming house. By this point, she had no vacancies with four tenants; again, her reputation as an excellent cook born in the wild attracted the business. Despite the desperate times, there was a continuous stream of boarders, some for short stays, others much longer, depending on their situation. There was much work to be done as a result. With Mariko's help, however, Yoshiko did find some time to enjoy herself.

Chan-to, chan-to, chan-to. The familiar rhythms of the folksong "Tokyo Ondo" chimed through the hot, humid August night, and the dancers in their bright kimonos moved in concentric circles around Powell Ground, their choreography as graceful as leaves falling from trees. It was Obon, the Buddhist festival of the dead, and Yoshiko revelled in the memories.

Obachan, you never left Japan, never deserted your family. I never should've left. The hanging girl torments me nightly. I am lost, perhaps I can only come home as ashes scattered upon the back of the Kuroshio. I offer incense to you. The Buddha is always near. Within the smoke, He will reach you. Namu Amida Butsu. Namu Amida Butsu. Namu Amida Butsu.

She hadn't gone to *omairi*. What was the point? She had no relatives buried in Canada. She remembered how bored she was during the cemetery visitation on the mountainside in Kiyama. How she craved to feel that boredom again: with the comfort of her entire family surrounding her and the feeling of continuance with the sea of grave markers before her, many with her family name printed on them.

At least she could enjoy the *Bon* dance. The exaggerated movements of the *kaporei* dancers made her laugh. The jutting jaws, the pointed hands, the outstretched legs snapped into position by swiveling hips. Their moves were filled with exuberance, especially Fukushima-*san*, a shrunken old man from Kagoshima who had the look of the simpleton about him. The regal Kawamura, on the other hand, in his navy blue kimono with gold leaf fan, moved smoothly from position to position in the sophisticated Tokyo style.

The creeping shadows of evening brought out the glow of the *cho-chin* suspended on wires webbing the park. The crowd roared its encouragement of the *taiko* players in their pounding and the *shamisen* musicians in their strumming. The respected Nakatsu-*san* sang in her high-pitched voice, competing with the shrill insistence of the *fue* players as her dark kimono of maple leaves and wind fluttered to the beat. ·

Yoshiko felt the flush of happiness come over her in the light atmosphere of the park. No feebleminded child embarrassing her time and time again in school. There had been more than one occasion when that *gaijin* teacher had called her in for "a talk," a talk she never understood. At least during the summer, Mariko remained at home, away from prying eyes.

Here there was no worthless, drunken husband and none of the pressures of running a rooming house. Around the outer circle, Yoshiko expected to see one *odori* dancer in particular who would make the evening perfect.

The young woman, whom she hadn't seen since last summer, would probably be dressed in a white and purple kimono, decorated with persimmon leaves, dancing gracefully, no doubt, with determined concentration, her hair done up in a pretty sweep around her head with hanging adornments atop and to the side, and her face powdered white and highlighted by dark eyebrows and crimson lips. Yoshiko looked for her – her cousin, Akiko.

ॐ

Obon 1934

Akiko Hayashi had married Etsuo Watanabe shortly after her cousin Yoshiko had left for Canada in May 1920, in an elaborate ceremony, perhaps the most elaborate Kiyama had ever seen. It was assumed by the villagers that the Watanabe patriarch was overjoyed to have someone marry the second of his nearsighted sons. But no one could confirm such a rumour, especially since it sounded like a joke.

The cherry blossoms seemed to fall in the path of the bride. Her dark kimono and pristine-white *tsunoka kushi* upon her head glistened in the bright sunlight. Her lips, moist with the colour of passion, were set in a field of purity symbolized by the white powder masking her face. Great quantities of delicacies made lovingly by the hands of so many female relatives lay invitingly before the awestruck couple. The myriad guests were suitably impressed.

Akiko lifted her eyes to the heavens and thanked the Shinto gods for their blessing and then shed a tear or two for her favourite cousin lost in the wilds of a *gaijin* world.

It wasn't quite two years later when Akiko and her husband boarded the *Manila Maru* bound for Canada. It had been impossible for Akiko to inform her cousin since Yoshiko herself had not written to anyone in Kiyama or Mihama. In her naiveté she thought nothing of it, feeling secure that she would just run into Yoshiko soon after she had arrived in Vancouver.

The truth was she and her husband lived in Steveston, a fishing village far enough away from the city to make coincidental sightings unlikely. Etsuo, despite his nearsightedness and bulbous nose, was a studious man with a keen sense of business, which allowed him to become in quick fashion secretary on the board of the Steveston Fishermen's Association. Although not entirely handsome, his intellect and compassion made him quite attractive to Akiko, who depended on her love to quash the rumours that her husband had attained his position through flattery. For her, he possessed a certain confidence that told her they would be prosperous in the long run even if they had to move to foreign soil. They're just jealous is all, she reasoned.

In the meantime, Akiko, in her relative isolation in Steveston, a town that reminded her greatly of Japan, had one day referred to the Vancouver Japanese telephone book put together by the *Tairiku Nippo*, checking for a familiar name amongst the boarding house owners, but to no avail.

After a time, she forgot about finding her cousin.

The air was heavy with humidity and flies buzzed about persistently. Luckily, the breezes came out with the evening darkness. It was the time of Obon and the community forgot their troubles temporarily. The federal and provincial governments were passing laws to prevent the Japanese from prospering at the expense of the "true Canadians," during this time of economic depression. That no longer mattered, at least for this one night; they came together to celebrate the immutability of change.

Akiko prepared her kimono for the communal Bon Dance in Vancouver's Powell Ground. She was part of the group representing the Steveston Buddhist Church dressing upstairs in a private room of the conveniently located United Church (used by special permission for the overflow dancers). Others dressed in the Buddhist church at Cordova and Heatley.

A chartered bus had taken the group to the park in the east end of the city, which the Buddhist Church members had decorated with a lattice of paper lanterns strung on wire. Kaburagi-*san*, the well-known carpenter's oldest son who had taken over the business after his father's mysterious disappearance, had built a covered pavilion, a *yagura*, raised to overlook the anticipated crowd in the middle of the dirt field, and set up a public-address system powered by a gas generator underneath the structure.

After the quick service in the park led by the amiable Reverend Ishiguro, the *odori* dancers took their places. They represented several groups from all over the area: Steveston, Vancouver, New Westminster, Fairview, Kitsilano, and as far away as Marpole, Abbotsford, and Haney.

The musicians stood poised over the taut *taiko* skins, the *fue* were placed to the lips, and the *shamisen* hummed with anticipation. Even the pesky flies seemed caught frozen in the moment. Then a downbeat, and the music began. The Bon Dance was set in motion.

It was in the first turn of the great circle of dancers that Akiko heard a familiar voice.

"Akiko-chan! Akiko-chan!"

She broke her concentration to look into the nearby crowd. Amid the blur of faces, one emerged with startling clarity. It was Yoshiko.

"Yoshiko-chan! Yoshiko-chan!" she squealed as she waved to her. The older dancers behind her scowled, but Akiko didn't care. She broke away and ran awkwardly, the *kimono* binding her legs together.

In a matter of moments, she embraced Yoshiko. Remembering Japanese convention, she self-consciously disengaged and bowed deeply several times. "Yoshiko-chan, I've been trying to find you!"

"You have? I've been right here," she laughed as her face beamed in the lantern glow.

"You never write," chided Akiko as the two walked away from the celebration, reunited at last.

They entered the community hall of the United Church beside the kitchen where the ladies were preparing a light, refreshing meal of *somen* noodle soup for all the performers and volunteers after the Bon Dance had concluded. The two cousins sipped tea at a wooden table as they caught up with each other, talking of events both recent and long past. Largely because of her kimono, Akiko sat demurely with legs held tightly together. She could see that Yoshiko had taken on the hard appearance of a life of labour, but something of her girlish personality remained intact. Despite the thin streaks of grey, her hair seemed as black as the night they had first talked about coming to *America* and her eyes appeared utterly happy, though devoid of the innocence of youth.

"So you have your boarding house," Akiko said with almost a sense of relief. "Your family?"

"Oh, my husband is on Vancouver Island somewhere. He comes in from time to time when a contract is up and he has to wait for the next one."

"You must miss him terribly," she said without irony.

Yoshiko noticeably shifted.

"Any children?" A smile cut across Akiko's expectant face.

"Yes. She's ten, almost eleven."

"A wonderful age. Where is she?"

"Not here," she said abruptly. "She's sick. Back at home."

That didn't sound convincing to Akiko, but she let it stand, deciding not to pursue it in case she caused her cousin uneasiness.

"How's ..." Yoshiko began, then stopped herself.

"How's what?"

"How's the family back in Japan?"

Akiko looked away. "Well, the last letter I got, everyone was all right."

"My family?"

Her cousin squirmed uncomfortably. "You don't know, do you?"

"Know what?" she asked with trepidation.

"Your okasan. I'm sorry, Yoshiko-chan. Your oka –"

"Died?"

"Two years ago." Akiko looked askance as she saw grief come over Yoshiko. Between the two cousins, a quiet sorrow descended.

Okasan. *The nervous, tender eyes. The soft hands. The curve of her back.*

The perfume of her so near while she told a bedtime story. So warm, so comforting. Goodbye. Goodbye.

A familiar voice came drifting in through the open street-level windows. Both women, grateful for the distraction, turned their attention toward the grounds. Hisaye Furuya had taken the microphone and began to sing "Defune" ("Departing Ship"), the latest popular song to come from Japan.

"Such a wonderful voice," Yoshiko sighed sadly. "Come, let's go."

Akiko could not help but follow. She herself loved the song and admired the young singer, who had a natural talent and an imperious air about her. Hisaye Furuya held her head high and looked down upon the crowd as she sang.

As the two cousins stood in front of the pavilion, they listened blissfully as a sense of nostalgia came over them.

> *This evening, as the ship leaves,*
> *I watch with tear-stained cheeks;*
> *the snow is falling on the dark waves.*

The song's melody absorbed them. Sitting so close together, the two cousins both felt the warmth of family surrounding them. The years shrank to nothingness.

❦

Obon 1935

The lyrics and minor-key melody came back to Yoshiko on the wings of a gentle, dark breeze. She thought about the years since her own ship had set sail. The *cho-chin* paper lantern light flickered in the cooling wind that swept across the night sky. There was also hurtful laughter to be heard.

> *Kuroshio-san, have you betrayed me too? I saw you flow into this land — this land of white devils, cruel husbands, and harsh life. I thought it a good sign. Yet I am cursed with a child ripped from me, damaged by birth. The Black Current engulfs but does not purify.*
>
> *Maybe Okasan was right. "Why do you want to go to such a place?*

There's nothing there but devil men and obake women. Only gaijin live there."

They had promised each other to come visit one another. They had promised to introduce family members and be close once again. But neither had kept that promise in a year, so Yoshiko watched with great anticipation for Akiko to come around in the circle to her. But she was not there. She never appeared.

☙

In the darkest part of the boarding house, deep within its shadowed recesses, Mariko sat huddled in a corner, the palms of her rough, stubby hands rubbing her eyes hard. Her body shook with undefined sorrow. She released her hands and began tearing at her hair, the long, matted strands shredding easily. She closed her sore eyes tightly and then tipped over with her face flat on the floor, her arms behind her back, sobbing profusely.

Most of the chores had been completed but incompetently. The floors had been washed and polished with great areas missed. The beds of boarders made clumsily. The dishes more or less clean. Piles of laundry remained, not only the household's but also those of customers taken in for extra money. She knew her mother would beat her when she returned that evening after the Bon Dance.

"Naniyo?" Her mother's voice cried out in dismay late in the evening, her seething anger reverberating throughout the house. "Mariko! Mariko!" Yoshiko shouted at the top of her lungs. "Where is that useless child?"

Mariko pulled her legs back underneath her as she cowered beneath the staircase. Doors opened; furniture was pushed aside. Somewhere from out of the darkness, her mother roughly grabbed Mariko's wrist and dragged her out into the open space of the hallway.

She screamed as her mother pulled her over her lap and pulled down her *dorosu*, exposing her pale, white buttocks. A lump then caught in her throat and her eyes spiked with horror – she had heard the rasp of a match igniting.

"Yaito!" Yoshiko screamed. Mariko felt nothing for a second but then the pain of concentrated fire at the tip of a lit incense stick to her skin

209

exploded her senses. The smoke of burnt flesh and incense curled into her nostrils. *The Buddha is always near.*

Mariko shrieked a trapped animal's plight.

Mariko's only escape from her home life was at Strathcona School, a large, gothic-like elementary public school constructed of red brick, with gargoyle flourishes about the eaves and a catacomb of hallways inside. She made no real friends, but there were those who were kind to her – Hanako Kagawa for one, who had sat behind Mariko since the third grade. From time to time, they walked home together.

"Next year should be a good one, Mariko," said Hanako just before the start of summer vacation. "Grade five. I can't wait!"

Mariko said nothing. Seldom saying anything at the best of times, talking about school was particularly embarrassing because she should have been going into grade seven. Starting late and failing a grade had kept her back. She was particularly aware of the age and height difference between her and her classmates and therefore spent a lot of time just listening to the talkative Hanako.

"This summer it'll be the same old thing. Working at my parents' store. Probably going on a trip to Salt Spring to see my cousins. What're you doing?"

Mariko winced at the expectation to answer and closed her arms in on herself. She knew what the summer had in store for her.

"Oh, you'll be at the boarding house," Hanako said in lieu of a response. "I'm sure you'll find something fun to do."

Strathcona was Mariko's escape, but it was not a sanctuary.

During the preceding school year, Mariko had Mrs. MacGregor as her fourth grade teacher – a tall, middle-aged woman with severe looks made even more severe by her pulled-back hair and horn-rimmed glasses. Although Strathcona's motto was "The School with Many Nationalities but Only One Flag," Mrs. MacGregor did everything in her power to make her classes truly "Canadian." With the school population about eighty percent Japanese, she felt it was her duty.

"Line up," she commanded one day. She stood at the front of the classroom, ruler in hand, surveying her students like an overseer.

The young nine-year-olds nervously obeyed by standing before the front blackboards with the line reaching around the corner to the tall windows.

"Hands up!"

Immediately they stuck their hands, plump and innocent, up in the air. Their breathing became heavier in nervous anticipation. Mrs. MacGregor slowly walked along the formation, letting her eyes roam over the extended palms, her ears attuned for any comment.

Suddenly Mariko stepped forward, her legs pressed together, one palm still out. "Missus? Missus? I must go *shi-shi*!"

Mrs. MacGregor glared and rushed forward. The ruler came down swiftly, striking the base of Mariko's thumb. "No Japanese!"

Mariko pulled her hand back, instantly nursing it with the other, and trembled. Mrs. MacGregor then proceeded to hit each and every student in line. "No Japanese will be spoken in this classroom!" she thundered.

Successive students held back their tears despite the impulse to cry. Then a sudden, guttural groan drew everyone's attention to the end of the line. Mariko stood shivering with pain and shame as her teacher gasped at the sight. She had wet the floor.

14. Monday, April 1, 1940

Etsuji Morii smoothed out the newspaper flat on the wide, rectangular table in the board room of the Nippon Club building. It was late at night as usual and cool with a heavy spring storm outside. Morii had withstood the lethal rain, but the needle-sharp raindrops had soaked him through to the bone. In his still-damp three-piece suit, he read the paper quietly in the shadow of the dull light. He strained his eyes as a consequence, but the words before him were easily guessed at.

Although the black and white photograph accompanying the article of interest was grainy, he could make out some of the *keto* faces. There were two interrogation officers present as was the coroner, a man Morii did not know. The others stood with their backs to the camera.

The *oyabun* read the article, deciphering much of the detail despite the complicated use of English.

CORONER'S JURY FINDS JAPANESE GIRL IN FURNACE WAS MURDERED
Verdict Rejects Police View Mariko Miyamoto Killed Herself

After deliberating for more than two and one-half hours, a coroner's jury indicated that Mariko "Mary" Miyamoto, 16, the Japanese girl whose body was found in the furnace of her home early in March, had been murdered.

"She came to her death as a result of multiple blows to the

head and body, same having been brought about by some person or persons unknown to us," the verdict read, after an inquest which occupied eight hours on Friday afternoon and evening.

Despite the fact that Detective-Inspector A.S. Hann and Detective A. Gibb, who worked on the case, expressed their personal convictions that the girl had committed suicide, the jury rejected the theory and reopened the mystery death.

After much questioning through an interpreter of the mother, Yoshiko Miyamoto, who could not speak English, little light was shed on the case. No motive for either murder or suicide was adduced during the hearing.

In a bizarre coincidence, the father, Jinsaburo Miyamoto, was found dead in the CP railway yards, stabbed three times and then decapitated by a passing train, a day after the daughter's death, but any connection to his daughter's death has been ruled out. Investigators have concluded he fell victim to foul play. He was a known drunk in the Japanese area.

Three residents of the boarding house at 232 Jackson Avenue agreed the girl was normal and healthy, had no enemies, and no apparent reason for doing away with herself.

Evidence of Inspector J.F. Vance, police scientist, and detectives indicated the furnace was cold when the girl's body entered it through an aperture measuring 13 inches by 10. They noted that the victim's chest and shoulders, where her clothing contained rapeseed oil, were severely burned, while the remainder of her body, including her hair, was not touched by the flames.

Dr. W.A. Hunter, coroner's physician, who conducted the autopsy, said he found the skull and cheek bone fractured and both arms broken. To the jury, he expressed the opinion this could have been self-inflicted while the girl struggled in the heat of the furnace. "If you believe the suicide theory," he added. "Of course, it's more likely someone attacked her."

Inspector Vance explained that analysis of oil found on the girl's red sweater showed it to be similar to a half-gallon can of rapeseed oil, used by Japanese for cooking and religious purposes, which was later found in the house. He said unburned matches found below the body in the furnace were of the same type as other matches in the home, and that a safety pin used to tie a sheet of oil-soaked paper to her sweater was similar to other pins in the house.

Running shoes worn by the dead girl had slight traces of rust on the soles, the rust corresponding with that on the top of the water pot below the furnace door, he said.

Rapeseed oil, the inspector declared, is not a volatile oil but is a substance that burns slowly with intense heat. Marks of burning on the body followed the course of the oil on her clothing.

Yoshiko Miyamoto, the distraught mother of the girl, discovered the body and consulted with community leaders before revealing her discovery to the police who had gone to her boarding house to question her about her dead husband. Throughout the proceedings, she stated emphatically that her daughter was in good health and normal mentally.

Although Japanese witnesses were unanimous in describing the girl as cheerful and in the habit of playing with other children, Inspector Hann said his investigation indicated the girl was not allowed out of the house except to attend Strathcona School. He suggested that she had to work in the household from six in the morning until school started and until late at night after school ended. After she helped to prepare dinner and washed the dishes, he said, she had to launder clothing and knit sweaters.

– *The Daily Province*, April 1, 1940

Morii sighed, then slumped in disappointment. His last chance to divert attention had failed. The police detectives had failed Gill. Gill had failed him. He had failed Yoshiko Miyamoto. Koji Okihara had failed her – and she had failed Mariko. All seemed relatively unimportant, except for the fact that he had in all probability failed his community, the Consul General, and perhaps even the Emperor himself. He wondered if he really didn't deserve the respect, tribute, or redemption he so craved. The Miyamoto incident had the potential to bring down all the Japanese.

The police would surely continue the investigation until a murderer was found. Thoughts raced through his mind. *If they don't arrest that* damned Miyamoto woman, he reasoned, *they could turn on me as Giru-san's "fall guy." Should I put them on to Okihara?*

He also feared that any probe of the Powell Street area could turn up all sorts of things. Just what they wanted. But then he remembered a piece of advice he had recently given. *This is not the time to think of my reputation.* His duty was clear: he had to prevent everyone from the corner grocer to the Emperor himself from losing face. But could he do it? The question joined the swarm of questions buzzing about his head. He knew what failure meant.

Dressed in pure white judo-gi, he sat cross-legged before the sun, preparing for it to explode. He loosened the canvas belt and exposed his midriff. He looked up at Rikimatsu and nodded to him. The yojimbo raised his sword.

The Japanese don't know half of what I do for them, Morii considered. Could this be the end? The thin edge of the wedge. My community, my world ruined by one weak woman and some greasy gigolo?

Out of the darkness, he aimed his gleaming knife at the fleshy part of his abdomen.

For a time, his initial plan had worked. Sgt. Gill had approached the police investigation unit assigned to the case with thick envelopes of money – the infamous "boxes of chocolate," for those in the know – and was apparently successful.

෴

Monday, March 18, 1940

Shortly after the grisly discovery of the girl's body, detectives Hann and Gibb announced to their superiors and to the newspapers that Mariko Miyamoto had committed suicide. When pressed for further details, they concluded that the daughter, isolated from society, had felt severely guilty and humiliated over doing so badly at school. They also cited the many occasions she had disgraced herself in front of her classmates and teachers. In a state of depression, she had pinned to her sweater a piece of blotting paper soaked in cooking oil and climbed into the furnace with matches. "The Japanese have an acute sense of honour. Apparently they can be driven to ludicrous lengths to get rid of any sense of shame," Detective-Inspector Hann opined.

When Morii first heard the explanation the Friday before Hann and Gibb's announcement, he blew up at Sgt. Gill.

"*Jisatsu*? Are you ...," said Morii, struggling for the right word, "*kichigai*?" He was obviously distraught and incredulous over this turn of events and poured himself his third shot of Canadian Club whiskey.

"If you mean suicide, Mr. Morry, that is precisely the reason I suggested." Gill answered calmly, even though he had rushed to the Showa Club, perhaps unwisely, directly after the police had interrogated Yoshiko Miyamoto that Friday morning.

"You think she put self in furnace?" Morii scoffed.

"What I think is irrelevant. You don't know the Occidental mind except that you should know the police don't understand the Oriental mind. But they think I do. I simply told them what you've told me on several occasions. Orientals would sooner commit suicide than live with shame. So believing the girl killed herself is no great leap of the mind, especially after I found out certain things from her elementary school teachers."

Morii remained unconvinced.

"It was the only way I could think of to keep the police from suspecting and hauling in other Japanese," Gill explained.

The *oyabun* simply grunted, then downed the rest of his whiskey.

"They released Mrs. Miyamoto."

"They let her go?" Morii said.

"She's home now."

Suddenly Morii erupted with joy and grabbed the bottle by the neck to pour Sgt. Gill a tall one. And before drinking, he stood up and danced a little jig, much to the surprise of the good sergeant.

Hann and Gibb's story was faithfully translated in the Tuesday, March 19 edition of the *Tairiku Nippo*. Sgt. Gill had done it! Morii was so delighted with himself that he headed for the little house on Jackson during the anonymity of night and, despite the hour, knocked on the door. Questions about Yoshiko's husband, Jinsaburo, still nagged him.

After a time, a tentative, frightened voice came from inside. "Who is it?"

"Miyamoto-san? Morii desu." He tried to sound lighthearted.

The door creaked open slowly, and Yoshiko peered around the edge.

"Miyamoto-san!" he exclaimed as he held up the *Tairiku Nippo* in front of her tired, shrunken face. "I'm sorry about the late hour, but while I was reading the newspaper, I remembered I had promised a visit to you."

The door opened wide as the triumphant *oyabun* entered and removed his overcoat and derby to hand to his reluctant host. Her face sagged in the dim hallway as if the very shadows weighed upon her. There were many sleepless nights under the eyes, and the body in that premature stoop he found unattractive had grown frail. Her feet shuffled along the frayed carpet as they sat down in the front living room.

"You see. You see, Miyamoto-san, your faith in me has paid off!" Morii boasted. "The police won't bother you again."

Yoshiko remained silent, her head down, her hands limp in her lap.

"My people have found your ... friend, Okihara Koji."

Life suddenly sparked in Yoshiko's eyes. "Where? What have you done with him?" she asked, her voice pleading with an edge of both desperation and accusation.

Morii rose to his feet. "In *San Francisco*. The bakatare was in the Naniwa-ya, my oyabun's bar, bragging about his adventures in *Vancouver*. He was easily spotted."

Yoshiko slumped further into the sofa. "Can you bring him back?" she asked despondently, as if she already knew the answer.

The *oyabun* turned his back on her. "He can't come back here or stay in *San Francisco*. He'll be taken care of."

Yoshiko fell to her knees and grasped at the leg of Morii's pants, almost clawing at him. "Bring him back!" she screamed. "Oyabun, I'm begging you, bring him back! Please, bring him ... I live with ghosts here."

"Naniyo!" Morii shouted. Her manoeuvre had nearly knocked him over. He pushed her away, only to have her crawl back and grab him once more. He pushed again and she fell against the sofa, dissolving into tears.

Morii stood over her, his mouth tightening. "Funny thing," he said, "that boke-nasu says you killed your daughter and your husband."

A glint of fear entered her eyes.

"You did kill her," he continued. "What else can I believe? You show no concern for your daughter ... your only child. All you want is that kusotare Okihara."

Yoshiko shook her head. "No, no."

"Then tell me what happened. Tell me or so help me...." Morii hands curled into fists.

"We were in bed together around noon," she began slowly, her voice meek. "After finishing ... finishing our lovemaking. But then she came in with that stupid look on her face!" she said, her voice rising, almost spitting with venom. "That stupid, stupid look. I'll never forget it." She turned away. "What was she doing home ... in the middle of the day? Why did she have to open the door? I heard her giggling and I ran after her. I couldn't let her tell anyone. She's so stupid, she would've easily.

"She screamed and ran. That kuso child. That urusai, useless child. She ran to the top of the stairs, tripped and ... fell down the stairs." Her story finished, her emotions subsided to a monotone again.

"You pushed her?" Morii asked. *Sato's body in a heap at the bottom of the stairs.*

"Maybe I pushed her ... maybe ... no. I don't know. I just knew she was dead," she said. "Koji ... he was the one who said we had to do something. If the police were called, everyone would know about us and we would face the hangman's noose. He was the one who came up with the furnace to get rid of the body and the plan for someone else to take the blame.

"Late that night, well past midnight, Jinsaburo came home ... drunk as usual. He was bleeding from fighting. After he fell asleep in his bed, Koji came out of hiding and stabbed him until he was dead. Don't you see? That way I could say Jinsaburo did it ... take the blame for everything and all our troubles would be taken care of. He was a useless drunk ... you know. After it was done, Koji took Jinsaburo's body and some money from me, and told me to wait for him. And so I have, ever since."

Morii squinted at her, trying to glean truth. He was shocked by her candor, as well as her lack of remorse. "So you're saying Okihara killed your husband?"

"Yes," she said with finality.

So easy to kill, maybe even to murder. He felt the urge to punish her but he soon realized that wouldn't exact justice. He could see she was wallowing in her own hell, her eyes vacant, her body beaten down. *Such is her karma.* The light within her seemed to have faded to a flicker. Maybe that was punishment enough.

"Thank you ... for telling me," he said awkwardly, not really knowing what else to say. "I know it wasn't easy. Don't tell anyone ... especially the police," he advised. "So you understand, Okihara-san cannot come back."

She was obviously not listening, gazing instead at the ceiling above them. Morii couldn't help but look up himself. From one of the beams dangled the frayed remains of a rope. He shook his head and the image disappeared. An illusion. He immediately dismissed it as insignificant.

"Miyamoto-san. Miyamoto-san!" he said, trying to get her attention. "Did you hear me? He cannot come back!" he repeated emphatically. "Why do you want him? He's a gigolo and he duped you, don't you realize that? And you played the fool so well."

Jolted out of her stupor, she stared at him, not understanding.

"He used you to get money and sex. He didn't love you or even want you."

Her lips trembled, "But he was looking for a job —"

"A job? Why would he look for a job when he had a fool like you to pay his bills, to buy his clothes, to feed him with all your good food? To give him a place to live, rent-free? Don't you think Soga-san would've hired a man like him in a minute to be a floorwalker at his store? Don't you know he worked for a time for my oyabun in San Francisco? Why do you think such a man would come to this hick town?"

The questions rained upon her as she pleaded. "Oyabun! Oyabun," she repeated, sobbing all the while.

Morii, usually intolerant of female frailties, held back his anger. "You should feel lucky you're not going to hang for this," he advised. "The police won't bother you anymore. Do you understand that? Get it into your head, we cannot bring him back. He's gonna disappear," he said ominously. "Forget him."

Yoshiko stopped crying and retreated into herself again. Morii sensed a moment of vulnerability and took advantage. "You should appreciate what I've done for you," he said. "I could've been the one in jail, charged with two murders, I still might be. Are you aware of that? Are you?"

She didn't respond.

"You are obligated ... to me. Consider how to fulfill that obligation." He continued despite her vacant eyes. "Sometime, maybe next year when this has all died down, you will sign over this house to me as a token of your gratitude," he said as a matter of fact. "And you can come to work for me at the Hinomaru. You'll get an apartment, token rent. You're a bit old but I've always thought you're good looking. Still not bad. You can dye your hair, put on makeup. And stand up straight! Make you look young again. Maybe you can manage the place for me.

You're good at running a business. Goodnight, then."

From the hallway as he donned his coat and hat, he looked back at the open family altar, the *butsudan*. Pressing his hands together in *gassho*, Morii bowed quickly and muttered the *Nembutsu*. Before turning to leave, he looked at Yoshiko as if to say one last thing. Her mouth was moving, emitting no sound. He shivered at the sight of a ghost. The *oyabun* shrugged, letting it go, and with a skip slammed the door behind him as if he had just won something.

⌘

April 1, 1940

All bets were off with the announced autopsy on the 22nd of March, the Friday after Detectives Hann and Gibb had proclaimed their conclusions. Things were made even worse when Morii read the results of that autopsy in the April 1st edition of the *Daily Province*.

"Oyabun, I think you oughta read this," Rikimatsu said as he held up the offending newspaper.

Morii did a double take at the headline and grabbed the entire paper. He didn't want to read it there in the Showa Club, reopened the week after his release. Instead, he quickly butted out his cigarette, quickly downed his *biru*, and headed for the door.

"Oyabun? Oyabun?" Rik-*san* called. "What'd it say?"

"Nothing!" Morii scoffed. "Take care of the place." He knew his *yojimbo* couldn't read English but had recognized the photograph. After entering the street, he headed straight for his Nippon Club office. He needed time to think and understand the implications of what the newspaper article said.

CORONER'S JURY FINDS JAPANESE GIRL IN FURNACE WAS MURDERED
Verdict Rejects Police View Mariko Miyamoto Killed Herself

He just knew it – that suicide story was just too ridiculous to believe. You'd have to be pretty stupid to swallow that one, even if you are a *gaijin*. But what were his options now? Sgt. Gill, transferred to Ottawa, could no longer help. *Rikimatsu, Moriyama, Tanaka? Aki?* No one, in fact, to turn to. One thing he was convinced of was the fact that the police had written off Yoshiko Miyamoto as a suspect. He had been told she gave a convincing performance during the interrogation, speaking in a garbled Japanese, screaming out of control from time to time.

Morii stood over the boardroom table surveying the newspaper article and shaking his head, incredulous at the events of the last week. *Her daughter dead, her husband dead, and all she cares about is that worthless Okihara. Her daughter just sixteen. I saved that damn woman's life. She should be grateful to me.* His mind flashed once again to the young Yamamoto in 1921 – he was only seventeen. *Why shouldn't I give her to the dogs?*

Koji Okihara had been taken care of by the Black Dragon Society in San Francisco. He would never be seen or heard of again. The sacrifice of one silly woman's sanity was worth the elimination of such a threat to the Japanese community. Besides, there were several women in San Francisco who wanted revenge in their own way. They were the reason Okihara was in Vancouver in the first place. Morii's *oyabun* could not turn down so many women's requests for justice.

At one time, Okihara had worked as a messenger for Hideo Kameoka, the *oyabun's* fat *yojimbo* in San Francisco, but his taste for the finer things in life soon drew him into the life of a gigolo, preying on the vanities of petty, vulnerable women. Eventually, his smooth ways got the better of him and he had to flee town.

But who to hand over to the police? Did Okihara truly kill Jinsaburo as Miyamoto-*san* had said? And was it really his idea about the furnace? Did it really matter? Morii knew the police needed someone, a "fall guy" as Sgt. Gill once said. *Okihara? Can't risk bringing him back. He's dead. He knows too much. Too much scandal. The keto newspapers would have a field day if they had the chance. Miyamoto Jinsaburo? Did it really matter which?* Both were beyond the clutches of the law. *Could it be me? How about Rikimatsu?* He chuckled at his own joke, deciding on what had become the obvious choice.

After a time, Morii noticed the lateness of the hour and imagined the office shadows on the walls undulating like waves over his consciousness. He smiled, knowing this Miyamoto woman's salvation would go a long way in getting what he wanted above all else. He will have done his duty and not suffer the indignity of failure or the consequences. *Namu Amida Butsu.* Black waves broke above a current, an unrelenting current running along Powell Street.

15.

On a clear day in 1935, Yoshiko learned through the Buddhist Church grapevine that her cousin Akiko, had given birth to twins. If such were true, then it was understandable why Akiko had not tried to contact her in the year since Obon, or so Yoshiko reasoned. On the other hand, she had no desire to see her cousin with her children. The thought of bearing witness to domestic bliss percolated in her stomach. Her only consolation was the fact that both babies were girls.

She remained at home, making no attempt to get in touch with Akiko, intensifying instead the torment of her own daughter whenever she thought of her two anonymous and therefore idealized nieces.

"You useless child!" she screamed at Mariko, who had scrambled underneath the first-floor stairs seeking refuge.

"Not my fault, Mama!" she protested, her hands webbing her face in an effort to disappear.

Yoshiko clawed at her with a broom. "Ahotare! Can't you do anything right?" She lunged demonically at her daughter with all the strength she could muster.

Mariko's misdemeanour did not matter; Yoshiko was beginning to take pleasure in meting out the punishment.

Fate, however, soon turned once again. On a cold, blustery day during the winter of 1939, Yoshiko sent Mariko to Union Fish to buy fresh rock cod for dinner.

"Don't let anything happen to the package!" Yoshiko threatened with an intense glare on her face.

Mariko shook her head vigorously. "No, nothing will happen," she said meekly.

"Just try to do this right. I called Okazaki-san, so he knows you're coming," Yoshiko said as she wiped her hands on her soiled apron before reaching into her pocket.

Mariko ran to the door in an effort to obey right away.

"Bakatare!" Yoshiko cracked.

Mariko stopped in her tracks and looked back.

"You forgot the money," she said, holding out her hand.

Mariko inched back, pulling her flowered dress material tight with one hand while reaching out with the other. In one swift move, Yoshiko gave her daughter a five-dollar bill with one hand and a slap to her face with the other. "Get your coat on! It's freezing out there."

Mariko ran to the door, choking back tears while holding a hand to her enflamed cheek.

She'll be the death of me, Yoshiko intoned to herself. Mariko had forgotten her overcoat.

About a half an hour later, Yoshiko noticed that her daughter had not returned, a ten-minute errand at most. The rice was just about ready, the vegetables prepared. She knew her boarders would be arriving home shortly, expecting dinner.

"That useless child," she said. *What am I going to do with her?* she pondered as she hurried down the hall toward the front room. From the *butsudan*, she selected a long incense stick and matches and laid them out on the coffee table as she sat down on the couch to wait. *A yaito will teach her. Maybe two.*

There was a rustling at the front door. She rose to her feet and prepared to confront her errant child. The blind, wooden door refused to open. She swore under her breath as she decided to expedite matters and fiddled with the stubborn knob herself. When she finally succeeded in opening it, her words caught in her throat.

"Naniyo?" said a familiar if startled voice. "Do you scare everyone who comes to the door?" Jinsaburo, dressed in denim work shirt, lumberman's jacket, thick wool pants, and boots, all heavy with grime, stood in the doorway with a tattered leather valise resting beside him on the porch. He appeared weary, his face sullen, weather-beaten. The residue stains and odour about him spoke of a recent drinking binge, which, no doubt, caused him to teeter on his feet as he held his stomach, indicating upset.

"You're back," she said coldly. She was not about to offer her husband any help because of his maladies.

"Aho! Of course I'm back. And none too soon." Jinsaburo staggered into the hall and threw off his plaid jacket. "I've heard how you're frittering away all my money."

Yoshiko flushed with anger. "What do you mean, *frittering away my money?*"

"Look at this house! Expensive, needless ornaments everywhere! Useless things everywhere!" accused Jinsaburo, his face wildly animated as he surveyed the front and dining rooms. "So this is what you do with the money I send you!" he said, shaking unnaturally. Spitting and coughing traces of blood into a withered handkerchief, he continued his diatribe. "No letters. No nothing. But I hear things. Oh yes, I hear things about you."

"Things? What things? What dirty mouth says this?" she asked.

"*Nem mind.* Just know this, I'm here to stay and start enjoying the things my money has bought!" Jinsaburo took two wide steps into the front room and flopped onto the couch. He sank into the cushions gasping and coughing.

Yoshiko fell into a stony silence as she brought in the valise. Letting it drop by her husband's side, she glared at him in disgust, her arms hanging limp by her sides. The almost visible vapours rising from him were almost too much to bear.

A sense of defeat settled in her. It was a step backwards, upsetting her sense of accomplishment. His return was an added burden already heavy with a useless daughter always underfoot.

"Is that otosan?" asked an innocent voice. Mariko had slipped into the house, having seen the open front door. She was shivering and pawing at her hair, trying to straighten it out.

"Damare," Yoshiko cursed. "Prepare a bath and make up the bed in your room."

Mariko looked up at her mother with tentative eyes as she offered the package of fish.

Yoshiko let out an exhausted sigh and accepted the package, no longer caring why Mariko was late. She spoke in a more charitable tone. "Prepare the bath and change the sheets on your bed, child. I'll get supper on the table."

Mariko appeared puzzled.

"Your otosan'll be in your bed and you'll sleep with me tonight."

Mariko cracked a broad smile, possibly anticipating the warm sheets and comforting presence of her mother, before dashing hastily into the depths of the house.

Just as Yoshiko turned to deal with the unwelcome Jinsaburo, he was on her.

"Where's my money?" he screamed as he roughly grabbed her by the blouse. "I know you've got it in some bottle around here." His eyes were filled with rage and contempt. "I need it now!"

His sour breath and fetid body odour made her gag. She let go of the package of fish and buckled under his weight. She pushed against his chest to keep him away, horror gripping her and not really believing what was happening.

The two spun around the room until he pulled her into the adjoining dining room. Then all of a sudden he let go of her unexpectedly and grabbed something from the large table in the middle of the room. "What the hell is this?" he asked menacingly, holding up one of the green teacups in front of Yoshiko.

She gasped. "No! Put that down!"

"How much did this kuso thing cost? Too much, no doubt," he barked in a slurred voice.

"That's a wedding present from my okasan!" A panic swelled in her like rising flood water.

"Bakayaro! That kuso family of yours!"

"Put it down! Put it down!" she repeated, hiccupping in tears.

"Down? Down? I'll put it down," he answered as he flung the cup against a wall, shattering it into a shower of jagged pieces. "Wasting my money. I'll show you." Jinsaburo then swept the dining table clean with his arm, knocking the rest of the tea set and pot to the floor.

Electricity coursed through Yoshiko as she let forth a scream she never thought possible. Grabbing a long-necked vase from atop a nearby cabinet, she swung it in the air, hitting her husband squarely in the temple with a satisfying thud. He reeled back on his heels, then fell flat on his back.

Catching her breath, Yoshiko rolled up her sleeves and stood over him. "You kusotare!" she gasped. "You'll never hurt me again." A sense of satisfaction came over her as she looked closer and inspected her husband's head. *Is he dead?* she asked herself hopefully as blood oozed from the web of broken and bruised skin. Savouring the moment, she allowed the desire harboured deep within her to bubble to the surface.

With laboured breathing, Jinsaburo lay in a deflated lump. Years of alcohol abuse had robbed him of his strength. He had become a ghost of his former self.

Yoshiko turned away from her husband and bent down to pick up a large fragment of the teapot, its green colour faded almost to white, its gold trim chipped and worn. *Gone. Bachan never left her home, never deserted her family. I've been robbed of my proper fate.*

The sound of sobbing made Yoshiko look up. Mariko was standing in the hallway, shaking, her face wet with tears. She had seen everything.

As Yoshiko had expected, Jinsaburo quickly became an embarrassment to her. Not that he did anything to disrupt the operation of the business, as he slept well past noon every day and then stayed out deep into the wee hours every night. It was the fact that he became known as the local drunk, the *nonbe*, that bothered Yoshiko.

Often he was found in the gutter by the clubhouse of Powell Ground by other drunks, who dragged him across the length of the park to the boarding house porch. Children often teased him, which caused the women at the neighbouring United Church and her own Buddhist Church to voice their concerns.

"Miyamoto-san?" asked Toshii Fukunaga, the timid and plump *fujinkai* member who had first befriended Yoshiko years ago. "Morii-san would like to talk to you."

Yoshiko, put upon and nervous, followed the messenger into a large but cluttered anteroom of the church. Misao Morii stood tall in her new spring outfit, a long beige skirt, white chemise, and matching jacket. Her imperious gaze was always the same, even when confronting a potentially stressful situation.

"Miyamoto-san," she said slowly, as if taking in and assessing Yoshiko's state of mind. "Won't you sit down?" Morii-*san* herself did not sit, opting to stand to maintain the upper hand, no doubt.

Yoshiko sat down in a heavy chair opposite. Keenly aware of her frayed jacket and mismatched scarf, she folded her arms on her lap, trying to hide the telltale signs of her financial state.

"Miyamoto-san, I asked to have a word with you because something troubling has come up involving you."

Yoshiko listened more out of fear than respect for what was about to be said.

"Not you so much but your husband," Morii-*san* added to correct herself. "These are the things that try a wife's patience, I know, but something has got to be done. Oh yes, I know he's not the only one, but he seems to be wanting to disgrace himself constantly in front of our children."

Yoshiko shook her head as if in despair.

Morii-*san* softened her position even more. "I know, I know. Something has got to be done," she repeated gently. "He's becoming an embarrassment to you, to the church, and to me."

Yoshiko looked at her, somewhat confused.

"Yes, myself included. I cannot talk of our community with pride at places like ... say ... the Consulate with men like your husband ... littering the streets now, can I?" Morii-*san* paused. "Perhaps I should speak to my husband."

"Oh ... no," Yoshiko stammered. "Please, let me handle him."

"But my husband is somewhat familiar with the world your husband frequents."

"Yes ... I suppose he is, but I can...." She was at a loss for words, the fear of indiscretion.

"All right Miyamoto-san, I'll leave my husband out of it, but please do something and soon."

She walked toward the door. "I must leave now. The fujinkai executive has been invited to the Consul's house ... in Shaughnessy Heights," she added emphatically. "So I will say goodbye." Her voice carried from the hallway to Yoshiko. "I will keep my eye on you."

Her last words seemed cold, with the hint of a threat attached to them.

A threat that was at best an idle one to Yoshiko. She could and would do nothing about her wayward husband. And what if Mori-*san's* husband was called upon? Even if the *oyabun* banished them again, she would stay. She had a legitimate business to run. What was he going to do, take it away from her? There are laws in Canada.

So she lived within herself, indifferent to her husband's comings and goings. His room, formerly Mariko's, became stained with his alcoholic excesses: sweat, vomit, urine. The sheets were changed only occasionally, Yoshiko preferring Jinsaburo to wallow in his own excretions.

She had two consolations in this miserable state of affairs. The first was clearly seeing her husband's fear of her in his manner as he left the house mumbling to himself, hunched over and with eyes averted. She allowed a smile to dance about her lips because she knew he was not getting any money from the household; in fact, she didn't know where he was getting his money and didn't care. *Maybe the oyabun, Shintani long dead.* The second consolation was the blueberry tarts at the Three Sisters Café. Most afternoons when she wished to indulge herself, she walked to the restaurant with the broad display window and the wide Venetian blinds in front and salivated over the prospect of biting into the sweet orbs.

The Three Sisters Café was situated on the corner of Jackson and Alexander, on the border between decency to the west and the red-light district to the east, and owned by the Yamada sisters, Hatsuko, Satoye and Kifumi. The eldest, Hatsuko, seemed to have a permanent scowl on her face, appropriate since she was always pessimistic. "Life is suffering," she used to say in her typical gruff manner. Though only in her early forties and still attractive in a weathered, experienced way, she appeared much older with world-weary eyes and rough olive complexion. In contrast, her two sisters were quite youthful: Satoye with a clear complexion and no-nonsense look; and Kifumi, the youngest and prettiest, with long shimmering hair, a pale oval face, and voluptuous body.

They were orphaned as teenagers, their parents having perished in a cabin fire on Vancouver Island. After leaving the orphanage in Victoria, the three sisters drifted and eventually became *joro*, working for Kiyoko Tanaka-Goto, the infamous and extraordinary Madam of the Powell Street area.

In time, they had cannily made enough money to buy the café and went out on their own, setting up shop there and using the upstairs bedrooms for their business trysts. Satoye, the middle child, had a practical approach to life, and so took care of the restaurant side of the business, keeping the books and setting the menu.

Her attitude was quite popular with a certain kind of man who frequently "discussed" things with her upstairs. In fact, the beauty and accommodating nature of all three sisters became well known among the fishermen and lumbermen and thus a steady clientele was born. Local teenage boys used to hold the crude notion that if "you wanna lose your cherry, go to the Three Sisters! They'll take care of you."

Yoshiko, through the ever-present gossip, knew the reputation of the place and scowled every time she passed by, though if truth be told, the illicit nature of the place held a certain fascination for her. In any case, she was often lured to the counter with its four red leatherette and metal stools on afternoons she wanted to escape the drudgery of boarding house business and her family situation. The blueberry tarts, advertised on a chalkboard sign outside as if they were a temporary special, were mouthwatering in appearance, with bright, luscious Okanagan Valley berries on top of overflowing custard in a light and flaky crust. "Mezurashii," she called them – "rare" – often adding, "Sugoi-ne?" – "Isn't it wonderful?"

The only irritation was the conversation, which tended toward the unseemly.

"Miyamoto-san," Satoye started, her face bright with the anticipation of a new audience, "how's that husband of yours? I haven't seen him around here lately."

The thought of Jinsaburo having a business tryst here made her throat constrict. She did not respond.

"It's just that he used to be here all the time …"

Her mind retreated. *Don't let him take away your dignity.* Years ago, her skin had become inert to his touch as her spirit had died in the bedroom.

"I was just wondering," Satoye continued.

"Satoye! Don't bother the customers," chastised Hatsuko. "Can't you see she doesn't want to talk about her dorakumono husband?" "Playboy": a euphemism for the drunkard he really was. Hatsuko pushed her sister toward the kitchen as she turned to Yoshiko and offered a contrite smile. "I'm sorry, Miyamoto-san. My sister doesn't know about life. Husbands can make us suffer so. It's like I always say, life is …"

Her words disappeared into the fog of Yoshiko's indifference.

Through the streets, through the front doors, down the hallways, into, around, and out of the rooms, the current flows quickly, easily. Absorbed by the flesh, the skin, the blackness seeps into all while thoughts meander

and remain. Life is suffering. The Buddha said so. The Kuroshio brings us
all to so much suffering in this damnable existence. Yet the hearts of men
continue to swell with desire.

Clouds moved in over Vancouver, a premonition of autumn rain. The coastal mountains appeared ashen as if ready to crumble, the twin lion peaks uncomfortable on their perch. It was October 1939 and the heaviness of the weather oppressed Yoshiko, making her restless.

When she pushed against the glass and wooden door and entered the brightness of the Three Sisters, she felt her outlook lighten. She made her way to a table in the corner as Hatsuko waited on her. The matronly proprietor patiently stood at her shoulder, not saying a thing but with her pad and pen ready.

"Blueberry tart," Yoshiko ordered as usual, "and black coffee onegaishimasu."

Hatsuko grunted as she wrote down the request. Then a voice called out to the oldest sister from the counter.

A man was perched on one of the cherry-red leatherette stools like he owned it. Not an ordinary man of the lumber and fishing industries. His shaving balm hovered about him and drifted throughout the room, acting like an introduction. Sharply dressed, he wore a beige suit, inappropriate for the season and location but attractive in its flamboyance.

Hatsuko went over and bent down slightly to hear the man's request and, unexpectedly, she snickered and scurried back to Yoshiko's table.

"Miyamoto-san, would you mind it if that gentleman over there sits with you?"

"What?" She was caught off guard.

"He's new in town and doesn't like to eat alone. Would you mind?"

"No ... no, I wouldn't," she said, still taken aback at the audacity yet intrigued at the same time.

Hatsuko smiled broadly and motioned for the man to come forward.

"Okihara Koji, desu," he said, bowing sharply as an opening gambit. His gleaming teeth dazzled, and his complexion was clear. This was not a man who laboured hard for a living. "I've just come from *San Francisco* to see what prospects there are here."

"*San Francisco?* You've come from such a wonderful city to here?" Yoshiko said with some skepticism. Something about him seemed familiar but she couldn't put her finger on it.

"Have you ever been there?"

"Well, no –"

"Well then, you must understand, for a salesman like me, I must find new territory."

"What do you sell?" She found herself forgetting about her beloved dessert for the moment to concentrate on this most unusual man.

"Just about anything I can. Myself, for example."

Her cheeks blushed warmly and she looked away, raising a hand to hide her sudden redness. It was a good thing Hatsuko brought Okihara's lunch at that moment, allowing Yoshiko to recover.

They spent the next two hours discussing the local attributes. At the end, Okihara graciously paid for his guest's tart.

"Oh no, I couldn't accept," she protested.

His hand touched hers. "Please, I insist," he said as he placed the money on the table. "Perhaps I can see you another time?"

It was the eyes, his soft, beautiful eyes. She hadn't thought about them in years, but surely this was not the same man of some twenty years ago. *No, not possible.* Yoshiko's skin tingled as she found herself, despite her misgivings, saying yes. "Afternoon … any day," she said with some reluctance. "232 Jackson, just down the street."

He beamed and sat back in his chair, looking like a satisfied cat.

Less than a week later, there was a knock at Yoshiko's door at two-thirty in the afternoon. She was alone. Mariko was in school. Jinsaburo was beginning his drunk at the Showa Club and her boarders were out.

In the intervening days, she had thought about the beautiful stranger, hoping he would come calling, yet dreading it at the same time for the gossip it would generate. A delicious dilemma. It was a pipe dream, she finally decided. Did she deserve such happiness?

She opened the door to Koji Okihara, dignified in his dark fedora, long coat, pleated pants, and polished shoes. Such a grand sight, Yoshiko couldn't help but smile.

"Miyamoto-san, I was calling on the United Church and I thought I would call on you since you invited me."

"Oh … yes … yes, I did." She gestured for him to enter and scanned the street before she closed the door. "The weather is turning bad these days," she said after him as she tried to straighten out her hair and smooth her plain housedress and stained apron into a presentable condition.

"Turning bad?" he chuckled as he removed his coat. "I haven't seen the sun since I got here! Not so different from *San Francisco*, actually."

"This is a nice coat," she remarked as she ran her hand along the smooth surface.

"*Cashmere*," he said in practiced English.

"Ka –?"

"A nice coat," he smiled at her.

"Here … sit in the front room. I'll bring some tea."

Not knowing quite why, she nervously fumbled with the tea leaves and pot, nearly dropping one of her new green cups.

The tea was piping hot when she served it to him with *hana arare*, crunchy rice crackers flavoured with soy sauce and sugar. He blew the liquid cool before his lips gingerly touched the lip of the cup. She sat on the sofa beside him and gazed at his smooth face, noticing the long lashes, high cheek bones, and prominent chin. *Beautiful eyes. No, he's not the same man.*

"Miyamoto-san?"

Yoshiko seemed startled at the intrusion of his voice. "Oh … would you like some farina cookies?" she stammered.

"Aw … no … no, thank you. I was asking about Soga's Department Store. Do you think they're looking for salesmen?"

"Yes! Yes!" she said eagerly. "Someone of your obvious skills will find a job there."

"Well, that's very nice of you. I'll make enquiries."

The afternoon seemed to fly by and, before long, Koji Okihara noticed the sunlight had waned and announced he had to leave. Yoshiko by this point found herself sitting very close to him, so close in fact she could feel the space between them. Whether she had moved toward him or he toward her, she couldn't recall.

"I should go," he whispered.

She was disappointed the time had gone so fast, but she also knew he was right. Mariko should've been home by now, but as luck would have it she was, no doubt, dawdling somewhere. Closing her eyes and bowing her head, she unconsciously moved her thigh, brushing against his momentarily.

He lifted his hand and cupped her cheek.

His touch jolted her, but she did not move away. Much later, she fancifully wondered if he had a mole on his shoulder.

In the next moment he was gone, but with a promise to return soon.

That night, the house sank into a deep quiet. Mariko was only too happy to share the bed in her mother's room, warmed by the apparent change-of-heart toward her and frightened by the *oni* beast that hibernated in her room and growled and snapped at them when aroused. She had never been close to her father, but only now did she realize why. He held in his heart an unspoken dislike of her, but for what reason, she did not know. Mariko was so relieved each day when he left the house not long after he had awakened.

As Mariko got into bed, she looked at her mother intently.

"What's wrong?" Yoshiko asked suspiciously. "You want something?"

"Okachan, tell me a story."

"A story? How old are you?"

"Okachan, please! Please tell me a story. Please?"

Yoshiko sighed and lay down searching the ceiling as Mariko tensed in anticipation.

… the bonsan Genno stepped away from the Death Stone and demanded of the spirit, "Who are you?"

A great voice came forth as a rumbling of thunder. "I am the demon which dwelled in the Jewel Maiden. Through her I have plotted the ruin of Emperors, Princes, and Kings who come under her charms."

A bright light emanated from within the stone. Genno cowered and fell to the ground. Inside the aura, he saw the form of a fox change into a beautiful maiden.

She appeared before him. "Prince Hazoku once paid homage to me. He died in his bed that night. In Great Cathay, I was known as Hoji, consort to the unfortunate Emperor Tzu. He died in battle with the taste of victory in his mouth," she said gleefully. "At the Imperial Court I was the Jewel Maiden, concubine to the Emperor. The weakness of men sickens me and so I bring them death."

"You killed all those great men?"

"All but the Emperor Toba. The Sorcerer Kamo foiled my plan."

"You must stop this," Genno insisted. "Where is your compassion for all living things?"

"Where was their compassion for me? For their fellow human beings? I had a family once. My father bore the strength of a thousand men. My mother had the beauty of the goddess Izanami. She bore several children, all beautiful and bearing gifts for the world. We were all tossed into the fires of Yomi at the whim of a 'great man' who couldn't defeat my father or win my mother. I was the one fated to wreak vengeance, show no compassion."

Overcome by her story, she began to weep over the Death Stone, crumbling it into pieces, breaking free the bright, clear light which surrounded her and transformed her once again into the fox.

Genno threw his head back as he shielded his eyes from the intense glare. Straining through the painful light, he could make out the fox running straight into the sunburst. It soon disappeared and the light died, leaving him alone.

Snoring interrupted the story. Yoshiko looked down at her daughter and saw that Mariko was sleeping contentedly in the moonlit darkness, her body warm to the touch, the simple look on her face enraptured by some dream. Yoshiko smiled as a mother.

Okachan? Yoshiko had never been called *Okachan*. The child's voice still grated with that irritating pleading tone she had so hated, but it hadn't bothered her as much this time. Perhaps it reminded her of the time of children's stories.

Oka, tell me a story like when I was a child. You haven't called me 'Oka' since you were ten. So will you? Tell me a story? Tell me one about a fox.

The closeness of her mother's voice remained with Yoshiko as she envisioned a corpse burning in the funeral pyre. A quiet sorrow settled in her consciousness. She soon felt her thoughts drifting to the kitchen with its pungent smell of rotting food; through the hallway, the airless corridor as still as a coffin; and into the dark front room, with all the possibilities created that day – though the spectre of the hanging girl haunted those expectations.

She imagined her pliant cheek against his clean-lined jaw and her breasts against his sculpted chest. A fox leered lasciviously. Her flesh flattened and then pressed into his crevices like soft dough. Her hands traced the curve of his muscled upper arms. Her legs opened to him. She moaned in reverie and squeezed her eyes. His scent filled her senses. But then she became aware of droplets coming from above: tears of blood.

A loud bang announced Jinsaburo's return in the recesses of deep night. Yoshiko frowned and lay still in bed, thanking the Buddha that the *kusotare* hadn't awakened Mariko or any of the boarders. As he stumbled down the hall, her anger festered. His every bump, misstep, and curse churned the acid in Yoshiko's stomach. Her forehead breaking out in a cold sweat, she could almost smell the alcohol haze, the pain of the past.

He pulled her to the ground by the hair, the shimmering waterfall disrupted by the sudden violence. He slapped her continuously as he tore at her clothes. She tasted blood and sputtered out red saliva as she uttered a soundless scream. He forced her legs open and her flesh went inert. Dead to the touch, dead to the emotion. He held her face tightly as he vomited curses and stale whiskey over her body. Her eyes turned white in the onslaught.

Though he had become too weak to dominate Yoshiko in any way, Jinsaburo was still an enormous burden. And the past is the past. Was there any escape from this poor excuse for a man, this monster, this *oni*? Death, she concluded. But whose?

At the beginning of the following week, a familiar knock came to the front door, confident yet hardly aggressive. Again, she let Okihara-*san* in with more excitement than trepidation coursing through her body. She actually was happy for the first time since daydreaming aboard the *Canada Maru*, and why shouldn't she? She had been promised much, been betrayed deeply, worked hard and long, and suffered many indignities. It was perhaps her time.

And again, she couldn't fathom how or when, but she soon sat close to him, the electricity palpable between them. The conversation meandered, but she wasn't listening anyway, captivated as she was by his eyes, the long lashes, the soft colour of the pupils. She felt the palm of his hand on her cheek again, cupped within its warmth. Her stomach prickled with anticipation. The thighs touched and she closed her eyes. A kiss. Her mouth opened to a second kiss.

She caught her breath as a hand grasped her breast. She didn't object; she welcomed the touch.

"… somewhere private …" was all she heard.

"… upstairs … empty room at top …" was her fragmented and breathless response.

The sensation of being lifted in the air and carried upstairs made her dizzy.

The room had been temporarily vacated by Hideo Yoshida, an itinerant labourer who was working in a copper mine up north near Cumberland. It was crammed with furniture, like most boarding rooms. The one window was open to the prevailing wind of fresh air, expelling the well-kept secrets and drawing in joy and anticipation.

The two of them burst into the room and fell to the bed to begin disrobing each other. Each territory of bare skin was attacked by the mouth of the other until they lay in each other's arms naked and willingly vulnerable. She moved to feel his entire presence as her fingers brushed over and then manipulated a bump, a blemish perhaps, or was it a birthmark; in a determined effort to see, she found it was diamond-shaped. Letting go of all control, she raked his back with her fingers, nearly drawing blood; she hoped she had.

The blood, a thick black blood, rushed down the body and rivered off the thighs. Both sets of hands created temporary dams, diverting the flow that streamed like the Kuroshio across the Pacific. The couple wallowed in the pool that formed on the bed, their bodies covered with its wetness. Wave upon wave of pleasure came over them.

The hanging girl laughed.

She heard him wince and felt him grab at limbs and abdomen. Her eyelids fluttered; her pupils went to white. She tasted salt, tingling with every touch, biting her lower lip. She moaned at the moment of connection and screamed at release.

అ

Christmas 1939 was a time of magic. Yoshiko, deciding to embrace the Canadian tradition fully for the first time, agreed to purchase a tree and she and Mariko spent a pleasant evening setting it up in the front room by the family altar.

"I know all about *Christmas*, Kachan! *Langley*-san ... I mean, *Mrs. Langley* taught us."

"Don't let it touch the butsudan, Mariko-chan," warned Yoshiko in a voice of uncustomary sweetness.

Mariko was quick to adjust the tree accordingly. For the holiday season, she took to wearing bright dresses and bows, even washing her hair regularly although she still had a hard time keeping it properly combed.

Yoshiko too displayed a much happier demeanour, even as Jinsaburo maintained his routine of drinking until unconsciousness. In fact, he was no longer the community disgrace but the community joke and very few concerned themselves with him. Those who did found sport in speculating where he was getting his money. *Probably from the wife but she's not suffering in any way. I heard he's afraid of her. She beats him from time to time! It's true! He's been in Chinatown a lot. Maybe he's working for the gambling bosses down there.* The Buddhist Church women, including Misao Morii, left well enough alone. If this man wanted to destroy himself, there was nothing they could do except keep their distance. Even the children laughed at him in the street, teasing him by chanting, "Nonbe-san! Nonbe-san! Nonbe, nonbe, nonbe-san!"

In the past few months, Yoshiko had come to accept Mariko as she was. She still punished her daughter for some inadequacy in her housework, but the punishment was not so severe. She didn't even concern herself with her daughter's lack of success in school. Mariko was sixteen and still in grade eight. But no matter what, at the end of this year, Yoshiko reasoned, she would be finished with school and work at the boarding house full time. *Enough is enough.*

The ladder reached the top of the seven-foot-tall tree that sparkled with coloured lights, glass bulbs, and tinsel. Mariko held her breath as she scaled the heights with the star ornament in hand. Reaching over, she felt a tremor and paused before trying again. The ladder shimmied but then held fast.

Yoshiko smiled at her daughter while holding the wooden legs steady. At times she had to admit to herself that she enjoyed Mariko's love for her.

Christmas morning, the house seemed filled with magic. Mariko scampered down the hall to the front room.

"Okachan!" she called to the back room. "Okachan! Come. Come."

A drowsy Yoshiko trudged into the room and winced as Mariko turned on the ceiling and Christmas lights, glass candles bubbling inside their enclosures caused by the heat generated within the ornaments.

Mariko bent down underneath the tree to pull out the brightly packaged presents. She shook each box in turn, hoping for precious treasure, and tossed aside those she deemed useless.

"Mariko, don't be so greedy!" Yoshiko admonished. "Just open them."

Mariko laughed gleefully when she found the prize – a shiny green and red metallic gift tied with a red bow and marked with her name. The gaily-decorated paper disappeared in two rips. What was revealed took her breath away – a *kokeshi*, a wooden doll painted red with jet-black hair.

"Ya sugoi-ne!" she said in wonderment. "Arigato, okachan! Arigato." She held the doll tightly to her and squeezed her eyes, close to tears.

In the weeks to follow, Yoshiko would observe her daughter with wonder. Mariko became very attached to that simple toy, playing with it endlessly. She even gave it a name.

"Kiyomi-chan," she said, "we must behave for okachan. You can help me wash the floors today. Maybe we'll get to eat some manju if we do a good job!" She caressed its head like a mother does her child.

Yoshiko sighed. *Maybe that was all she needed.*

But that was to come. For the moment, she just sat back on her legs and let the happiness of Christmas day fill her.

The days folded into nights into days until Oshogatsu was imminent. On December 31, Yoshiko uncharacteristically sang in the kitchen as she prepared the following day's New Year feast. It was an old song from Japan she had almost forgotten. In between choruses, she chuckled over the memory of preparing *mochi* at the Miyamoto estate in Mihama. *Jeez, that was hard. I should've slipped and hit that fat, good-for-nothing Hisa onesan.* For this year's celebration, she went to the Buddhist Church's community *mochitsuki* and watched the men pound the rice as an army of *fujinkai* ladies made the dumplings to sell.

Mariko, wearing her new outfit, a red sweater and high-top running shoes, danced and skipped throughout the house, nearly knocking over furniture with her oversized shoes. Yoshiko frowned at her daughter but continued to sing, while at the same time deciding that she would return those sneakers to the store at the first opportunity.

For her part, Mariko had gone on another trip to Union Fish for an emergency purchase of shrimp. Yoshiko had spent a great deal of time and care in finding the ingredients for the Oshogatsu feast but the shrimp, the jumbo kind with abundant crimson roe accumulated on the legs and abdomen, was not available New Year's Eve.

The long, uncut *futomaki*, its black *nori* skin glistening in the kitchen light, lay side by side on the cutting board like the day's catch of fish. Also awaiting the New Year's Day guests were the *sekihan*, its good-luck red beans nestled snugly throughout the rose coloured rice; the *nishime*, filled with rolled kelp for good fortune, carrots for long life, squash for good thoughts, yellow *daikon* pickles and other cooked vegetables; and the *kamaboko*. Yoshiko was especially proud of the *maguro*, its plump, red tuna flesh sliced thin and placed on a bed of lettuce. There was the preparation for the *tempura*, *tai* fish, and Cumberland *chow mein* left to do (that would take her long into the night), but the actual cooking could take place in the morning.

Yoshiko swelled with pride as she gazed at the generous spread of food. *As good as any the Miyamoto clan ever made,* she thought.

Unlike the uncivilized Canadian *gaijin*, the Japanese dutifully upheld the tradition of paying respect at Oshogatsu. The men, just as in Japan, would make the rounds of visiting friends and bosses alone while their women stayed at home to serve these guests drinks and the delicacies they had prepared the night before.

At about eleven o'clock in the morning, the first of these visitors to come to the Miyamoto table were the upstairs boarders: Hideo Yoshida, Takeshi Takahashi, and Tsuyoshi Sumida, young jacks-of-all-trades; and Tosuke Kato, one of the pair of boarders Yoshiko had met during her first stay at the Taniguchi back in 1920. When he had first come to her door a few months earlier, she recognized him immediately. His thinning hair and slightly stooped body pointed to a premature dotage, but he was still the same person underneath it all. He was as before in the logging trade but had injured his back recently, and needed an inexpensive place to stay and recuperate. His current boss, Yosuke Jikemura, had agreed to pay for his room and board within reason until he was able to return. Yoshiko gave him a special rate.

The guests gathered around the feast were full of conversation. Yoshiko and Mariko had pulled the large mahogany table out from against the wall, allowing enough chairs for several guests at the same time. In the kitchen, the cut vegetables and shrimp tails were gilding in the cooking oil of a deep fryer, the appetizing smell permeating the house.

Everyone clapped as Yoshiko brought in the golden *tempura* on a large platter decorated with maraschino cherries on lettuce. She stood in her full-length apron, the one given her by the late Yaeko Ebisuzaki all those years ago that concealed her faded Britannia Beach green dress, and bowed to the applause.

"Oishiso dana!" said Kato. "It looks so delicious!"

"Nani-mo nai ga tabenasai!" she claimed with false modesty. "There's nothing here but eat anyway!"

Their enjoyment filled Yoshiko with a sense of accomplishment and happiness, yet she couldn't help but feel a spot of pessimism as well. *1940, perhaps the last best year of my life ... it can't ... last.*

"Well, should I or shouldn't I?" Yoshida asked "old man" Kato.

"What?"

"Join the army and go fight."

"The Canadian army?"

"They won't have you," Takahashi offered.

"Why not?" Yoshida snapped back. "There's a war going on!"

"Where? There's no fighting going on," Kato said.

The Phony War held no interest for the immigrant *issei* generation. It was a white man's war, after all. The Japanese campaigns in China and the South Pacific gave them a sense of pride, but for some of the younger *issei* and *nisei*, the war in Europe held much significance.

"So what? It's my country. If I want to prove my loyalty, I've got to go."

Kato reared in anger. "Aho! You're just a Jap to them."

"You sound like one of those baka nisei at that paper of theirs," Takahashi argued.

"Gentlemen," Yoshiko interjected, "don't talk politics today! It's not the time or place. Mariko, bring the men some beer!"

About one hour into the festivities, the front door pushed open with a bang. A hulking figure stepped in, as if encumbered by its own weight. Jinsaburo's hair was matted, greasy; his eyes wild with madness. His coat, dingy and rain-soaked, drooped to the floor.

"Wife!" he bellowed. "Wife!"

In a panic, Yoshiko rushed down the hall. "Jinsaburo! Be quiet! We have guests!" She could see he was not going to be intimidated by her this time. Alcohol had made him brave.

"So?" His mouth spewed out a stream of stale whiskey on his breath as he leaned into her. "I came home to wish you a happy New Year!"

Yoshiko pushed him away in revulsion. "We have guests," she repeated.

"Miyamoto-san?" called Kato from the dining room.

Fatigued, Jinsaburo propped himself up against the wall.

"Go to your room," she ordered. "And try not to disturb my guests," she whispered as she returned to the dining room.

"More rice, Yoshida-san?" she asked, putting on a cheerful façade. "Daughter, serve him!"

Mariko stood in the corner, eyes wide open. She knew her *nonbe* father was home and didn't know what to do. Yoshiko ignored her and parceled out a generous portion of steamed rice into Yoshida's bowl. The young man raised an eye at the amount but said nothing.

The conversation resumed for a time, but it came to a crashing halt when a malodorous presence entered the room. Jinsaburo flopped into a chair at the table and glared at the gathering. "You bastards!" he snarled. "You came here expecting free food. Eating up my money."

The four guests shifted uncomfortably. Mortified, Mariko suddenly bolted for her room.

"Take my money, take my money," Jinsaburo repeated as his head sank to the table. "Must go to the kuso Chankoro." His voice faded to a sputter. "Never the luck ... never...."

"It's time I leave," Kato announced. "Kawabata-san is expecting us."

The others nodded in agreement. As they thanked their hostess in unison and left, Yoshiko sat absolutely still, not even acknowledging their departure. When quiet settled again, she glared at her unconscious husband from her chair. A nauseating mist rose from his body. She was determined not to cry, stifling any tears with a quick sniffle. He would never make her cry again. Her mind filled again with dark wishes.

That familiar knock at the door. A cold tingle irritated the pit of Yoshiko's stomach. She left Jinsaburo in a heap at the table and scurried down the hallway. Taking a breath, she opened the door. Koji Okihara, a beautiful smile on his face, stood in the vestibule, immaculately dressed as always. His crushed velour fedora matched his luxurious full-length coat, and he wore shiny patent-leather shoes. He bowed before her.

"Shinen omedeto —"

"Okihara-san, please come in," she said.

They had continued their affair in the months since they had first met at the Three Sisters Café. Yoshiko had become increasingly jealous of their time together but had been very careful not to be seen with him in public, certainly not at the church or any community event. Koji for his part had been just as discreet, although there was a time coming when things would have to change.

Yoshiko quietly led him to the front room, where they sat down on the sofa. Koji relaxed against the satin pillows and softened his gaze while she removed her relatively spotless apron in an effort to make herself presentable.

Yoshiko, though happy to see him, was keenly aware of her husband not five feet away, and so kept a respectable distance from Koji on the couch, her eyes downcast.

"Okihara-san," she said in a hushed tone, "you can't stay here long. My husband." She pointed toward the dining room.

"Him?" Koji cocked his head. "He doesn't seem to mind!" he snorted, then stood up and sauntered over to check on the slumped body at the table. "You don't mind that I keep company with your wife, now do you, Miyamoto-san?"

"Shhh!" she admonished.

Koji laughed out loud as he returned to the couch.

"I'm sorry. I know we haven't been … together lately," she said, her cheeks blushing intensely.

"I understand. The room's let out —"

"He'll be gone in a week!" she said while reaching out to touch his hand.

He didn't accept the invitation. "Which brings me to a point I wish to make." He shifted away from her. "I think I should move into that room."

"What?"

"I'm paying too much at the Empress and your room is empty at times."

Her mind raced. "But … but if people found out!"

"No one will. I'll just be one of your roomers. Your best-dressed roomer, but just one of your roomers nevertheless!" he said, smiling.

She wasn't amused. "But what about my husband? My daughter?"

"Two people you care little about," he said, dismissing them with a wave of the hand. "Do you care for me?"

"But they're right here in the house," she whispered.

"They've been here all along and still they haven't noticed anything. Am I right?" He leaned back into the sofa, smirking with confidence. "Now, do you care for me?"

"Well … well, yes, of course."

"Don't you enjoy our time together?"

"Yes … yes," she stammered.

"Then let me stay here. We'll be together always. Like we were married."

Yoshiko rubbed her forehead. She hadn't even considered such an idea but all of a sudden now it seemed possible in her mind. She bit her lower lip, letting his hand fold into hers. She had been happy, she reminded herself. But living together – she thought of the infamous Rev. Shigeno. Flirting with scandal started to excite her.

"Maybe," she said tentatively.

"Then it's settled."

"Wait," Yoshiko insisted. "I can't think."

Koji held her hand. A silence settled between them, filled with both foreboding and accord.

"So I'll move in after the room's vacated."

Yoshiko nodded, but she couldn't look at him.

"Shall we eat?"

Feeling awkward sitting at the table with her drunk, unconscious husband and her bold lover, Yoshiko found refuge in the kitchen preparing a new batch of *tempura*. She could hear Mariko in her bedroom whimpering. Best place for her, she thought as the shrimp batter turned golden brown. *Her kokeshi, her comfort.*

"Nineteen-forty looks to be a good year," Koji said as he lifted a *maki-zushi* to his mouth. *The last best year.*

"Have you found work, Okihara-san?" Yoshiko asked, trying to keep up the pretense of casual conversation.

"Well, no, but prospects are good. Soga-san may have something for me in the spring. He said so himself."

From time to time Jinsaburo moaned and shifted slightly but never regained consciousness that day – not even when Koji dragged the *nonbe* to bed, a most onerous task that wrinkled his tailor-cut suit.

"Don't you clean up in there?" Koji said when he returned, brushing away the imagined filth from Jinsaburo.

"No one sees it except him and he doesn't mind," she answered.

"I must be going now," he announced. "Come see me to the door."

In the quiet shadows of the alcove, Koji took her into his arms. She struggled a bit but the pleasure and the anonymity made her bold.

"It's a good idea," she said in a rough whisper.

"What is?"

"You moving in here." Her chest swelled with emotion. "I don't know what people –"

"I wonder … do you have any money?" he said, interrupting the sentiment.

She pulled back in surprise once again. "What?"

"The rent's due and I'm a little short this week. I'm beside myself. Anything will do," he said sweetly as he casually reached out his hand.

"Well." She retrieved her apron and searched the pockets to find a five-dollar bill, change from an errand she had Mariko perform.

"That'll do. I'll pay you back." He slipped the bill inside his suit and left Yoshiko without another look.

16. January 1940

Mariko Miyamoto had not found much success in school. Besides the many humiliating experiences in the classroom, her grades were still poor. Her *keto* teachers at Strathcona were not sympathetic and hadn't helped. It was too late anyway since they had assumed the young sixteen-year-old was in the last half of the last year of her education. And her eighth grade teacher, Mrs. Langley, like her close friend Mrs. MacGregor, terrified her students with the familiar diatribes against the Japanese.

"Damn," Mrs. Langley cursed loudly after breaking a pencil at her desk. "Must be made in Japan!" she concluded, her face contorted as if irritated by a bad smell.

Mariko lowered her head in shame. She frequently kept her head down, in order to avoid calling attention to herself.

With her mother finally treating her with some kindness, home had now become her refuge. She slept contentedly in the same bed with her *okachan* and sometimes watched her sleep. All she wanted was her mother's love, to be accepted by her. Mariko thought she was the most beautiful woman in the world, especially in contrast to her own mis-shapen face with its bent nose, thick lips, and crooked mouth.

One night, as her mother slept, Mariko gazed upward to the window in the far wall, to the shadows playing with stray moonbeams. The ticking of the clock kept her company as she herself slipped into sleep. In her fading thoughts, she imagined the adjacent room, its own black heart holding the *oni* beast within its confines. She instinctively pulled the covers over her head to escape the danger – the ample folds of sheets and her mother's new camisole fragrant with her body perfume and warmth. *Safe in my cave. No oni's gonna get me.*

With March came the milder weather when Mariko discarded her heavy coat and donned her favourite red sweater with tiny yellow daisies sewn into it. She revelled in the light and skipped home every afternoon, sometimes tripping over her oversized running shoes.

One day, there was a teachers' meeting, so the students were dismissed from class just after lunch. Mariko had forgotten to tell her mother, but didn't care. Enjoying the freedom of the afternoon, she skipped home as usual; the sun was high, bathing the streets with its radiating warmth. She was alive and free. *Okachan will find something for me to do! Maybe I can play with Kiyomi-chan!* – her Christmas *kokeshi*.

Mariko quietly opened the front door. She padded down the hallway, which had a peculiar yet familiar fragrance: a fancy scent, belonging to the new boarder – Okihara-*san*. She didn't like him; he paid too much attention to her mother. All of sudden she heard a sound, unidentifiable but from somewhere.

From upstairs? "Okachan?" she called softly, discreetly, as she moved to the foot of the stairs. No response, but the sound persisted. Voices … someone's upstairs, she decided as she started up the stairs. Voices not saying anything. She strained to hear clearly. Moaning. Grunting. Suffering.

At the top landing, she determined that the voices came from behind the second door, Okihara-*san's* room.

"Okachan, I know it's you. Are you playing a trick on me?" she called. "What're you…?" The hinges yawned when she swung open the door. What she saw caught her by the throat as acid pooled and bubbled at the back of her mouth.

෨

Friday, March 8, 1940

Yoshiko Miyamoto's life certainly had taken a turn for the better when Koji Okihara moved in as a boarder. He paid no rent but there were obvious compensations for her, especially when he came home afternoons after inquiring about jobs in the morning. In the beginning, she felt guilty about the illicit affair but then reasoned why she shouldn't. Koji was her true love, the diamond mole proved that. And if life wasn't fair – *life is suffering* – it was up to her to make it right: she had been tricked into abandoning the comfort of home and family and saddled in a loveless marriage to a brutal man. Her deformed daughter was an embarrassment but a tolerable one because of Koji. At least now she had the semblance of a real family.

Yoshiko had some concerns, especially with the amount of money Koji "borrowed." At first, she feared he was gambling and was sure of it when he mentioned Shibuya's, the clothing store below the Showa Club. Money was tight since the transients who were her bread and butter were mostly out of town at this time of year. It was much to her relief when she found that he had been spending the money on new clothes, like a homburg or a silk shirt. Expensive and perhaps frivolous, but at least it wasn't gambling. Besides, he needed good clothes to get a job, she rationalized. And she was sure he would pay her back.

The man I will marry is adventurous and has the strength of ten men. His eyes are clear and black like coal. His hair, long and dark like fertile earth. He's tall and proud of his accomplishments, as seen in his straight back and flexed muscles. He has lived in the land of white devils and obake women and is their master. And I will be his wife.

Lying in bed with him as the sun slanted through the window blinds offered her much satisfaction. The horizon of his back as he lay on his side intrigued her. The skin was like a baby's, smooth and blemish free. She often ran her hand along his spine, to the left shoulder blade, where she traced the diamond-shaped birthmark with a finger. She hadn't told him of her premonition on the *Canada Maru* all those years ago during the voyage over in 1920. It was her secret, a convergence of fate and the supernatural.

At some leisurely moment, Yoshiko reached over to the side table and took out a familiar item from the drawer. The photograph – stained, creased, and cracked, but the image of a young girl looking askance with parasol remained discernible.

She had kept it all these years, never looking at it for too long since it reminded her of a lost home, her girlish dreams and foolish hope. Most times, she just glanced at it, knowing full well what it was but unwilling to deal with the consequences. The picture simply mocked her. Finally, she buried it deep in her trunk along with her wedding kimono.

With a renewed purpose, she had retrieved it recently and hid it in his drawer. "Koji-san," she started, coquettishly.

Koji yawned and didn't turn around.

"There's something I want you to have," she continued as she gingerly held up the picture to her lover.

Koji rolled onto his stomach and let out a sigh. He took the photo and inspected it casually. "You?"

"Yes, my picture-bride photograph."

"You were young then," was his only comment.

She forgave the slight, given that the photograph was with its rightful owner at last, and returned to caressing his back.

"A fine catch I am," Koji said. "I'm no better than your lying drunk of a husband. It'd be better if I had a job. Then we could do something about our situation."

"Don't you think ... I mean perhaps you're not looking hard enough –"

He twisted around to face her. "You think I like owing you money?" He went on the offensive as if anticipating criticism. "No one in this hick town appreciates my talent."

The frustration in his voice frightened her, so she immediately embraced him. Slowly pushing her to the bed, he kissed her with open eyes. Yoshiko's own eyes floated upwards as pleasure overtook her. Time slowed to a standstill as they moved to the friction of sex. Their emotions rose to a climax when the bedroom door flew open.

"Oka! Oka! Oka!" shrieked a young voice.

The bodies released from one another and Yoshiko slid off the bed, her face flooded with horror.

Mariko, repelled by her mother's and Okihara-*san's* nakedness, bolted down the hall.

Yoshiko gave naked chase. *Useless child. Urusai child.* Three steps and she was just about upon her at the top of the stairs. *Kuso child.* She lunged at her daughter. In the split second before contact, her mind flashed between two possibilities: grab the sweater or push the back. *Grab or push.*

With a scream, Mariko tumbled down the stairs. Yoshiko fell hard, hitting her elbows on the wooden flooring. She let out a cry of pain, then sat up, pressing the palms of her hands against her cheeks. She saw her daughter at the bottom of the steps, both of her arms bent in an unnatural position, her neck obviously broken.

Yoshiko knelt beside Mariko who was lying very still, appearing strangely at peace. Bringing her camisole, Koji soon joined her from upstairs.

"Is she dead?" he asked tentatively as he pulled his *yukata* tightly together.

A coldness settled in her stomach. "Yes," she answered softly, standing up.

"Why'd you do it?" Koji asked.

"Do what?" she answered.

"You didn't have to push her down the stairs."

Yoshiko grabbed at Koji, her eyes fierce. "I didn't!" she screamed. "She fell. I chased her and she tripped at the top of the stairs. I was nowhere near her. It was an accident."

Koji didn't respond. The two of them simply stood over the body, trembling at the ramifications of what had just happened. The coldness of loss was in the air; the end of a dream.

Our glorious lovemaking. Koji makes love to me like no other. I melt in his presence. He knows the contours of my body and traces every one with the delicacy of summer wind. And when I look into his eyes, I sink into their blackness like I was slipping into the ocean's depths, making me feel alive. Alive in our lovemaking! Every nerve tingles as I ache for his next touch.

Yoshiko's mind raced. *The child was born to curse me.*

I tried to reach her, grab her, save her, but I wasn't in time. I saw her slip and tumble down. She was a lifeless lump at the bottom of the stairs by the time I reached her. That's the story. Even so, people are gonna talk about us. We won't be able to be seen anywhere together. Koji will have to leave town. I'll never see him again. What am I going to do? What?

She really wasn't sure if she had pushed Mariko, but she felt no guilt over what had happened, she might have done her daughter a favour. It was possibly better she had died, she reasoned, than to have to fend for herself in later years.

She began to feel everything slipping away from her, just as she imagined Japan slipping away from the deck of the *Canada Maru*, all those years ago.

There are few certainties in life and those who indulge in such a luxury live in a fool's paradise. Yoshiko had learned that years ago. But the incontrovertible priority now was not to lose Koji.

"They'll think I did it," Yoshiko concluded, breaking the silence.

"Who?" Koji asked.

"Everybody."

"But you said it was an accident."

"It was. I told you so! But don't you see? They'll think I did it once they find out about you ... like they did with Reverend Shigeno and that woman he took in." Yoshiko started to pace back and forth.

"What are you talking about?" Koji asked.

"The Nodas too," she continued. "They're such gossips. And at the church! Fukunaga-san, Morii-san, that snob. Her and her precious Consulate friends, they'll make trouble for me —"

"Look, maybe I oughta move out," Koji suggested, alarmed by her mounting paranoia.

"No! No, you can't!" Yoshiko asserted. "Don't give up so easily. I swear I'm not gonna lose you because of this damn girl."

"But this changes everything," he said.

"Why aren't you listening to me?" she pleaded, her brow now moist with sweat. "Nothing's changed. Not if I fix things."

"How are you gonna do that?"

"I don't know. I'll think of something ... I'll think. Pick her up," she ordered, her face now hardened with sudden conviction.

"What? Why?" Koji asked.

"Pick her up," she repeated sternly, glaring at him with grim determination.

Koji, fretting to himself, obeyed and struggled to lift the lifeless body gingerly. "What're you thinking?"

"We're gonna get rid of the body."

"You can't do that." He bristled at the implications.

"Do you want our life together finished? Because that's what happens if she's found!"

"Then you pushed her?"

She moved to touch him, but she felt him shudder and shift away. Her eyes widened. "Word'll get out about us. Don't you see? This useless child torments me, even in death."

"But ... but the police!"

"They'll never know about this."

"What? How? Even if I were to agree to this, what's going to happen when they do find the body? And they will find the body!"

"Not where I'm going to hide it. Follow me."

After rummaging through her room and the kitchen, Yoshiko went down to the damp, musty basement that was cluttered with the debris of her nomadic years in British Columbia. Her original steamer trunk containing her *nigiyakana* wedding *kimono* lay dormant in the corner covered with cobwebs, dust and dreams, having remained unopened for years.

At the back, the silent black coal furnace sat brooding, its tentacle pipes leading to all parts of the house. Yoshiko shivered, then carefully pulled open its door, the black hole, an *obake's* mouth gaping as if waiting to be fed.

Koji struggled as he dragged Mariko's body behind until he crouched down on the floor, breathing hard. "You ... you can't do this!" he complained, almost pleading. "It was bad enough you ... okay you didn't, but...." Feeling dizzy, he steadied himself on the back of a nearby chair.

"We have no choice," she said coldly, her mind very much made up. "I have no choice." She had worked too hard to let it now all slip away so easily.

"But she's your only child!" he said, even though the words sounded ridiculous in the wake of what had already transpired.

"A dead child. She doesn't care what happens," she whispered callously. "It's my time. No one's going to deny me that."

Lifting the corpse into the furnace opening, Koji found it too narrow but, with some effort, managed to force the body through it and onto a bed of coal. He nearly gagged.

"Be a man!" Yoshiko admonished. She took a deep breath before reaching inside with the oil can she had brought from the kitchen and tilted it just enough to soak a square piece of blotting paper she had already fastened to Mariko's sweater. The thick liquid spread like black flood waters across the paper and oozed onto the sweater. Her daughter's eyes were open and glassy, as if pleading. From somewhere about her person, Yoshiko produced a figurine and placed it beside the body. It was Kiyomi-*chan*, Mariko's beloved *kokeshi*. Her vision blurred as she turned away. *Useless girl.*

Koji questioned her with his eyes.

"It'll make the fire burn better," she said. After wiping her face with her sleeve, she lit the paper and closed the door with the slam of finality.

The couple sat on the sofa as the dull light of day crawled toward evening. Spring cloud cover seemed to underscore the gruesome crime they had just committed. Koji kept rubbing his hands together, not caring that his pants and shirt were smudged with coal dust. Yoshiko sat staring into space, even though the sound of a dull thumping came from down in the basement every so often. She could only imagine what was causing it.

The flames feasting on the body, consuming the flesh, charring the bones. The body twitching, squirming to get away, before relenting. Banging the sides of the furnace. And all the while, the face peering out, asking why.

She began to rub her hands together as if in *gassho*, perhaps in a futile search for redemption. *Namu Amida Butsu. Namu Amida Butsu. Namu Amida Butsu.* She had no choice, was her only answer to herself. She had once wondered how far she was willing to go. Guilt could not touch her, but was she willing to go further?

Koji gathered the strength to speak. "What if … what if they find out?"

"They won't. Nobody saw and no one's going to be renting for awhile."

"Someone'll miss her … at school."

This gave her pause, and she clenched her fists in frustration. The one place Mariko was allowed to be in public. *She will be missed.* Yoshiko had been so desperate she had forgotten to consider that fact.

"They may never find her, but you must explain her disappearance," Koji insisted.

"Yes. Yes," she repeated, trying to think.

Then all of a sudden, the smell began. Through the furnace grills, the ductwork, the very floors themselves came the telltale odour of burnt flesh and hair. Koji became agitated. "I can't stand this!" he cried out and ran upstairs.

Yoshiko sat stoic as ever. "They'll never find her," she said aloud to herself. "She's disappeared. Her father. Yes." She smiled as the reek of foul deeds intensified, like a ghost rising through the floorboards.

In the quiet fall of night, the two of them were crouched down, waiting, sure in their resolve. The opportunity would surely present itself soon. But what if he decided not to stagger home? What if he was unconscious in some gutter somewhere? Then it would be tomorrow night. If not, then the night after. The time had come to settle accounts.

Just past three in the morning, when their eyelids were at their heaviest, there was a loud stumbling on the porch, then the sound of the door latch disengaging. In fell Jinsaburo.

"Kusotare!" he cursed, not caring whom he disturbed.

They could see him, the alcohol haze about his red-beacon eyes. He crumbled to the floor and, practically crawling, he made his way to his room. They resisted the immediate temptation.

Jinsaburo flopped into bed with some effort and let his consciousness drain in the exhalation. He began snoring in a matter of minutes.

Yoshiko advised that they wait awhile to make sure he was "dead to the world." Ignoring the word play, Koji fidgeted in anticipation. Soon enough, it was time. Watching Jinsaburo, she held her favourite cutting knife close to her bosom, her fingers caressing the sturdy wooden handle stained with the blood of choice cuts of *gaijin* beef. The lump in the dark was inviting. She stared at her husband coldly, dispassionately. She held no regret in her heart for what she was about to do, shaking not in fear but with great anticipation. A wave of pleasure came over her.

Twenty years of suffering. The promises made, the dreams clung to and the crush of disappointment. He was her husband, a man caught in the vortex of pride and failure, separated from family by an ocean, self-pity, and self-deception.

So what? He took away her dignity. Hokusai's Tsunami is about to crash and collapse, drowning all in its wake. Kuroshio-san will carry everything away, leaving no trace of anything – not even the memory.

The white eyes of the hanged girl formed before her. Her mouth cracked a sharp-toothed smile.

They never forgive.

Yoshiko's blade hovered over the body as she pulled the white sheet over him with one hand, the other remarkably steady. *Twenty years.* Jinsaburo was the one who was trembling now, she thought. *He's afraid.* The imagined fear in him pleased her.

The girl burst into a devil's laugh that blended with the roar of the sea, the Black Current crashing about the ears.

In the instant she heard the cacophony, she plunged the knife deep into the shrouded lump below. Again and again, she stabbed, his slight groans testament to the slipping away of life.

The white sheet, caught in stray light, grew black with the blood.

Her eyes remained cold and determined, even long after the deed had been done, but the implications started to weigh heavily upon her. Washing her hands under running water in the kitchen sink, she shook and muttered to herself almost in a kind of muted revelry.

Her father kidnapped her. I don't know what happened to my daughter. Please find her. Please! There's no telling what he'll do to her.

Koji in the meantime wrapped the sheets and blankets tightly around the body and with much difficulty gathered together the load over his back. Fortunately, the blood had not soaked into the mattress. With great effort, he struggled to get outside, letting out small grunts as proof of his burden, and carried the body away, avoiding the streetlights. He departed without saying a word to Yoshiko, leaving behind her photograph on the dining room table.

She stood at the sink still rubbing her hands together as Koji stole away.

After a day and a night of profound sleep, Yoshiko woke with a start the following morning. Her hand immediately searched for a familiar body beside her. Not Mariko's, but Koji's. With no one there, she bounded from the bed and ran to his room at the top of the stairs. No one there. His precious clothes and effects were intact, but he hadn't returned.

She returned to her room to dress. From her *nemaki* pocket, she pulled out her photograph, discarded by Koji "by accident," she reasoned, as reassurance of his return to retrieve it. In the closet, she found a faded red dress, frayed at the cuffs but made attractive by the glass buttons and beadwork. She dressed quickly.

Wrapped in her cloth coat, she stepped into the cold March wind. Aimlessly, she searched the streets for a while until she reached the Three Sisters Café. Through the window, she saw Hatsuko-*san* wiping down the counter.

"Yamada-san!" shouted Yoshiko as she entered.

Hatsuko looked up, startled.

"I'm sorry," Yoshiko said. "Sumimasen, have you seen Okihara-san?"

Hatsuko's face turned pale with concern and rushed to Yoshiko's side. "Miyamoto-san, come sit down. Have a cup of coffee," she offered as she helped the distressed woman into a chair. She then returned to the kitchen to get something else.

Yoshiko stared at the restaurant owner fussing about, at the same time letting the coffee steam her face. She turned her gaze to across the road at the row of silent houses, wondering if they held terrible secrets too. Gradually, she confronted the possibility that Koji was never coming back. She let her head slump to the table.

At that moment, Hatsuko returned with a slice of pie. "It must've been a terrible shock," she said, sitting next to Yoshiko.

"What're you talking about?" she asked.

"Your husband. I read about it in the paper."

"What?"

Hatsuko withdrew to the counter again, retrieved the morning Japanese newspaper, and showed it to Yoshiko.

A man identified as Jinsaburo Miyamoto was found dead on the CPR tracks. Police say he was probably hit by a train.

As soon as she saw the front-page story, Yoshiko collected herself, stood up, and walked to the door.

Hatsuko, believing she had done something wrong, took a step toward her but then stopped. "I'm sorry … I didn't know you didn't know.…" Her voice trailed off as Yoshiko closed the door behind her.

Invisible walls seemed to close in on her even with the open park in front of her and the wind whining in her ears. Without Koji, what good was her story about her husband and Mariko? Without Koji, there was no chance for happiness, no chance for family. There were few choices left: confess all to the police or *jisatsu*. In either case, she would end up dead. But perhaps there was another way: Etsuji Morii.

That ketsuno ana Morii. He is the one responsible. He condemned me to a hard life in the Interior. Jinsaburo didn't have to tell me. I knew all along. He owed the money to Morii. Who else? Everyone owes that bastard something. The oyabun, with his smooth tongue offering favours in his generous way and then cutting down the spirit like the sword master that he is. Like a devil giving with one hand and taking with the other.

But he'll help me now. He'll bring Koji back to me. He has to, or all of us will be made to bow before the ketojin! Oh yes, he will help me now.

And if he won't, I'll spit in his face and Koji and I will be together in the fires of hell.

She headed north past the Three Sisters but then thought better of it, deciding to walk west along Powell Street, the long way round to the Nippon Club.

The next day, the sky was full of rain and the streets were covered in shadows, as if cowering from the impending storm. A knock came to Yoshiko's front door. She scrambled to the front hall to answer it – *Koji!*

Instead, two police detectives greeted her, their badges in hand. Tall, husky, with combed-back hair, the two men seemed identical in appearance.

Yoshiko's English was rudimentary at best, but she showed them in out of respect for authority. She heard them speak, in that unfathomable language, and nodded to every question. Guessing what they wanted, she decided not to say anything.

The two men looked at one another and came to an agreement. Getting her coat and staging a pantomime, they asked her to come with them.

That she fully understood.

The small basement interrogation room of the Cordova Street police station was sparsely adorned. The windows were obscured by bars, holding everyone and everything inside. The sickly green walls seemed recently washed, mixing ammonia with evidence of old violence. Yoshiko felt ill at ease sitting alone on the single creaking chair.

As she waited, her mind filled with thoughts of Koji: his handsome face, his stylish clothes. She lingered over the question of their mutual fate.

Suddenly, the door yawned open and a small runt of a man entered with the two officers in tow.

"*Miyamoto-san*," he said in a comically high Japanese, "*I am Kawasaki Hideki*." He bowed curtly. "*Detectives Hann and Gibb want to ask some routine questions.*"

Kawasaki? Wasn't the immigration man named Kawasaki? she said to herself. *Do they all have the same name?*

"When did you last see your husband?" asked Detective Hann in a quiet voice.

"*When did you last see your husband?*" Kawasaki's voice was much more accusatory than the detective's, she judged.

"*I haven't seen him,*" she said with a worried look, "*two maybe three days.*"

"Not in three days," repeated Kawasaki in English.

"Three days? And you weren't worried?"

"*Why didn't you report this to the police?*" Kawasaki asked her.

"*I ... I'm sorry. He's a drunkard. I never worry about his whereabouts.*"

"*Where does he drink? Does he gamble there as well? Did he owe money?*" he asked in rapid succession. "*Perhaps the Showa Club?*"

"*He has stolen from me from time to time,*" she answered quietly. "*He worked at the Showa Club ... I think.*"

Kawasaki consulted with the two officers.

Yoshiko watched as the two *ketojin* towered over the interpreter. Among these Canadian giants, Kawasaki looked like a *kappa*, the troll that lives beneath bridges.

Hann turned to her. "Your husband is dead. Some boys found him on Sunday, beheaded near the CP railroad tracks.

"*Your husband was found dead two days ago. He's probably been dead since Saturday night.*"

"*Oh,*" she said dully. Her thoughts drifted to Koji. "*Where? How?*"

"*The CP railway yards. He was stabbed and then hit by a train.*"

She fell silent, feigning shock.

Detective Gibb spoke up. "It took a while to identify him. The train really mangled —"

Tears rolled down her cheeks as she sat absolutely still, half listening to the translation and waiting for the other shoe to fall. *Mariko is missing. Mariko is … should I tell? Jinsaburo did it.* Her eyes sparked out in defeat in the flat fluorescent light, causing the contours of her face to turn red and unattractive. But no words of accusation came.

Soon thereafter, Yoshiko was allowed to go home. Kawasaki himself escorted her out of the building as he offered his condolences.

"The police believe your husband was a victim of foul play," Kawasaki informed her in Japanese. "Witnesses say he had been drinking and was in a fight outside the Showa Club late that night. In all probability, it was over money. Your husband owed a lot of money to the Chinatown gambling bosses."

Her eyes grown dark, her skin sallow, she nodded quietly, appropriate in light of the tragic event. She wondered why there was no mention of Morii, but let the moment pass.

"The Chankoro will do anything for money. Probably hired Japanese thugs to collect."

At home, for the rest of the day, into the evening, and through the night, she sat, staring at the beams of the ceiling. The *karma* of what had happened weighed heavily upon her, bending her back toward the basement where Mariko's remains lay. She looked up suddenly, but no young girl was hanging from the rafters. She fell asleep where she sat.

She awoke to pitiful light attempting to penetrate the gloom of the house. A knock at the door. Koji! she thought again. She anxiously opened it only to find a middle-aged Canadian woman in a heavy wool coat. With not so much as a smile, the woman began speaking at her in the cursed English. Yoshiko closed her eyes and shut the door, the woman's irritatingly loud and angry voice carrying on even after the lock was engaged.

A final knock came early the following morning. By now, she somehow knew it wasn't Koji. In fact, it was Kawasaki and the two officers.

"*Miyamoto-san, it appears your daughter is missing,*" Kawasaki said, smiling a devil's smile. "*Her sensei from school said she came here yesterday to ask after her but couldn't get an answer. Where is she?*"

Yoshiko didn't answer, as if her lips were locked together, frozen with their secret. *My husband kidnapped.* Without Koji, all seemed futile somehow.

"Where's your daughter?" one of the officers said.

She hesitated, but then turned slowly around and started down the hall to the basement door in the kitchen. It yawned open like the entrance to a crypt.

Yoshiko soon found herself in the police interrogation room once more. In her presence, Detective Hann had issued an order to search the rooming house. He and Kawasaki late in the day entered the room with grim faces. After some consultation between the two, Kawasaki bent down to talk to her, but before he could get a word out, the door opened.

A tall, auburn-haired gentleman entered, his suit catching Yoshiko's eye. It was expensive, like Koji's. The man had an easy manner about him as he called the other two together. The three spoke in low conspiratorial tones. She heard the name "*Giru*" spoken but it was of no significance to her. The trio then stepped outside.

In a few minutes, Kawasaki alone returned and said, "You are free to go."

She looked at him questioningly.

"While we've been talking to you, an investigation team has searched your house and found no evidence of foul play. I also talked with your daughter's teachers … that is, the detectives did. They were told of her … difficulties in school, as it were." He coughed uncomfortably at these revelations. "In any case, we have all concluded your daughter committed suicide. I'm sorry to break the news to you like this, but you had to know."

Yoshiko sat, dumbfounded.

In the weeks that followed, the furor seemed to die down considerably. The papers, both English and Japanese, carried the sensational story about the Japanese girl committing suicide, which caused Yoshiko to laugh maniacally in the solitude of her house.

Life became normal again except for the lingering taste of scandal in the Powell Street area. Everywhere people strained to sneak a peek at her, whispered about her just within earshot as if they suspected the truth. *She did it … why didn't she kill herself? Didn't she want to die after losing him? Okihara … her boarder … the shame of it. I woulda killed myself and the daughter too. Woulda made sense. No, she did it because the daughter caught them. Oh. Useless husband, I bet he had something to do with it. Maybe he killed the daughter. What happened to him then? She killed him. No, he owed Morii. Remember, Rik-san beat him bad? No, if anybody, the Chankoro did it. Maybe they killed the daughter too, as punishment. No.*

Yoshiko's roomers moved out as a result of the grisly death and the house descended into a murky emptiness. Even her talent for frying beef "*gaijin* style" couldn't keep or attract them. She slept in Koji's old room, constantly searching for his scent and yearning for his presence.

Staring in the mirror one day, she noticed the curve in her back. Like her mother. What did she die of? she wondered. Guilt? Sadness? Loneliness? How much further was she prepared to go now?

Soon thereafter, during the evening of a sun-drenched day with a gentle breeze filtering through the trees, she heard a knock once more at the front door. Etsuji Morii greeted Yoshiko with a wide grin. Her business with him had been concluded, had it not? But no, she realized in the end business was never really over with the *oyabun*.

"We have an obligation here," he said slowly, insidiously.

A few days later on March 22, she read of the autopsy and inquiry into Mariko's death in the *Tairiku Nippo*, but the news didn't bother her. In fact, nothing bothered her. All that was left for her was the house, but with no boarders and her depressed state, the place had begun to fall into disrepair. Dust mounted in corners, on surfaces. Rust stains in sinks and toilets. Floorboards dulled and tiles, marginally protected by old wax, remained scratched and marred.

Alone again in her front room, Yoshiko replayed Morii's words over and over in her head. *Think about your obligation.* She didn't believe the *oyabun's* revelations about Koji at first, but then she had lied to him about Jinsaburo's murder. Why couldn't she answer? Maybe it was Koji's continued absence; she began to choke on the truth. All the men in her life, she realized, had betrayed her: her father should've known, Jinsaburo and Iwakichi had deceived her into marrying a bitter old man and coming to Canada, the *oyabun* waved his hand to exile her, robbing her of the best years of her life, and now he wanted to steal everything she had worked so hard for in the wilderness. All she had lived for were the promises made and dreamed about during girlhood. Koji was her last chance. But his was the worst betrayal. He preyed upon her like some scavenger and took everything from her, especially her dignity, and then broke her heart.

She held her picture-bride photograph up to the light. Where is Akiko? Haruko? Where is her mother ... and Mariko? All dead to her. She tore the picture to shreds. It was time to act.

The hanging girl's legs touched the surface of the water where the current pulled at them. The upper body swayed back and forth, twisting in the air. She finally broke free and disappeared into the black depths. Whitecaps remained on the surface as a haunting voice plaintively called out Yoshiko's name.

She selected a steady chair from the middle room and placed it directly beneath the centre of the front room ceiling. Next she went to the basement and found a long rope made of rough twine. She barely glanced at the furnace, its open mouth almost mocking her. The rope was thin but strong enough.

Tying a slipknot at one end, she tossed the other over an exposed rafter. It took some doing but eventually she secured it. After making a noose, she slipped it around her neck and perched precariously on the chair, straining to stretch to her full height.

She casually gazed at the ends of her fingernails, realizing they were the last things she would see of this world, but she remained calm with no sign of any second thoughts. A feeling of resolve braced her. Bringing her hands together in *gassho*, Yoshiko Miyamoto closed her eyes, recited the *Nembutsu*, and stepped into oblivion.

She heard the crash of furniture around her before feeling the hardness of the floor. Something heavy struck the back of her head. The rope had snapped. Tilting her gaze up to the ceiling, she saw the hanging girl: the eyes, white with malice, directed toward her – the gaping mouth full of jagged teeth bursting forth with an unearthly laughter in a sustained tone of ridicule.

She slid across the floor to cower beside the couch. A white, clear light emanated from the body, nearly blinding her as she turned away. She forced her head around to face it again and saw that the light had fractured into its component parts. Through the glare, Yoshiko shrank before a collage of chaotic colour until the figure of a distorted and monstrous fox emerged running toward the shining, sunburst horizon. After the display subsided, she felt a cold rain, like accusing fingers, on her cheek. *Pera pera* drops at first, growing steadily until water streamed down to the body below. Her skin seemed to shrivel as the drizzle turned into a downpour. She lowered her head with the weight of the onslaught and her body convulsed in tears when she realized what her fate was to be.

After the storm, above the city, the neat wooden houses of North Vancouver and the proud twin lions, a gleaming rainbow shone as an arc of deceptive promise.

Epilogue

FATHER IS KILLER OF JAPANESE GIRL IN FURNACE

Police announced today that Jin Miyamoto, a Japanese man known to police, killed his daughter, Mariko Miyamoto, 16, who was found in the furnace of her home early in March. Detective-Inspector A.S. Hann and Detective A. Gibb concluded their investigation of the case after extensive interrogation of witnesses to a brawl in the Japanese sector.

Jin Miyamoto, 52, suffered a severe beating on Powell Street over gambling debts on March 7, the night before his daughter's death. The next afternoon, he returned home looking for the money to pay that debt. In the attempt to steal it, he beat his wife, Yoshiko Miyamoto, into unconsciousness and then turned on the daughter. He struck her repeatedly until she was dead. In an effort to evade arrest, he placed the child in the furnace and ignited it. Yoshiko Miyamoto was spared as her husband fled the scene shortly after disposing of the daughter's body.

Evidence revealed that he was not able to pay the debt when approached by his creditors a second time and was stabbed three times and dumped in the CP railway yards at the foot of Burrard Street. A late-night train decapitated the body.

The assailants are unknown. Detective Hann suspects they have flown the province.

– *The Daily Province*, April 30, 1940

Glossary

aho, ahotare	foolish, stupid
ah ra, ah re	feminine and masculine expressions of surprise: "Heavens!," "Goodness!"
baka, bakatare, bakayaro	a fool, an idiot; or, as an expression: "You idiot!"
biru	beer
boke-nasu	Japanese Canadian expression: stupid
Buddha Dharma	the teaching of the Buddha
Canada Shimpo	*The Progressive Canadian*
–chan	form of address to children or a younger loved one
Chankoro	the Chinese (pejorative)
chi chi	baby expression for breast
chikusho	a curse: "Goddamn it!"
chinpoko	(vulgarism) a small penis
damare	(vulgarism) "Shut up!"
da-me	an expression: "No good."
–de	preposition: at
defune	departing boat
desu	auxiliary: "That is so"
dojo	an exercise hall
Eigo wakarimasen	"I do not understand English"

eta	the untouchables
futomaki	a thickly rolled sushi
gaijin	a foreigner, an alien, usually referred to Caucasians
ganbatte nasai	"persevere!"
gassho	two hands pressed together in supplication
high kara	expression: highfalutin
Hongwanji	mother temple of the Jodo Shinshu sect of Buddhism. Located in Kyoto, Japan.
honto	true, genuine
inari-zushi	sushi wrapped in fried bean curd
issei	immigrant generation of Japanese Canadians; first generation
iyarashii	distasteful, unpleasant, disgusting
jikeidan	a vigilance committee
kamaboko	boiled fish paste
kame, kame, kame-san, kame-san yo	turtle; verse from an old Japanese children's song
kaporei	exaggerated and comic style of folk dancing
karma	the cycle of cause and effect
kashiya	a confectionery store
kawaiso ne	"Isn't that pitiful?"
keto	a white person (pejorative); (literally) hairy human
ketsuno ana	(vulgarism) asshole
kichigai	madness, craziness, lunacy
Kurombo	a Negro (pejorative)

kuso, kusotare	(vulgarism) "You shit! You son of a bitch!"
kyabin	Japanese Canadian term: cabin
Maru	title of an ocean going ship (similar to H.M.S. or U.S.S.)
Meiji era	1868–1912
Momiji	maple leaf
montsuki	formal five-crested kimono
mukashi, mukashi, omukashi	a very long time ago; once upon a time
nabeyaki udon	fried noodles
Namu Amida Butsu	a Buddhist expression: "I rely on the Buddha of Infinite Light and Life."
Naniwa	former name of Osaka, Japan
naniyo, nani, nanja	an expression: What?
ne	an expression: "You see"; "You know"; "Isn't it?"
nem mind	Japanese Canadian phrase: never mind
nemaki	pajamas, night clothes
nembutsu	an expression of gratitude to the Buddha (Namu Amida Butsu)
nesan, onesan	elder sister, waitress
nigiyakana	garish
nisei	first generation of Japanese Canadians born in Canada, considered to be second generation Japanese Canadian
nonbe	a slang expression: town drunk
obachan	a grandmother
obake	an apparition, a monster, a spook
obasan, oba	an older lady, an old hag

okasan, oka, okachan	mother
omairi	commemoration ritual
onegaishimasu	an expression: "Please do me the favour of ..."
otosan	father
pera pera	chatter; onomatopoetic sound of rain
Rennyo	(1415–1499) 8th Abbot of the Shin Buddhist sect
sa iko	expression: "All right, let's go!"
saibashi	(vulgarism) term coined by the Japanese in prewar British Columbia (may relate to the Saiwash Natives)
Sentaku	laundry
shikataganai	an expression: "It can't be helped"
shimatta	an expression: "Damn it!"
Shinen omedeto	"Happy New Year!"
Showa era	1926–1989
so ka	an expression: "Is that right?"
so ne	an expression: "Oh, that's right."
sumimasen	thank you
Tairiku Nippo	*The Continental Times of Japan*
Taisho era	1912–1926
urusai	annoying
Yamato-damashii	the spirit of ancient Japan
yoshi	an expression: "Okay!" "All right!"
yokkoriso	an expression when exerting effort: "Oh!"
Yomi	hell
yukata	an informal kimono

Acknowledgments

The author wishes to thank the following for their insight, stories, love, and friendship: Dr. Tane Akamatsu, Dr. Midge Ayukawa, Bruce Hunter, Dorothy Kagawa, Martin Kobayakawa, Kuan Foo, Helen Koyama (great illustrations), Frank Moritsugu, Roy and Kay Shin, Momoye Sugiman, Gloria Sumiya, Toyo Takata, Yusuke Tanaka, Dr. Brian Watada, Dr. Hideki Watada, Jim Wong Chu, Harry Yonekura, Dr. Misao Yoneyama, and my father Matsujiro Watada.

The author also wishes to acknowledge the support of Arsenal Pulp Press (thanks for giving me the confidence to continue writing), *Ricepaper* magazine (past and present), and the Toronto Arts Council's Writers Program.

Terry Watada is the author of numerous books of history, fiction, and poetry, including *Daruma Days, Ten Thousand Views of Rain, Seeing the Invisible,* and *Bukkyo Tozen: A History of Buddhism in Canada.* His latest poetry book is *Obon: the Festival of the Dead.* He lives in Toronto.